CHRISTMAS RANSOM

B.J. DANIELS

CANYON KIDNAPPING

CINDI MYERS

MILLS & BOON

First Published in Great Britain 2022
by Mills & Boon, an imprint of HarperCollins*Publishers* Ltd
1 London Bridge Street, London, SE1 9GF

www.harpercollins.co.uk

HarperCollins*Publishers*
1st Floor, Watermarque Building,
Ringsend Road, Dublin 4, Ireland

Christmas Ransom © 2022 Barbara Heinlein
Canyon Kidnapping © 2022 Cynthia Myers

ISBN: 978-0-263-30365-0

1122

This book is produced from independently certified FSC™ paper to ensure responsible forest management.

For more information visit: www.harpercollins.co.uk/green

Printed and Bound in Spain using 100% Renewable electricity at CPI Black Print, Barcelona

CHRISTMAS RANSOM

B.J. DANIELS

This one is for my brother Charley, who knows what happens when you fall for the wrong woman.

Chapter One

The whole desperate plan began simply as a last-ditch attempt to save his life. He never intended for anyone to get hurt. That day, not long after Thanksgiving, he walked into the bank full of hope. It was the first time he'd ever asked for a loan. It was also the first time he'd ever seen executive loan officer Carla Richmond.

When he tapped at her open doorway, she looked up from that big desk of hers. He thought she was too young and pretty with her big blue eyes and all that curly chestnut-brown hair to make the decision as to whether he lived or died.

She had a great smile as she got to her feet to offer him a seat.

He felt so out of place in her plush office that he stood in the doorway nervously kneading the brim of his worn baseball cap for a moment before stepping in. As he did, her blue-eyed gaze took in his ill-fitting clothing hanging on his rangy body, his bad haircut, his large, weathered hands.

He told himself that she'd already made up her mind before he even sat down. She didn't give men like him a second look—let alone money. Like his father always said, bankers never gave dough to poor people who actually needed it. They just helped their rich friends.

Right away Carla Richmond made him feel small with

her questions about his employment record, what he had for collateral, why he needed the money and how he planned to repay it. He'd recently lost one crappy job and was in the process of starting another temporary one, and all he had to show for the years he'd worked hard labor since high school was an old pickup and a pile of bills.

He took the forms she handed him and thanked her, knowing he wasn't going to bother filling them in. On the way out of her office, he balled them up and dropped them in the trash. All the way to his pickup, he mentally kicked himself for being such a fool. What had he expected?

No one was going to give him money, even to save his life—especially some woman in a suit behind a big desk in an air-conditioned office. It didn't matter that she didn't have a clue how desperate he really was. All she'd seen when she'd looked at him was a loser. To think that he'd bought a new pair of jeans with the last of his cash and borrowed a too-large button-down shirt from a former co-worker for this meeting.

After climbing into his truck, he sat for a moment, too scared and sick at heart to start the engine. The worst part was the thought of going home and telling Jesse. The way his luck was going, she would walk out on him. Not that he could blame her, since his gambling had gotten them into this mess.

He thought about blowing off work since his new job was only temporary anyway and going straight to the bar. Then he reminded himself that he'd spent the last of his money on the jeans. He couldn't even afford a beer. His own fault, he reminded himself. He'd only made things worse when he'd gone to a loan shark for cash and then stupidly gambled the money, thinking he could make back what he owed and then some when he won. He'd been so sure his luck had changed for the better when he'd met Jesse.

Last time the two thugs had come to collect the interest on the loan, they'd left him bleeding in the dirt outside his rented house. They would be back any day.

With a curse, he started the pickup. A cloud of exhaust blew out the back as he headed home to face Jesse with the bad news. Asking for a loan had been a long shot, but still he couldn't help thinking about the disappointment he'd see in her eyes when he told her. They'd planned to go out tonight for an expensive dinner with the loan money to celebrate.

As he drove home, his humiliation began to fester like a sore that just wouldn't heal. Had he known even then how this was going to end? Or was he still telling himself he was just a nice guy who'd made some mistakes, had some bad luck and gotten involved with the wrong people?

Chapter Two

There was nothing worse than having to stop by work on her day off less than a week before Christmas. Or so Carla Richmond thought as she entered the bank to the sound of holiday tunes. She waved to her best friend, Amelia, then to one of the other tellers before she hurried into her office. She didn't bother closing the door since she wasn't staying long. They were having a true Montana winter, she thought as she shed her snow-covered coat, hat and gloves. She hoped she could purchase the rest of her Christmas gifts and make it home before the snowstorm got any worse.

That's why she hoped to make this quick. As executive loan officer, Carla took her job seriously, especially the privacy part. That's why she'd panicked this afternoon when she'd realized that she might not have secured a client file yesterday before leaving work. She was always so careful, but just before quitting time she'd been distracted.

Yesterday, she'd looked up to find Davy Colt leaning against her doorjamb wearing a sheepish grin and the latest rodeo belt buckle he'd won. It wasn't like she'd missed the way his Western shirt hugged those broad shoulders or the way his jeans ran the length of his muscled legs and cupped that perfect behind. He held his Stetson in the fingers of one hand. His blue gaze danced with mischief as he hid his other hand behind him.

She hadn't seen him in months, not even in passing, so being caught off guard like that had come as a shock, though a pleasant one. A while back, in a weak moment, she'd made the mistake of asking his brother Tommy about Davy. Was that why he was standing in her doorway? she'd wondered at the time.

Mentally kicking herself, Carla had wished she hadn't asked Tommy about his brother. Why hadn't she left well enough alone? She'd made a clean break from Davy and since nothing had changed…

"Hey," he'd said. "Bad time? I don't mean to bother you."

"You aren't bothering me." She'd closed the file she'd been working on and shoved it aside. "Is there something…" That's when he'd drawn his hand from behind him and she'd seen what he'd been hiding. "Is that—"

"Mistletoe," he'd said with a shy, almost nervous grin. He'd stepped into her office, bringing with him the scent of pine and the crisp Montana air. She'd breathed it in as if she'd never had oxygen before. "I got to thinking about you on my way into town. I pinched the mistletoe from the doorway of a shop down the street." He'd glanced at his boots. "It reminded me of our first Christmas together." When he'd looked up, he'd shrugged as if embarrassed. "Guess I was feeling a little nostalgic, the holidays and all. You get off work soon?"

Was he asking her out? Heart bumping erratically against her ribs, she'd checked the time. "In twenty minutes." That's when she'd remembered that she'd promised to meet a friend for an early dinner. She'd groaned because she'd already canceled on this friend the last time they'd had plans. "But I'm meeting a friend."

Had he looked as disappointed as she'd felt? "No problem. I'm home for a few days over the holidays." His denim-blue gaze had locked with hers for several breath-stealing moments. "Tommy mentioned something about seeing you, and I thought…"

Carla had nodded, although she'd had no idea what he'd thought since he hadn't finished whatever he was going to say.

He'd set the mistletoe on the corner of her desk. "Maybe another time."

She'd tried to smile around her disappointment as he'd settled his Stetson back on his thick dark hair. Every one of those Colt brothers was handsome as sin, but Davy… Well, he had always been her favorite.

He'd met her gaze and she'd felt the heartache of the past settle over her. "Merry Christmas, Carla." And he'd been gone, leaving her with a familiar ache that had gotten worse since their breakup.

Belatedly she'd realized she should have told him that she had the next day off. Not that any good would come from getting involved with Davy again.

But just seeing him and hearing that he remembered the two of them together way back when had her heart floating. Her brain meanwhile was digging in its heels, arguing that picking up where the two of them had left off would be a huge mistake that she would regret.

She'd had a crush on Davy Colt from as far back as she could remember. When he'd finally asked her out in high school, she'd felt as if she had filled with helium. Her feet hadn't touched the ground for weeks.

Her mother hadn't been as thrilled. "I've heard stories about those Colt boys," she'd said, but Carla had assured her that Davy wasn't like that. She'd believed in her heart that Davy was The One. She'd imagined them married with kids. She'd pictured a perfect happy-ever-after—until he'd told her that he wasn't going to college with her at Montana

State University, even though he had a rodeo scholarship to attend. He was joining the rodeo circuit instead.

The romantic bubble had exploded with a loud *pop*. He'd rodeoed throughout high school, but she'd never imagined he planned to make it his occupation. Except she should have. Look at the rest of his family, all the way back to his great-grandfather who'd been a Hollywood Western movie star back in the 1940s and '50s. Ridin' and ropin' was in his blood, and being on the road following the rodeo circuit was the life all the Colt brothers had chosen as if it were their destiny as well as their legacy.

Carla, on the other hand, had been raised by a single mother who had barely finished high school. Because of that, Rosemary Richmond was determined Carla would get an education so she had options. Her mother hadn't wanted Carla to end up like her, in a low-paying job living from paycheck to paycheck. Rosemary had said from the time Carla could remember that her only daughter was going to college. Her mother had worked so hard to make that happen.

Carla had had no choice. While it had broken her heart, she'd ended the relationship with Davy and headed for college, where she'd majored in business and finance and graduated with honors. She'd had her pick of jobs.

But when her mother had gotten sick, Carla had taken a job at the local bank in Lonesome to help take care of her. And after she'd died from the cancer, the rest was history. She'd stayed in Lonesome, seeing Davy from time to time—but only in passing. She'd always wondered if she'd made a mistake choosing a career over the cowboy she'd loved. Still loved, if she was being honest.

That's why it had been such a shock when he'd come into the bank to see her. Was it possible he still felt the same way she did about him?

After he'd left, she'd sat at her desk fighting emotions until she'd grabbed her things and hurried to meet her friend. All the time, she'd kept reminding herself that Davy was only home for the holidays. His life was far from Lonesome. Who knew when he'd be back? She had to quit pining away for the rodeo cowboy.

Now as she looked around her desk, she realized that the file she'd thought she left there yesterday afternoon was nowhere to be seen. She took her key and unlocked the file drawer and was flipping through it when she saw that she *had* put the file away. But she had no memory of doing it. Her mind had been a million miles away—just like it was now. No, not quite a million miles. More like the distance from the bank to the Colt Brothers Investigation building down the street.

Davy Colt would be staying there in the apartment over the business, at least for a few days. Then he'd be riding in Texas after the holidays and who knew where after that, since she tried not to keep track of the rodeo circuit schedule anymore.

Her brain and heart were still at war since his visit yesterday. She told herself he would be busy with family. She might not even see him again before the holiday was over. She figured that, after yesterday, maybe he'd changed his mind about whatever thought had prompted him to stop by her office.

She picked up the mistletoe on the corner of her desk, but couldn't force herself to throw it away. She put it back down. Maybe he'd stop by work tomorrow or the next day. If he came in looking for her, she was sure that the other loan officer, Amelia Curtis, or one of the tellers would let him know that she'd be working right up through Christmas Eve, in case Davy wanted to stop back by.

Even as she wanted desperately to see him again, she

knew how dangerous that could be. Davy was serious about only one thing—rodeo—and spending time with him would only lead to another heartbreak.

As she started to reach for her things to leave, someone in the lobby screamed and then the whole place broke out in what sounded like panicked alarm. Carla looked up. Standing in her doorway was a masked man in a Santa suit holding a semiautomatic rifle. The Santa mask—complete with big white beard and red hat—covered his entire head. The only thing visible was the shine of his dark eyes through two small holes and the ugly slash at his mouth as he rushed toward her.

Chapter Three

The plan had come to him in the darkest, most desperate hours of night. He hadn't been able to sleep in the weeks since going to the bank for the loan and realizing that there would be no Christmas miracle. No Hail Mary pass. No one to bail him out. And if he didn't do something soon, Jesse was going to leave him.

As he lay awake, he kept replaying the day he'd gone to the bank for the loan with so much hope, misplaced or not. Before he'd left that afternoon, his girlfriend, Jesse, had told him how handsome he looked in his borrowed button-down shirt and new jeans. It had made him smile despite how scared he'd been to ask a bank for money.

But like Jesse had said, what did he have to lose? A lot, he'd discovered, because when he'd returned home empty-handed, Jesse had run out onto the porch. She'd been wearing a new dress for the celebratory dinner they had planned. She'd looked so happy, so hopeful.

"Did you get the loan?" Her expression drooped as she must have seen the answer written all over his face. His shoulders slumped as she let out a choked sob and turned away as if she didn't want him to see her cry.

He'd rushed up the steps and taken her in his arms, holding her as if she was all that was keeping him rooted to earth.

"They're going to kill us!" she said between sobs. "Look what happened the last time they came for a payment." She felt stiff in his arms. When she pulled back to look at him, he saw her disappointment in him like poison in her eyes. She pushed him, then balled her hands into fists and pounded against his chest until he pulled her to him so tightly that she finally slumped in his arms and sobbed.

"I bet you didn't even go to the bank and ask," she cried.

"I did. I talked to Carla Richmond, the executive loan officer." Jesse had stopped crying and was listening, but he had no more to say. He wasn't about to tell her that he'd thrown the forms away without even filling them out. He shook his head. "Don't worry. They won't kill us. I'll take care of it."

He could feel the distance growing between them in the quaking of her body. She'd trusted him and look what a mess he'd made of it. They hadn't been together long. He still couldn't believe that a woman who looked like her had given him a second glance.

They'd met at a bar in another town. The next morning, in the light of day, he'd figured that would be the end of it. But when he'd asked her if she wanted to come home with him, she had. She'd only balked a little when he told her he lived in Lonesome. It had been her idea to move out of the trailer he was renting and into a house. She'd gotten a job right away. He'd really believed that Lady Luck was finally on his side.

That day after he'd been turned down at the bank, he'd held Jesse until she quit crying and he'd felt all the fight go out of her. His shirt had been wet with her tears. He'd wanted to be this woman's hero from the moment he'd met her and brought her back to Lonesome four months ago. He'd told himself he still could. He would think of something. He couldn't lose her.

"I need to go to work," she'd whispered, pulling back to look down in what could only be disgust at the new dress she'd bought.

"Call in sick," he'd said, afraid to let her go. All he had thought about was curling up naked in their bed, holding each other until they fell asleep.

Her job paid the rent and kept the lights on. His new temporary one would keep them fed and buy gas for their vehicles. With luck, they would have enough money at the end of the week to hold off the loan shark. Between the two of them they were slowly going broke because of the foolish mistakes he'd made. Worse, she was right. The last time the men had come for the money, they'd almost killed him and had threatened her. The next time they came would be worse.

Who was he kidding? There was no way he'd have enough money to hold them off. They would kill him, but his real terror was what they might do to Jesse if she were home. Probably the best thing she could do was leave him. He knew she'd thought about it. Maybe this would be the straw that broke the camel's back.

"I have to change," she'd said, pulling away. "I can't lose my job."

He'd watched her walk away, his gut cramping at the thought of her leaving him for good. He kept a pack of cigarettes that he'd swiped from one of the men he'd worked with. Jesse hated him smoking. But once she'd left…

She'd come out dressed for work. She'd fixed her face and pulled her long blond hair up into a ponytail. As with every time he'd looked at her, he was always stunned at how beautiful she was. How had he gotten so lucky? It still astounded him, and he knew he would do whatever it took to keep her.

"It's going to be all right, baby," he'd said as he'd quickly stepped to her and leaned down to kiss her. He'd thought she'd pull away, but instead, she'd looped her arms around his neck and pulled him down to her. The kiss had started a fire in his belly that slid lower. He'd thought of their bed just inside, thought of her naked.

"I'm going to be late," she'd said as she drew back. Their gazes had met for a long moment.

"Don't lose faith in me." He hated that his voice had broken.

She'd shaken her head and given him a weak smile. "I know you will think of something. You working tonight?"

He'd nodded. A lie. He'd quit the night stocking job at the grocery store in town when he'd realized it wasn't enough to get him out of trouble—and that Jesse was right. Maybe the simpliest answer had been to go to the bank for a loan. He'd picked up the temporary job through the rest of the holiday—one he had planned to quit once he'd gotten the bank loan.

The truth was that even the loan wouldn't have held off the goons for long. He was just as good as dead.

He'd been so down that day after going to the bank. He'd thought for sure that he'd lost Jesse. His words had felt like sawdust in his mouth. "I'd understand if you left me. I wouldn't blame you at all."

He couldn't have the men stopping by for the money and finding her home alone.

To his surprise, she'd said, "You aren't getting rid of me that easily. You'll think of something, Jud."

After she'd left, his throat parched from the cigarettes he'd smoked, he knew what he had to do. He'd been left no choice. But the plan hadn't come together until he'd talked it over with Jesse. It still amazed him how she'd known so much about robbing a bank. She'd been angrier with Carla Richmond than he'd been.

"She deserves this for not giving you the loan," Jesse had said. "She's probably had everything handed to her all of her life. How dare she. Someday she's going to get what's coming to her."

BEFORE CARLA COULD SCREAM, the Santa-suited robber rushed around her desk to grab a handful of her long hair and drag her toward the lobby. She saw others already on the floor and felt the panic that seemed to suck all the air out of the room. Amelia was crying and so were the tellers. They all looked terrified where they lay.

"On the floor!" the man bellowed, using his hold on her hair to throw her down. Carla stumbled, landing hard on her side, pain shooting across her shoulder as the breath was knocked out of her. "Facedown!" he yelled and kicked her in the side.

She flattened herself facedown on the floor, fighting the pain as she gasped for breath. She tried to see if the others were all right. A teller was sobbing as she emptied out her till into a large bag, the kind Santa might carry toys in, and moved on to the next one. The bank had been about to close, so there were only a couple of customers on the floor, two older women frozen in fear. In all the racket, she could hear the bank manager trying to reason with one of the robbers.

There appeared to be three robbers, all in Santa suits and rubber masks. They wore white gloves on their hands and tall black boots, exposing no skin except for those holes where their eyes peered out—and that slit for their mouths.

One of the robbers had a gun to the bank manager's head as he led him back toward the vault. The other robber finished loading the money from the tills, then ordered the teller onto the floor to lie down with the others as he followed the bank manager toward the vault. Carla saw that the robber had an extra bag with him along with the one full of money from the tellers' tills.

She knew she must be in shock because her thoughts seemed to veer all over the place. Bank robberies were rare. The rule of thumb was that if a bank hadn't been robbed in a hundred years, then it was due. This bank hadn't been robbed in almost a hundred and twenty. She thought about how much money was in the vault and groaned inwardly. They had more money than usual because of the holidays. Had the robbers known that?

Stay calm, she chanted silently. *Stay calm.* She realized she was trembling. Her shoulder and side ached, and her scalp hurt from where he'd dragged her by her hair. She wanted to touch the spot on her head, to rub it, but was afraid to breathe, let alone move. Instead, she tried to concentrate on staying calm as she heard crying and praying, and the man yelling at everyone to stay down or die. No one wanted to die here today. Not right before Christmas.

Her gaze flicked up to the man who'd dragged her from her office. He'd moved off to the side, his semiautomatic rifle trained on those on the floor some distance away from her. He seemed nervous and kept shifting on his feet and pulling at the back of the mask.

She watched as he reached up under his fake white beard and scratched hard at his neck. She caught sight of what appeared to be a red rash and realized he must be allergic to whatever material the mask was made of.

But the rash wasn't the only thing she'd seen when he'd raised the mask. He had a tattoo low on his neck. There were two *J*'s with an odd-shaped heart between them. *J* loves *J*?

Even though she was sure that she hadn't made a sound, he quickly adjusted his mask and spun in her direction, leading with the business end of the rifle in his hand. She saw from his expression that he'd realized his mistake in lifting the bottom of the mask. Carla had quickly looked away, but she could feel his gaze boring into her. Did he know what she'd seen? Her heart pounded harder, her breath more ragged. She feared he knew as she heard him advance on her. "I told you to keep your head down!"

Chapter Four

Jud couldn't believe what had just happened. But the moment he'd seen her expression, he'd realized that she'd seen something when he'd lifted the Santa beard to scratch his neck. His tattoo! The foolish woman. She'd tell the cops. He tried to tell himself that the law wouldn't be able to track him down by some silly tattoo, but even as he was arguing the point, he knew he couldn't take the chance.

Jesse wouldn't wait for him if he went to prison. Hell, she was barely hanging on as it was. If he could pull off this bank job, they'd leave the country. Maybe go to someplace warm, sit on a beach and watch the sunset. Jesse would like that. He could finally make her happy. Maybe they'd even get married.

He'd asked her to marry him, but she'd put him off. He was no fool. He knew that she was hoping for something better. With his share of the money, he could be better. He could give her more than some drunken sentimental gesture like a tattoo. He'd wanted her name embedded into his flesh, but hadn't had enough money according to the tattoo tech. Maybe if he hadn't spent so much on the booze before coming up with the idea…

Swearing under his breath, he tried not to scratch his neck again, but this mask and beard were making him hot and itchy. He wasn't sure how much longer he could stand having it on. He felt as if he couldn't breathe. All he wanted to do was rip it off and scratch his damned neck.

He glanced anxiously toward the short hallway to the vault. What was taking them so long? He quickly looked back at Carla Richmond. He thought about what Jesse had said about her. Worse, he figured Carla was smart. Too smart for her own good. But she'd made a mistake that was now going to cost her her life.

The thought made him a little sick. But how could he let her live now? Even if the cops couldn't track him down because of the tattoo, she might remember him from the day he'd come in for the loan. He swore under his breath again. If only he hadn't lifted his mask. If she'd done what he'd told her to do... It was her own fault. He hadn't wanted anyone to get hurt.

Glancing toward the vault again, he was about to yell back to see what was taking so long when two Santa-suited figures came out, pushing the bank manager ahead of them and forcing him down on the floor near the tellers.

The larger of the two looked up, signaling that it had gone well. "Let's go!" Buddy called and started toward Jud, carrying a bulging bag filled with money. Eli was right behind with a tote that looked just as full.

For a moment, Jud felt a surge of joy and relief and pride. It had gone just as Jesse had said it would. His good mood didn't last though as he looked down at the executive loan officer at his feet. He couldn't leave her here alive.

Jud swung the end of the rifle at her head, his finger on the trigger. It wasn't like he had a choice. He hadn't had a choice his whole life.

OUT OF THE corner of her eye, Carla saw him standing over her with his weapon pointed at her head. She could hear him breathing hard under the mask and she knew. He was going to kill her. She'd seen his tattoo. She squeezed her eyes shut and held her breath, but all she could think about was Davy. Hadn't she been holding out hope for years that somehow they would find a way to be together? She felt scalding tears behind her lashes.

"I said let's go!" She opened her eyes and could see that the other two robbers had joined them. "Whatever it is you're thinking about doing, don't," one man said. He was taller and broader than the one with the tattoo. She could feel the tension between the two. "We need to get out of here."

"I can't leave her here," he said, his finger still on the trigger. "Not alive."

"We said no one gets hurt."

"Then I'm taking her hostage."

"No. You're not."

Her arm was suddenly grabbed, fingers digging deep into her flesh as she was jerked to standing. He spun her around and locked his arm around her throat. Nearly lifting her off her feet, he said, "She's coming with us."

Carla heard the screech of tires. She saw a van pull up out front. The driver honked the horn. Somewhere in the distance, she thought she heard sirens. The larger of the men swore and said that someone had pushed an alarm and they had to get out of there.

The robber holding her began to drag her toward the door. She'd watched enough crime television shows to know the last thing she could let this man do was take her out of the bank and into that van. She tried to fight him, but his hold on her throat was cutting off her air supply.

The bank manager was yelling something at the men. One of the robbers was threatening him, telling him to stay down or he would shoot him. Someone on the floor was sobbing loudly now. Someone else began to scream.

Then someone else screamed. She realized that the second scream was coming out of her mouth and her terror rose. The time for remaining calm was over.

Frantically she clawed at the arm clamped around her neck, but the Santa suit was thick and she found little purchase as the man dragged her toward the door and the waiting van.

Chapter Five

"Mistletoe?" James Colt laughed, and his brothers Tommy and Willie joined in.

"Hey, I was thinking fast on my feet, okay?" Davy said. He'd been taking a ribbing from his brothers for as long as he could remember. They'd always been close but had grown more so since their father's death. They had the classically handsome Colt features, dark hair and blue eyes, and the reputations to go with them—the wild Colt brothers, as they were known in Lonesome, Montana.

Even if they hadn't been rodeo cowboys like their father and grandfather, most mothers in town didn't want them dating their daughters. Davy didn't think it mattered that both James and Tommy had settled down recently, become private investigators and were now married.

"That is so cheesy," Tommy said of the mistletoe. "So what happened?"

"I hope you got the kiss," Willie said, eyeing him speculatively. "That was all you were after, right?"

His brothers knew how heartbroken he'd been when Carla had ended their relationship years ago. "Like I said, spur-of-the-moment. I'm not sure what I had in mind. Maybe to just say hello. Maybe I thought we could have a drink together, talk old times, I don't know."

They were all gathered in the Colt Brothers Investigation

office. It had changed since his father, Del, had started the PI business almost ten years ago—before his death. James and Tommy had moved the office downstairs, keeping their father's desk and large leather office chair.

There were two bedrooms now upstairs for when Davy and Willie were home. They would have been welcome to stay with James or Tommy at their homes, but they preferred the upstairs apartment on Main Street, Lonesome. They all had memories of spending time in the office with their father.

"So did you get around to asking her out?" James had been the first to leave the rodeo circuit. After getting involved in one of their father's old cases, he'd decided he wanted to be in the PI business.

Davy looked down at his boots. "Just my luck she already had a date."

Willie shook his head. "You sure you want to go down that path again?"

He wasn't sure. That was the problem. It's why he'd stayed away today. "What's this about you joining the sheriff's department?" he asked, hoping to get the focus off him.

"Stop trying to change the subject," Willie said.

All of them looked toward Willie. "Davy's right," James said. "I distinctly remember you saying you were never going to become a private eye. Too dangerous, you said."

"You'd just spent a night in jail, as I remember," Tommy interjected. "So yeah, what's up with you joining the sheriff's department?"

"I needed a change and we have enough PIs in the family," Willie said with a laugh.

James narrowed his eyes at his brother. "This wouldn't have anything to do with Dad's death, would it?"

"Enough about me," Willie said, standing to walk over to the window that faced Main Street. Davy looked past his brother. Lonesome looked so picturesque with its quaint old brick buildings, Christmas decorations and snowflakes falling to the distant sound of holiday music.

"Willie's right," James said, letting Willie off easy, Davy thought. "I'd think long and hard about revisiting that love affair. As Dad used to say, there are a lot of Buckle Bunnies out there. It isn't like you have ever been short of female company."

Davy sighed and shook his head. There were always cowgirls who followed the circuit. True enough, he had no problem getting a date. But none of them were Carla.

"Remember, she was the one who broke up with you because she didn't want to be married to a rodeo cowboy," Tommy reminded him, as if he could ever forget.

"Can't blame her," James said. "What woman in her right mind would?"

"Unless something has changed?" Tommy said.

Davy shook his head. "There are too many broncs waiting to be ridden."

"Or bucked off of," Tommy said with a laugh.

"Well, I have a few more years." He was young, the youngest of the brood. He wasn't ready to settle down, he kept telling himself. But he'd never gotten over Carla, and lately he'd been thinking about her more and more. When Tommy told him that she'd said to tell him hello, he'd gotten his hopes up that they might still have a chance.

"Did Carla at least seem glad to see you?" Tommy asked now.

Davy shrugged. "I was too nervous to notice."

Willie had grown quiet, almost reflective, for a few minutes. "Davy, you're ruining our bad reputations," he joked. "I'm getting the feeling that you're still hung up on this woman."

Davy groaned and got to his feet. "Maybe I'll go out for a while, do some Christmas shopping—"

"And maybe stop by the bank before it closes?" Tommy asked with a grin.

At the sound of distant sirens, Willie turned toward the front window again. "Speaking of the bank, it looks like something's happening down there."

Chapter Six

For a moment, Jud didn't know what hit him. He'd been dragging Carla Richmond toward the door, determined to take her hostage, when he heard the pop as one of his ribs cracked from the butt of Buddy's weapon. His own weapon was jerked from his free hand. Gasping for air, he was forced to loosen his leverage on the woman.

After that, everything went south. Carla, no doubt seeing her chance, elbowed him hard in the same spot Buddy had nailed him. The last of his air rushed from his lungs. He doubled over and the woman slipped from his hold to collapse on the floor.

He had only a few seconds as she hurried to scramble out of his reach. In that instant when she'd looked back from the floor, something had passed between them. She'd known he was going to kill her, and he'd known that she would tell the cops what she'd seen.

He kicked her, catching her temple with the toe of his boot. The blow flipped her from her hands and knees to her back. Her head struck the marble floor with a crack and she lay motionless. People began to scream and cry louder. There was shouting and he could hear some of the bank employees getting to their feet and scrambling for cover. If he'd still had his weapon, he would have turned it on all of them—starting with Carla Richmond.

But Buddy grabbed him, propelling him toward the front door of the bank before he could finish her off. The sound of sirens filled the air as the three of them stumbled across the snowy sidewalk to the diminishing sound of Christmas music and into the waiting van at the curb. Their getaway driver, Rick, sped off even before the van doors closed.

Jud looked back through the glass front of the bank. There were people kneeling next to Carla. From what he could tell, she still wasn't moving as the getaway vehicle roared down the road. All he could hope was that she never would again.

"You idiot," Buddy snapped as he pulled off his mask and threw it down on the floor of the van as they sped out of Lonesome—headed for the mountains. "What were you thinking?" he demanded as he struggled to shed his costume. Like the rest of them, he wore a T-shirt and jeans underneath. "The plan wasn't to take a hostage."

Jud glared at him, holding his side. He'd already ripped off his mask, each breath a torture as he scratched angrily at his neck. "Plans change."

Buddy swore, chucked his costume past Jud into the very back of the van and turned away to look out the side window. "I knew better than to get involved with this because you screw up everything you touch. You always have— ever since we were kids."

"We got the money, didn't we?" Jud insisted as he too shed his costume between fits of scratching at the rash breaking out everywhere the costume had touched bare skin.

"The money won't do us any good if we're locked up in prison, or worse, dead. You could have gotten us all killed back there," Buddy snapped.

"He still might," Eli said and pointed out the windshield. Ahead of them, Jud could see the railroad crossing—and the approaching train. At their rates of speed, both the train and the van would reach the crossing at the same time. He swallowed back the bile that rose in his throat.

He and Jesse had researched their escape, knowing it was the only chance they had of getting out of Lonesome and evading the cops. They would hit the bank and head for the train crossing. He'd timed the robbery so they would get across the tracks before the train by a few minutes. Anyone following them would have to wait for the entire length of the train to pass before following them.

Because of that small window of time, he'd known how dangerous trying to beat the train was going to be. A thirty-car freight train hitting a vehicle would be the same force as a car crushing an aluminum soda can. It would take the train a mile before it came to a complete stop.

Add to that the fact that the train was about six feet wider than the rails. That meant an extra three feet on each side of the locomotive that could clip the van even after the back tires cleared the rails.

The timing had been crucial. Now he saw that trying to take Carla Richmond hostage had cost them critical time and might end up being the last reckless thing he'd ever do.

"Are we going to make it?" Eli asked, his voice breaking as Rick tried to get more speed out of the van as they raced toward the crossing. Lights were flashing, but there were no crossing barriers. The county had talked about adding them after Del Colt had been killed at this spot, but it hadn't happened.

The roar of the train and the locomotive horn was deafening in his ears. It was so close that Jud could see the panicked look on the engineer's face. The man had already hit the brakes, but there was no stopping the train in time to miss the van.

Rick had the gas pedal pressed to the floor. As the van

bounced over the first rail, all Jud could see out the side window next to him was the massive front of the train's engine. They were all going to die. After an initial spike of panic, he felt almost relieved that his life would be over. Except for Jesse. He'd let her down, the one good thing in his life.

The van felt as if it were flying as the back wheels bucked over the second rail. Jud thought for sure the engine would catch the rear panel of the van, ripping it off and sending them cartwheeling through the air.

The train roared by behind them as the van kept going and Rick fought to keep the vehicle on the road at this speed. Jud realized he'd been holding his breath. He let it out, feeling shaky and sick to his stomach. He'd never come that close to dying. He sat back in his seat and tried to breathe. The pain in his chest was excruciating, and now that he was going to live, he was furious with Buddy.

Eli swore next to him, looking as shaken as Jud felt. "You sorry son of a—" Eli looked like he wanted to punch him. "You almost got us killed. If we hadn't beaten that train across the tracks…"

"I didn't get us caught or killed. Instead, I made you money. You knew the risk." He could feel Buddy's gaze on him again.

"You're right. I don't know what we were thinking. We definitely should have known dealing with you was more than a risk," Buddy said. "I still can't believe you were going to take that woman as a hostage." His gaze narrowed. "What were you going to do with her?"

Jud said nothing. He'd had to make a decision. Kill her where she lay or take her hostage. "I didn't have a choice. My mask slipped. I think she saw my tattoo. Once I realized she could make me…"

Buddy swore. "This just keeps getting better."

"Don't worry. If she's still alive, I know who she is. I'll take care of it."

He saw Eli and Rick exchange a look with Buddy as if he was the one who'd planned this. Buddy said, "You'd better hope she's still alive. Otherwise, they'll never stop looking for us for murder on top of armed robbery." Buddy swore. "What were you thinking? She can't ID you from that crappy *JJ* tattoo. Unless you've had your name and phone number tattooed on you since we last saw you. Or maybe your Social Security number."

Jud gritted his teeth. In a few minutes, he would see the last of these guys and he'd be rich. "Maybe I overreacted," he said sullenly, hating Buddy all the more for putting him in a position where he had to back down. "But Jesse watches this TV show where they find people with a whole lot less than an obvious tattoo."

Buddy shook his head and turned away to stare at the road ahead. Jud saw that they were almost to the spot where they would divide the loot and part company after one final step. He couldn't wait. He could feel his skin burning from wearing the ridiculous costume. At least one of his ribs felt broken. And Carla Richmond might still be alive. The only good news was that, with luck, he'd never see these men again. He regretted bringing them in for this. Once he had his share of the money, he and Jesse would leave the country.

As he shifted in his seat, he felt the pain in his side from Buddy's gun butt. It made him all the more furious that Buddy seemed to think he could tell him what to do.

"You don't know that she made you," Buddy was saying as the van came to a stop in the middle of the forest where an SUV and Rick's motorcycle waited for them. They would take the SUV to the spot where they'd left their vehicles. Except for Rick, who would stay behind and burn the van with the costumes and their weapons inside it. All the evidence would be gone, including any evidence on the unregistered weapons. While the rifles wouldn't burn, they couldn't be traced back to them.

If Carla Richmond hadn't seen his tattoo, the robbery would have gone off perfectly. Now he was going to have to deal with her. The thought made his stomach roil.

"Don't be a fool," Buddy said as if he could read his thoughts. The man opened the passenger-side door to climb out but hesitated to look back at Jud. "The cops can't prove anything. Just forget about the woman, take your share of the money and make a new life for yourself. If you're smart, you'll leave Jesse behind. You wouldn't have gotten this deep in trouble if you weren't trying to keep her. Let her go. Women are a dime a dozen. Especially ones like Jesse." As Buddy stepped out, Jud saw the bulge of a handgun stuffed in the back of his jeans.

The plan had been that no one would bring extra weapons. Were the others now carrying as well?

"Thanks for the advice," Jud said between gritted teeth as everyone climbed out of the van, taking the bags of money but leaving their weapons behind to go up in flames. He picked up his fully loaded semiautomatic rifle from the van floor where it had been dropped.

As his feet hit the dirt, he saw Buddy give a nod toward the others. They started to turn as Jud said, "Buddy, you should know that I've never been good at taking advice." As Buddy reached behind him for his weapon, Jud saw the others about to do the same thing.

He told himself that they'd given him no choice as he hit the trigger, opening fire on all of them before they could get off a shot.

Chapter Seven

Carla woke confused, head aching. She blinked. The room seemed too bright, the light like an ice pick jammed between her eyes. She closed them again. Shifting in the bed, she realized that it wasn't just her head that hurt. Her whole body hurt. She pried her eyes open to slits. Where was she?

"Carla."

In that one word she heard so much relief and concern that she felt her pulse jump, and yet the moment came with more confusion. *"Davy?"*

As she opened her eyes, she turned her head and winced in pain. Davy was sitting in a chair next to her bed. The sight of him was as incongruous as the realization that she was in the hospital. She closed her eyes again.

She heard him rise from the chair and come to her side. With her eyes still closed, she asked, "What happened?" Her voice came out a whisper and suddenly she was aware of how weak she felt as he took her free hand.

When she opened her eyes again, she saw that her other hand was hooked up to tubes and machines that beeped noisily.

"You're safe now," he said, gently squeezing her hand in his two large ones. *Safe?* His hands felt warm and calloused, hands she remembered. She tried to sit up, but he urged her back down. "Just stay still. The doctor is on his way."

She closed her eyes again, trying to make sense out of all of it. She was in the hospital, she'd been hurt, Davy was here. The last was the most confusing. It was as if she'd been teleported back in time and she and Davy were still together.

Opening her eyes, she heard someone come into the room and felt Davy release her hand and say, "She just came to."

"How are you feeling?" asked a male voice. She focused on the sixtysomething doctor. Dr. Hull had delivered her his first year in Lonesome. He'd met the love of his life, a local woman, and had ended up staying all these years in their tiny Western town.

"I have a terrible headache," she whispered, as if speaking loudly would make it worse.

"We'll see what we can do about that," the doctor said.

"I don't understand what happened."

"You have a concussion and some minor bruises and swelling." He met her gaze. "You don't remember?" She shook her head and then wished she hadn't. "What's the last thing you remember?"

Her gaze shifted to Davy's concerned, handsome face. She remembered him coming into her office. Or had that been a dream? She couldn't be sure.

"Do you remember me stopping by the bank to see you?" Davy asked.

So it had been true. "Yes."

Dr. Hull looked relieved, then nodded and smiled. "When was that?"

"Yesterday," Davy said, making her start with surprise.

"How long have I been in here?" she asked, feeling her fear rise. What had happened? Why couldn't she remember? Had there been a car accident? Had anyone else been hurt?

"Earlier today," the doctor said.

"Tell me what happened." She tried to sit up again, but the doctor placed a hand on her shoulder.

"Easy," he said. "You don't remember anything about the bank robbery?"

She lay back. *Bank robbery?* A flash of memory. Santa standing in her doorway. She frowned as the image blurred and disappeared. Her mind filled with questions that flew in and out like a flock of birds. She tried to grab hold of one, but it only made her headache worse. "Was anyone else hurt?"

"No," the doctor said.

"Did they get away with the money?"

He nodded. "But the FBI is on the case, so you need not worry. You just concentrate on feeling better."

"Why can't I remember?"

"The blow to your head," Dr. Hull said and patted her arm. "You just need rest so your brain can heal and your body as well." He started to turn away but stopped. "An FBI agent is here, wanting to ask you questions about the robbery." Of course. She knew the FBI investigated bank robberies and had since they became a federal crime in 1934 thanks to John Dillinger and his gang. "Don't worry, I'll send the agent away for now."

For now? She looked to Davy. "I can't help the FBI. I don't know anything. I can't remember any…" Her voice broke.

"Do what the doctor said. Get some rest. Your memory will come back. Or it won't." He must have seen her worried look. "Come on, I've landed on my head enough times that I know how this works. Worrying about it doesn't help, trust me. Just close those beautiful blue eyes. I'll be here if you need me."

She didn't want to close her eyes, but she could feel a strange kind of exhaustion trying to drag her under. "How…" She was going to ask how it was that he was here. But the thought whizzed past and was gone. "You're sure no one else was hurt?"

"Everyone is fine. You apparently got the worst of it."

"What if I can't remember?" Her words sounded slurred and took all of her energy.

"The feds will find them probably before you wake up, so you have nothing to worry about."

Nothing to worry about. Why didn't she believe that? A memory played at the edge of her consciousness. Dark eyes peering out at her from Santa's face. She shuddered as sleep dragged her under.

HIGH IN THE MOUNTAINS, Jud watched the van burn. There'd been several cans of gas in the back to use to start the blaze and make sure nothing was left but charred ashes. One can had been used inside the van. Another had been dumped on the three bodies. He'd been right. All of them had been carrying guns. All of them had been going for those guns when he stepped out of the van.

Was the plan to double-cross him? Or had they brought weapons because they didn't trust him?

Not that it mattered now. But it showed how little they thought of him. So much for former childhood friends. He kept thinking about the things Buddy had said about him. Worse, what he'd said about Jesse. The man couldn't have been more wrong. Jesse was the real deal. His stomach ached at the thought of how close he'd come to losing her. He'd known that he would do anything to keep that from happening. Look at what he'd already done. He and Buddy had known each other from the old neighborhood. It hurt that he'd been put in a position where he had to kill him. Sick at heart, his stomach roiling, his ribs making every move hurt, he pushed the thought away.

This hadn't been part of the plan, he thought as he watched the flames consume the bodies and the van and motorcycle. But now it was over. Time to move on. Any moment the gas tank on the van would blow. He feared that the smoke from the flames could be seen from miles away. He had to get going. He'd already loaded the bags of money in the SUV.

After climbing behind the wheel, he started the vehicle and drove to where his pickup was waiting for him. As part of the adjusted plan, he left the SUV with the keys in the ignition. With luck, someone would steal it—just as they had done.

He checked the time. Jesse should be getting ready for her night shift. He'd hoped to be back to the house before she left for work. She would be worried since he hadn't taken her call earlier. She would have heard about the bank robbery. By now, everyone in the county would know. He thought about calling her to let her know that he was fine. But he feared she would hear the truth in his voice. Better to head home, get cleaned up, calm down and then call her.

When she got off her shift, he would be waiting for her with the money. All of the money. They could make love in the middle of it if she wanted. There was enough to last them a very long time if they were careful.

Not that he'd taken the time to count it, but he knew it was a whole lot more than he'd been planning on since there was no splitting it. Now he didn't want to part with any of it. Once he tied up the one loose end, they could get out of town before anyone was the wiser. They could start a new life together. Jesse would like that. Or maybe they would just leave right away and forget about Carla Richmond. With blood already on his hands, the idea more than appealed to him.

From now on, only happy thoughts. The money would make sure of that. No wonder rich people always looked so pleased with themselves. The first thing he was going to do was buy Jesse an engagement ring with a huge diamond on it.

He remembered Buddy's voice from the day they got together to plan the robbery. "Don't do anything foolish like flashing the money around when this is over. It would be just like you, Jud, to go buy a sports car that you'd never be able to afford on your income and get the feds onto us."

Another reminder that Buddy thought he was smarter than him. But then again, Jud was still alive and rich and Buddy was toast. He turned on the radio to drown out his former friend's voice in his head, anxious to get home.

He thought about Jesse's face when she saw all the money. He planned to make her smile for the rest of her life—even if he had to knock over another bank to do it.

Carla Richmond broke into his thoughts like a recurring toothache. He turned up the radio, hoping to catch the news.

When Carla opened her eyes again, Davy was asleep in the chair beside her bed. She had time to study him. She'd fallen in love with him not because of how drop-dead gorgeous he was. He was a good-hearted cowboy. Unfortunately, the rodeo had stolen his heart long before she'd come along.

He stirred as if sensing she was awake. Smiling, he pushed himself up, then winced and grabbed the back of his neck to rub it.

"What time is it?" she asked, her throat dry.

"Nine thirty." She looked past him to see darkness beyond the windows.

"You slept all this time in that chair?" she asked.

"I wasn't about to leave you until I knew you were all right."

"I'm fine. You should go home and get some sleep. You heard what Dr. Hull said." She smiled despite her headache. "All I need is rest and I'll be good as new." At least she hoped so. She saw his expression. "I appreciate you being here though. Thank you. But I won't have you sleeping in a chair anymore."

"I suppose I could use a shower," Davy said and took a whiff of himself. "That's really what you're telling me, huh?"

She shook her head, surprised that it didn't hurt as much. "Before you go, have you heard anything? Have they caught the robbers?" She saw from his expression they hadn't. "I'm still confused. Dr. Hull said no one was hurt? Just me?"

Davy seemed to hesitate before he stood and stepped closer, then said, "Apparently one of the robbers decided to take you as a hostage."

The memory came back like a bolt of lightning. Her hand went to her throat as she remembered being in a headlock, fighting for breath while the other robbers argued with him to let her go as he tried to drag her outside. "There was a van at the curb."

"So your memory is coming back. That's a good sign."

"But something happened, and he had to let me go. After that…there's nothing."

"Hey, that's progress," Davy said excitedly. "I can tell you feel better now that you can remember more."

Did she? He would know that not being able to remember would drive her crazy. She prided herself on being capable, self-reliant, independent. Having a dark hole in her memory and lying in a hospital bed made her feel vulnerable and afraid. Davy would know that about her. Unless he'd forgotten.

"When he let you go, he kicked you and you fell back, hitting the floor hard with your head. At least that's what I heard. One of the tellers saw the whole thing. She was terrified that they were going to take you hostage."

Not half as terrified as she'd been, she thought.

"But it's over and you're doing great," he said, still looking worried though. "Are you sure you don't want me to stay?"

"Yes." She needed to be alone, to try to piece the rest of it together. What had she been doing at the bank in the first place? Wasn't it her day off? "Go."

"Well, I'm coming back later to make sure you're okay," he said as he picked up his Stetson. As he started for the door, it opened.

Carla saw Dr. Hull and two other men enter. FBI agents? They stopped for a moment to speak to Davy. She couldn't hear what was being said, but when Davy looked back toward her, there was worry in his expression.

"What's going on?" she asked the moment Davy left and the men came to her bedside.

"These are FBI agents Robert Grover and Hank Deeds," the doctor told her. "They'd like to ask you a few questions."

She didn't feel up to answering their questions right now. A lot of it had come back, but there were still holes in her memory that worried her. "You told him that I don't remember, didn't you?" she asked Dr. Hull before looking at the other men. Agent Deeds was younger with blond hair and blue eyes, Agent Grover had gray at his temples with dark eyes and bushy dark brows the color of his hair. She had another flash of memory of dark eyes peering at her from out of a mask and shivered. Pulling the blanket up, she said, "I doubt I can be much help."

"Well, let's see if that's true," Agent Grover said, and the doctor excused himself to take a call, saying he'd be right outside her door. "What were you doing at the bank? Wasn't it your day off?"

She frowned. "I must have forgotten something and stopped by." Wasn't there something about a file? Why did she suddenly have the image of mistletoe on her desk?

"Do you go into the bank on your day off normally?" Carla shook her head. He asked how long she'd worked at the bank, then how long she'd been the executive loan officer. She told him. "You worked your way up pretty fast," the agent commented. "You sound like you're ambitious."

His question made a hard knot rise in her chest because she was suddenly concerned about where he was headed with this. It also had been a bone of contention between her and Davy. Her need to make something of her life had been one of their problems, the rodeo the other. "I suppose I am."

He laughed. "Looking at your school records, I'd say you definitely are."

"Having ambition isn't—"

He didn't let her finish. "Were you aware of how much money was in the vault on the day of the robbery?"

The question disturbed her. "I'm the executive loan officer, so of course I know. It's part of my job."

He smiled and nodded. "You're single, no boyfriend?"

Her heart began to beat harder. She definitely knew where he was headed with this. "I've been busy—"

"With your career," he finished for her. "Is it everything you thought it would be?"

She couldn't help being defensive since she'd chosen this life over Davy. "I enjoy what I do."

"Really?" He studied her speculatively. "Don't you have to turn down a lot of people who want a loan?"

"Not always. We try to work with everyone."

He looked down at his notes. "Why do you think you were the only one hurt during the robbery?"

"I have no idea. Maybe if I could remember everything that happened…"

"How about you tell me everything that you do remember," the agent said.

She'd seen the exchange between the agents and Davy just inside her door and now realized that something new had happened. "Have you caught them?" The agents shared a look. "Please, I have to know what's happened."

Agent Grover was studying her closely. "We found the getaway vehicle some miles from here in the mountains. It had been torched, no doubt to try to get rid of any evidence. A motorcycle was also destroyed in the fire." His gaze bored into her as he said, "There were also three bodies found incinerated next to it. We're still trying to identify them. One of the robbers got away, the one I suspect you know. The one who tried to take you hostage?"

"Why would I know him?" Carla stared at him as her heart took off at a gallop. She could have been in that van. She would have been one of those incinerated bodies. If one of the robbers hadn't stopped the man… The angry man in the Santa suit who'd dragged her from her office. She saw him in her memory now standing over her, lifting the big white beard to scratch at his neck.

The tattoo. It flashed in her mind. *J* heart *J*. That's why he'd wanted to take her hostage. He'd been afraid she could identify him. He would have killed her. He'd gotten away? He was still out there?

The alarm on the machine next to her began to go off.

"That's enough for now," Dr. Hull said as he rushed back

in. "Step outside the room, Agent Grover, Agent Deeds. Now." Then he turned to her. "You're having a panic attack. I need you to breathe, Carla." A nurse came racing into the room.

She closed her eyes, trying to blot out the memories that had suddenly rushed at her. That's why the man had wanted to take her hostage. He was going to kill her right there in the bank but changed his mind. He said as much to the others.

As frightening as that was, something else scared her more. The way he'd treated her from the moment he'd appeared in her office doorway. It had felt personal. It hadn't been random. He'd known her.

The next thought came hard and fast. But didn't that mean that she knew him? That she'd known the killer?

Chapter Eight

"How is Carla?" James asked when Davy walked into the office after showering and changing his clothing. He'd slept little after coming back to the office apartment. He'd waited until Carla was settled and safe—at least for now.

"She's in pain and doesn't remember what happened," Davy told him as Willie and Tommy came through the front door of the Colt Brothers Investigation building. "Also, she's scared. I just heard that they found the getaway van and three bodies. There's a chance that the man who wanted to take Carla hostage killed them and is now on the run. I spoke to a couple of bank employees who stopped by the hospital to check on Carla. They said the robbers were arguing over the man taking Carla before they left." He turned to his brother Willie, who shook his head.

"I was just at the sheriff's department," Willie said. "No news, but there's a statewide manhunt that will probably be expanded before nightfall to the states around us. But so far, nothing."

"The feds are assuming that he's on the run," Davy said. "But what if he didn't run? What if he's local? What if he merely drove home?"

"Why would he stick around?" James asked, and they all shared a look. They'd all heard how the robber had been rough with Carla before trying to take her hostage.

"For some reason, he singled her out," Davy said.

"You think Carla's in danger?"

He nodded. "Everyone seems to think he might have known her, had some reason to treat her more roughly than the others."

"Is it possible she might have information that could lead to his arrest?" Tommy asked.

Davy swore. "Well, if she does, she doesn't know it. She says she can't remember a lot of it, but she was talking in her sleep. She saw something, something that has her scared. I think it's why he tried to take her hostage. I'm not going to leave her alone until he's caught." He saw his brothers exchange glances again. "What?"

"Maybe you can stay with her 24/7 at the hospital, but what happens when she's well enough to go home?" James asked. "Davy, you're already dead on your feet, not to mention you'll be leaving right after Christmas."

"You can't stay with her 24/7," Willie broke in. "We'll take turns. I'll go to the hospital now. Tommy?"

His brother nodded. "Just call me and I'll come relieve you."

"I'll help too, but it doesn't solve the problem," James said. "We can't do this indefinitely. We have no idea when or even if this man will be caught."

"Let's do what we can now and cross that bridge when we come to it," Willie told him. As the oldest, he'd always been the calmest in a disaster. It didn't surprise Davy that he was going into law enforcement. All three of his brothers had quit the rodeo now. It was only a matter of time before he hung up his spurs as well. He didn't want to think about any of that right now. All his concern was for Carla.

"The FBI agents were interviewing her when I left," he said. "Hopefully they'll find the robber quickly."

"Get some rest, Davy," Willie ordered as he left. "I'll stay with her until Tommy relieves me."

How could he rest knowing a killer was out there? One who had hurt Carla and might be back to finish the job? He realized he was exhausted. He'd gotten little sleep the night before because of thoughts of Carla, even before the robbery. All that time in the chair next to her bed had left his neck aching. Between that and worry, he hadn't slept much.

He went upstairs, knowing Willie wouldn't let anything happen to Carla. He'd drifted off for a while, then he'd spent some time talking to bank employees. Those who'd witnessed the robbery had been given the day off. Lonesome was such a small town it hadn't been hard to find out who to talk to and where to find them.

They all told the same story. It had looked as if Carla had been targeted by one of the robbers. The words *unnecessary roughness* and *seemed to single her out* had kept coming up.

"He was determined to take her as a hostage," a bank teller had told him. "I mean, he wasn't going to leave without her. If one of the other robbers hadn't hit him to make him let go of her…"

Davy knew there must have been a tie-in between Carla and the robber. What if she knew him? Why beat her up and want to take her hostage? Had she maybe recognized his voice or something about him and he'd realized it? If he'd taken her hostage… Then she would be dead right now.

Davy felt as if the clock were ticking. If the robber, now killer, thought she knew something about him, then he wasn't finished. He wouldn't know that she couldn't remember. Davy cautioned himself that this was all speculation.

Either way, Carla had to remember, he thought, feeling the urgency. She had to help the feds catch him. Until then, Davy couldn't shake the feeling that Carla was in danger.

He quickly reminded himself that Willie was sitting outside her hospital room to make sure she was safe. He'd insisted. As long as she was in the hospital, one of them would be keeping an eye on her, but once she got out…

Davy told himself they'd cross that bridge when they came to it. In the meantime, he'd do whatever he could to help find the robber turned killer.

Jud was headed home after lying low until the time he usually came home since quitting his night job. He'd just started to turn down his street when he saw a vehicle he didn't recognize behind him. He made a quick turn and then another and another. When he looked back, there was no one following him, but his heart was pounding. He couldn't even imagine how many people were looking for him or what would happen if he were caught.

He took a long way to the house he and Jesse rented. He knew she'd be at work. He parked and realized he couldn't just carry two huge bags of money into the house. Not in this neighborhood. He covered the bags on his floorboard with an old blanket, then let himself into the house. It was almost dark. He'd wait. The truck was locked, and he figured in this neighborhood no one stole from each other since they were all piss-poor.

After showering, he pulled on a white T-shirt, some faded jeans and an old pair of sneakers. He wadded up his smoky, bloody clothing and picked up his boots and socks. He hated to part with the boots since they had sentimental value, but he knew he had to. Who knew what kind of evidence was on them?

In the backyard he put everything into the burn barrel and set it on fire. He quickly stepped away and went back into the house. The sneakers would have to do until he could buy new boots. He smiled as he remembered that he now had money. He could buy a good pair. Hell, he could buy two pairs.

He tried to call Jesse, but her phone went to voice mail. He checked the time. Her shift would have just started unless she'd been called in early. He decided he'd stop by her work, something he rarely did after she'd asked him not to.

But he had to see her to tell her that he'd gotten all the money and that everything was going to be all right. As he parked at the rear of the building in a spot for employees only, he saw her standing just outside with another employee, who was male. The man was smoking and laughing at something Jesse had said. They both wore scrubs. Jealousy reared its ugly head to see her laughing with another man, but he tamped it back down.

Jesse said something to the man, who stubbed out his cigarette and hurried back inside as Jud got out and sauntered toward her. He checked his expression before he reached her. If he acted jealous, they'd argue about it. He didn't want to fight with her. They had more important things to discuss.

On the way here, he'd heard on the radio that one of the bank employees had been taken to the hospital. He couldn't be sure it was Carla. The bank manager was old enough that he could have had a heart attack. But he had a bad feeling the patient upstairs was Carla Richmond. Which meant that she wasn't dead. Not yet anyway. He had to know her condition.

As he neared the employee entrance of the hospital, he caught a whiff of food coming from the cafeteria and realized the patients would be getting their meal trays soon.

Chapter Nine

Jud walked toward the back steps where Jesse had been laughing with the man. He kept his head down until he got his emotions under control. He didn't want her to see that he was jealous, or worse, now that they had all this money, that he was uncertain what to do next. He was also scared that he hadn't covered his tracks well enough.

But the moment he lifted his head and his gaze met hers, he saw that she knew. Her eyes were wide, the words coming out on a breath. "You got it?"

He swallowed and nodded, hating that he was going to have to tell her everything. If he lied, she'd know it. It was like she had a sixth sense when it came to him. He didn't want to talk about killing Buddy and the others. She would see that it had gutted him. He quickly told her what was important.

When he got to the part about Carla Richmond seeing his tattoo, the one he'd had done on a boys' trip to Butte, she'd sat down hard on the top step.

By the time he told her about trying to take the executive loan officer hostage and Buddy interfering and then later going for his gun, Jesse dropped her face into her hands.

He sat down beside her, wanting to take her in his arms, but he was half-afraid to touch her. This couldn't be the end of them. He had all this money. What if she decided to go to the cops? He started to tell her his plan for the two of them to leave the country and make a brand-new life for themselves, when she lifted her head.

Jud was surprised to see that she hadn't been crying. Instead, she was dry-eyed. Nor did she look angry. He felt confused and almost afraid. Maybe she would rise and march inside and tell someone to call the cops. Or maybe she would—

"Carla Richmond's on my floor," she said, so calmly he felt a chill wriggle up his backbone. "I'll take care of it. From what I've heard, she doesn't remember anything. You need to get the money off the floorboard of your pickup, Jud. Remember that hike we went on just outside of town? That little rock cave?"

He remembered the two of them naked as jaybirds before winter set in next to that cave as he screwed her against one of the rocks.

"Hide the bags in the cave. Then tomorrow you need to go to work."

He started to argue that neither of them ever had to work again, but she cut him off.

"We need to act as normal as possible. You go to work as if nothing has happened." She rose to her feet. "I got called in for a double today. They'll be serving dinner. I need to go. So do you."

"Jesse—"

"Don't worry. I'm going to help you. But those two bill collectors stopped by earlier. When you go back to the house, the men could be there. Before you put the money in the cave, take out just over fifteen hundred dollars from the bag with the money from the tellers' tills. Those will be the bills not banded. Tell your associates you hocked some stuff or sold your grandmother's knickknacks and that you can get more. That should hold them off for now."

"But Carla Richmond saw my tattoo. If she tells the feds... I think we should leave town now."

She cupped his face in her hands, forcing him to meet her eyes. "Like I said, I'll take care of it. Leave everything to me."

He stared at her. She wasn't upset with him. She wasn't going to leave him and never look back. She wasn't going to the cops. She was going to help him.

For the first time since the robbery, he felt as if he could breathe. He bent to quickly kiss her and headed for his pickup, his step lighter. Buddy had been wrong about Jesse, Jud thought with a grin. She was definitely the woman for him.

BY THE TIME a woman in scrubs brought her dinner, Carla knew she was getting some of her strength back because she was hungry. Her headache had lessened, and she was starting to feel more like her old self—until she remembered everything that had happened to her at the bank and how close she'd come to dying. Then she had to be careful not to have another anxiety attack.

Davy said she was safe now, but she didn't feel like it. Nor did she think he believed it. Why else did he think she needed either him or his brothers stationed outside her hospital room door?

The door opened and she got a glimpse of Willie Colt out in the hallway. He winked at her and gave her a thumbs-up as a young, attractive blonde in scrubs brought in her dinner tray.

"Hope you're hungry," the woman said cheerfully as she began to arrange the tray in front of Carla. "How are you feeling?"

"Better."

"That's good." The blonde finished with the service and

seemed to hesitate. "I heard what happened. How awful."
The aide took her hand and squeezed it quickly before letting go. "You must have been terrified."

"I was."

"Your memory of what happened has returned?"

Carla shook her head. "Just bits and pieces, but enough
to be terrified all over again."

The blonde tsk-tsked and shook her head. "Well, it's over
now and you can put it all behind you. Enjoy your dinner.
I'll be back to pick up your tray." She smiled. "So you'd
better eat everything."

Carla returned her smile, promising to do her best.

At the door, the young woman turned to look back at
her. "There's an FBI agent outside and a friend of yours.
I'm going to tell them that you're eating and that they need
to leave you alone."

"Thank you," Carla said as the aide left.

Why was the FBI agent waiting to talk to her again?
She'd told him that she didn't remember anything. Which
wasn't quite true, she realized. But when she replayed their
conversation in her head, she realized the agent suspected
the robbery had been an inside job—and that she'd been a
part of it. No wonder he'd rattled her.

Not that she couldn't see why he was suspicious. Why
had the robber only hurt her? She recalled looking up and
seeing him standing in her office doorway as if he'd come
looking for her. His reaction to her seemed too aggressive
even from the start. She couldn't shake the feeling that he
knew her and had reason to dislike her. Had she turned him
down for a loan? Could he be someone from town, someone
who had a grudge against her for some reason? Someone
she'd offended back in high school?

She'd just assumed the robbers weren't from around
Lonesome. But what if they were? What if the man who'd

attacked her lived in Lonesome? She thought of the tattoo on the man's neck. She was sure that she'd never seen it before. But most of the time it could be covered, she thought and frowned. She remembered greasy-looking longish dark hair that had escaped the mask covering his head.

So he could have a house down the street. He could be the man who waited on her at the grocery store or the one with the low ponytail who delivered her mail. He could be anyone and she wouldn't recognize him until it was too late. That made this situation all the more frightening.

But the FBI agent had it all wrong. She wished she knew how to convince him of that. He needed to be looking for the robber turned killer and not spend his time coming after her.

Her stomach growled. She realized that the last thing she'd eaten was Christmas sugar cookies a friend had dropped off that morning as she was headed for the bank and shopping. While she was feeling stronger, she knew if she hoped to feel like herself again she had to eat. More than anything, she wanted to feel strong and capable again—not vulnerable and scared like she was right now.

She began to uncover the small dishes on the tray.

THE TWO GOONS who'd roughed him up the last time were waiting for Jud when he returned home—just as Jesse had warned him. Before he'd left the hospital parking lot, he'd taken Jesse's advice and had the fifteen hundred and sixty-five dollars from the bank tills ready. He'd left the rest of the money in the small cave and had driven home, prepared with the story about stealing his grandmother's jewelry and knickknacks. He must have looked like the kind of guy who would steal from his grandmother because they bought his story—just as Jesse had said they would.

One of the goons had cuffed him hard upside the head,

warning him he'd better have the rest next week, before they drove away. By next week he planned to be miles from here, he thought as he rubbed the side of his head and went inside the house.

The past few days had exhausted him. He went to bed early, determined that when he arrived at his delivery job in the morning, no one would suspect anything.

Still, it would be hard pretending that nothing had happened. He'd planned the robbery around the two days he had off.

The moment he clocked in and headed to the loading area, he heard people talking about the bank job. He couldn't help feeling superior as he joined everyone and began loading boxes into his truck.

"I wonder how much money they got away with," one of his coworkers was saying. "How much money does the Lonesome bank keep in the vault?"

He listened to them speculate and smiled to himself. He enjoyed this. He kept thinking, wouldn't they all have a cow if they knew just how much the score had landed— and that he had every dollar of it?

There were five of them busy loading the trucks this morning. Because of the upcoming holidays, there were more packages than usual, which was why he'd been hired. The only time he felt uncomfortable was when they talked about the deaths of the robbery accomplices.

"Pretty cold-blooded to kill them all like that," one of the men said.

"Greed. You know that's all it was," another said.

Jud bit his lip to keep from saying anything.

Their only female coworker added her two cents. "Bet he was the one who almost killed Carla Richmond. He was the kind who would kill his accomplices."

Jud had never liked the fiftysomething know-it-all

Cheryl. "What makes you think it was a man? Could have been a woman."

That got a burst of laughter and put his female coworker on the defensive.

"Well, now he has all the money," she said.

"Wonder what he'll do with it," someone said.

"Spend it," another said.

"If it was a woman, she'd be smart enough to hang on to it and bide her time," Cheryl said as she hefted a large box onto her truck.

The others scoffed and Jud joined in.

"Anyone heard how Carla is doing?" she asked.

One of the young men spoke up. "My girlfriend's cousin is an orderly at the hospital. He said she can't remember anything. She has a concussion. But that doesn't mean that her memory won't come back."

Jud hoped that wasn't true. "I had one of those. I never could remember what had happened to me." He glanced up. No one was paying him any mind. They seemed to think that his interest had been in the concussion part of the story.

"She probably can't help the feds catch the robbers anyway," one of the men said. "I heard they had on Santa suits that covered everything. Doubt they'll ever catch the one who's left." Jud could only hope.

"I heard the robber who hurt her had tried to take her hostage," Cheryl said. "Wonder what he had against her?"

"Or what he had against his accomplices," another added with a laugh.

"He might have just been having a bad day," Jud said and wished he hadn't, although that didn't stop him. "Or maybe they turned on him, pulling a gun with a plan to kill him. It could have been a double cross that ended with him being forced to defend himself."

Their boss had come out then and everyone fell silent

and kept working. But he could feel Cheryl giving him the eye as if she knew more than she did. It was boring and repetitious manual labor. But it wasn't hard, and it paid the bills—just barely, and had he not been a temporary employee for the holidays, he would get an extra week's vacation after five years.

The thought made him laugh out loud, which only made Cheryl squint her eyes at him. He didn't care. He had a ton of money hidden outside town. He wouldn't be needing that extra week of vacation. Let these fools break their backs day after day here. Judson Bruckner was putting this hick town behind him soon.

The trucks were almost loaded. He was glad he'd come into work. It was interesting hearing what people were saying, especially about Carla Richmond and what she might—or might not—have told the feds.

"I won't feel safe until he's caught," a coworker said as they finished up and he slammed the rear door of his truck. There would be more to load tomorrow and a ton of packages to deliver. "Robbing the bank was one thing, but killing his accomplices?" The man shook his head. "If he's still around, I'd feel better if he was caught." The others agreed.

"But why would he stay around?" Cheryl asked.

"I agree," another said. "I'm sure he's long gone from here."

"I know I would be," one of the men added. "I'd be anxious to spend all that money."

"Which would get you caught," Cheryl said in that annoying tone of hers. "Some of that money is marked. I had a friend who worked in a bank. You know they keep marked money at every bank just in case they get robbed."

"I didn't know that," one of the men said. "So he can't spend that money? That would really suck."

"Couldn't he tell which bills were marked?" Jud asked

as casually as he could over the sudden rush of his pulse. He'd heard about bank employees dropping into a robber's bag a container of ink that blew up. He'd checked the bags when he'd gotten the money out for the goons. All the bills were just fine.

"They're not marked like that. They keep bills that have consecutive serial numbers they watch for. Everyone will be looking for those bills," she said. "He'll have trouble spending the money—even years from now—and not getting caught."

Jud ground his teeth. Why hadn't he known that? Had Buddy? Had the others? He thought of the bags of money and swore silently. Carla Richmond would have known that. She would have known it the whole time they were robbing the bank. That woman.

Then he had a thought that stopped him dead. He'd just given over fifteen hundred dollars of the money to Wes and Fletch, the two goons who worked for the loan shark.

His blood ran cold at the thought of what would happen if they pocketed some of the money, tried to spend it, were arrested—and told their boss where they'd gotten the cash.

He reminded himself that Jesse had been specific about him taking the money that had come from the tellers' tills. He hadn't, but it was probably fine.

CARLA WAS PLEASED to see that every lid she lifted on her food tray revealed something that looked and smelled delicious. She really was hungry. She hoped the aide was good to her word and kept the agent out of her room until she'd eaten. She'd already decided that because of the aide's promise, she would take her time.

Eventually, she would have to tell the FBI agent about the tattoo. She had her doubts whether he could find the man based on it though. But it was a clue. She'd bet that the man's name started with *J*. That had to be something, right?

She lifted the last lid to see what she had before she took her first bite and swallowed back a scream. On top of what smelled like a brownie lay a napkin. Someone had written in black marker TALK AND YOU DIE.

Chapter Ten

Reflexively, Carla slammed the lid back down as she fought the tears that came on the heels of her shock—and terror. Past her initial alarm came a chilling thought: she wasn't safe here. Not even with an FBI agent and Willie Colt outside her door.

Worse, she knew why she'd been left the note. The man from the bank robbery. He knew that she'd seen his tattoo. He feared that she could identify him. That was why he had been so desperate to take her hostage. He'd wanted to kill her and would have if she'd gotten into that van.

But how did he get a note onto her food tray? Did he work here or did he know someone who did? Not that it mattered. She wasn't safe, and if she told anyone about what she'd seen—

Agent Robert Grover stuck his head into her hospital room doorway.

"Up for a few questions while you eat?" he asked as he stepped into the room, with his partner Deeds right behind him.

Carla made angry swipes at her wet cheeks and pushed away the food tray, her appetite gone. She tried to pull herself together and decide what to do.

As long as she was in the hospital, she wasn't safe. The robber knew what room she was in. How else would he have been able to sneak her the note? He could be a nurse. Or an orderly. Or work in food service. He could be so close that he had seen the agent enter her room just moments ago.

Her thoughts were immediately at war. Wouldn't the smart thing be to tell the agent everything and let him track down the man and put him behind bars? Maybe J, as she now thought of him, had left fingerprints on the dish or the food tray. If he had a record…

But even as she considered it, she reminded herself that Agent Grover thought it was an inside job. He was busy looking at her as a suspect. He might think the tattoo was just a stalling tactic on her part, something to keep him busy tracking down red herrings instead of looking more closely at her.

If she talked, J would know and he'd be coming for her right here at the hospital. Right when she would be at her most vulnerable.

She kept her mouth shut about the note out of terror. After FBI agents Robert Grover and Hank Deeds left, the blonde aide came in to take her tray as if she had been waiting outside in the hallway—as anxious for him to leave as Carla had been.

"You hardly touched your dinner. Is everything all right?" She didn't wait for an answer as she started to reach for the dessert dish lid with the note under it. "You sure you don't at least want your brownie?"

"No!" She'd said it a little too sharply, because the young woman looked at her with concern, but pulled back her hand without lifting the lid. "I'm just not hungry. Please take it and throw it all away."

"If you're sure," the blonde said before picking up the tray. "Maybe you'll be hungrier in the morning. Did I hear that you're going to be released tomorrow afternoon? At least you'll be with us for a while longer." The young woman smiled. "That's good news, even though I'm sure you're anxious to get out of here. Once you get home, maybe then your appetite will return."

Carla watched her go, feeling even sicker than she had been earlier. She wasn't being released until tomorrow afternoon. If she lived that long, she was going home to an empty house. Not only did she live alone, but also her house was outside town. Her closest neighbor was a half mile away.

She thought of her cozy little house, which had always been her sanctuary. Now it felt ominous, set back off the road, the home surrounded by dense pines on three sides and large boulders at the edge of the river on the other. How quickly the privacy and quiet turned into something else—a place where she wouldn't see the killer coming until it was too late.

How foolish she'd been to think it was over. She'd thought that she'd dodged a bullet when J hadn't taken her hostage, when she'd awakened in the hospital and realized it was only a concussion and she was going to live.

Then she'd read the note. It was a reminder that he not only hadn't forgotten about her, but that he could get to her at any time, even later when she was sleeping.

Carla could feel her pulse thumping hard just beneath her skin as the reality of her situation hit her. She had a killer worried that she might give him away to the feds. She had a federal agent who thought the robbery had been an inside job with her help. She wasn't safe. Not here in the hospital. Not anywhere until J was caught.

Maybe she should have told the agent. Maybe if she'd shown him the note… It was too late now. Worse, she doubted J would trust her to keep her mouth shut. Which meant he wasn't finished with her.

When Davy walked through her hospital door and

rushed to her bedside, she threw her arms around him. She was so glad to see him.

"HEY," DAVY SAID, unable not to grin as he held her. It felt good having her in his arms again. He told himself not to make more of it than it probably was. Carla was scared after her ordeal at the bank. Who wouldn't be?

"I wasn't expecting that kind of reception, but I liked it," he joked as he pulled back to look at her and sobered. "What's happened?" He could feel her trembling and swore he could hear her heart pounding it was beating so hard.

She looked toward the door. She was biting at her lower lip, tears welling in her blue eyes, and all the color had leached from her face.

"Talk to me," he said, drawing her attention back to him. He'd never seen her like this in all the years he'd known her, including the intimate ones. "You're scaring me."

She let out a strangled bark of a laugh. "*You're* scared? No one's threatening to kill you."

He stared at her in confusion. He'd talked to Willie before coming into her room. His brother had sworn that the only people who'd come into her room were two FBI agents and a food server. "You were threatened here at the hospital?"

As she nodded, she brushed at her tears. "There was a note on my dinner tray."

"You still have it?" he asked and looked around. The tray was gone. When he met her eyes again, he knew that so was the note. "How long ago was this? Maybe I can still—"

"No, I don't want you getting involved," she cried.

He shook his head. "Carla, I am involved. You're in trouble and I'm here for you. Tell me. What was on the note?" He listened as she described it. TALK AND YOU DIE.

"He's here in the hospital," she cried. "He can get to me at any time."

"No, he can't," Davy assured her, angry with himself for leaving her room. Not that it would have kept someone from getting the note to her. But at least they would have the note to give to the feds. "I'm not leaving you alone again."

She groaned, but no longer appeared to be trembling. "You can't protect me. Not from a killer. Or the FBI."

"What are you talking about?"

"The FBI agent who questioned me? I can tell he thinks the robbery an inside job and that I was involved." She buried her face in her hands. "If only I hadn't stopped by my office on my day off…"

"Don't." He took her hands in both of his. They felt cold. He rubbed a little heat back into them and thought about the winter they were together. She had always had cold hands and feet. He'd been more than happy to warm them up for her. "You can't rewrite history. I've done some of that and all it does is make you feel worse." He frowned. TALK AND YOU DIE. "Carla, why would the robber think you know something he doesn't want you telling the law?"

She looked away for a moment, swallowed and then met his gaze as if making up her mind. "I remembered something about the robbery. He had a tattoo, the man who tried to abduct me." She described it. "I'm assuming his name starts with *J*. Maybe so does his partner's."

"Did you tell the agent?"

Carla shook her head. "I was too afraid."

"Tell me about the tattoo."

"It was on his neck close to his shoulder. It was fairly crude. A *J*, then a heart and another *J*. The heart was a little sloppy and the ink had settled in the bottom of it."

"You need to tell the FBI agent."

She looked close to tears. "How is it going to help?"

"I'm not sure," Davy said. "But it's something. What about his voice? Would you recognize it if you heard it again?"

She shook her head. "It was muffled because of the mask and beard."

He questioned her about the size of the man. Average in every way. She hadn't gotten a good look at the other men. She thought one of them, the one who acted like the boss, had been larger, stockier.

"Who do you know whose name begins with *J*—other than my brother?"

She shook her head and winced. He could tell her headache had come back and was starting to hurt again.

"Try not to worry about it," he said. "I'm staying right here to make sure you're safe. No one is going to get to you."

She met his gaze and tears again flooded her eyes. "Davy, I'm being released from the hospital tomorrow."

He didn't have time to react before there was a knock at the door and a blonde in scrubs stuck her head in. She had an armful of flowers. So did the candy striper behind her.

"I'm sorry—you have company," the blonde said as she put down two vases of flowers and took three more from the young candy striper behind her. She placed them around the room. "Seems you have a lot of friends."

He watched the aide fuss with one of the bouquets. "Is this the woman who brought your dinner tray?" he whispered to Carla, who nodded. "Excuse me," he said to the blonde. "Were you in charge of her dinner tray?"

The woman looked surprised. She carefully straightened one of the vases before she said, "The patient said she wasn't hungry and asked me to take it away. If she's changed her mind, I'd be happy to get her another tray."

He shook his head. "Where is that original tray?"

She seemed confused. "I took it down to the kitchen. By now the dishes have been scraped clean and loaded in the dishwasher." She looked past him to Carla. "Did you leave something on the tray that you didn't mean to?"

"Never mind," Davy said and felt the woman's gaze turn to him. Something like anger flickered in those blue eyes before she dropped her lashes.

"I'm sorry, but visiting hours are over," she said to him.

"I'm not visiting. I'll be staying as long as Carla remains in the hospital."

The blonde aide raised a brow. "Sure? I can't imagine you would be comfortable—"

"No problem."

It wasn't until she'd left that he saw Carla frowning at him as if surprised by his reaction to the attendant. "At this point, we have to suspect everyone," he said. "She had access to your dinner tray." Carla's eyes widened in alarm. "I didn't see a name tag, did you?" She shook her head. "I'll get James and Tommy to find out who she is."

He moved to the side of her bed. "In the meantime, I'm not going anywhere. Don't worry." But even as he said it, he was more than worried. He had feared that her life might be in danger. Now they knew it was.

Chapter Eleven

Carla told herself that she couldn't do this as she listened to Davy inform the doctor that he would be sleeping in the reclining chair next to Carla's bed. The last thing she wanted was for him to spend his Christmas holidays here in this hospital. But she couldn't send him away either. His being here made her feel safe and less afraid.

Her head ached and she felt sick to her stomach. She hated feeling so vulnerable. She was the one who helped others—not the other way around. She didn't like asking for help. Especially from Davy Colt, the man she'd given an ultimatum to all those years ago.

But she'd never had a killer after her before. Was this going to be her life until the masked man was caught—if he was ever caught? Running scared and being afraid of everyone who crossed her path? "I can't do this," she said when Davy got off the phone. "I can't ask you to either."

She was so grateful to him, but what if the killer wasn't caught? Davy couldn't put his life on hold. She wouldn't allow that. He didn't have that many more years to rodeo. She knew what it meant to him and felt sick at how she'd demanded he give it up if he loved her. She'd forced him to choose—and he had, breaking both of their hearts. He'd begged her to come on the road with him, calling it an adventure they would talk about when they were old.

But she'd refused, telling him he needed to grow up and quit being so selfish. She cringed now at the memory. Given the way she'd treated him, she had no right to ask him to keep her safe now.

"Hey, you didn't ask," he said as he moved to the bed. He brushed a lock of her hair back from her forehead, his fingertips gliding over her skin and sending a shiver through her. "I'm here for you. Don't worry. The feds are looking for him and my brothers are beating the bushes for information on him. We've got this."

She couldn't help the relief that welled inside her. "Thank you, Davy."

His gaze softened. "Just try to get some rest. I'll be here."

As silly as it seemed, she was exhausted. She closed her eyes. Davy was here. He was the only man who'd ever made her feel completely safe. Within seconds, she drifted off into a deep, dreamless sleep.

WHILE CARLA SLEPT, Davy placed a call to the Colt Brothers Investigation office and filled James in on the latest information, including the tattoo and note.

"She needs to tell the FBI agent about both," James said.

"I agree, but not until she's out of the hospital. We can't take the chance that J will find out. We know he has access to her here. Better for her to tell the agent after she's at home. Not that I suspect the feds are going to like it."

James agreed. "The agent is definitely going to be skeptical about this new information. She just now remembered the tattoo? As for the note, because she didn't keep it, there is no evidence that she's telling the truth. If he already suspects she's involved, he's going to think she's lying to cover up something. But don't worry, if the feds don't follow up on this, we will."

"Think you can get information on hospital employees with names that begin with *J*?"

"I'll do what I can," his brother said. "As for the tattoo clue, it could be an old girlfriend, so don't hang too much hope on the second *J*. The first *J* could be a nickname. Unfortunately, Tommy and I are both working other cases too and Willie is training over at the sheriff's department. Do you think you can hit the tattoo shops?"

It would give him something to do besides worry. The problem was, he couldn't leave Carla. He'd have to take her with him.

"The tattoo doesn't sound all that memorable," James was saying. "Have Carla sketch out what she remembers. I'll let you know if I get the hospital employee list."

Davy knew James was right. Neither lead might be all that helpful, another reason the feds would suspect her. "She's getting released from the hospital tomorrow."

"What are you going to do then?" his brother asked.

"I'm not sure," he said, looking toward the hospital bed where she was sleeping peacefully for the moment. "I'm not sure what she'll *allow* me to do. She's scared right now and still healing. Once she is strong again… Well, you know how she is, and given our history, well, it's not like we've ever agreed on the future."

"Don't you have a ride coming up in the New Year?"

"I can't leave knowing she's in danger."

James sighed. "Davy, have you considered what you're going to do if this case isn't solved for months or maybe ever?"

"I guess I'll cross that bridge when I get to it."

He could hear his brother's concern in the silence that followed.

"Well, we'll all do what we can to help. Keep us in the loop."

A silence fell between them but neither disconnected. "I suppose you heard," Davy said. "The reason the robbers were able to get away from the cops was because of the train crossing where Dad was killed."

"I heard. Sounds like at least one of the robbers was familiar with that unregulated crossing and maybe even knew its history," James said.

"Which could mean he's a local."

"Yeah." His brother was silent for a moment before he said, "The two cases aren't tied together."

Davy didn't answer for a moment. "I know. It just brings it all back. You still working on Dad's case?"

"You know I am. Tommy's helping. We're trying to get the file on the case now that we have a new sheriff. Our lawyer thinks we should be able to since Dad's death was ruled an accident."

"Except that we don't believe that."

"No, we don't."

JUD HAD TRIED to call Jesse numerous times during work, but the calls had always gone to voice mail. He'd left messages. "Call back. I need to know what's going on." Each message had sounded more frantic, but still she hadn't returned his calls.

He was thinking the worst had happened when he finally finished his shift and drove home. As he came down the street, he looked for any vehicles he didn't recognize. Maybe the feds had already made him. He knew that was a long shot. They couldn't have this quickly. Not based on a tattoo—and that was if Carla Richmond had told them what she'd seen.

Even if Carla remembered him coming into the bank for a loan weeks ago, she didn't know his name. He'd never given it to her. Nor did they travel in the same circles. He also hadn't left any fingerprints or DNA at the bank. Or in the getaway car.

Knowing all this still didn't give him any peace of mind. Too much was at stake. He hated loose ends. That's why he was glad that he'd parted ways with Buddy, Rick and Eli. He'd learned a long time ago not to trust anyone. Like his old man used to say, two people can keep a secret—if one of them is dead.

No one even knew that he'd robbed the bank.

Except Jesse.

The thought made his pulse spike. She wouldn't turn on him. He trusted her with his life, didn't he? He thought about how well she'd taken the news earlier. But what if she'd just been pretending?

His breath came out in a rush of both relief and worry when he saw her sedan parked by the house. The curtains were closed in the front window, a light glowing behind them. There were no other vehicles around. He thought about driving around the block to make sure none were idling in the alley. But if he had, he'd feel guilty about not trusting her, so he pulled in next to her car.

He and Jesse were cut from the same cloth, his mother would have said. From what little she'd told him about herself, he knew that neither of them had ever colored inside the lines. They'd always taken the easiest way, no matter how many rules they had to break. Some people would have thought that dishonest, but he knew that he and Jesse just thought of it as surviving in a world that was against them since birth. His mother would have said he was making an excuse for his despicable behavior. But then his mother was no saint herself, was she?

Jud cut his pickup's engine and sat for a moment, staring at the front door. He wouldn't know if she'd betrayed him until he got out and went inside. If she had… Well, then he'd be going to prison. That's if he got lucky and didn't get the chair. Fortunately, Montana hadn't executed anyone in a long time. He didn't want to be the one they fired up Old Sparky for.

On what felt like a long walk to the house, he realized electric chairs were a thing of the past—at least in Montana. They'd gone to lethal injection a long time ago, he now remembered hearing. That didn't relieve him much as he opened the front door of his house expecting to see Jesse sitting in the living room with the feds—after making a deal.

Chapter Twelve

Jesse came out of the kitchen bringing the smell of fried chicken like a cloud around her. He could hear music playing at the back of the house. It could have been any other day. Except that Jesse hadn't brought home takeout. She was apparently *cooking* dinner.

Not just that. She looked happy.

Jud frowned as he glanced past her, still expecting the feds to come bursting out, weapons drawn and a SWAT team hiding in the alley.

"I hope you're hungry," she said, smiling as she leaned in to kiss him. "I made us a special meal to celebrate. Smarter than going out for dinner."

They were celebrating? He wondered if this was his last meal before he ended up behind bars. It dawned on him that making a deal with the feds was just one way she could have betrayed him. There was also Leon Trainer, the loan shark who'd sent the goons to collect his debt. She could nark him out to Leon.

He realized that Jesse had all kinds of ways to come out of this on top. He thought of the other women he'd known. None of them would have given a thought to double-crossing him. Did he really believe this one was different?

"What are we celebrating?" he asked, the words coming out slow and awkward.

"Are you kidding?" She laughed, making him feel as if he should go out and come in again. Had she forgotten how much trouble they were in? Leon's goons wouldn't hesitate to refresh her memory. Good luck convincing the feds that she wasn't involved from the beginning.

"Carla Richmond didn't tell the feds."

He shook his head as if to clear it. "How do you know that?"

Jesse grinned. "I know because I took care of it."

He suddenly had a vision of her holding a pillow down on Carla Richmond's face at the hospital. "How did you—"

"I'll tell you over dinner. Come on, I don't want the chicken to burn."

Like a sleepwalker, he followed her into the kitchen. She had the table set and candles burning. She wasn't kidding. This was a celebratory dinner. He just wished he felt like celebrating after the day he'd had.

But he wasn't in handcuffs. Yet. And Jesse was cooking. His stomach growled as she put a bowl of real mashed potatoes on the table and motioned him into his chair. He couldn't remember the last time he'd had anything but instant potatoes from some drive-through.

She plated the fried chicken, put it down next to the mountain of potatoes and then she brought out a bowl of corn. He could see the can still sitting on the counter, but he wasn't about to complain that it wasn't fresh from the cob.

"Eat," she said as she joined him.

He began to load his plate, not sure how much longer he could wait to hear what was going on. "Jesse—"

"Not until you take a bite of my chicken. My grandma used to make the best fried chicken. She taught me how. I'd thought I'd forgotten." She loaded her own plate while humming along with the song on the radio.

He took a bite out of a drumstick. It was delicious and

he said as much. She beamed at the compliment. He took another bite and asked around it, "Come on, Jesse, what did you do?"

"I made sure she got the message."

He listened while she explained how she'd gotten a note onto Carla Richmond's dinner tray and been the one to bring the woman's tray to her hospital room.

"You should have seen her face when I went back in to get the tray," Jesse said and laughed. "She was scared spitless. Couldn't eat any of her meal." She took a big bite of the mashed potatoes, still grinning.

"How do you know she didn't tell the feds?"

Jesse gave him an impatient look. "Because the note was still on top of the brownie. Don't you see? If she was going to tell, she would have taken the note and shown it to the federal agent. He was right outside her door waiting for her to finish her meal." She shrugged as if all this was child's play for her. "When I came in to take her tray, the lid was still on, the note under it. She could have given it to the feds, but she didn't. She got the message." She laughed, then sobered. "There's one problem though."

He had to wait as she took a bite of her dinner. He wondered if she'd heard about some of the money being marked.

"There's a long, lanky cowboy with her," Jesse said as she chewed. "Davy Colt? You know him?"

Jud swore. "Everyone in four counties around us knows about the Colt brothers. They're wild rodeo cowboys." At least they used to be, he realized. He'd lived in Lonesome long enough to know who they were—not that he'd ever met any of them. But he'd heard about them. "Two of them took over their father's old private-investigation business on Main Street. I think another was just hired as a deputy sheriff."

"Should we be worried?"

He gave it a moment's thought. "Naw. I doubt bronc riders know what they're doing out of the arena."

She gave him the eye for a moment as if trying to tell whether he was being truthful or just trying to mollify her. "Well, Davy Colt seems to think that Carla might be in danger. He's staying the night with her at the hospital." She blew out a puff of air, lifting her blond bangs from her forehead. The kitchen was small and hot. They usually ate takeout in front of the television in the living room.

"You think she told Davy Colt about the note?"

Jesse shrugged. "Depends on how much she trusts him. They seem close but not like they're involved. There's something between them though. He's way too protective. You sure he and his brothers won't be a problem?"

"They don't have anything because she doesn't have anything. If she knew who I was, she would have already told and I'd be behind bars."

"What about that tattoo?"

He shrugged, playing it down. "So she knows our names start with *J*. Good luck finding us—even if she does talk to the feds."

"She'd better not or she'll regret it," Jesse said.

He was beginning to think that Buddy had been right. "The only way they'll catch us is if I make a move on her."

Jesse didn't seem to be listening. Instead, she had a strange look on her face, her eyes narrowed, her lip caught in her teeth. "Carla's being released from the hospital today. I'll know if she talks."

CARLA OPENED HER eyes to sunshine streaming in the hospital room window. She couldn't believe that she'd slept through the whole night. For a moment she forgot where she was. When it all came back in a rush, she sat up abruptly.

"Easy, Sleeping Beauty," Davy said as he approached.

He'd been standing on the far side of the room by the window. She hadn't seen him until he spoke. Her expression must have given her away. "You thought I'd left."

She started to deny it but stopped herself. "I was just startled for a few moments."

"Have I ever given you reason not to trust me?" he asked, frowning.

"No." She chastised herself. If anyone wasn't trustworthy, it was her. Davy had trusted her, thinking they had a future all those years ago. Then she'd given him the ultimatum—her or the rodeo. She'd known it was a mistake the moment the demand left her lips, but there had been no taking it back.

She'd never forgotten the hurt she'd seen in his eyes. He'd pleaded with her not to make their relationship an either-or. But she'd been adamant, determined to make him choose. When he hadn't, she'd broken up with him and started dating Levi Johnson. She'd known about the animosity between Davy and Levi. It was one of the reasons she'd jumped at going out with him when he'd called. News of her breakup with Davy had spread fast and Levi had moved quickly.

Carla realized fast that she and Levi had both wanted to hurt Davy. After a few dates, she'd told Levi that she couldn't see him anymore. By then Davy had gone back to the rodeo circuit, so he probably hadn't even known anyway.

That she'd purposely tried to hurt him was one of her deepest regrets. That he had now slept in her hospital room on the visitor's chair to protect her only made her feel worse about the past.

"I've given you reason not to trust me though," she said quietly.

Davy shook his head and gave her a smile. "All water under the bridge."

She felt tears sting her eyes and had to look away as the doctor came in to tell her she could get dressed to go home. It was no surprise Davy had had one of his brothers get her clothes from her house.

"I'm going to step out into the hall while you change," Davy said, pretending he didn't see how close she was to crying.

Carla changed in the bathroom once he was gone. The clothing she'd been wearing the day of the robbery was now in the hands of the feds. Davy had picked up her coat, hat and scarf from her office at the bank.

As she came out of the bathroom, she saw an aide waiting with a wheelchair. Not the same aide who'd brought her food and flowers yesterday.

"We can have your flowers sent to your house if you like," the woman said.

Carla felt ashamed because she didn't want to take the flowers. She'd hardly acknowledged the ones from her boss and coworkers. Her life had been so much about her work that she'd let other friendships go, hardly ever seeing old friends who'd stayed in town. How had her life become so small? And now there was a killer threatening to destroy it?

"Could you share the flowers with other patients?" she asked the aide, who quickly nodded.

"I have some elderly patients who would love them," the woman said, pulling all the cards from the bouquets and handing them to her. "I'll take care of it."

As the aide wheeled her from the hospital room, Carla saw Davy waiting for her just outside the door. Sometimes she forgot how handsome he was with his longish dark hair and those incredible blue eyes. But what struck her most was how genuine he was. It made her heart ache for what could have been and the lost years between them.

DAVY HELPED CARLA into his pickup and hurried around to slide behind the wheel. He knew this woman, so he could tell that she was uncomfortable being dependent on him. And yet she was scared and didn't want to be alone.

He knew she would balk when he suggested he stay at her house—at least for a while. James was right. It could take months for J to be found. Worse, he might never be caught. If so, Carla would have to look over her shoulder the rest of her life. She would never feel safe. Davy couldn't bear that for her, knowing how she prided herself on her independence.

"This isn't the way to my house," she said after he'd driven only a few blocks.

"Nope." He turned down the alley and came to a stop behind the Colt Brothers Investigation building. Shutting off the motor, he turned toward her. "I want you to stay here for just a little while. James and Tommy redid the upstairs apartment. There's now two bedrooms and two baths." He was talking fast, hoping he could get out his plan before she stopped him. "I'm staying up there, but I'll give you all the space you want. Please say you'll at least stay here until you're cleared to go back to work."

He took a breath. He could see her fighting the idea. "Or at least through the holidays. You'd be doing me a huge favor. You know how my brothers are. They'll cut me some slack with you around."

She sighed and looked over at him. Her expression said that he wasn't fooling her. She knew why he wanted her to stay here—in a place that he would find easier to protect her.

"Just until I'm cleared to go back to work," she said. "I

had some time off coming anyway. After that, you go back
to the rodeo, and I go home. Agreed?"

Davy saw that he had no choice but to agree, so he nodded. The truth was, if the killer wasn't caught, he couldn't
see how he could ever leave her.

Chapter Thirteen

Jud felt as if he was being watched—and had since the robbery. He especially hated doing any shopping in Lonesome, but Jesse had asked him to pick up a few things on his way home. How could he say no to a quick stop at the local grocery store?

Fortunately, it wasn't very busy. Maybe if he hurried… He brushed a lock of hair back from his face as he glanced through the frosty glass of the ice-cream freezer in front of him and tried to remember what kind of ice cream she'd asked for. There were dark circles under his eyes. He hadn't slept well. Last night, he'd awakened to find Jesse lying next to him, staring at him. When he'd started to ask if something was wrong, she'd closed her eyes and rolled over.

He studied his reflection. He looked older too, he thought, as if he'd aged ten years since the robbery. Out of the corner of his eye, he saw a figure standing a little off to one side behind him. His breath rushed out of him and he half turned to reach for the pistol at his back, but then he saw who it was. Not Davy Colt or any of his brothers. Not the local sheriff or his deputies. Not the feds.

Just an annoying old woman.

He silently cursed her for scaring him. His heart pingponged around in his chest as he released his hold on his weapon and said, "You need something, Mrs. Brooks?"

"I need to know why you have a gun stuck in the back of your jeans," she snapped.

"Keep your voice down." He glared at her. She was old and frail and a little more hunched over than he remembered, but that tongue of hers was sharp and lethal. The worst busybody in the entire county had just seen him staring at himself in a freezer glass door before going for his gun. She seemed to be waiting impatiently for an answer as if it was any of her business.

"These are dangerous times," he said. He'd started carrying the gun, except at work. "I'm sure you heard about the bank being robbed."

"Not to mention the robber's accomplices being murdered," she said, still eyeing him suspiciously.

"Exactly." He turned back to the freezer, opened the door and took out a quart of vanilla ice cream. "Jesse's making peach cobbler. Got to have ice cream," he said, hoping to change the subject. "Better get this home before it melts." He started to step past her, but she grabbed his arm in her clawlike fingers.

"Jesse Watney?" She spat the name out like a mouthful of dirt. "I heard a rumor that she was back here. So you've hooked up with her. Guess you've lost your mind. She ever mention that family of hers, who used to live not far from here? No? Suppose she wouldn't want to scare you away. Bet she hasn't mentioned her sister, who went missing, either." Cora Brooks chuckled. "Wonder why she kept that from you."

"I think you have her confused with someone else. Jesse isn't from around here. All her kin are down in Idaho."

"That what she told you?"

He wanted to wipe that knowing smile off her face. "My ice cream is melting." He stepped past her.

"Best watch your back," Cora called after him. "You

have no idea who you're living with." She let out a cackle that raised the hair on the back of his neck. "I'd keep that gun handy if I were you."

"What was that about?" the checkout woman asked.

"Just Cora. You know how she is," he said, more shaken than he wanted to admit.

"She seems to have nothing to do but butt in to other people's business," the checker said. "Half the time I don't think she knows what she's talking about."

Jud wondered about that. "You've lived here your whole life. You ever know anyone named Watney?"

The woman thought for a moment before she counted out his change and handed it to him. "You sure it was Watney? I remember a family that lived back in the mountains. But I thought their name was Welsh. Or maybe they were Welsh. I just remember my grandmother talking about them. I think one of them was murdered or disappeared. There was something everyone was whispering about." She shrugged. "That what Cora was giving you a hard time about?"

"Like you said, she probably doesn't know what she's talking about."

IT HADN'T TAKEN Agent Grover long to find her. Carla had just gotten settled into one of the bedrooms over the Colt Brothers Investigation office when he and Agent Deeds had shown up downstairs demanding to see her.

Not long before that, she'd made a list of clothing and other items she needed from her house. Willie had gone to take care of that while Tommy had asked her to draw the tattoo as close to the size, shape and design as she could remember.

"I'm no artist, but I'll try." She'd been glad to do it. They were trying so hard to find J, she'd do whatever she could to help them. Carla knew the only chance she had of getting her life back was for the killer to be caught and locked up.

She'd just finished the drawing when James called to say the agents were waiting downstairs.

"James and I talked about this. I think you should tell him everything," Davy said. "It doesn't matter if he's skeptical or suspicious. The feds' best chance of catching this man is with all the information. But maybe you should have a lawyer present."

Carla shook her head. Although not looking forward to another interrogation by Agent Grover, she wasn't ready to lawyer up. She felt it would only make her look guiltier. She said as much to Davy.

"Well, at any point during the questioning that you change your mind, ask for your lawyer. Give me your phone." He put in his cell number. "All you have to do is hit this button, and I'll come in and make sure the next time he talks to you will be with your lawyer present."

"Thank you."

"You don't have to thank me."

But she did, she thought even as she knew she'd never be able to thank him enough.

The agents were sitting in the office downstairs when she and Davy came through the door. James suggested they talk in the conference room at the back.

"We'll speak with Ms. Richmond alone," Grover said.

"You might want this," Tommy said and stepped toward the copy machine. He handed the agent the copy he'd made.

"What is this?"

"A tattoo. Carla will fill you in," Davy said.

The agent scowled at them before ushering her back into the conference room and closing the door. He tossed the copy of the tattoo she'd drawn onto the large table and pulled out his phone as Agent Deeds pulled up a chair.

Carla took a seat some distance from them, waiting for Grover to ask his first question. His expression had her on edge. She wasn't used to anyone not trusting her—let alone not liking her for no apparent reason other than a false belief that she was a liar and a crook and in league with a killer.

"What's this?" he asked, indicating the paper with the drawing on it.

"It's the man's tattoo—at least the only one I saw," she said.

He shoved the drawing over to Deeds. "So you're starting to remember, huh?" he asked after he had his phone recording their conversation. "Now you remember a tattoo. How is that possible, since as I understand it, the men were completely covered in their Santa costumes?"

She told him about the robber scratching at his neck and exposing the tattoo.

When she finished, he said, "That's it? That's all you remember?"

"I remember the robbery, but I didn't see the man who tried to take me hostage other than the slash in the mask for his mouth and the holes for his eyes." She hesitated, already knowing how this was going to look. "His eyes were dark. I saw the tattoo when he lifted his false beard to scratch his neck."

"That's it?" Grover said as he looked again at her drawing.

She swallowed, seeing that he thought she was making all of this up. What would he say when she told him about the note? "Something happened while I was in the hospital."

The agent looked up in surprise. Even Deeds seemed interested.

"Someone put a message on my dinner tray last night. It read 'Talk and You Die.'"

"Where is the note?" Grover asked, just as she knew he would.

She mentally kicked herself for not keeping the note, but at the time she'd been so shocked and terrified knowing that the killer could get to her even in the hospital that she'd just wanted it gone.

When she told him that he nodded, his mouth twisting in a smirk. "So you didn't keep the evidence that might help us find the person who robbed your bank and killed three of his associates."

Carla bit her lip. "I was scared. I'm still scared. I'm the one he almost killed. If he'd taken me hostage the way he'd wanted to..." Her voice broke.

"When's the best time to rob a bank?" Agent Grover asked.

The question was so out of the blue that she stared at him. "I beg your pardon?"

"Isn't there more money in the vault at Christmastime than any other time because a lot of businesses like to give cash bonuses?"

"I don't know where you heard that," she said, but she could see that he already knew the answer. It was true. As one of the top financial officers, she knew there had been more money in the vault than usual. Had the robbers hit the bank any other day, it wouldn't have been the case. Was that why he thought someone employed by the bank had given the robbers this information, making it an inside job?

"But it's true, isn't it," he said, eyeing her. "The day those men walked armed into your bank was the perfect time to rob a bank that hasn't been robbed in more than a hundred years."

She pushed back her chair and rose.

"We aren't finished here," Grover snapped. "Let's stop playing games, Ms. Richmond. You know exactly who robbed the bank. Isn't that what you were doing in the bank on your day off? Isn't that why you were the only one who ended up in the hospital? Make it look good. Isn't that what you told him? You saw the perfect way to—"

"You couldn't be more wrong. I'm going to say this one more time. I had nothing to do with the robbery. From now on, I won't be talking to you unless my lawyer is present." She had her hand in her pocket, gripping her phone, and she pushed the button as the agent started to argue the point. Davy's phone rang in the other room and an instant later he came through the door.

Davy looked at her face and turned to Grover. "I think we're done here."

Grover rose slowly, his gaze locked on her. Deeds got to his feet. He gave her a "what did you expect" look before they started out of the room. "I wouldn't leave town if I was you, Ms. Richmond," Grover said over his shoulder. "I suggest you get yourself a lawyer, because we'll be back."

"I THOUGHT YOU said we didn't have to worry about the Colt brothers," Jesse demanded the moment Jud picked up the call later that night after she'd gone to work.

He could tell from the background noise that she was standing outside on the back steps at the hospital and that she was smoking and not even trying to hide it from him. "What's going on?"

"The administrator's assistant told me that James Colt asked for the names of all the hospital employees. Why would he want those unless she talked?"

"He's just fishing. He's looking for someone whose name begins with *J.*" He laughed, relieved that's all it was. "So there's no problem. They aren't looking for Debra Watney."

She lowered her voice. "But if the feds get involved, they could find out that I'm not who I say I am." Jesse had used her twin sister's name and nurse's aide experience to get the job at the hospital.

Jud had questioned her at the time, asking, "What happens if your sister shows up or applies for a job somewhere else?"

"We don't have to worry about Deb," Jesse had said. "It's all good."

Now he thought about what Cora Brooks had said. Was Debra the missing sister?

"The last thing I need is the feds snooping around here," Jesse was saying.

He told himself that the fear he heard in Jesse's voice had nothing to do with a missing sister. Cora Brooks didn't know what she was talking about. "You're not going to be working there much longer anyway."

Did he have to remind her that they had a ton of money in a cave? Or that she was the one who'd insisted they continue working at their jobs as if nothing had happened? She'd made a good argument, even though he couldn't wait to blow this town, this county, this state, maybe even this country.

But she was right. If she quit now, she'd look guilty and the hospital might dig deeper. Same with his boring job. He hadn't been completely truthful on his application either.

"Did you drive by her house?" Jesse asked.

They'd discussed this and she'd warned him to stay clear of Carla Richmond and her house. "You told me not to." He'd driven past earlier. The sidewalk hadn't been shoveled since the latest snowstorm. There was a fresh set of tracks where someone had driven in, gotten out and gone inside the house. Large prints, like a man's boot size. The tracks had gone in and come back out.

"Well, if you did drive by there, you'd realize that she isn't there," Jesse said as if knowing he'd lied. "She's staying with the Colts for the holidays above that office of theirs." He wondered how she knew this. "So there is no getting to her until she returns home."

"I think it's a sign that we shouldn't wait," he said. "We should get the money and leave. She told the feds everything she knows and nothing has really happened. We're in the clear. Why press our luck?"

He waited for her to agree or put up an argument. All he got was a cold, dead silence. "Jesse?" He thought maybe she'd already disconnected, before he heard her let out an angry sigh.

"I've got to go." This time she did disconnect.

Jud swore under his breath. He knew that sigh. Jesse was in this now up to her neck. He'd told himself the Colt brothers weren't going to be a problem and now they were. In the meantime, he needed to find out just how hot the bank money might be. If he'd given marked bills to the loan shark, he should hear about it soon. This day just kept getting better.

Before work, he'd spent some time on the computer at the town library. He'd quickly learned what a fool he was. Marked bills, he'd discovered, were often not really "marked." Instead, banks kept bills with sequential serial numbers—in the tills of the tellers. Once those bills were mixed with those from the main vault, there was no telling which bills were marked and which weren't. Apparently a countrywide bulletin was issued to all retailers to watch out for those serial numbers.

So now he realized he may have given the wrong people marked bills.

Jud hated feeling so asinine. It made him angry and that anger found itself aimed at Carla Richmond. She knew all of this. She'd known it the day of the robbery. That's why he'd driven by her house. He hadn't known what he was going to do. He knew he'd be smart to just let it go. But it made him angrier that he couldn't get to Carla even if he wanted to.

So he'd passed her house and gone to work feeling out of sorts long before his conversation with Jesse. He felt worse after her second call.

"I was right. Your bank girl talked," Jesse said without preamble. "The feds know about the note. They're interviewing everyone with access to her food tray. I'll be called in at any moment."

"Lie." It was the best advice he had to give. "Tell them you didn't know anything about it. You can handle this."

"It just makes me so angry that she talked to the feds after I warned her not to," Jesse was saying. "She can't get away with this."

Alarmed by her tone as well as her words, Jud tried to calm her down.

"Easy. We don't want to do anything rash, right? You're the one who said we had to keep our heads and play it cool."

"I'm getting paged. I have to go." She disconnected, leaving him still alarmed and worried. Jesse could handle this, he assured himself. Unless she let her anger get the better of her, and he knew from experience how dangerous that could be. He'd almost blown the bank job because he'd wanted to punish Carla Richmond for not giving him a loan he hadn't even applied for. At least now he had a good reason to hate her and want to harm her.

He didn't even make an excuse this time for driving past her house.

Chapter Fourteen

"Are you feeling all right?" Davy asked when Carla said she was going upstairs to lie down. "Maybe you checked out of the hospital too soon."

She scoffed at that. "I couldn't get out of there soon enough. I'm fine, really. I just tire quickly." He offered to go with her to make sure she made it upstairs.

"Davy, I can climb stairs by myself. Please, I feel helpless enough."

"Sorry." He let her go and went back to the office.

"Everything okay?" James asked when he walked in.

"She's still weak from her injuries." But he knew that wasn't the real cause. Like him, she was worried. The feds seemed to think the robbery had been an inside job. Agent Grover especially thought it was Carla. "She needs a good lawyer. You know one?"

"Slim pickings in Lonesome," his brother said. "You might want to try Missoula. I'll ask around. How soon do you need one?"

"Yesterday," Davy said. "What about the lawyer helping us with Dad's case?"

"Carla needs someone who specializes in defense cases," James said. "Especially with the FBI involved."

Davy was worried about her, and he knew that his brother saw it.

"Might have trouble finding one over the holidays," James said. "Could be a problem."

That wasn't the biggest problem, Davy thought. After giving Carla some time alone, he climbed the stairs, hoping she'd gotten some sleep and was feeling better. At least he hoped she was upstairs and hadn't sneaked out. It would be just like her to feel like she was too much trouble and go home, scared or not.

As he entered the apartment, he saw that she was up and awake. He also saw that she looked anxious. She'd always been so independent. Not like other girls at high school who had to be with their boyfriends 24/7.

Before he could speak, she said, "I'm sorry I snapped at you earlier." He started to wave it off, but she continued. "You know me. I can't stay locked up here like a princess hiding in her castle."

"This space is nice, but it's no castle."

"You know what I mean. I'll stay for a few more days until I'm more myself, but I'd at least like to go over to the house and pick up a few more things. Willie brought everything on my list, but if I'm staying longer…"

"Sure. I'll take you." He realized that she was going to make it harder for him to keep her safe, but he was surprised that she'd agreed to come here to begin with. Not that he'd given her much choice. He and his brother Tommy had picked up her car from where she'd parked it downtown and taken it back to her house. He hoped she wouldn't want it yet. "Whatever you need."

"I'm not trying to be difficult."

"You're not. I would feel the same way." Their gazes held for a few moments. He did know her, intimately. Or at least he had a long time ago. Had either of them really changed all that much? He didn't think so. She looked more rested. He could see that she was feeling better, getting stronger and more like her old self. So it would surprise him if she stayed even a few more days.

"Then I want to be part of the investigation," she said. "I overheard you and James talking about tattoo shops. I want to come along."

Davy's first thought was to argue all the reasons she would be safer not to, but he could see that she'd made up her mind and he didn't like leaving her here alone with everyone out of the office. "Sure, if you're up to it."

He saw her visibly relax. He knew she would feel better being involved, but still he worried. The killer was out there. He could be anyone on the street. They wouldn't know until it was too late.

She was quiet on the drive to the small house she'd bought outside Lonesome. Covered in snow, it looked like a fairy-tale cottage in a snow globe. Davy parked in the unplowed driveway and took in his surroundings. Dark shadows hunkered in the snow-laden pines that sheltered the house on three sides. He was glad he'd talked her into coming back to the office, even though he wasn't sure how long he could keep her there. But out here at the house, it would be hard to keep her safe unless he moved in, something he really doubted she would allow him to do.

After getting out, they walked through the fresh snow to the front door. *No tracks*, he thought. But that didn't mean that someone hadn't been here, hadn't checked out the place for when they planned to come back.

Carla unlocked the door and they entered the foyer. They left their snowy boots on the mat by the door, and he followed her through the house. It struck him how much this place reflected her personality. Everything was neat and clean, the colors bright and sunny. There was no clutter. It appeared every furnishing had been handpicked over time to give the place a warm and welcoming feel.

It drew him in more than he wanted to admit. He'd been living out of a camper in his horse trailer all this time. He couldn't help but feel a sense of pride and admiration for Carla. She'd done what she'd set out to do. She'd made a good life for herself.

And yet he knew this wasn't what she had planned. She'd had higher aspirations, but had to put those on hold to come home to Lonesome and take care of her mother. She'd wanted to make something of herself, while he had just wanted adventure—and her to share in it as his wife.

Davy felt that old ache. He'd wanted her more than his next breath. But he couldn't give up his dreams any more than she could hers. Still, he found himself wondering what their lives could have been if they'd married in these past ten years. Couldn't they both have had what they wanted and still found a way to be together?

He scoffed silently at that as he looked around the house. Could he not see that Carla had wanted permanency, security, a place to call home? She'd never wanted his transient lifestyle. For her it wouldn't have been an adventure at all.

Like she'd said back then, they wanted different things. This house stood as an example of how true that was. Except for one thing. They had wanted each other. Did they still?

She came out of the bedroom with a small bag that warned him she wouldn't be staying long with him at the office.

"Got everything you need?" He watched her glance around the house before she nodded. She had roots, a home she clearly loved, a career. He would have taken that all from her had she come with him on the road. They'd chosen the trajectory of their lives back then based on what they wanted out of life. Thanks to a robbery and a killer on the loose, those lives had intersected again. But for how long?

Once the killer was caught, Carla would be going back
to her life and he'd be going back to his. Even as he thought
it, he knew that he wouldn't come out of this experience
unchanged though. But changed enough to find a way to
be together? Or again brokenhearted and alone?

He turned his thoughts to finding the killer. With James
and Tommy both busy on cases and Willie down at the sheriff's department as part of his training as deputy, he and
Carla would hit tattoo shops with the sketch she'd made.

"I thought we'd start with the local tattoo shop," he told
her once they were back in his pickup. "And if no luck
there, branch out."

Carla said nothing. She was looking in her side mirror
as if she thought someone might be following them.

Davy glanced back. All he saw was a delivery truck
behind them.

CARLA LEANED BACK and closed her eyes as they drove back
into Lonesome. She hadn't been able to sleep at first when
she'd gone upstairs at the agency earlier. She'd felt restless
and had found herself moving around the apartment, studying the posters and photographs.

She'd seen them as a teenager when she and Davy had
been together. The movie poster was of his great-grandfather Ransom Del Colt, an old Hollywood Westerns star.
There were flyers from Davy's grandfather's Wild West
shows. RD Colt Jr. had traveled the globe ridin' and ropin'
until late in his life.

Del Colt, the brothers' father, had only stopped rodeoing because of an injury. He was the one who had started
the investigation business. He was also the one who had
taught his four sons to ride a horse when they were probably still in diapers.

As she'd moved around the room, she'd seen the Colt

family legacy on the walls. Each generation had passed on that love to the next. Rodeo and horses and competition were embedded deep in the brothers' genes. Had she really thought she could get Davy to give that up? What had made her think she had the right?

Well, he'd made his choice all those years ago and it hadn't been her. That's what made this so hard. The past was almost palpable between them. She knew it was why he felt he had to protect her. It wasn't because of any residual feelings for her, she told herself. Yet she kept thinking about the day he'd come into the bank. Had he wanted to ask her out? If only he had. If only they could have started over then.

Feeling the weight of everything after she'd looked over the posters in the room, she'd finally lain down. As she'd drifted off, her last thought had been how desperately they both needed to get back to their lives before they tried to rewrite history—and got their hearts broken all over again.

JUD FOUND JESSE waiting for him when he got home from work the next day. She'd traded schedules with a friend, apparently, so wasn't working her late shift. She seemed calm after being questioned by the feds about the note on the food tray.

"You think they believed you?" he asked as he joined her on the couch. He didn't smell anything cooking and wondered if she'd gotten takeout or if he'd misunderstood and had been expected to pick something up.

She shot him a look. "Why wouldn't they? Do I look like someone who would lie?"

He wasn't about to touch that. At first glance, no. But he'd gotten to know her. He'd seen below the sweet, shy, blond exterior.

She got right down to business. "We have to assume that

they know about the tattoo and will start looking for the person who inked it." He'd never told her where he'd gone. He'd just come home with a tattoo. She might have thought a friend had done it because the tattoo was so simple. "The question is, how long before they track it back to you?"

Jud scoffed. "How would they do that? I didn't have it done around here." He could feel her gaze boring into him. "As many tattoo artists as there are in the state…" He shrugged. "Maybe if it were a unique design…"

She'd been sitting cross-legged at the end of the couch, but now she rolled up onto her knees and crawled toward him. He tried not to flinch when she jerked back the collar of his shirt to expose the tattoo.

"Why is your neck all red?" she asked, as if afraid to touch it.

"I told you—the Santa costume gave me a rash. I was itchy. I had to scratch or go crazy."

She made no comment, simply ran the tip of her finger over one *J*, then the heart. He was waiting for her to finish by tracing the other *J* when she said, "What's that at the bottom of the heart?" as if she'd never paid much attention to the tattoo before.

He'd gotten the painful tattoo for *her* as a symbol of his love. He bit back the bitter taste in his mouth that urged his tongue to lash out at her. "It's another, smaller heart."

"It looks black, but it has something in it. Something squiggly. Maybe it's just a mistake, but it looks like a snake."

"What is your point?" he snapped and pulled away from her, buttoning up his collar as he tried to tamp down his growing impatience with her. He'd gotten the tattoo for her, he'd robbed the bank for her, he'd gone back to work instead of taking the money and leaving—all for her. So things hadn't gone as planned. That was life. Learn to live with it. He had.

"Who did your tattoo?" she asked, after going back to the other end of the couch and picking up her wineglass. Even that annoyed him. She couldn't drink beer with him and had to have wine like she was someone he really doubted she was. But even as he thought it, he realized he didn't know much about her.

He couldn't help but think about what Cora Brooks had said. Was it possible her family had lived up in the mountains around here? Cora had made them sound like survivalists or criminals or squatters. Nothing good. Jesse had never wanted to talk about her family.

Then again, maybe Cora didn't know what she was talking about. Maybe Jesse came from money. Maybe all her relatives drank wine. She could have been royalty for all he knew.

Except that she was with him, which told him she didn't come from money any more than he did and there wasn't a royal bone in her body.

"It was just a shop on the street in Butte. I don't even remember its name." There was no reason not to tell her. Then again, she didn't have to know everything, especially about that night.

"You don't remember which shop." Clearly she didn't believe him. She turned to glare down the length of the couch at him. "You might not remember the shop, but there will be paperwork. Paperwork with your name on it."

He wondered how she knew so much about tattoos, since as far as he knew, she'd never had one. But now she had him worried. He tried to remember what information he'd given the tattooist. He vaguely recalled signing something. A consent form? Had he shown his driver's license? Maybe— he wasn't sure. He'd had way too much to drink, and his friend had plied him with more as he'd egged him on. Jud had been feeling no pain—at first—and had been glad that he hadn't had enough money for Jesse's whole name. He'd gotten what he could afford. Something simple and quick. So who cared what was at the bottom of the heart?

"Maybe you should try to remember and get to the artist before the feds do, don't you think?" Jesse said.

Only if the feds find out where I got the tattoo, he thought. What were the chances?

Jesse sighed and asked as if reading his mind, "Haven't you taken enough chances?"

He didn't bother to answer. He could tell that nothing he could say would make a difference. Only one thing would appease her. He shook his head, even as he knew he would do whatever she asked. Worse, she knew it.

Chapter Fifteen

Davy had little hope that they could track down the person who'd given the man the tattoo, but they had to try. The tattoo was simple, nothing unique about it that he could tell from the sketch Carla had drawn.

He'd had to park off Main Street because of the lack of parking with Christmas so close. Even the sidewalk was fairly crowded as they headed to Lonesome's only tattoo shop. He found himself looking at everyone they passed and trying to keep himself between them and Carla. Earlier, he'd considered just emailing all the tattoo parlors within a hundred-mile radius with an accompanying shot of the tattoo, but he'd learned that people were more forthcoming in person.

The shop wasn't much more than a hole-in-the-wall with one chair and one artist. The sign in the window read only Tattoos. The owner's name was Big John, a burly former state-champion wrestler who'd done time in Deer Lodge for check fraud. It was in prison that he'd apparently gotten hooked on injecting ink under other people's skin, where it stayed forever.

"Davy Colt!" Big John bellowed when he saw him. "You finally decided to get a tattoo." He laughed uproariously and slapped him on the back before saying hello to Carla. It was a small town and Big John had gotten his start-up loan at her bank, she'd told Davy before they entered the shop. "Not afraid of an angry bull, but a little needle…"

Davy had heard all of this before. Big John had been trying to get him and his brothers tatted for years. He hoped to get this over with as quickly as possible. He pulled the sketch from his pocket and held it out to the tattooist.

"This is what you want?" Big John asked with a chortle.

"No, I need to know if you did this design."

The man looked insulted. "A child could have done that."

"So I'm taking it that you didn't. Who might have done it?"

The tattoo artist was shaking his head when Carla spoke up. "I know it's really basic, but I think that little squiggle at the bottom inside the tiny black heart could be a trademark or just a slip of the needle."

Davy shot her a look, surprised she knew something about tattoos.

"I did a little research on my phone," she said without looking at him.

Big John considered the two of them before he took the sketch and held it up to the light. Stepping over to a tray next to his chair, he picked up a large magnifying glass and studied the sketch more closely. He nodded and handed the paper back.

"You're right. It could be a trademark sign. If so, then I know the so-called artist. An embarrassment to our craft. Bad for business, you know," he said, giving Carla a nod.

"What's inside the tiny black heart?" Davy asked.

"Up close with a magnifying glass on the tattoo itself it could be a tiny broken heart with an *S* in it," Big John said. "Some artists put a little of themselves into every tattoo they do, kind of like a signature at the bottom of a canvas."

He handed back the sketch. "So let's talk about a tattoo for you, Davy Colt. I could do a bucking horse."

"I see enough of those, but thanks."

"Still afraid of needles, huh? Your girlfriend here wasn't afraid."

Davy didn't think Carla could surprise him more. "You got a tattoo?" Her face flamed.

"You haven't seen it yet, huh?" Big John laughed and winked at Carla. "He's in for a surprise, huh."

"Can you tell us where we can find the tattoo artist who might have done the tattoo?" she asked, clearly anxious to change the subject.

"If I'm right, Butte," Big John said with a sigh. "The name of the shop is Sam's Pit. Get it?"

"After the Berkeley Pit," Davy said. A former open-pit copper mine, The Pit, as it was known, was a mile long and a half mile wide and held fifty billion gallons of toxic water. It was a lasting symbol of mining gone wrong. Only 19 percent of cities were more dangerous as a place to live because of the toxic pit.

"Sam is really Samantha Elliot," Big John said with a chuckle. "You'll find her rather interesting. You might want to take a sidearm just in case she doesn't like the looks of you. Or take Carla here with you." His belly laugh followed them out the door.

"I DON'T WANT to talk about it," Carla said the moment they were outside Big John's tattoo parlor.

Davy glanced over at her as they walked back to where he'd parked the pickup. She knew that grin. She also recognized the curiosity in those blue eyes of his. He was dying to know about the tattoo along with what and where it was. She should have known Big John would say something.

Holding up both hands in surrender, Davy said, "I won't mention your tattoo again." But that wouldn't stop him from thinking about it, she thought, feeling her cheeks redden again.

"So when do we go to Butte?" she asked, hating that he could get under her skin so easily.

"We can go today. I need to stop by the office and see if James is back. He might have heard something from the hospital," Davy said as they climbed into his pickup. "I'm anxious to find out the name of the blonde aide who brought you your dinner tray—and then took it away."

Carla knew she'd messed up by not keeping the note. She wanted to blame her concussion and that she hadn't been thinking clearly. That probably had played a part in it since she'd been feeling so vulnerable. But she knew it had also been fear. Just the thought that the person who'd hurt her could get to her even in the hospital…

"It's not your fault," Davy said as they drove the few blocks to the Colt Brothers Investigation building. Fortunately, there was parking in the back alley. "You were recovering from a head injury and you were scared."

She wished he would stop reading her mind. It had always been like this between them. She had thought it would have changed in all the time they'd been apart. "Maybe the feds could have gotten fingerprints or—"

"Not likely."

"But it would have been proof," she cried.

Davy glanced at her. "Or the agent would have suspected you wrote it yourself."

She groaned. He was right. She had to let it go. They now had a lead on the tattoo. Once they had J's full name…

AFTER DAVY LEFT Carla's overnight bag upstairs in her room, they went down to the office to find James sitting behind the large desk. "Good news," he announced when he saw them. "I just got the list of hospital personnel and information about who's nearing retirement and vacation schedules."

Davy quickly moved to look over his brother's shoulder at the computer screen. It didn't take long to sort the names by the initial *J.* Carla joined him.

There was one Jennifer and one Jane. Jane worked in medical records and was about to retire. Jennifer was a young nurse's aide who was on Christmas vacation all week in Mexico.

Disappointed, Davy said, "Did you get the name of the blonde aide? She not only brought Carla's dinner tray, but also took it away."

"I thought you might be onto something when you first mentioned her," James said. "When I asked who had delivered Carla's tray, it turned out that one of the aides had volunteered to take it to her, saying she felt sorry for Carla after what had happened at the bank."

"Sounds like a red flag to me," Davy said.

"Her name is Debra Anne Watney. She's been there more than two months now and is a model employee," James said. "Apparently it's not unusual for her to help out in any department, and she's very compassionate with patients."

"She seemed *nice*," Carla said.

"And her name doesn't start with *J*," James pointed out unnecessarily. "But like I said, the tattoo could be about an old girlfriend."

Davy shook his head. "I felt like there was something off about her. I'd like to find out more about her." He told him about what they'd learned at the local tattoo parlor. "Big John thinks it might have been inked by a woman named Samantha Elliot at Sam's Pit in Butte."

"The tiny heart at the bottom might be her trademark," Carla said.

"I think you need to tell the feds," James said.

"We wanted to talk to her first," Davy said.

"Might be better to let them follow the lead. If it came from Carla and it pans out…"

"You think it might get Grover off my back," she said and James nodded.

"And if they don't take it seriously?" Davy demanded. "I think we should make sure and then tell the feds. If it turns out to be another dead end, Agent Grover is going to be even more suspicious of Carla."

"You make a good point," James said. "Still, I'd call up there and make sure the tattooist hasn't taken off for the holidays. Hopefully the woman will be able to help you. In the meantime, Willie said he'd help, but he had a ride-along down at the sheriff's department. Tommy's on a stakeout. I'll see what I can find out about Debra Anne Watney."

"Willie really is going to become a deputy sheriff?" Davy said, shaking his head.

James nodded thoughtfully. "I hope he knows what he's doing." He quickly changed the subject. "Lori called earlier. She and Bella are asking about our plans for the holidays. They were thinking Christmas Eve out at the Worthington Ranch and New Year's Eve to at least begin at our place," James said. "They're delighted Carla will be coming. But we'd also like to have you guys out to our house for dinner one night as well."

Davy looked over at Carla. "You game?" He hoped he didn't have to remind her that she'd promised to stay with him for a while.

She hesitated only a moment before she nodded. "Sure. Thank you."

"Definitely Christmas Eve at Bella's," Davy said and smiled, thinking of their last Christmas together. Now he and Carla would be spending Christmas together again— just not the way he'd often dreamed.

CARLA COULDN'T HELP being disappointed that the hospital employee list hadn't been fruitful. But it had been a long shot. J could have a friend who worked there, although she couldn't imagine the sort of person who'd agree to put a note like that on her tray. Surely that person would know through Lonesome's grapevine that she'd been through enough trauma with the bank robbery. No way would anyone think the note was funny or just a harmless prank.

James was going to check out Debra Anne Watney, but Carla thought that too would be a dead end. She didn't see it leading anywhere since there had been nothing threatening about the blonde aide. Nor did the woman's name begin with *J*. Carla would have been much happier if they had more of a lead on J.

She'd been thinking about another possible way to find him. She stepped into the conference room and called her boss, president and manager of the bank, Larry Baxter. After he'd asked how she was and said how glad he was that she was out of the hospital, she asked him for the favor she'd been thinking about.

"I know it's against bank privacy rules, but I have a feeling that the man who attacked me at the bank might have come in recently for a loan," she told him. "If I could go through the latest requests that I've had to deny…" She could hear her boss trying to let her down easy. "If not all of them, then any whose names start with the letter *J*."

"Why *J*?"

"I saw the man's tattoo. I believe his name begins with *J*. I know this request is unorthodox but—"

"I'll tell you what," Larry said. "I'll go through your files and pull out all the ones starting with *J*, first and last name. I'm sure you told the federal agents this so they'll be asking for the same information at some point. But," he said, lowering his voice. "Because of the circumstances,

I'm allowing it for your eyes only, and this stays between the two of us."

"I think it would be best if you let me know when you have the list ready," she said. "No need to send it by email. I could meet you at the coffee shop down from the bank."

"You're beginning to think like a criminal," he joked.

"I wish that were true. Then maybe I'd know what the man will do next."

"How about coffee this afternoon? Two?" Larry asked and she quickly agreed. They wished each other well before he disconnected.

"I need to do some Christmas shopping" she told Davy, knowing he was going to try to stop her. "I don't have anything for your family."

"My family doesn't expect gifts from you, especially under the circumstances." She merely looked at him until he said, "I suppose it won't do any good to mention how dangerous it is with all those last-minute shoppers crowding the stores and us not knowing which of them is a killer?" He must have seen that it didn't.

She knew she couldn't keep the truth from him. "I'm also meeting my boss at the coffee shop down from the bank at two. He'd prefer I come alone since it's bank business." Davy groaned. "You could drop me off, watch the shop from across the street in the bar and I could text you when I'm done. It shouldn't take long." She gave him a broad smile and saw him weaken.

"You're not an easy woman to keep alive, Carla Richmond."

"I appreciate you trying though," she said. "But you aren't always going to be around. Maybe it would be best if you changed your mind and walked away now so—"

"Not happening." He met her gaze. "Just to be clear, I'm

not changing my mind. I don't want to see anything happen to you if I can prevent it."

She sighed. "Davy, I know this isn't how you planned to spend your holiday."

His blue eyes darkened. "Plans change, Carla. You should know that. Ten years ago I planned to marry you. If I'd had my way, we would be married right now. It wouldn't have been the life you had planned though, but I'd be just as determined to keep you safe as I am now."

She couldn't speak around the lump in her throat.

"Now that we have that settled, let me try to reach Sam's Pit tattoo shop again. I know that the shop is open. I left her a message to say we were coming. If I can't reach her, we'll have to drive to Butte tomorrow. She could be busy doing a tattoo and not taking calls. But I'd feel better if I could reach her before we take the drive."

IT WAS NO coincidence that Samantha "Sam" Elliot's mother named her after the baritone heartthrob who just happened to be in a Western on the hospital room television the night Sam came into the world.

Over the years though, Sam had done everything possible to erase that Hollywood image when it came to her appearance. The truth was, her body was the direct result of her love of food, alcohol and tattoos. A massive woman, she had a deep voice and a laugh that carried for at least four blocks. She loved life and she lived as if there were no tomorrow.

As for the tattoos, Sam had once thought that she'd become a famous artist. She could laugh about that now, but it had hurt when critics called her talentless. That, however, turned out to be true. It was after her first tattoo that she realized she'd found her calling. Since then she'd covered almost every square inch of her body with her art and others'.

That's how she'd found her career path. With her robust personality, her decorative flesh and her limited talent, she'd made a name for herself in the regional world of tattoo artists. She'd even put her own stamp on it with the tiny black hearts she put in every tattoo she inked. Inside that black heart was a tiny *S*. It was her trademark.

She never forgot a tattoo. So she recognized Jud the moment he walked in, right after her last customer had left and she was about to close for the rest of the holidays. She had a great memory. It would take her a minute or two to recall his last name though, without looking it up in her file. But she remembered that, when he'd come in originally, he'd been drunk and so had his friend with him. He'd wanted something for his girlfriend and asked what he could get for… He'd dug some crumpled bills from his pocket and shoved them at her.

She'd almost turned him away. But there was something pathetic about Jud. So, feeling sorry for him, she'd told him what she could do. It wasn't much, but then again his money didn't even cover her time.

She'd have wagered that he wouldn't be a return customer even before she'd sat him down in her chair that first time. He'd had trouble sitting still, so it hadn't been her best work. Some people couldn't take the pain. But Jud was in lust with someone named Jesse. He was merely trying to make a statement, so Sam had helped him out.

When he walked in now though, she got the feeling that things hadn't worked out. He looked so unhappy she thought he'd come to ask about redesigning the tattoo or covering it up since Jesse was now nothing more than a bad memory.

That's why she was surprised when he said, "That form I signed? I need it back." He glanced toward the adjoining room where the file cabinets were kept.

Her cell phone began to ring. She looked toward it resting on the table off to her right. It had rung earlier, but she'd let it go to voice mail because she'd been busy with a customer.

"Your consent form?" she asked, wondering why he would want it and if she could even find it as she took a step toward her ringing cell phone.

Before she could reach it, she saw the gun he'd pulled from behind him. "The consent form, *now*."

She saw then that he wasn't just unhappy. He was clearly agitated. Was he on something? Her phone rang again. He snatched it up and threw it across the room, where it landed on the chairs used for those waiting their turn. Fortunately, it had quit ringing.

"Jud, I'll be happy to give you your form. I file them by last name. You'll have to remind me—" She saw his surprise that she knew his first name. That's probably why she hadn't seen the blow coming, when in retrospect she should have, she thought. The butt of his gun broke her cheekbone and cut her nose, which began to bleed profusely.

She stumbled back, crashing into her table of tools. They scattered noisily across the floor. She was trying to get to the chairs and her cell phone when he hit her again. The room dimmed. She tried to speak, but nothing came out. As she began to slump to the floor, she saw him coming at her again. He appeared to be crying, his face flushed, spittle flying from his lips as he attacked. She felt nothing after the fourth blow.

Chapter Sixteen

Jud had been home for hours pacing the floor as he waited to hear from Jesse. He'd tried calling her, but all his calls had gone straight to voice mail. The last time he'd talked to her, she'd been about to be called in to be questioned by the feds again. He was losing his mind and was about to go look for her when he heard her come in through the front door.

"Where the hell—" He caught himself even though he wanted to strangle her. Instead, he rushed to her, taking her in his arms. She smelled of booze, answering his question about where she'd been. But why hadn't she called him? She had to have known how worried he was.

He wondered who she'd had drinks with. Some other man? He held her tighter and realized that she was trembling. Letting go, he stepped back to study her face. At first he'd thought she was scared. But he quickly realized that she was furious. For a moment, he thought it was with him. It wouldn't be the first time. But he tried hard to keep Jesse happy. He'd dated a lot of women, most of them walking out on him once they really got to know him.

Jesse was different. She was worth keeping. It was one reason he'd taken the mind-numbing delivery job even temporarily. It was another reason he'd decided to pull off the bank job. He'd promised himself he would do whatever it took to make this one stay.

"Want to tell me what happened?" he asked as he followed her into the kitchen.

She opened the refrigerator and took out the wine bottle. As she poured herself a glass, she finally looked at him again. "I got grilled by the feds. They already knew I was the one who took in the dinner tray and picked it up from the first time they talked to me. Again, they wanted to know what I did with it. What they really wanted to know was if there was a note with it."

"What did you tell them?" he asked as he followed her into the living room.

She kicked off her shoes and sprawled on the couch, leaving him just enough room to sit, if he didn't mind her feet in his lap. "What do you think I told them? That I wrote the note?" She shook her head. "I said like I did the first time that I didn't see any note. At least one of the feds believes me. He asked what Carla had said to me. I told him again that she said she wasn't hungry and to get rid of the tray." Jesse smiled. "I could tell that they suspect she lied about there being a note."

"So it's all good," he said, sighing in relief. So why was she so upset? She looked angrier than when she'd come home.

"No, it's not all good, Jud." She bit off each word. "Carla Richmond drew them a sketch of your tattoo. They were showing it around to everyone, asking if they knew anyone who had a tattoo like that."

"No one did, right?"

"That's not the point. The point is I warned her to keep her trap shut." She shifted on the couch, her expression going dark. "That woman is as good as dead. She should have done what I told her."

He was no fan of Carla Richmond either, but all he really wanted was for this to be over. "I think we should take the money and leave." He'd been thinking about it all the way home from Butte. It was time to get the hell out of Dodge. Not that he thought anyone could connect him to what had happened at the tattoo parlor. He'd gotten his forms and destroyed them on the way home. At least for this, he was home free.

He didn't want to wait around until the loan goons got arrested in case the money he'd given them was marked. Mostly, he was ready to start spending some of that cash— the unmarked cash. "We can go anywhere we want. I was thinking—"

"We're not going anywhere, not yet," she said, sitting up. She pulled her legs into her and wrapped her arms around them. She wasn't as angry now. Somehow it made her scarier. "I'm not leaving until she's dead."

He hoped she was merely venting. "That's not going to happen as long as she's staying with Davy Colt."

Jesse nodded. "Eventually she'll have to go back to her place. No one crosses me. No one." Her gaze met his, and he had to fight hard not to flinch. "I'm going to make something to eat." She got up and left the room.

He sat for a moment listening to her bang around in the kitchen before he got up and followed her. He couldn't let her go off half-cocked. She'd get them both arrested.

"Jesse, you're making me nervous," Jud said as he watched her chopping up carrots. She was angry and waving the knife around as she cursed and fumed. "I can't let you do something you'll regret," he said.

"Then cut up the carrots yourself," she snapped, throwing down the knife.

"That's not what I was talking about," he said, quickly pulling the knife and then sliding the cutting board and the rest of the carrots across the counter out of her reach. "You can't kill Carla Richmond."

She glared at him, and he was glad he now had their only decent knife. "That's your problem, Jud. You don't stand up for yourself. You would have never robbed the bank if I hadn't put the idea into your head." Was that true? She had been nagging him relentlessly. "Just once, don't you want to prove to people that you have a backbone?"

He thought of what he'd done in Butte and grimaced. "I can't see how killing that woman would help matters," he said, only to have her turn toward him with a look in her eyes that chilled him to his very core. "I'm not saying we can't kill her," he amended quickly. "But we have to plan. We don't want to get caught, right?"

Her mouth was set in a stubborn line. "What are you suggesting?"

"That you let me take care of it." He thought of the day he'd had—all the blood—and tried not to gag. "You didn't ask me about my day."

"You have blood on your shoes," she said and met his gaze. "What is there to ask?"

He looked down, shocked to see that while he'd stripped out of his bloody clothing, tossed it into the wash and changed as soon as he got home, he'd put on the same shoes. He swallowed back the bile that rose in his throat. With the other bank robbers, it had been self-defense. They would have killed him for the money if he hadn't killed them first. But the woman at the tattoo shop...

"All I'm saying is that I have more experience with this than you do," he said.

Jesse laughed and cocked a brow at him. "You sure about that?"

He wasn't. He thought her more than capable of murder though, especially when she was angry. He could hear Cora Brooks again warning him about Jesse. Buddy too.

"Then you're going to handle this before we leave?"

she asked, crossing her arms over her chest and glaring at him as she waited.

At this stage, he thought it unnecessary to kill Carla. It was risky and foolish, but right then he would have said anything to mollify Jesse. "You know she can't hurt either of us since she's already told the feds everything she knows." Jesse's eyes narrowed to slits. He could see that there was no talking her out of this. "I'll take care of her, though I don't think it's necessary." Jesse began to tap her foot. "I'll kill her, okay?" The tapping stopped.

Jesse took the knife, cutting board and carrots from him. She carefully chopped up the rest and dumped them into the pot. "When? When will you do it?" she asked, still holding the knife.

IT WASN'T UNTIL Carla came back downstairs after getting ready for her meeting with the bank manager that she heard. As she walked into the office, she saw Davy on the phone. From his expression, she knew something had happened— and it wasn't good.

"What?" she asked the moment he disconnected from the call.

"That was the Butte Police Department. They heard the message I left on Samantha Elliot's voice mail," Davy said. She felt her eyes widen in alarm and tried to swallow. "She was attacked and her office destroyed. When I told them why we'd been anxious to talk to her…" He met Carla's gaze. "They think her attack might be related to the robbery and murders. She's in serious condition in the hospital. They don't think she'll make it."

She lowered herself into a chair as her legs threatened to give out under her. "This is his doing." The shock of the horrifying reality of this situation ricocheted through her. "He's covering his trail." She felt her eyes widen as her pulse thundered in her ears. "He knows that I told the federal agents about the tattoo." She felt tears burn her eyes. She'd drawn a picture of the man's tattoo and now the woman who'd inked it could die. "This is all my fault."

Davy moved to her, kneeling down in front of her to grasp her shoulders. "None of this is your fault."

"I told the agents about the tattoo. He knows I told. That's why that woman—"

"There's only one way he would know that you told the agents," James said. "J either works at the hospital or he knows someone who does."

"Which means he's local," Davy said as he rose.

"There was no one with a *J* name on the list though that fit the description," Carla pointed out. She felt as if she were trapped in a nightmare and couldn't wake up. But somehow she had to. They had to figure this out. They had to find him and stop him before… She shook off the rest of that thought as a tremor moved through her.

"Then more than likely he knows someone who does. Someone close to him. Just not with a name that starts with *J*," Davy said.

"I have to find him," she said as she pushed herself up from the chair. "If he applied for a loan at the bank and I turned him down…" His name had to be there. It was the only hope she had right now. She glanced at the time and wondered if her boss had those names. She felt as if the clock were ticking. She quickly made the call. He had the names and would meet her in ten minutes. "I need to go."

"I'm taking you in my truck," Davy said.

She started to point out that it was just a few blocks, but she saved her breath. He wasn't going to let her even walk down the street until the man was caught.

That's why she had to do everything possible to make that happen for both her sake and Davy's.

DAVY WAS SURPRISED that the meeting at the coffee shop was so short. Carla had gone in, ordered coffee and was joined only minutes later by an older man. They'd spoken for a few moments before he'd slipped her a manila envelope and she'd gotten up and left. Davy had been waiting for her parked at the curb, after earlier going in a few shops with her as she finished her Christmas shopping as if there wasn't a killer after her.

"I need to go by my house again," she said as she climbed into his pickup now. "If we're going to your brother's, I need more clothes. Sorry."

"You don't have to apologize. I'm happy to take you." He started the engine, just grateful that there was no talk of going back to her house to stay.

She snapped on her seat belt and without another word opened the envelope and began to go through what looked like copies of loan forms. She made sure he couldn't read them, but he thought he already knew.

"People you turned down for a loan?" he asked.

She shot him a look, and for a moment, he thought she might not answer. "This is highly irregular."

"So is a bank robbery and you almost dying and having a killer after you," he said.

Carla rolled her eyes. "Well, when you put it that way. Still, it would be best if you didn't know." She glanced at the sheets of paper she'd been given. "I thought maybe one of them might jog my memory. Only a couple have names that begin with a *J*. My boss gave me all of the requests over the past month. They're people I remember. He's not in here," she said and pushed the copies back into the envelope. "Neither are their spouses."

He could see how disappointed she was. She'd been counting on the man's name being in there. He hated that it was another dead end.

She sighed. "Also I need to go by the gift store. I have to do a little more Christmas shopping since my plans have changed."

"Under the circumstances, the last thing you need to do is go shopping for my family."

She shot him a look.

"Fine, but know I'll be at your side the entire time."

"Have you always been this stubborn?"

"Yes, but I think you already know that." Their gazes met and he could feel the chemistry sparking between them. He knew her as well as she knew him. They'd both been each other's firsts. They'd reveled in each other and the sex and had basically been crazy in love their entire last year of high school.

Then everything had gone south when he'd told her that he wasn't following her to college. He was joining the rodeo circuit. That had been the end for her. The end for them.

They'd parted, but so much of that passion was still simmering between them. He could feel it, stronger than ever. If she felt it, she didn't let on. But then, neither did he. He was home only for Christmas and then it was on the back of a bronco. They'd be fools to start up anything again. Letting her go way back then had been hard enough. He didn't want to do that to himself again—let alone to her.

"Stubbornness is something we have in common, among other things." He was no longer talking about stubbornness, and from her expression, she knew it.

"Davy—"

"Clothes first, then shopping? I will say again that my family isn't expecting gifts."

She looked away. "It's Christmas. Sometimes you get something you didn't ask for or expect."

He smiled at that, wondering if this time with her was just that.

Her gaze was on the snow-filled pines as he headed down the narrow two-lane road toward her house. There was fresh color in her cheeks. He smiled to himself. She felt the chemistry too. He'd bet his horse on it.

As they neared her house, he was again aware of how isolated her place was. Somehow he had to keep her from returning there until the killer was caught. He glanced over at her and shook his head. Ten years ago he'd tried to convince her that they belonged together and would find a way. Ten years ago they'd been in love. Did he really think he stood a chance of convincing her of anything now that they were no longer together?

JUD WALKED UP to Carla Richmond's house through the deep snow blanketing her sidewalk. He could see that she hadn't been here for a while. There were recent tire tracks in her driveway, so she'd at least stopped by. Or someone had.

But from the looks of the place, what he'd heard was true. She was staying with Davy Colt at the Colt Brothers Investigation building on Main. Apparently, the two had been tight in high school.

Still, he needed to scout out the place for when she returned. The rodeo cowboy would be leaving again soon. Right after Christmas probably, since from what Jud knew about the Colt brothers, Davy made his money on the rodeo circuit. Carla would have no choice then but to come home.

He trudged through the snow, carrying an empty box like it was a delivery just in case someone drove by and saw him. He knocked on the door and waited. While he did, he looked for any indication of an alarm system. This was Montana—hardly anyone had security systems unless they'd moved here from somewhere else and brought their paranoia with them.

Jud still didn't want to do this, he thought, as he peered

in the window through a crack in the curtains. The best thing he and Jesse could do was get the hidden money and skip the country. He didn't understand why they were still in Lonesome as it was. The longer they stayed, the more worried he was that they would get caught—especially if he did something stupid like kill Carla Richmond.

But he worried that if he didn't, Jesse might take matters into her own hands. He was still hoping that he could talk her out of it. He couldn't wait to put this hick town in his rearview mirror.

He was about to put the box down and walk around the house to check the back door lock when he heard a pickup turn into the drive. The last thing he'd wanted to do was be seen here. Fortunately, he was wearing his large company winter jacket and hat with earflaps even though the day wasn't that cold.

As DAVY DROVE UP, he saw a delivery man standing on Carla's front porch—and a delivery truck parked at the edge of the road. The man, seemingly startled, turned at the sound of the truck's engine. Davy parked in the driveway and he and Carla climbed out.

"Do you have a package for me?" Carla called as the man started to retrace his steps back down the sidewalk toward his truck—carrying the package.

Davy could see where the man had left tracks in the deep snow of the sidewalk to the front door. He made a mental note to shovel her walk before he left. It was supposed to snow again tonight. Davy wanted to be able to tell who'd been here after they were gone.

The delivery man looked down at the package in his arms and shook his head. "Wrong address," he said over his shoulder as he headed for his truck.

Davy started across the yard toward the man. "What

address are you looking for?" The man didn't answer, as if he hadn't heard. He disappeared inside his truck. A moment later, the engine revved and he took off.

"That wasn't weird at all," Carla said next to him.

"Yes, it was." He tried to see the plate number on the truck, but it was covered in snow and ice.

"It's a busy time of year," Carla said. "That's probably all it was."

Maybe, Davy thought. Yet when he'd driven up, he'd thought the man had been trying to see inside the house. Not necessarily suspicious, unless the homeowner had recently crossed paths with a killer.

"Tell me where your snow shovel is and I'll take care of your walk while you get what you need," he said, putting the delivery man out of his thoughts for the moment.

She smiled. "What is the point? It's supposed to snow again tonight and I'm not staying here."

Davy saw her eye him with suspicion. "A clean walk makes it look like someone's home. Just safer." That too was true. But he had a bad feeling that the delivery man would come back. He wanted to be able to check the tracks when they returned.

Carla shook her head. "You think that man was checking out the place to steal my silverware?" When he didn't answer right away, she said, "No, you think he might be…" She shivered and looked down the road where the delivery truck had disappeared. "If he comes back—"

"There will be fresh tracks in the snow. Snow shovel?" he asked.

She swallowed. "Garage."

CARLA LET HERSELF into the house. She'd left the heat on, but still it felt cold inside. She flipped on lights as she went, hating how easily she'd been spooked. She wanted to blame

Davy for scaring her. Was she going to have to be afraid of every delivery man who came to her door?

She had just started to gather more clothing for the rest of the holidays when her cell phone rang, and she saw it was her boss. "Hello?"

"Carla." The way he said that one word had her heart battering her rib cage.

"Has something happened?"

He cleared his voice. "Sorry, no, that is… I know you mentioned earlier how anxious you are to come back to work, but unfortunately, until the FBI's investigation is finished, I have to put you on administrative leave. You'll still be paid."

Unless I'm found guilty of being involved in the robbery, she thought. Then she would have to pay all of that back. That was the least of her problems, since she hadn't been involved. But could she prove it?

"I understand," she said, her voice breaking. She'd already lost so much, and yet her credibility and now her job hung in the balance? Not to mention her life.

"Also, I'd appreciate it if you shred those copies I gave you," he said, dropping his voice. "I'd just as soon no one knew about that."

"Of course. I didn't find anything anyway. But thank you for trying to help me." She disconnected and fought the sudden rush of tears. She'd almost lost her life and now she'd lost her independence. She would never feel safe again if the man wasn't caught. What if the federal agents felt they had enough evidence to charge her as an accomplice to the robbery and subsequent murders?

Fighting her growing fear, she finished packing. How was she going to get through the holidays? The FBI suspected her, Davy thought she was still in danger and, if that wasn't enough, how could she spend so much time with the man she'd almost married ten years ago and not fall in love with him all over again?

As if on cue, Davy came through the door smelling of the wintry outdoors. There were snowflakes in his hair and his dark eyelashes. He was flushed, his blue eyes sparkling. He stole her breath—just as he'd stolen her heart all those years ago. It wasn't as if she'd ever gotten it back.

Chapter Seventeen

Back at the office, while Carla unpacked upstairs, Davy called the delivery company with a fictional story about wanting to give their usual driver a Christmas gift. He asked for the names of the drivers who covered her neighborhood, and the woman said she'd have to get back to him.

As he hung up, James came in and he filled him in. His brother fell silent for a moment. "Are you that sure Carla is still in danger?" he asked.

Davy turned to look at his brother. He'd heard something in his tone, making the question more loaded than it might have sounded to someone else. "What are you asking?"

James raised his hands in surrender. "Has there been another threat made against her?" Obviously aware of the answer, he quickly continued. "So the killer could be miles from here by now."

"Or only as far as Butte," Davy snapped.

"I'm just asking about your endgame because I care about you. It's great that you want to protect her, but for how long can you do this?"

"If you're saying that I'm using this situation to be with her…" He saw that it was exactly what his brother was saying. He shook his head, feeling his anger flare inside him. "Why would I do that? Carla made her feelings clear ten years ago. Nothing has changed."

"Exactly," James said. "That's why we're worried about you."

"*We're?* So you've *all* been discussing my life?" he demanded as he raked a hand through his hair and angrily began to pace the room.

"Davy, we love you. You're like a brother to us." James's attempt to lighten the mood fell flat. "Come on, we just don't want to see you get hurt again. We never want to see you that brokenhearted. We're concerned that being thrown together like this… You aren't falling for her again, are you?"

Davy stopped pacing and laughed as he turned to face his brother. "There's no need to fall for her again. I've never stopped loving her," he said and left the office before his brother could ask how Carla felt about him.

CHRISTMAS EVE WAS busier than usual. Jud knew that the time he'd spent driving out to Carla Richmond's house and screwing around had been part of it. Mostly it had been all the packages that just had to get delivered before Christmas morning—which meant he had to work until his truck was empty.

He hated the holidays. Did people really need all this stuff? His mother would have said he was jealous. He didn't even want to think about his Christmas mornings as a boy. A sad-looking store-bought tree with several branches missing because his mom had gotten a deal on it. Under the tree was always worse.

The year he was eight, she'd gotten him a can of black olives. When he'd cried, she'd said, "But I thought you liked them."

It was dark by the time he returned his truck, left behind his hooded coat with the company's insignia on it, pulled on his ragged jean jacket and walked to where he'd parked his pickup earlier that morning. His entire body hurt, from the soles of his feet to the top of his head and all the way down his back.

All he could think about was a beer and Jesse. If he was lucky, she'd be in a good mood after he told her that he'd scoped out Carla's house and then she'd make him feel better. He realized that he hadn't bought her a present and tomorrow was Christmas. He'd been afraid to use the money. Not that he would have known what to get her anyway. She wasn't like the other women he'd known. She didn't care that much about clothes or jewelry.

When he thought about it, he wasn't sure what she cared about other than money. Well, he'd gotten her a ton of cash, hadn't he? Maybe he'd go pick up a bag from the hiding place in the cave and dump it in the middle of the living room and they could roll around in it. Jud smiled at that idea. Jesse had been in such a dark mood the past few days he was almost afraid of what he would find when he got home.

He was a few feet from his pickup when one of the dark shadows moved. He'd been so lost in thought that he didn't have time to react before the man he knew only as Wes had him in a beefy-armed headlock.

"What the—"

Wes tightened his hold, cutting off the rest of Jud's words. "Fletch was arrested after he tried to spend one of those twenties you gave us."

Jud closed his eyes. Wasn't this what he'd feared? Jud tried to talk, but couldn't get more than a strangled groan out, and finally Wes loosened his hold. "I don't know what you're talking about," he croaked out.

"Don't lie. I know you pulled the bank job. So where's the money?"

CARLA HAD TOLD herself that she wasn't in the mood for a holiday party. So it surprised her when she slipped into one of her two fancy dresses. She looked in the mirror and felt a rush of excitement. She smoothed the rich silky emerald green fabric down over her hips and felt her mood lighten for the first time in days. She wanted to enjoy this night, to forget about everything but Christmas and…and Davy.

"Carla?" The sound of Davy's voice outside her bedroom door made her swallow and take a final look at herself in the mirror. She'd put her hair up for the party and wore the pearl earrings Davy had bought her for Christmas all those years ago. She hadn't let herself wear them before now because of the painful memories of their breakup.

"Coming!" she called. Pushing back an errant curl, she took a deep breath and had to smile. She was nervous, she realized, because this felt like a date. She quickly reminded herself that Davy was only trying to protect her. He couldn't very well leave her here in the office apartment while he went to his family Christmas Eve celebration.

She warned herself not to make too much of this. It was like any other night. She was only playing dress-up for the occasion.

But then she opened the door and saw Davy. He was dressed in a Western suit, his thick dark hair brushed back to where it curled at his neck. He was wearing his good boots and he held his white Stetson between the fingers of his left hand.

What struck her was that he looked as nervous as she felt. He'd taken her in, his eyes widening in what could only be approval. He let out a low whistle and she felt her cheeks warm.

"Wow," he said, his eyes glowing. "You're *beautiful*."

She felt a little embarrassed. "Is the dress too much?"

Davy chuckled. "Not too much at all."

"I guess I should have asked if this was a casual or formal dinner."

His gaze met hers. "It's perfect. You look...perfect."

She swallowed. If this wasn't a date, she didn't know what was.

DAVY HAD BEEN at a loss for words when Carla stepped out of the bedroom. He was struck by how gorgeous she was. The green dress accentuated her curves, diving at the neck to the swell of her breasts, tucking into her slim waist and skimming down over her hips to fall to midcalf. She'd piled her wild, curly mane of hair up, baring her throat, making him remember the feel of it on his lips. Several locks brushed her high cheekbones, making her blue eyes look wide and liquid.

If he hadn't been enchanted by this woman for years, he would have fallen all over again. He felt that old ache more acutely than ever. James was right—he was in dangerous territory.

"Ready? It's snowing," he said as he helped her with her coat. The faint, sweet scent of her familiar perfume whirled around him for a moment. He took a step back, finally admitting how hard this was. It was hell being this close to her and not being able to take her in his arms and make love to her. He took another step back.

When she turned, she seemed to see the battle going on inside him as if it were etched on his face. "Davy, I—"

He shook his head, stopping whatever she was about to say. "I already loaded the presents in the truck, if that's what you're worried about."

She studied him for a moment, then shook her head. "I guess we should go then."

He readily agreed. The upstairs apartment felt as if it had shrunk and was suddenly too close, too intimate. He was too aware of how bare she was beneath the coat, let alone the dress. He'd once known that body. It had matured in the years since, making it even more lush, more titillating. One more minute in this space with her looking at him like that…

Pushing those thoughts away, he headed down the stairs to his pickup, Carla following. Snow whirled around them, and he remembered another winter night and a stolen kiss. He almost reached for her, his desire to kiss those lips again so strong that he felt powerless over it.

Instead, he opened her door and she climbed inside. Closing the door, he stood for a moment breathing in the cold night air, comforted by the feel of the icy flakes melting on his face. Then, feeling as if he'd been kicked in the gut, he walked around the pickup and climbed behind the wheel.

All he had to do was get through this night without acting on his feelings. *Good luck with that*, he thought as he drove toward Worthington Ranch.

Jud told himself that Wes wasn't going to kill him—not if he thought he had the robbery money. He'd want to know where it was first.

"I don't know what you're talking about," he told the man, once Wes let up the pressure enough on his throat that he could speak clearly. He'd feared that he'd given the men marked money. Now those fears were realized.

What gave him hope was that the men hadn't told their boss where they'd gotten the money. Otherwise, Leon would be here instead of his henchman. Leon wouldn't have had him in a choke hold. Instead, Jud would have battery cables hooked up to parts of his body that would have made him regret being born.

"Where did you really get the money you said your grandmother gave you?" Wes demanded.

"I didn't say she gave it to me. I pawned some of her knickknacks and jewelry hoping she wouldn't miss them," Jud said with enough anger he hoped it would be convincing for Wes.

"What pawnshop?"

Jud told him it had been one in Missoula, where he let Wes believe his grandmother lived. Had she been alive. "Then I bought a few groceries, paid for gas, went home and gave you what I had left. So whoever pulled the heist could have already shopped at one of those places."

Wes eyed him suspiciously. "That's quite a story."

"Would I still be delivering packages if I had that kind of money?" Jud could see that the man wasn't so sure now. He was glad that Jesse had reminded him to use as many old bills as he could find in the bags. So Wes wouldn't have gotten all marked bills, which would help sell his story.

"If you're lying…" Wes said and let him go. "I'll be back for another installment."

Jud groaned. "I'll have to visit my grandmother again because I don't have it." He could feel Wes studying him. "It's Christmas. Can't you give me until after the holidays? My grandmother's in poor health. Once she crosses over, I'll get everything and can settle my bill in full."

"The boss won't wait that long. I'll be back." With that, the man left.

Jud let himself breathe for a few minutes after Wes drove away. He'd just dodged a bullet. But it didn't leave him much time. They couldn't chance giving Fletch or Wes any more marked money from the robbery. He had to talk to Jesse.

"We need to leave town," he told her when she came home from work. He related his encounter with Wes. "We have all this money. Enough time has gone by. Let's get out of here before another bill turns up from the robbery or Leon comes himself to collect."

"Not until you finish things," she said without looking at him.

"Jesse—"

She spun on him. "If you can't do it, I will. I warned her not to talk and she talked. I can't let that stand."

"Technically, she didn't even know it was you warning her."

"Are you serious right now?" Jesse demanded. "Tell me you aren't taking up for her."

He raised both hands. "I'm not. We're free and rich. Why take a chance getting caught because some dumb fool didn't do what you said?"

"It's about betrayal, standing up for yourself, not letting people disrespect you."

"But no one even knows that she disrespected you."

"I know," Jesse said, giving him a look that seemed to nail him to the floor. "I know and that's all that matters." With that, she turned and stormed into the bedroom.

Jud flinched as she slammed the door. His instincts told him to leave, to go get the money and keep going. Why did he always get involved with domineering women? Before he could move, she came out of the bedroom dressed in all black. He watched her walk into the kitchen and come back out with a butcher's knife.

"Jesse?" His voice cracked.

She stopped to hold the knife up. The blade caught the light. "I'm going to take care of this myself. Be ready to leave when I get back." With that she headed for the door, but stopped with her hand on the knob. "And, Jud, don't even think about leaving me behind. I moved the money." With that, she left.

THAT MAGICAL MOMENT standing outside in the falling snow was lost. All Carla had, along with the ache in her heart, was the memory of what she'd seen in Davy's expression. He'd remembered their kiss that Christmas together—just as she had. The cold, the snow falling around them. Davy had pulled her close for their winter kiss. Wasn't that when they'd both known that they were truly in love—the forever kind?

She closed her eyes now. Carla knew she wasn't wrong. He'd come close to kissing her. Her heart had started to pound, and she'd felt such a yearning… She hadn't realized how badly she'd wanted that kiss until it hadn't happened.

The drive to Worthington Ranch didn't take long. Neither of them spoke. What was there to say? Earlier she had almost brought up the subject of *them*, but Davy had stopped her. Because there was no them. She'd made her choice all those years ago. And he'd made his.

If I'd had my way, we would be married right now.

She'd heard the hurt and pain in his voice. If he'd had his way. She'd tried to imagine what their life would have been like with him on the road all the time, following the rodeo circuit. It wasn't what she'd wanted. It wasn't her idea of marriage and happy-ever-after.

And this is? the little voice at the back of her mind demanded. She hadn't met anyone else she wanted to spend the rest of her life with. Because she'd never gotten over Davy, she admitted to herself now. Being with him and yet not being with him…

She glanced over at him. He looked so handsome in his Western dress suit. She wanted to reach out and touch his arm and tell him—

"We're here," he said, and she looked up to see that he was pulling in front of the Worthington Ranch lodge.

SHE MOVED THE MONEY? Jud stared after Jesse for several moments, too stunned to move. He didn't have to guess where she was going—or what she planned to do. She was going to get them both arrested. He had to stop her, make her see that she wasn't being rational. How had this become about her and Carla Richmond?

He charged out into the darkness and falling snow in time to see her speeding away. He told himself that she'd come to her senses before she did anything, but he wasn't sure he believed that. He didn't know what to do. Maybe she was lying about moving the money, but somehow he didn't believe that either. Maybe he could find where she hid the money, take it and run. Not unless he wanted that crazed woman with the knife to come after him. Go try to stop her?

With a groan, he realized that he'd set all of this in motion the night he'd gotten involved in that poker game. Once he was in so deep, he'd thought for sure that he could dig his way out with just one more game—double or nothing. He hadn't realized who he was playing against. What had started as a friendly poker game had gotten ugly fast. If Leon hadn't offered to bail him out…

Jud shook his head, trying to clear his thoughts. He couldn't go back and change any of that. That's why he had to end this.

He grabbed his coat. Jesse would go to Carla's house and then the Colt Brothers Investigation office. She didn't know that she wouldn't find Carla at either of those places. Jud wouldn't have either if he hadn't seen Bella Worthington Colt in the grocery store parking lot. He'd overheard the conversation she'd been having with another woman as she'd unloaded her shopping cart into the back of her SUV.

All of the family were coming to her house tonight for Christmas Eve.

Jud started his pickup, his mind clearer than it had been in days. He thought about the day he'd walked into the bank to get a loan. Now he knew that it always had to end this way.

Chapter Eighteen

Carla had been quiet on the drive out to the Worthington Ranch. Davy was glad that she didn't feel the need for small talk. He wasn't sure he could have handled that. But he hated the awkward silence that had filled the cab of the pickup the entire drive. He didn't like leaving things this way between them. What had made him think he could spend this much time together and not get involved again? Being around her and not being able to touch her was pure hell.

He'd come so close to kissing her. He blamed the falling snow and cold for the memory. She'd called it their winter kiss. Like he could ever forget it. Or her.

She had no idea how many times after he'd first left her that he'd thought about quitting the rodeo circuit, coming back to Lonesome and proposing. He'd wanted her that badly. He still did.

It wasn't like he couldn't find a job. He'd recently been offered a position promoting rodeo statewide. Except he wasn't ready to quit the circuit. It was in his blood. Just another year or two, he kept telling himself. But then what? He had some ideas, one in particular he'd been thinking about more since coming home and seeing Carla.

What was a couple more years rodeoing? Like Carla

would still be single and waiting for him? He was surprised that some smart man hadn't already snatched her up.

As he pulled in front of the Worthington Ranch lodge, he was relieved that the drive was over. He'd had too much time to think about the almost kiss and his future. *Love shouldn't hurt. It shouldn't demand giving up your dreams*, he told himself as he got out and went around to open Carla's door.

He told himself that they'd chosen their completely different paths years ago. There was no going back, even as he felt his heart ache at the sight of her. Look what his stubborn determination had gotten him, he thought as he saw her avoid his gaze as they headed inside. She couldn't even stand to look at him.

The moment they'd hung up their coats and walked into the main room, James pulled him aside. "Have you heard?" Clearly, he hadn't. "It was just on the news. A man was arrested at the local convenience store trying to buy beer with a twenty-dollar bill from the bank robbery."

Davy couldn't help but get his hopes up. This might be it. The killer might already be behind bars. Then he and Carla would go their separate ways. Isn't that what they both wanted? "What's his name?"

"Fletch. He's a caretaker for that big ranch outside of town that was bought up by that corporation," James said.

Fletch? His disappointment must have shown. "So do they think he had something to do with the robbery?"

James shook his head. "Apparently not. He had an airtight alibi for the day of the robbery, and he's already been released. But the bills are surfacing, Davy. You might be right about the man still being in Lonesome."

Davy groaned as he looked across the room where Carla was visiting with Bella. As James said, if the bills were circulating locally, there was a good chance that the robber hadn't left town. Hadn't his gut told him that Carla was still in danger?

As if sensing him looking at her, she glanced in his direction. She looked so pretty, her cheeks a little flushed from coming in out of the cold into the warm ranch house.

"Please don't say anything tonight about this to Carla," he said.

"She's going to hear about it," James said. "Might be better if it came from you. If the bills are turning up…" James sighed. "I don't know about you, but I could use a drink."

Forty-five minutes and several drinks later, Bella announced that everyone should start heading into the dining room. Davy knew James was right. It would probably be better coming from him. But what he would give if they could just have this one night, he thought as he made a beeline for Carla.

EVERYONE BEGAN TO move toward the entrance to the dining room. Bella had invited family and friends, so the huge table inside would be full. Carla had tried to lose herself in the party atmosphere. Everyone was dressed up, tiny Christmas lights twinkled from the log rafters and holiday music formed a background for the laughter and chatter.

She'd wanted to enjoy herself tonight. To let her hair down, so to speak. She needed this. But earlier she'd seen James pull Davy aside. From their expressions it wasn't good news. She'd wanted to go to him and find out what had happened, but Bella had approached her. By the time that conversation ended, Davy had disappeared.

That's why she was startled when he suddenly reappeared beside her. Ahead of her, the crowd was milling toward the dining room. He touched her arm and indicated that he wanted to talk to her. She felt her heart drop. Hadn't they said enough earlier? Or maybe he wanted to tell her what he and James had been discussing. Either way, she feared it was bad news.

Not tonight, she wanted to say. Not tonight in this beautiful home on Christmas Eve. But she also knew that whatever it was, she needed to hear it. Could she even pretend for one night that there wasn't a killer after her?

She turned toward him as the others disappeared into the dining room. "I saw you talking to James. I know something's happened."

"That's not what I wanted to talk about."

"Davy, we can't keep going over the same old grou—"

He touched his finger to her lips to silence her and pointed upward. She frowned since she'd been bracing herself for bad news. When she looked up, she blinked at the sight of mistletoe hanging from one of the log rafters above them.

Her gaze dropped to his. She looked into his amazing blue eyes, fringed with dark lashes. The man was drop-dead gorgeous. But it was that kindness in those eyes, that caring, that love. She felt her heart lean in. What would one kiss hurt?

"Carla, it's Christmas. Could we just enjoy this time together?" he asked as he brushed a lock of her hair back from her eyes. "Can we put our differences aside? We used to be good friends before we became…" He seemed to hesitate. Lovers? "More," he finished. "Can't we just enjoy the holidays together like old friends?" His gaze met hers and practically burned her with its intensity.

Carla wanted that desperately—no matter how dangerous. Davy Colt was a good, loving man. He'd dropped everything to protect her. One night without the past pushing its way between them sounded like heaven. She nodded and he pulled her to him.

The kiss was sweet and soft—at first. But then it changed

as he drew her closer, arousing emotions so strong that she found her arms around his neck. He deepened the kiss and she surrendered so willingly that it shocked her. But she couldn't stop herself. She met his tongue with her own, the taste of bourbon and champagne like an accelerant fanning the flames.

They could never be just friends again. They would always be lovers. The thought breezed past as he whispered her name against her lips like an oath. Or a curse. She felt her nipples harden beneath her sheer dress. Her heart took off at a gallop as she pressed the soft swell of her breasts to his rock-hard, solid chest and heard him moan. Her heart drummed in answer.

Wrapped in each other's arms, locked in the passionate kiss, neither of them heard anyone approach.

"Excuse me," Willie said, clearing his throat. "I told Bella it was probably the mistletoe. Guess I was right."

Davy and Carla sprung apart like teenagers caught on the sofa. But when they looked at each other, the fire still burning inside her, she began to laugh. Davy joined in.

Willie chuckled, shaking his head as he turned to go back to the dining room. "Christmas Eve dinner is being served, in case either of you are interested." He mumbled something under his breath, which only made them laugh harder.

As Willie disappeared, Davy turned toward her. "I guess we should…" He waved a hand toward the dining room.

"Yes, I suppose we should." Carla knew her face was flushed, her lipstick smeared. "I should probably stop in the ladies' room first." She bit her lower lip, the kiss still raging through her veins. But it had felt so good to laugh. To laugh together, like they used to before she'd broken both of their hearts. "You go ahead. Tell them I'll be right in and they shouldn't wait."

He smiled at her. "I'm not sorry."

She knew he meant the kiss and how they'd gotten carried away. She shook her head. "Me neither." She had to clear her voice. "I'll hurry." With that she escaped to the restroom.

Once the door closed behind her, she stepped in front of the mirror. Her cheeks were flushed, her eyes bright. She felt as if she were floating. It was as if all they'd needed was a little Christmas magic like in the movies. A sprinkle of pixie dust and they found their way back together.

The thought made her shake her head. It wasn't pixie dust, but she had to believe that all of this had happened for a reason. The bank robbery right before the holidays had thrown them together. *Maybe it was meant to be*, she told herself, even as that tiny rational killjoy Carla on her shoulder argued that this would only lead to heartbreak. She mentally swatted the pesky voice of reason away. There was no fighting fate, right?

Yet she saw the truth in the mirror as the kiss's effect began to lessen. Nothing had really changed between her and Davy. She would never ask him to choose between rodeo and her again. Had he stayed in Lonesome for her, he would have ended up resenting her. The thought broke her heart.

She'd thought she could forget for one night about what was going on in her life. But that was impossible. Being here with Davy didn't help. He was a constant reminder of how temporary and off-kilter everything was right now—and how it could get so much worse.

As much as she appreciated him being with her, she didn't want him involved. What if the killer did come after her and Davy tried to stop him? She couldn't bear the thought that she might get the man she loved killed when he should be miles from here.

Fate might have thrown them together, but it was temporary. How had she forgotten that in his arms? As she headed for the dining room, she knew in her head and her heart that what fate had given them was a few precious days together—and nothing more.

DAVY SLIPPED INTO the dining room. "Sorry to keep you all waiting. Carla's right behind me. Just had to make a stop." He picked up his wineglass and took a drink. His body vibrated from the kiss, from the rush of desire still thrumming in his veins. Hadn't he known that if he kissed her, all those old feelings would be there? Their chemistry had always been so strong. They'd started as friends long before they'd become lovers years ago. That foundation was still there. He'd take a bullet for this woman.

"Is there news on the robbery?" Bella asked, drawing him back.

"Apparently one of the marked bills has turned up," he said and put down his empty wineglass.

"That's good, right?" Lori asked. "So they have the man."

James shook his head. "He had an airtight alibi and the police let him go. It appears the bills are circulating in town though. Which could mean the man is a local. Also that he might still be around." Davy felt everyone look to him.

"Why would he still be here?" Bella asked, frowning.

"That we don't know," Davy said and was glad when his wineglass was refilled. He picked it up and turned it in his hands. "He might not be finished with Carla."

Bella let out a cry. "That's horrible. Why?"

Davy shook his head. "We're trying to find that out."

"How is she doing?" Lori asked. Davy was sure she'd quizzed James but she was just being polite by asking.

"She's strong. This is hard for her. She's always been

so independent and self-reliant. She's anxious to get back her old life."

"I'm sure you are too," Lori said. "Don't you have a ride coming up right after Christmas?"

They all turned as Carla came into the room. When Davy saw her expression, he knew that she'd heard the last part and was just as keen as everyone else to hear his reply.

"There are other rides," he said and got up to pull out Carla's chair.

The moment he was seated again, she said, "He isn't going to miss any rides." Carla was smiling as she looked over at him, but he caught the unshed tears glistening in her eyes. "I appreciate how wonderful he's been, but he's a rodeo cowboy. He has to do what he was born to do."

"But what if the killer hasn't been caught by the time he has to leave?" Bella asked, sounding worried.

Davy started to say something, but Carla cut him off. "Neither of us can put our lives on hold until that happens. It might be months, even years or never. Once the investigation is over, I'll be going back to work."

She said it with such ferocity that Davy couldn't help staring at her in surprise before she added, "The bank has put me on administrative leave until then."

He hadn't known. He reached for her hand under the table and squeezed it, but after a moment she pulled it away. He could see her fighting tears. She'd worked so hard to get where she was. This was so wrong. None of this was her fault.

His cell phone rang. He checked the screen, apologizing as he pushed back his chair and stood. "I need to take this. I've been waiting for this call."

Once outside the room, he accepted the call from the delivery company. Earlier, he'd left a message, needing to know which delivery drivers worked in Carla's area. Now he listened as a woman told him. No name that started with *J.*

"Thank you for getting back to me. Merry Christmas." He disconnected. Another dead end. He'd been so sure that there was something strange about the man he'd seen standing on her doorstep with the package. It might have just been a case of a wrong address as the man said.

Davy sighed. He had to question his instincts. He'd also thought for sure that James would find out something suspicious about the nurse, Debra Watney, but he hadn't. Apparently, he'd been wrong about her as well. He'd become so suspicious since the robbery, since there was a killer out there who'd hurt Carla and might still be in town and not finished with her.

But he knew the kiss also had him worked up. The earth had moved for him. But had it for her? If so, then how could she keep denying what the two of them had together? She seemed anxious to get rid of him again.

He felt that old frustration. But he also had to admit that there was some residual anger in him because she hadn't given them a chance ten years ago. He regretted the years they'd spent apart. He looked over at her. Had he really thought anything had changed? He told himself that he couldn't do this again.

She wanted him to leave right after Christmas? Wouldn't that be the smart thing to do? But as he thought it, he knew it was already too late to keep his heart from getting broken all over again.

Davy took his seat again and looked into her eyes. He realized that he wasn't going to let her push him away. Not this time. He reached over and took her hand as he leaned close. "You're not getting rid of me that easily. Not this time."

HIS WORDS SENT a shiver through her. He squeezed her hand. Their gazes locked, stealing her breath. The kiss earlier proved how dangerous it was for them to be together any longer. Why postpone the inevitable? He needed to go back to the rodeo circuit, and she needed to get her job back.

But at the back of her mind, she kept hearing that voice of reason. What if the robber wasn't caught? What if she couldn't go back to her job? For years she'd lost herself in her pursuit of a career. Even with the detour back to Lonesome when her mother got sick and later died, she'd managed to stay in a job using her degree.

Her mother used to joke that her daughter would thrive no matter where she was planted. Often Carla felt like a stubborn weed that fought its way to the sun no matter what she had to overcome. She wasn't one to give up easily.

Yet she'd given up on Davy.

She looked into his eyes and knew that she couldn't again. As painful as it would be when they finally parted again, she wanted this time together. She concentrated on the food as dinner was served by chef Roberto. She'd heard Bella saying what an amazing cook he was. Everything was delicious.

For the rest of the meal, the conversation stayed clear of the robbery. Bella wanted to know if Carla would like to come out and ride horses with her. Carla said she would love that. She hadn't ridden for years but hoped it was like riding a bike.

"You used to love riding," Davy said. "It was something we had in common."

"With any of the Colt brothers you have to love horses," Bella said with a laugh. "Fortunately, I do."

The conversation moved on to babies, with Lori pregnant with a daughter and Bella and Tommy trying to get pregnant. Carla again felt Davy's gaze on her, but she didn't dare look in his direction. Was he thinking that if they'd gotten married right out of high school, or even after she'd finished college, they could have had children of their own now?

The thought made her sad and stirred that desire in her for a family of her own. But there was only one man she'd wanted to have kids with. Davy Colt. Except with Davy on the rodeo circuit, she would have been a single mother—like her own mother.

That wasn't what she had wanted. That hadn't been part of her dream. But the passion of their kiss still thrumming through her veins demanded to know why she was still hanging on to that old dream, since she'd never been able to fit Davy Colt into it.

THE NIGHT WAS BLACK. Low clouds pressed down on the road between the banks of dense pines that lined the road. The pickup's headlights punched a shallow hole in the darkness ahead. Inside the truck cab, Davy felt too close, and yet Carla could feel an ocean between them.

"I know you're angry with me," she said at last, needing to break the tense silence. She didn't know what to blame. The kiss? Or what she'd said at dinner?

He glanced over at her, looking surprised. "Is that what I am? Angry?"

"You tell me." She saw his jaw tighten along with his hands on the wheel, but he didn't speak. "I wish we could just be friends again, but I can't see how we can. That kiss proves it, doesn't it?"

"It was just—" he started, then shook his head no. "Like hell it was," he amended quickly, looking over at her. "What that kiss proves is that we're still in love, Carla. Have been for years. When are we going to quit denying it?"

"I'm not denying it. We just want different things."

"Oh, right, that's why we broke up."

"Would you please stop doing that," she snapped. "And stop pretending that you don't know why I broke up with you."

Davy sighed. "I thought we wanted the same things—marriage, a house, kids, a life together. I thought we were in love."

"We were." Her voice broke. She didn't want to argue, but she couldn't let the past lie between them like a dead body they were both trying to ignore. "What kind of life would that have been with you on the road all the time?"

"I wouldn't have been on the road all the time. Other people make it work—truck drivers, pilots, commercial fishermen. But that wasn't what you wanted, was it?"

"No," she admitted and felt tears sting her eyes. "Breaking up with you was the hardest thing I've ever done. It broke…" Her voice choked again as well and she had to look away. "It broke my heart to walk away from you." She felt him look over at her and swallowed back the tears that threatened to fall.

"You didn't give us a chance," he said quietly, the pain clear in his words.

"You don't know how badly I wanted to." She looked over at him as she was enveloped in the memory of the kiss, of his arms wrapped about her, their bodies molded together in the heat of passion. The worst part was that she still did want to.

The moment their eyes locked she knew she could no longer fight her feelings for him. "Davy." The word came out a plea. She wanted to throw herself into his arms and tell him that she'd never stopped loving him and plead for them to find a way to be together. She opened her mouth, but what came out was a scream as she saw headlights headed right for them.

Chapter Nineteen

At Carla's scream, Davy's gaze returned to the road, only to find himself blinded by the set of headlights bearing down on them. "Hang on!" he cried and jerked the wheel hard to the right. The cab interior filled with light. He braced himself for impact as he caught a flash of the vehicle as it whizzed past his driver's-side window.

To his amazement, the vehicle barely missed the rear of the pickup as he and Carla crashed into the snow-filled ditch. The front tires dropped down into the wind-crusted depths. Snow cascaded over the hood to cover the windshield as the pickup buried itself before coming to a stop.

"Carla," Davy said, glancing over at her. "Are you all right?" Her face had lost all color and she was hanging on tightly if her white knuckles were any indication.

"I thought for sure that car was going to hit us," she said haltingly.

"That was way too close." He glanced over his shoulder and saw a pair of taillights disappearing down the road. "The driver didn't even stop. Must be drunk or…"

She looked over at him then. "It wasn't a drunk driver. It was him, wasn't it?"

Davy wanted to argue but couldn't. The car had been headed unerringly at them. If he hadn't jerked the wheel and put them in the ditch, the vehicle would have hit them head-on. It would have been a suicidal mission—if it was J. He'd caught a glimpse of the pickup as it had sped past. While he hadn't seen the driver, his impression in that split second was that there'd been a man behind the wheel. A man wearing a baseball cap.

As Carla began to cry, he unsnapped his seat belt, then reached over and did the same with hers before pulling her into his arms. She was trembling and fighting tears. His heart was still pounding. He told himself that whoever had run them off the road wouldn't be back to finish them off, but he was glad that his .22 pistol was under the seat. If anyone came down the road from that direction, he would be ready.

"This is killing me," Carla said through sobs against his shoulder.

"I know. I'm so sorry." He knew being a suspect in the bank robbery was added to her pain. That and not being able to get back to her job, her life. She'd always been so independent. She'd always been so strong. He knew how hard this was on her.

"It's going to be all right," he said as he ran his hand over her hair and held her close. "I'm here for you."

At those words she pulled back, her eyes brimming with tears as she shook her head. He could well imagine what she wanted to say. The last thing she wanted was to keep him from going back to his life, the life he'd chosen over her.

"Carla," he said, his heart breaking for her. "I'm sorry this is so hard on you, but I'm not letting you out of my sight until this monster is caught. I'll put the past aside if you can quit worrying about the future. Maybe we could find some common ground because—let's face it—we still feel the same, don't we?"

She nodded, tears filling her eyes. "Yes."

He smiled then and touched her face as he pulled her

close. "We're going to get through this." She nodded against his chest, then sat up to wipe her tears. He saw her gather herself, her strength and determination taking over again, before he reached for his phone to call for a tow truck.

JUD LOOKED OUT the window, angry that Jesse had taken his truck. "What did you do?" he demanded, worry filling him with dread as she walked in the door. He could tell by her flushed face and the brittle brightness in her eyes that she'd done something. He didn't dare guess what.

Jesse shook her head angrily as she swept past him. She took off her coat, kicking off her boots on her way and leaving a trail of snow behind her. "Someone had to do something, and since you don't have the—"

"What did you do?"

She pulled the knife from her coat pocket and tossed it onto the table beside the couch. His gaze shot to it, his heart hammering as he looked to see if there was blood on it. There didn't appear to be.

When Jesse spoke, she spit the words at him. "I tried to kill her." She wiped the spittle at the corner of her mouth. "I drove right at them, but unfortunately, they swerved. I left them in the ditch. I should have gone back and finished them," she said, shaking her head. "But I wasn't sure he wouldn't be armed."

Jud groaned. "Don't you realize what you've done? The word on the street was that the feds were looking for me in Washington State. Some of the heat was off and now…" He swore. "What was the point of that?"

"It made me feel better." She glared at him, daring him to say that wasn't good enough.

"None of this makes any sense. You do realize that, don't you?" He shook his head. "We should be miles from here.

Staying around to make you feel better..." He didn't finish as her eyes narrowed.

"I told you. I'm not leaving until she's dead."

"Then be smart. There is no way to get to her right now. Once she moves back home—"

Jesse's laugh cut him off. "You really want to wait that long? Because I don't. Anyway, how do you know the cowboy won't move in with her and you'll have another excuse not to finish this?" She shook her head. "If you ever want to see that money again, you'd better do something and soon."

WHEN JAMES HEARD what had happened, he insisted Carla call Agent Grover.

She wasn't surprised when the agent again didn't believe her.

"Probably just someone who had too much to drink on Christmas Eve," the agent said on the phone call. "We have reason to believe that your J might be in Washington State."

The "your J" grated, but she didn't let the agent get to her. When she asked what made him think J was in Washington State, he said he couldn't say but that he would be returning to Lonesome soon for a talk with her, so she'd better have a lawyer.

She hung up more frustrated than ever and repeated what the agent had told her.

"There were several arrested for drunk driving," Willie told them. "It's possible that one of them was responsible for running you off the road."

"The good news is that if they have a lead out in Washington State, then last night was only an accident," James said.

Carla knew that, like her, Davy wanted to believe that's all it had been. She'd made a few calls to attorneys, leaving her number since most were out of the office until the end of the year. But she felt better since making the contact. Hopefully, Agent Grover would find J out in Washington and that would be the end of it.

By Christmas morning, both she and Davy were in better spirits. Davy had picked up a small decorated tree for the upstairs apartment and she woke to Christmas music. They exchanged presents.

"It's just a little something that I saw that reminded me of you," he said when he handed her the tiny wrapped package he'd taken from under the tree.

For a moment, her heart had begun to drum as she remembered another small box he'd given her all those years ago—one with a diamond engagement ring inside.

She quickly unwrapped the box and opened it with trembling fingers, telling herself Davy would never make that mistake again.

"Do you like it?" he asked, sounding worried.

"It's beautiful," she said with relief as she picked up the silver bracelet from its nest in the box. "I love it." It was delicate, with one tiny star dangling from it.

"For making wishes," he said, seeming a little embarrassed.

She looked up at him, feeling her eyes sting, and asked him to help her with the clasp. Then she handed Davy his present. She'd gotten him a new leather belt for the many buckles he'd won over the years.

He immediately put it on. It fit perfectly, just as she knew it would. "I'll wear it tonight at James and Lori's. You haven't forgotten that we're invited for dinner, right?"

They'd both gone to the small kitchen after that to make a Christmas breakfast. Davy had thought of everything. He seemed determined to make her forget her problems—at least for the holidays. It was almost working, Carla thought.

After their near collision, they'd both gone out of their

way to avoid any mention of the past or the future. They both had seemed to adopt a "one day at a time" philosophy.

For Carla, it was strange. She'd seldom taken time off from work, accumulating weeks of vacation time. She realized that it was kind of nice not to have to wake to an alarm clock, not to have to go to work.

The feds were apparently convinced that J had left town with the bank money and gone to Washington State. The focus of their investigation had moved—at least temporarily. Maybe that *had* been a drunk driver last night.

What bothered her was that Agent Grover still believed that it had been an inside job—with her helping the robbers. She'd heard that he was looking at several former employees at the bank—one who now worked at the hospital.

She'd quit fighting Davy about returning to her home—at least for the time being. Instead, she told herself that these days together were a dream, one she didn't ever want to wake up from. For most of her life, she'd spent it looking to the future, planning what it would be like.

When it hadn't turned out anything like she'd planned, she'd been devastated. But now she could see just how different she and Davy were. He lived more day by day, and she was beginning to see the value in that. It was something she'd never done before—not looking to the future, but just enjoying one day at a time.

She'd also come to realize that she'd been living around her job. Without it, she felt adrift. Now with all this time on her hands, she saw that even on her days off work she'd had a list of things to do and would check them off. She'd kept so busy she'd never questioned if she was truly happy.

Being here with Davy without lists and a schedule was truly her first holiday. She tried hard not to remind herself that it had to end. Instead, she couldn't wait to open her door and see Davy every morning. Also, there was usually coffee.

This morning was no different. They finished breakfast. He handed her a cup of coffee before clearing away their dishes. "Remember what we used to do over the holidays?"

She remembered building snowmen, hanging on to the bumpers of cars and sliding down the streets, climbing snow-laden roofs and jumping off into deep drifts. She also remembered making love in his pickup one very cold, starry night.

"You're going to have to be more specific," she said, curious where he was going with this.

"Sledding," he said and grinned as if he'd known where her mind had gone. "Although the thought of getting you in the back of my pickup…" He laughed and she joined him.

"Neither of us want that," she said. They made eye contact for a little too long before she pulled away. They were falling back into their old, easy relationship. She'd forgotten what good friends they'd been. They could tell each other anything and everything. It was nice to be close again.

They'd avoided any more mistletoe though, being close again but not that close. Not that Carla couldn't feel that combination of chemistry bubbling between them. She knew Davy felt it too. When they'd parted last night to go to their separate bedrooms, Carla had had to bite her tongue to keep from calling him back to her.

But this was nice, them being friends again. She told herself that she'd be a fool to let it go further. While they'd agreed to make the best of this time they had together, she knew he'd suggested it to keep her mind off the robbery and the investigation and the killer.

She just hoped the feds were right and the killer was long gone from Lonesome—and her.

Chapter Twenty

Jud slept in late since he didn't have to work Christmas Day—and he was in no mood to deal with Jesse after last night. By the time he got up, she had left for the hospital. All he could think about was the money. If he found it, he would be in control of his life again. It was his way out.

He tried to think like Jesse, expanding his search and starting with her car, which was now in his driveway because she'd taken his pickup, saying her car was out of gas. Unfortunately, she was too smart to hide the money in such an obvious place. But at the same time, it would be just like her to hide it in front of his nose.

Back in the house, he tore the place apart. Winded and sweating, he stared at the mess he'd made. No money. What if she'd given it to a friend for safekeeping? He immediately discarded that idea. Jesse didn't have any friends that he knew of, especially any she would trust with money.

No, she'd hidden it. He'd start in the rocks up in the mountain near the cave where he'd initially stashed it and work from there.

But when he opened the door, he was shocked to find Cora Brooks standing out by Jesse's car. "Mrs. Brooks?" he asked as he approached her.

"This is her sister's car," Cora said, pointing at the small sedan. "Her sister Debra's car."

He hadn't known that. Jesse had taken her sister's identity right down to her checking and savings accounts—and her car, apparently. How was that possible? Unless...

"They're identical twins, you know," Cora said with distaste. "But only in looks. I'd always hoped that Debra would turn up." She shook her head. "Realizing what Jesse has done... Debra is dead, isn't she?"

He figured it was the reason Jesse had taken not just her car but her life, including the job as an aide at the hospital. "I wouldn't know anything about that," he said.

The old woman sneered. "Thought I'd have a chat with her." Cora tried to see around him inside the house, which he'd just torn apart.

He blocked her view. "She's not here, and I was just going to work."

She gave him a once-over, as if wondering where he went to work dressed like he was, in old jeans and a T-shirt. He was going to tell her it was none of her business, but that had never stopped Cora.

"I'll tell her you stopped by," he said and started back toward the house, hoping she'd take the hint and leave.

"Don't bother," she said and turned to leave. "I'd rather surprise her. Maybe I'll pay her a visit at the hospital. I heard she's working there." Something about Cora's smile chilled him to the bone. He'd heard that she had a bad habit of finding out things about people and then extorting money from them to keep silent. Hadn't she almost gotten killed last year because she'd tried to blackmail the sheriff's brother? Or maybe that was just a small-town rumor.

He watched her head down the street and flag down the senior citizen bus, which pulled up to stop for her. Once she disappeared inside, he went back in for his winter coat and boots. He should probably warn Jesse about Cora. He pushed the thought away. He had bigger fish to fry. He had to find the money and outsmart Jesse.

Once he was rich, this hick town would never see him again—and, he realized with relief, neither would Jesse.

DAVY COULDN'T REMEMBER the last time he'd been sledding. He'd had to borrow a sled from old friends in town before driving up into the mountains where he and Carla used to go. They could have gone to the sledding hills around town, but he wanted to be alone with her. He was still worried, even though the feds seemed convinced she was safe. He felt better when they weren't around a lot of other people. Not that it necessarily felt safer.

It had been his idea for them to put the past behind them and just be friends again for the holidays. He'd had good intentions. He'd wanted to keep Carla's mind off the killer. But he'd also wanted this time with her. If this was all they had, then he'd take it.

He just hadn't realized how hard it would be. They'd grown close again, so close that taking her in his arms and kissing her seemed like the most natural thing. Sometimes the way she looked at him… He felt that old firestorm inside him. He wanted her so badly it hurt.

On the drive into the mountains, they fell into a companionable silence. He saw Carla looking out the window, taking in the snowy winter landscape as if seeing it for the first time. He wondered if she hadn't had her head down working for so long that she'd forgotten to look around her—let alone to have fun. He was glad that he'd suggested sledding.

After he parked the pickup, they made the hike up the open mountainside, with him pulling the sled behind him. The sky overhead was cerulean blue without a cloud anywhere, the sun turning the snow into bejeweled waves. The slope was perfect for sledding—and yet not so steep that they had to worry about avalanche danger. Also, they were entirely alone up here. The fresh snow on the narrow road up hadn't been disturbed.

The cold air came out in puffs as they reached the top and caught their breaths. He looked over at Carla. "Ready?"

"I haven't done this in years."

"Me neither. I think it's like riding a bike though," he joked. "Let's find out. Hop on." He held the sled on a flat spot at the top to make sure it didn't take off until he was ready. Once she was situated, he gave the sled a shove and jumped on at the last minute. Putting his legs on each side of her, he wrapped his arms around Carla's waist and pulled her against him as the sled took off.

Snow blew up in an icy wave as they careened down the mountainside. He heard her squeal and then laugh. He pressed his face against her shoulder, feeling the cold and the exhilaration. They'd both needed this, he thought.

The sled slowed and came to a stop. Carla turned to look at him, all grins. Her cheeks were red from the cold, her eyes bright. Snow crystals clung to her lashes and the locks of hair that had escaped her hat.

Davy felt himself grinning as widely as she was.

"Can we do it again?" she cried.

He laughed. "We can do it as many times as you want to."

They both scrambled off and began the trudge back up the mountain. The next few times were as exhilarating as the first one. But this time, when the sled slowed and finally stopped at the bottom of the mountainside, neither of them moved.

"That was amazing," she said and leaned back into him. "Thank you for this." He nodded, unable to speak around the lump that had formed in his throat. She shifted on the sled to face him. Their gazes locked and he felt a rush of heat course through him. Her hat and coat were covered in snow. He brushed one frozen lock of her hair back from her face.

"Carla." He said her name like a plea, an oath, a prayer.

SHE KISSED HIM. His lips were cool at first—just like her own. She breathed in the scent of him, the pines, the cold. They'd shared other winter kisses that year they were together. But this one—this one was pure joy.

It felt like that first winter kiss of so long ago. Except this one was so filled with pent-up passion it felt like igniting a rocket. Desire swept through her like the sled had careened down the mountainside. The thrill was there along with the heat as she straddled him, cupping his frosty face in her hands.

She heard him unzip her coat and moments later his hand snaked up under her sweater. His ungloved fingers were warm against her naked skin as they moved upward to cup her breast. She felt her nipple harden to an aching peak even before his fingers slipped inside her bra. A blaze of heat rushed through her veins to her center, and she felt herself go molten.

"I think we should take this to the pickup," Davy said, pulling back from the kiss. His gaze met hers. "Unless you want to stop now."

She shook her head. She could feel his desire pressing into her through her snow pants. She wanted this, needed this, felt as if she would scream if they stopped now. The voice of reason could be heard warning her in the back of her mind, but her need was stronger. "Pickup."

They rose and began stripping off their outer snowy clothes before they reached the truck. Once inside, Davy started the engine and turned on the heater, but Carla knew they didn't need it. Her body felt on fire, and when he touched her again, she groaned with pleasure.

He was easing off her shirt when he saw the tattoo over her heart. It was small and delicate, but when she felt him start, she knew he recognized it. "Carla?"

She felt shy, peeking at him through her lashes. "I know it's silly, but I wanted something that would remind me of you and our dreams. Don't you remember? You gave me your great-grandfather's old branding iron." It had felt like a promise for the future at the time. "That night, you told me about your plans for Colt Ranch. The brand is your family history, your legacy. Now it's part of my history as well."

He shook his head as he gently ran a calloused finger across the tiny brand over her heart before lifting his eyes to hers. "Oh, Carla." He pulled her to him, wrapping her in his arms. "I love you with all my heart. I always have." He drew back to kiss her, and she felt the chemistry between them rocket through her.

When they were teens, their lovemaking had been a concoction of jacked-up hormones as they raced to a climax. Now Davy took it slow, as if revisiting all her pleasure points, teasing her nipples into rock-hard points and sucking them until she leaned back with a cry of release. It was as if he could make love to her all afternoon and the rest of the night.

When they finally came together, Carla cried out, heart thundering, body quivering as the pleasure roared through her in waves. He reached over and turned off the engine. Then he held her, the two of them catching their breaths, the silence of the winter day around them. Snowflakes fluttered past the steamed-over windows.

"I wish we could just stay right here forever," she whispered.

"Then we have to get a bigger truck," Davy said, his arm around her. He stretched out one long leg, then the other, and they both laughed. They weren't kids anymore, but it was nice revisiting their youth in the cab of his pickup again. The truck began to cool quickly.

"No regrets?" he whispered, and she felt him turn to look at her.

She met his eyes. "None." She leaned up to kiss him on the lips. "None," she repeated. He smiled then and pulled her closer.

Carla could hear the unspoken questions between them as the pickup chilled and Davy started the engine again and they began to dress. Had it been a mistake? How could they not do this again and again until he left? But would they regret it, if not today, then tomorrow or the days ahead?

"I suppose we better get going," Davy said as he climbed out to retrieve the sled. They were going to James and Lori's new house on what was known as the Colt Ranch. The original homestead cabin was gone and so was the double-wide trailer the boys had used when they were home. But the land was still there, with plenty of room for each of the brothers to build their own lives on.

Years ago, Carla remembered Davy talking about someday building a house for them on the ranch. His great-grandfather had run a few cattle on the land at one time. His grandfather had kept stock in the corrals.

Davy had always said he would come back to the ranch when he quit the rodeo. He'd talked about making it a working ranch again, either raising cattle or horses. Like rodeo, the place was part of the Colt brothers' legacy. At one time the ranch had been part of her dream as well, the blueprint she'd had for her perfect life. But Davy hadn't fit into her perfect plan so neither had Colt Ranch. Still, like Davy, it had a place in her heart.

Carla thought about that as they drove back toward Lonesome.

CARLA HAD GROWN quiet on the drive out of the mountains. Davy worried that instead of bringing them closer, their earlier lovemaking would drive them even further apart. That was the last thing he wanted.

He was still blown away by Carla's tattoo of his family brand. The chemistry between them had been undeniable. He still wanted her and knew that he would the rest of his days.

But he wasn't fool enough to think it was enough, he told himself as he turned onto a narrow county road that cut through the snow-filled pines. His pickup's headlights punched a hole in the growing darkness, but only yards up the road. This time of the year it got dark by five o'clock. With the weatherman calling for more snow, the night was pitch-black.

"Are you okay?" Davy asked, glancing over at her. He saw her nod. "I'm still planning to come back, you know. I always thought... I hoped..." Their gazes met and he saw that she knew what he'd hoped because she had the same hope.

"Davy."

He heard her unbuckle her seat belt and start to slide across the bench seat toward him. His foot went to the brake.

The cab of the pickup exploded, filling the air with tiny cubes of glass and the shriek of twisted metal. The impact from the right side of the pickup shoved the vehicle into the pines next to the road. He heard wood splintering. A limb struck the windshield, shattering it, as the pickup came to an abrupt stop.

Chapter Twenty-One

"Carla!" Davy cried as his brain fought to understand what had happened. They'd been hit. The passenger-side door was caved in, and Carla lay in his lap. If he'd been going any faster… "Carla!"

She sat up, blinking at him in confusion. He could see her in the light from the dash. "Are you hurt?" With relief he saw her shake her head.

"I don't think so. What happened?" she asked.

"I'm not sure." He glanced back and saw what had hit them. A huge truck sat halfway in the old logging road, the headlights shining out at odd angles. He thought he could hear the engine still running.

With a shock, Davy saw that the passenger-side door of the truck hung open.

"I… I think I'm all right," Carla said, then winced. "But I think I might have—"

He didn't hear the rest of her words as he caught movement beyond what was left of her side window. A man dressed in dark clothes, hood up, was looking at them as if to see if they were…hurt? Still alive? Then suddenly, the man turned and ran down the road behind them.

Before that instant, Davy had assumed the crash had been an accident. Like the other night, this hadn't been an accident.

He swore, then grabbed his door handle and shoved his shoulder against it. But the door, wedged tight against the pine trees, didn't budge. He realized that he wasn't getting out that way and quickly smashed the rest of the windshield and climbed out over the hood. "Stay here," he said back at Carla. Once his boots hit the ground, he took off running after the man.

It had begun to snow, visibility dropping quickly. Not that it would have made a difference. He hadn't gone far when he realized that he'd lost him. The figure had cut off into the pines. Davy could see the man's footprints in the snow, but only in the ambient light of the large rig's headlights. Once he stepped into the dark pines, he couldn't see anything.

He turned back, heart pounding. If only he'd thought to grab his flashlight. And his gun from under the seat. He hadn't been prepared. He told himself he would be next time, because just as he'd feared, this wasn't over.

By the time he reached the pickup, he could hear the sound of sirens. Carla must have made the call. Fortunately, they weren't far from town—just like the last crash. He looked into the pickup and saw her cradling her right ankle. "I think it's broken," she said, pain in her voice. He could tell that she was trying hard not to cry.

"I'm so sorry," he said and reached through her side window for her hand and squeezed it as she met his gaze.

"I was so afraid that you would go after him into the woods. It was him, wasn't it?"

"I think so," he said, hating how close they'd come to the killer—how close they'd come to almost catching him. The sound of sirens grew louder. Flashing lights came about the bend in the road. "It's going to be all right," he said to Carla, but neither of them believed that.

THE NIGHT BECAME a blur of flashing lights and sirens. Carla swam in and out of pain as she was extricated from Davy's wrecked pickup. She still didn't understand what had happened. The EMTs gave her something for the pain once she was on the stretcher and they'd stabilized her ankle. She closed her eyes, welcoming the easing of the pain as the drugs did their job.

It wasn't until she opened her eyes that her terror returned. In alarm, she saw that they were taking her back to the hospital. "No!" she cried and tried to get up.

"As soon as they get a cast on your leg in the ER, I'll get you out of there," Davy said. "I promise."

She closed her eyes, but couldn't shake off the memory of flying broken glass, the sound of metal screaming and looking back to see that a huge truck had T-boned Davy's pickup. Worse was the memory of Davy going after the man while she called 911 because she couldn't help.

True to his word, he stayed by her side even when his brothers rushed down to the hospital to make sure they were both all right. "How are you feeling?" James asked her.

The pain pills had her a little loopy, but unfortunately, she could still feel her ankle. "I feel like I've been hit by a truck."

"It all happened too fast," Davy said. "I never saw it coming."

"But you're all right?" Tommy asked when he saw Davy favoring his left side. Carla hadn't realized he'd been hurt in the crash. So like Davy to brush it off.

"My body got slammed into the driver's-side door. The EMTs checked me out. I'm fine." He touched the left side of his head. "My head apparently connected with the side window. Dazed me."

"Which explains why you went after the driver of the truck rather than wait for the law," Willie said.

"Aren't you guys wanted somewhere?" Davy asked his brothers, but he smiled when he said it. She loved how close they all were. She'd always wished that she had siblings.

Tommy and Willie started to leave, calling back, "Feel better, Carla."

James had pulled Davy aside. She couldn't hear all of their conversation, but enough of it to know that the driver of the truck that had T-boned Davy's pickup hadn't been found yet.

"This proves that he's still in town and that he's going to continue coming after Carla," she heard Davy say. "He's waiting for her to return to her house, for me to go back to the rodeo circuit and leave her alone."

James said something about him being wrong about Debra Watney. She caught the words "model student" and "excellent work history," then "she left her last job abruptly apparently, because of a family emergency."

Davy shook his head. He'd been so sure there was something off about the woman, Carla thought as he raised his voice. "Well, someone at the hospital put that note on Carla's food tray. The killer wanted her to know he could get to her at any time. The only reason he hasn't is because I've hardly let her out of my sight. But clearly he's not giving up and it looks personal to me."

James nodded. "Apparently he's fine with killing you as well."

"I'm going to find this man if it's the last thing I do."

"You're a rodeo cowboy. No offense, but you have no training for this. Let the feds handle this. Let us see what we can find out. Don't—"

Davy shook his head. "For whatever reason, he wants her dead. Which means he'll come for her again. I plan to be ready this time when he does. Nothing you can say will change my mind."

His brother gave him a hug, whispering something to him before he left.

"How's our patient?" Dr. Hull asked as he came in as James left the room.

"Sore. My ankle hurts."

He nodded. "I'll order you some pain medication. How's the head?"

"It aches some. I think I hit the steering wheel with it."

He shook his head. "At least this time you didn't get another concussion, so that's good. I've ordered you a pair of crutches. Have you ever used crutches before?" She shook her head. "I'll get you into a walking cast as soon as I can. Knowing you, you won't like being immobile, but best to take it easy for a while. No stairs."

"I'll take her home to her house," Davy said. "No stairs."

"I know you'll take good care of her." He winked at Carla and left the room.

She looked over at Davy. "How can you take me home? Your truck—"

"I borrowed a truck. I've got this."

Carla shook her head. "Do I have a say in any of this?"

"I guess it will depend on how well you get around on crutches," Davy joked. "But as long as I can outrun you? Then I guess not."

"Davy." It came out a plea. "Doc said I can get in-home help if necessary. You can't keep taking care of me."

He shook his head. Carla would have argued further if FBI agents Grover and Deeds hadn't come into the room. Grover asked Davy to wait outside.

"Carla?" Davy asked.

She nodded. She'd sworn she wouldn't talk to them again without an attorney present, but she hadn't been able to get one yet. "I'll be fine, since I don't have much I can tell them," she said.

Davy said, "I'll get a wheelchair so you can get out of here. I won't be long." He scowled at the agents as he left the room.

"Did I hear you say you don't remember this any better than the robbery?" Grover glanced around the room. "I don't see your attorney."

"I haven't been able to get an attorney, but we can make this quick. I didn't see anything last night. But it wasn't an accident. The man I call J tried to kill me and Davy as well."

"You know that for a fact?" asked his partner.

"There aren't that many people who want me dead," she snapped.

Grover seemed to consider that. "Why would the same person who robbed the bank steal a truck to run into you? He's got the money. Why would he take the chance of getting caught? Unless there's something more he's afraid you're going to tell us."

She groaned. "I've told you everything I know. I was warned not to talk to you, and someone ran us off the road and now crashed into us. What does that tell you?"

"A falling out among thieves?" Grover said and smiled as if joking. They both knew he wasn't.

Carla shook her head and winced. "It doesn't matter what I tell you. You don't believe me. You're convinced that I'm involved in all this."

"Clearly, you are involved," the agent said.

"Not the way you think." She closed her eyes for a moment. "I told you everything I know."

"You didn't tell us about Samantha Elliot until she was in the hospital in a coma," he said.

"She's still alive?" Carla couldn't help her surprise. Last she'd heard, the woman was in serious condition. Maybe she would make it and give them a name or at least a description of the man who attacked her. Carla couldn't help but believe the man's name started with a *J*. "Did you find J's name in her files?"

"The office was ransacked and a lot of files destroyed," Deeds said. "The Butte police are going through them trying to match the tattoo to the one you told us about. But we suspect the attacker took the file."

"Been to Butte recently?" Grover asked.

"No. Why would we share that information with you if we had anything to do with this?"

"Because you thought she may not have survived. Isn't that right? Now she has a guard outside her hospital room door. Should she regain consciousness and remember her attacker..." He left the rest hanging as a threat.

"I hope she does and remembers not just her attacker but that he is the man she tattooed *J* heart *J* on," she said. "That will be the only way this will ever be over since you aren't looking for this man."

"We are looking for him," Grover said, sounding like he was losing his temper. "But you have to admit. You have given us very little."

"What about the truck that hit us last night?" she demanded. She saw the agents exchange a look. Her heart fell.

"The truck was stolen," Deeds said. "We suspect the driver was wearing gloves. Everything was wiped clean."

"So you have nothing," she said and closed her eyes.

"Ms. Richmond," Deeds said. "We might be able to get you a deal if you tell us the truth. We know you didn't kill those other men. I really doubt you or Davy Colt tried to silence Samantha Elliot. Give us the man's name, turn state's evidence against him and—"

"I can't do that, Agent," she said, opening her eyes with a groan. "If I knew who he was, you would already have his name and he would already be behind bars. Now please, leave. After the holidays I'll get a lawyer before we talk again."

"We're going to keep coming back until you tell us the truth," Grover said. "Think about making a deal, Ms. Richmond. I'd hate to see you spend the rest of your life behind bars. So either hire a lawyer or…"

"Or what?" she snapped.

"Or wait until we arrest you and one will be provided for you." Grover signaled his partner and the two left her room as Davy came in with the wheelchair—and a pair of crutches.

Chapter Twenty-Two

Jud wasn't surprised to find Jesse waiting for him when he finally got home late the next morning. He figured she'd already heard about what had happened last night. She might have been close enough by that she'd heard the sirens or maybe even seen the flashing lights of the cop cars. She might have even chased the ambulance to the hospital to find out who was inside—and whether or not they were going to survive.

He wouldn't have put it past her.

That's why he half expected her to have the butcher knife within reach as he came through the door. He hesitated as he closed the front door behind him.

She was sitting in the dark waiting for him. He could feel her rage. He stayed where he was as his eyes adjusted and he could see her shape more clearly.

As he decided how to handle this, he watched for any movement. He might have only an instant between when the blade of the knife caught a slice of sunlight through the crack in the curtains and when she was on him.

"Where have you been?" she asked quietly.

It had been close to daylight before he'd been able to get Jesse's car where he'd left it. He'd been cold and wet. He'd started the engine and turned on the heater and must have fallen asleep. He awoke when the engine died. He'd run out of gas. He'd had to hike into town with the gas can he kept in the back, since this wasn't the first time something like this had happened.

"I think you know where I've been."

She smiled, her teeth shining in the darkness. "While you were messing up my plans, did you also check to make sure the money wasn't where you left it?"

He wanted to turn on a light so he could see her better, but he was afraid of what she might see in his eyes. He would have been home hours ago, but of course she was right—he'd been searching for the money.

"You didn't think I believed that you moved it? By the way, why did you do that? Don't you trust me?"

She made a sound of displeasure before she said, "You know why I moved the money." She waved a hand through the air, as if that covered it. "I told you I would handle things with Carla Richmond if you didn't." Her tone was scarily reasonable. He hadn't seen the butcher's knife out of her reach for a while now.

"I didn't want blood on your hands too," he said. "I did it to protect you."

Her laugh could have shattered crystal. "But you didn't kill her. *Surprise.*"

It was a surprise. He'd T-boned Davy Colt's pickup on the passenger side hard enough to kill her. Now he was even happier that he hadn't turned on a lamp. For sure she would have seen his disappointment that this wasn't over—and right on its heels, his relief that he hadn't killed another person to get out of this mess.

"I had a plan, Jud," Jesse said. "It would have worked too. I was waiting in the alley behind Colt Brothers Investigation. I was waiting for them to come back. She and her cowboy would be dead now. But you had to…*protect* me. I don't think you trust me anymore."

He looked down at the floor, no longer shocked by anything she did. But he didn't want her to know that he'd gone to the spot where he'd hidden the money. She would take that as a betrayal, and he already knew how she reacted when feeling betrayed.

Last night, he'd heard sirens and an ambulance. "She has to be badly injured."

She shook her head. "A broken ankle and a bump on her head. So no, Jud, you failed, and we're not leaving until it's finished."

"It *is* finished," he said, raising his voice. He saw her shift on the couch. He could no longer see both of her hands. "Jesse, I'm begging you. She's not worth it. Let's get the money and leave." He took a wary step toward her, then another. "Staying here will only get us arrested or killed. Please, let this go."

She snapped on the lamp next to the couch, stopping him in his tracks and momentarily blinding him. He blinked and saw that she wouldn't be happy until Carla Richmond was dead.

He wasn't sure he cared about trying to make her happy anymore, but if he wanted the money, he had no choice. He had to kill Carla Richmond—and soon. The problem was that the woman seemed to have nine lives.

Then he would deal with his other problem. Jesse. She was right about one thing. He no longer trusted her. He wasn't all that sure that she wasn't planning to take off with the money without him. Or worse, kill him.

"The good news is that she'll have to go home now to her house—and on crutches," Jesse said. "Even you should be able to handle that."

He watched her get up from the couch. Both of her hands were empty. No butcher's knife. That should have relieved him, except that she was now headed for the kitchen.

"I hope you're hungry," she said over her shoulder. "There's leftover stew."

His first instinct at that moment was to forget about the money, the women, everything and just cut and run. Maybe if he'd had a full tank of gas in the pickup he would have.

"Starved!" he called after her, telling himself that he would outsmart her. "Something smells good," he said, coming up behind Jesse as she pulled a bowl of stew from the microwave and set it on a trivet on the table. He put his arms around her and pulled her against him. At least she didn't have the knife on her. But if he wanted the money and to live to spend it, he'd have to make sure the knife didn't get stuck between his ribs.

CARLA LOOKED DOWN at the cast on her leg and wanted to cry. Crutches? She thought her freedom had been taken away before this. Now she really was in trouble. She was a sitting duck. Finding the man should prove easy. She could just sit and wait for him to come. It wasn't like she could run.

Now Davy felt he had no choice but to stay with her. How could things get worse? They were both trapped. But the worst part was that when J came for her again, Davy would try to stop him. She could get the man she loved killed.

Dr. Hull and Davy helped her into the wheelchair. Her other option was, as Dr. Hull had suggested, getting a nurse. Carla wanted to laugh out loud. Someone from the hospital—a place she was now terrified of? It would just be her luck to bring the killer or his accomplice into her home.

But at the same time, she hated that Davy felt he had to take care of her. She couldn't bear to think of how this was going to end. Davy couldn't stay and protect her forever. Nor would she allow him to.

"Ready?" he asked as he took the wheelchair handles.

"This isn't what I wanted." She sounded close to tears and felt them pool in her eyes.

"You don't always get what you want. Sometimes you get what you need."

She recognized the verse. He'd sung it to her all those years ago—before they'd parted. "Something tells me that we aren't talking about this current situation."

He smiled as he pushed her out of the room and down the hall to the elevator. "I should have fought harder ten years ago. This time, you can't push me away."

Davy drove her home to her house. As he pulled into the drive, she said, "I overheard you talking to your brother. James is right. I'm not your responsibility. I don't want you risking your life for me or putting it on hold any longer." Her voice broke as he parked and turned off the engine. "I'm not going to be responsible for keeping you from what you love." She took hold of her crutches.

"You aren't keeping me from what I love, Carla. Stop fighting me, because you can't change my mind." His gaze burned into her. "Now let's see how you do on these crutches. I cleaned off the sidewalk of snow earlier, but it will still be icy. You sure you don't want me to carry you to the door?"

She looked at him, aghast, and it made him laugh.

"Just a thought," he said, grinning, and he got out to rush around and open her door.

Carla was determined to make it to the house on the crutches. If she fell... Well, she just wasn't going to fall. She was awkward, but she didn't fall. She felt a rush of pride when she even managed the front steps to the porch. True, Davy was right behind her and would have caught her if she'd even wobbled, but she'd made it on her own.

He reached into her purse, pulled out the keys and

opened the front door. She had to prove to him that she would be all right. She had to believe that J would be caught and that she would do fine on crutches until Dr. Hull put her in a walking cast. She had to believe that when Davy left, her heart would somehow survive.

Once inside, she turned to him. She looked into his denim-blue eyes. All of the Colt brothers had the same thick head of dark hair and blue eyes that ranged from faded denim to sky blue. They were all pretty much built alike as well, and all wanted to believe that they were the most handsome of the bunch. Close in age, they spent years confusing their teachers and the town.

But Carla knew that Davy was the most gorgeous of the Colt brothers. He was also the kindest, sweetest and most thoughtful. That she'd let him walk away ten years ago... That she was going to push him away again...

Before she could speak, he said, "Why don't I make us something to eat?" He moved past her on his way to the kitchen.

"Wait. You cook?" If true, this made him even more irresistible.

He stopped to turn. "You keep underestimating me."

It was true and they both knew it. He would make someone a great husband. She felt it to the tender center of her heart. She almost said that, but knew she couldn't joke about him being with anyone else. She held his look for a few moments, then moved past him on her crutches. "I'm not even sure there is anything to cook in the fridge."

JUD HAD BEEN called in to work for a few hours and had readily agreed. Anything to get away from Jesse for a while. Not to mention it took the pressure off him to deal with Carla Richmond.

On the way back home that afternoon after cashing his

paycheck, Jud realized with everything that had been going on, he'd forgotten that one of Leon's goons would be coming by for a payment. Wes knew what day Jud got paid. He almost turned around—until he saw that Wes was standing by his big black SUV—with a headlock on Jesse. Her hands were bound in front of her with duct tape and so was her mouth.

Heart jumping to his throat, Jud sped up. He couldn't let Wes kill her. Jesse was the only one who knew where the money was. He wheeled in next to the SUV and jumped out.

"Let her go," Jud cried and tried to pull Wes off her. Two men Jud had never seen before tumbled out of the SUV and grabbed him. "What the hell is going on?" he demanded, becoming even more afraid.

"Leon wants all of his money *now*. I'm taking your girlfriend as collateral. You ever hear of collateral damage, Jud?"

Jud tried to break free of the men holding him as Wes shoved Jesse into the back of the SUV. "Wait!" he cried as the two men released him and climbed back in the rig to shove Jesse down on the floorboard and slam the door.

Wes came toward him so quickly that he didn't see the incoming fist. It hit him in the gut, dropping him to his knees on the driveway. He gasped for oxygen, unable to speak.

"Let us know when you have the money," Wes said, crouching down next to him. "Your girlfriend told us that we'd already have our money if you had taken care of things. I suggest you do what has to be done, Jud. You have twenty-four hours. Otherwise, we'll take care of her and come back for you."

"Don't kill her," he managed as Wes climbed into the SUV, started the engine and roared away.

Jud couldn't believe this was happening. Only Jesse

knew where the money was. His mind raced. Why hadn't she given them the payment? What the hell was going on? Had she lost her mind?

He watched Wes drive away with Jesse—and his only way to pay the debt before the twenty-four hours were up.

Wes thought that this was about getting the money from his dying grandmother. But Jud had gotten the message loud and clear. Jesse wouldn't pay off Leon—not until Jud took care of Carla Richmond. No matter what he did, the woman wasn't giving up. If he'd had any doubt about her mental state, he no longer did. Cora Brooks was right. There was definitely something wrong with Jesse Watney, a flaw that he had foolishly overlooked—and now deeply regretted.

His back against the wall, he had twenty-four hours. Otherwise, he could kiss the bank money goodbye. He'd risked his life for it. Not that he didn't realize that even if he did what she wanted, Jesse might still double-cross him.

But he told himself that over his dead body would Jesse get away with all that money as he decided to end this.

Chapter Twenty-Three

Agent Grover got the call from Butte on his way back to Lonesome.

"Samantha Elliot has regained consciousness," the doctor told him. "She is determined to speak with you. She had me call the number on the card you left for her."

The phone was handed over. He listened as she told him that she'd done some work for a man named Judson Bruckner. "He's the one who attacked me."

Just to clarify, Grover asked, "What did the tattoo look like?"

She described the one that Carla Richmond had said she'd seen during the robbery. *J* heart *J*. He recalled the drawing she'd done of it.

"You're sure he's the man?"

The tattoo artist cursed at him. "I never forget a face—or a tattoo. It just took me a minute to recall his last name. If he had waited, I would have handed over his paperwork. Stupid fool. When you catch him, I'd be happy to identify him in a lineup and testify against him."

The woman had no idea how lucky she'd been, since if true, Judson Bruckner had already killed three men. He thanked her and quickly did a background check on the suspect. Judson was currently renting a house in Lonesome and temporarily employed by a delivery company for the holidays. He drove an old red pickup. Grover scribbled down the plate number. His rap sheet showed that he'd had a few run-ins with the law, but nothing close to armed robbery and murder.

As he disconnected, he started to call the sheriff's department in Lonesome, but hesitated. He was on his way back from Washington State. He could be in Lonesome in a few hours. He wanted to make this bust himself because he had one very important question for Judson. Who inside the bank had helped him? Because someone had, and he knew that for a fact. He couldn't chance that the local law enforcement would screw up the collar, so he just kept driving, anxious to finally get to the truth.

CARLA COULDN'T IMAGINE how the two of them could live together in her small one-bedroom house. It felt too intimate, Carla thought as she agilely glided across the floor on the crutches past Davy. She stopped to look back at him. "See? I'm fine."

He nodded. "You're better than fine." His gaze was hot and sexy and full of promise.

She felt a rush of desire. How long before the two of them were making love in her double bed as snow fell outside? She shook off the image. It would be fine for a while, but eventually he would resent her for keeping him here. It didn't matter that none of this was her fault—or his either. They'd been thrown together because of an armed bank robbery and a killer who had his own reasons for wanting her dead, apparently.

But how was she going to get Davy to leave if the killer wasn't caught? Because she couldn't keep him. He wasn't hers. Too much of his heart was still taken by the rodeo. If anyone could understand that, it was her. Look how hard she'd worked to succeed, giving up everything but work to prove herself.

Carla leaned on her crutches and opened the refrigerator, surprised to find it stocked. She looked back at Davy, who was lounging against the doorjamb, watching her. "You did this," she said, feeling even guiltier. This man had dropped everything to make sure she was safe, and now this?

"Actually, Lori helped. She thought we might be hungry since we never made it out to their house for dinner."

"And she apparently worried that we might be thirsty," Carla said, pulling out a cold bottle of wine as she balanced on one crutch.

Davy grinned. "Looks like she thought of everything."

Suddenly she wasn't hungry, even though the food stocked in the refrigerator looked delicious. There was only one thing she wanted. She started to close the refrigerator door.

The back door exploded, flying open with the shriek of splintering wood and breaking metal. The first shot was deafening in the small kitchen. Behind her, she heard the bullet hit the wall, burying itself in the Sheetrock. An instant later, the second shot hit the china cabinet in the corner, glass shattering before the bullet made a thwack sound as it burrowed into the wood at the back of the display case.

Carla dropped the bottle of wine in her hand. It hit the tile floor and shattered like a gunshot, sending glass and wine flying. She started to move back, but was shoved into the open refrigerator as Davy dove for the back door. A bullet lodged itself in the refrigerator door she was holding open.

She fell back, dropping one of her crutches as she tried not to come down on her casted leg. She clutched at the refrigerator shelves and screamed, "No!" at Davy. But her cry was drowned out by the fourth shot in the seconds since the back door had been smashed open.

Those terrifying few moments though were nothing compared to the silence that followed. Carla could feel the aching cold of the night coming through the open back door. But over the thumping of her pulse, she heard nothing.

"Davy?" Fear made her voice break and tears rush to her eyes. She reached down and picked up the fallen crutch and awkwardly moved out from behind the refrigerator door, through the spilled wine and glass, terrified of what she would find.

The back door stood open to the night. She could see snow melting just inside it where the man had stood. Past it, she saw two sets of tracks that disappeared into the darkness.

"No!" she cried again and launched herself at the door, only to find that she could see nothing beyond the tracks in the light coming from the kitchen. Nor could she hear anything.

She spun around, searching the floor for a moment, praying she wouldn't find it. But there it was. Blood. Three drops of it, all leading to the back door.

Stumbling into the living room, she searched frantically for her purse and cell phone. She remembered that Davy had brought it in. She looked around, praying that any moment Davy would come through that back door.

Fighting tears of fear and frustration, she spotted her purse and moved quickly on the crutches toward it. She had to toss them aside to get to her purse and the phone inside.

As she was digging for her cell, she heard a noise and looked up. In that instant, she would have done anything to see Davy standing there. Instead, what she saw turned her insides to liquid. To her horror, the blade of the large knife in the hooded figure's hand caught the light as the hood was thrown back and the blonde aide from the hospital rushed at her.

DAVY FELT THE searing pain in his shoulder—but not until he'd run through the fallen snow, chasing the man who'd shot him. He became aware of the cold along with his ragged breaths as he ran. He followed the sound of branches brushing clothing ahead of him and tried to ignore the pain.

The clouds were low, the night black. He couldn't see movement ahead of him, but he knew he was gaining on the killer. Ahead, he saw a faint light through the pines and realized that the man had veered off to the right—toward the river.

Davy had no idea how far he'd run. It had happened so fast that he hadn't had time to think when he'd rushed the man, only to have him fire a final shot and turn and run. Davy had felt something smack hard into his left shoulder, but hadn't let it stop him. This time, he wouldn't let the bank robber turned killer get away. He was determined to catch this man if it killed him.

He was breathing hard, so at first he didn't realize that he could no longer hear the man crashing through the pines ahead of him. He pulled up for a moment to listen. That's when he heard a cry of surprise, followed by a scream that ended abruptly in silence.

Rushing toward the sound, he came out of the pines into the open and stopped as he saw where he was—standing on the cliff above the river. He listened, hearing nothing but his own blood rushing through his veins. He stepped closer to the edge of the cliff, aware of the trampled snow at his feet.

Even in the darkness he could see the sheen of the water's surface below him and, at its edge, something dark crumpled down there in the rocks. He waited for what he knew was the hooded figure who'd tried to kill them to move as he pulled his cell phone from his pocket and hit 911. The figure didn't move.

As he turned back toward the house, following his own footsteps through the snow, he realized that his shirt was covered in blood. He began to move steadily, anxious to get back to Carla. An engine revved somewhere in the distance. Surely Carla would stay at the house and call the cops.

He began to move quicker, suddenly afraid, suddenly having doubts. J, whoever he was, was dead, lying at the edge of the river. There was no way the man could have doubled back. But what if the man had had an accomplice at the hospital? Davy began to run. He heard an engine rev. He ran harder. Finally, he heard sirens headed this way.

By the time he reached Carla's house, he saw the flashing lights of SUV patrol cars pulling into the drive. The back door still stood open and he charged through it. He could hear the sheriff's deputies knocking on the front door.

Through the doorway, he could see into the living room. His pulse jumped. He saw evidence of a struggle. A lamp lay broken on the floor next to one of Carla's crutches.

"Carla!" He was calling her name, his voice cracking with fear, as he rushed through the house. "Carla!" Her purse was on the floor by the couch, the contents—including her cell phone—scattered across the floor. The deputies were pounding harder at the front door. He rushed to it, facing his greatest fear.

Carla was gone.

Someone had taken her.

J? But if true, then who was that lying dead at the edge of the river?

The second *J*.

Chapter Twenty-Four

Davy felt as if he were in shock—from the loss of blood, from the loss of so much more. He'd been taken to the hospital, where the bullet had been removed from his upper arm and the wound bandaged.

He was anxious to be released. While his brothers and most of the sheriff's department were looking for Carla, he had to get out of the hospital so he could find her. Not that he had any idea where to look.

But right now there was a sheriff's deputy outside his hospital room door, apparently to keep him there. Federal agents were on the way to question him.

The moment Grover walked in, Davy could tell he was angry, demanding to hear what had happened in detail from the beginning.

"This is a waste of time," Davy had snapped after he told the agents everything that had occurred. "Now can we please find Carla?"

"I'm sure she's long gone," Grover said and seemed surprised that Davy was still anxious to leave to look for her. "You don't get it, do you? The robbery? Judson Bruckner had inside information from someone working at the bank. We know that for a fact. We believe that information came from your girlfriend."

"You're wrong. From the very beginning she told you

she had nothing to do with it," Davy snapped. "We were almost killed by that man. You found his body lying down on the edge of the river, right?"

Grover nodded. "Which is unfortunate. I really wanted to ask him about the missing money. But apparently, it and Carla Richmond are gone."

"How can you think that? There were obvious signs of a struggle when I got back to the house," Davy said.

"Maybe too obvious," Grover said.

Davy shook his head in irritation. "Someone took her."

"Who do you think that was?" Deeds asked. "You said that you were chasing a man in a hoodie. Was there someone else with him?"

"Just because I didn't see anyone else..." Davy raked a hand through his hair. He felt sick to his stomach. His brothers had warned him, and he hadn't listened. He should never have gone after the man. He should never have left Carla alone. Now someone had her.

"So, who is he, the man at the bottom of the cliff? Have you been able to ID him?" The moment he asked the question, he saw the answer on the agent's face. "You know already?"

"Samantha Elliot, the tattoo artist who inked him, regained consciousness and gave us his name. I was on my way back here to question him."

"But if you know who he is, then you should be able to find out who he was working with," Davy said. "The note on Carla's tray at the hospital... Does he work at the hospital?"

Grover shook his head. "His name is Judson Bruckner. He worked temporarily for a delivery company."

"I saw him," Davy cried. "He was looking in the window of her house. He had a package, but he said it was the wrong address and left before I could question him further." Davy couldn't believe he'd been that close to the killer, that close to catching him. If only he had, Carla would be safe now.

The agent looked at the small notebook in his hand. "You and Ms. Richmond, you hadn't had any contact for how long before the robbery?"

Davy shook his head, confused for a moment as to why the agent was asking him this. "I told you, I saw her the day before—"

"Before the robbery. I'm asking about before that. Had you had any contact with Ms. Richmond?"

"No. I stopped by the bank the day before the robbery to see her. Before that, I hadn't seen her in months. But what does this have to do with—"

"You have to understand my skepticism, Mr. Colt," Grover said. "You said Ms. Richmond wasn't injured during the shooting at the house, but you were."

"She had the refrigerator open. I shoved her against it, the door blocking any bullets, as I lunged at the shooter." He groaned. "Agent Grover, could we please quit wasting time? Carla is in trouble. If this Judson Bruckner didn't work at the hospital, then someone he knew does."

"Doesn't this remind you of the truck that hit you? Haven't you asked yourself how it was that neither of you were hurt?"

"One of us *was* hurt," he said through gritted teeth. He could feel time running out. They were wasting precious moments here while Carla… Who knew where or what was happening with her? "Carla's ankle was broken."

"Still, the way the side of your pickup was crushed, I'm surprised she wasn't killed."

"I was slowing down. She'd unbuckled her seat belt and was moving toward me."

"So she's what? Making a move on you, and out of the blue a big truck just happens to crash into your pickup on

Ms. Richmond's side at that exact moment? How lucky that she slid over by you just before that happened."

"You can't still think she had anything to do with this," Davy cried.

"Why not? Tell me…now that you've had time to think about this. Doesn't it seem strange that the shooter fired shots all over the place—except for the one that winged you, Mr. Colt?"

Davy swore. "You didn't see his face. I did. His eyes were wild and his hand was shaking. But all that aside, I've had enough of this. You're wrong. Carla's been taken. By someone connected to the killer. Maybe someone even more dangerous. Instead of talking nonsense, you should be trying to find her before it's too late." His voice broke at the fear that it might already be too late.

Grover shook his head. "Ms. Richmond knew I was onto her. She needed to disappear. Now she has." The agent got to his feet. "I'm sorry, Mr. Colt. I can tell that you care about this woman, but you're kidding yourself if you think she isn't involved. Why do you think the robber stayed in town this long? He couldn't leave without her. And he would have—if you hadn't run him over a cliff."

He started toward the door only to turn back. "Carla Richmond's gone and so is the money. She staged it so you'd think someone took her, struggled with her. But don't worry, we'll find her. However, you'd be smart to put this little…episode behind you. She used you." With that he turned and walked out.

DAVY COULD PRACTICALLY hear the clock ticking as he was finally allowed to leave the hospital. Now at least he knew J's name. Judson Bruckner. Apparently, he'd been living in Lonesome for a few years.

But who had taken Carla? All he knew was that she had

put up a fight. His gut instinct told him whoever it was had been working with Jud Bruckner. The other *J*? Someone who worked at the hospital?

But when James had gotten the list of employees, that had been a dead end.

Davy thought of the blonde nurse. He still thought there was something about her that bothered him. What if he wasn't wrong? The answer was here, he told himself as he went down to the hospital's main office.

"Can I help?" the woman at the desk asked.

"I'm looking for an aide who works here. Debra Watney?"

"I'm sorry, she isn't working tonight. Is there someone else who can help you?"

"Did you say Debra Watney?"

He turned at the deep, coarse female voice, recognizing the sound of it at once. It was the same one that had yelled at him and his brothers for stealing her apples from the tree near both of their properties. Davy groaned inwardly. Cora Brooks had been the bane of their existences for years and the worst neighbor a bunch of wild Colt boys could have. She'd threatened numerous times to shoot them with her shotgun loaded with rock salt.

Cora stood not even five feet tall, but she was a force to be reckoned with. He saw that her right wrist had been bandaged, which he realized might explain what she was doing here. "Why are you asking about Debra Watney?" Cora demanded.

He had to bite his tongue for a moment. Nosy old busy-body. "She's an aide who works here."

"Not likely," Cora said with a scoff. "She's dead."

Davy didn't have time for this. He started past her, but she grabbed his arm with her free hand. "Cora, I have to find this woman—"

"You aren't looking for Debra Watney," Cora said, dropping her voice and pulling him away from the nurse's station. "Her name's Jesse. Jesse Watney. I knew she was back in town, but I had no idea that she'd stolen her twin's name and profession." She clucked in disgust.

He'd frozen at the name—*Jesse*. Cora had to be wrong, and yet hadn't he been suspicious of the aide from the get-go? "How can you be sure her name is Jesse and not Debra?"

"I know, so just leave it at that. Debra disappeared a while back and hasn't been seen since getting into a car with Jesse. Jesse's the devil incarnate."

"Where can I find her?" he asked, telling himself that if he was right about the blonde aide, then what Cora was telling him just might be true.

"She's been living with Judson Bruckner in a house they rent on the edge of town."

He felt his heart kick up and then drop. Maybe Cora did know what she was talking about—but the aide wouldn't take Carla there. Too obvious. "Is there somewhere she'd go if she didn't want anyone to find her?"

"Probably back to the family hovel in the mountains."

"Around here?" he asked in surprise, and Cora nodded. "Can you draw me a map of how to get there?"

"I can do you one better. I'll show you." She must have seen him hesitate. "That's the deal. I go with you, or you don't get the information. I want to see her face when retribution comes knocking."

"Cora, it's going to be dangerous. You don't want to—"

"Of course it's going to be dangerous," the elderly woman snapped. "Jesse would just as soon kill you as spit in your eye. You underestimate her evil and you'll be dead as a doornail. I'm going." She started for the door. "We'll take my rig. I keep my stinger in it."

Davy wanted to argue, but he'd left the pickup he'd borrowed out at Carla's. He climbed into Cora's small pickup, as she pulled her shotgun off the rack on the rear window.

"Let's go get her," Cora said with obvious delight. "On the way, you can tell me why Jesse has your girlfriend." He started to tell her that Carla wasn't his girlfriend, but of course she didn't give him a chance. "What were you thinking not marrying her a long time ago anyway?"

CARLA SURFACED AS if from the bottom of a lake. She opened her eyes slowly, fighting to focus. Her brain felt foggy. For a moment, all she wanted to do was close her eyes and go back to the darkness.

But then her brain snapped in. Her eyes flew open, and she bolted upright to quickly take in her surroundings. The smelly, lumpy mattress she'd been lying on. The worn wooden floor. The log walls. The cloudy dust-coated old window. The snowy pines beyond it.

At the sound of something popping and cracking, she turned her head and saw the ancient rock fireplace, its face dark with layers of soot. A small fire burned at the back of it, sending out puffs of heat into the cold room.

"You're finally awake."

She started at the female voice, her head swiveling around to see the woman standing in the doorway. It all came back in a flash at the sight of the blonde aide. A gun dangled from the woman's right hand as she moved into the room and dragged over what was left of an old cloth recliner. She sat and leaned forward, balancing the gun on one thigh.

"Where are we?" Carla asked, her mouth dry and her tongue feeling too large for her mouth. Their conversation earlier tonight had been short, punctuated by the needle the woman had jammed into her arm as they'd struggled on the couch. Carla had been at a distinct disadvantage, given the cast on her leg. She vaguely remembered being half dragged out to the woman's vehicle. After that, nothing.

"Does it matter where we are?" the blonde asked.

She guessed not and tried to clear the fog still drifting around in her head. "You're the aide from the hospital." Carla frowned as she tried to remember the name James had told her. "Debra."

"You can call me Jesse," she said with a smile.

"Jesse?" She felt her pulse jump. "The other *J.* Of course."

"Jud and that stupid tattoo," Jesse said with a rueful shake of her head. "He's had his uses, I'll give him that, but let's face it—he's a dim bulb."

Carla gathered that Jud, the other *J*, wasn't here with them. She supposed that was something. "Why have you brought me here?"

"Why?" Jesse laughed. "You don't like the place? I grew up here." She glanced around, all humor erased from her face. "I swore I'd never come back here." Her gaze returned to Carla. "Because of you, here I am and here you are." Her face hardened. "You shouldn't have told the feds about the tattoo. I told you not to talk to them. You should have listened."

"You wrote the note." Her mind was taking its time clearing. Not that it helped. She had a cast on her leg and Jesse had a gun. The odds of getting out of here alive weren't good.

Jesse rose and began to pace the small room. "I spent my life being disrespected because of my family, my perfect twin, everyone—" She spun to face her. "People just like you who thought they were better than me."

"I don't even know you."

"You should have given Jud a loan."

She blinked. "He never applied for one." At least, not under the name Jud.

Jesse let out a rude sound. "Don't pretend you would have given him one if he had."

"I guess we'll never know." Carla looked around the room, afraid to ask what happened next. She had a bad feeling she already knew. But a small bubble of hope rose in her as she wondered why she was still alive. Jesse could have killed her back at the house. So why hadn't she?

The thought of the house brought a heart-dropping memory. "The last I saw my friend Davy, he was chasing a man out the back door of my house. I assume it was Jud." Since Jud wasn't here, Carla hoped that meant that Davy had caught up to him and was fine. "Do you know what—"

"Happened? Your guess is as good as mine. They might both be dead." Jesse shrugged. "It doesn't matter."

It did to Carla. She felt her eyes burn with tears. Wasn't this what she'd feared? That Davy would get injured or killed trying to protect her? But Jud could have gotten away, she realized. He could be headed up to this cabin right now. And Davy...? He had to be alive.

She realized Jesse was studying her intently, frowning as she did, as if surprised that she wasn't more terrified. If the woman only knew. But Carla was doing her best not to panic. It was her nature to keep control over her emotions. Except for when she thought of Davy.

"What? You aren't going to ask?" Jesse smiled as she sat back down on the edge of the recliner. Carla shook her head, pretending she didn't know what it was the woman was getting at. "Come on, don't you want to know what I'm going to do with you?"

"I would imagine you plan to kill me."

Jesse smiled, then cocked her head as if to listen before sending a glance toward the window and the darkness outside.

Carla realized that she was expecting someone. Jud? Of course. Her heart sank. She was waiting for Jud before she killed her. Or was it Jud who would be pulling the trigger?

Listening, she didn't hear anything. The deep snow was like thick cotton insulation, swallowing up sound. She was on her own with a gun-toting Jesse and possibly her even more dangerous boyfriend. If she had any hope of getting away from the Js, she had better come up with a plan.

She thought of Davy and her heart ached. Her life couldn't end here in this cabin deep in the mountains. If he was alive, he would blame himself. She couldn't bear the thought.

Over against the fireplace she saw an old branding iron that was apparently being used as a poker. How ironic, she thought, that the one weapon in the room other than Jesse's gun was a branding iron.

AS DAVY RODE SHOTGUN, Cora filled him in on what she knew about Jesse Watney and he told her what had happened back at the cabin. If Carla was in Jesse Watney's hands, then she was in worse trouble than if she'd been taken by Jud. Jesse had threatened her at the hospital, but that was mild compared to the stories Cora told him about the woman.

He was wishing he didn't know, fearing that he would be too late, that Carla was already dead. That is, if this woman named Jesse Watney had her.

When his cell rang, he quickly picked up, seeing that it was James.

"I just spoke with Agent Grover. What a... Where are you?"

"Probably on a wild-goose chase." He heard Cora grunt

in the driver's seat. "Judson Bruckner was living with a woman named Jesse Watney. We're on our way to Jesse's family cabin in the mountains right now."

"We're?"

"Cora's with me." The road was getting worse. "Got to go."

After he disconnected, he could feel the elderly woman's gaze on him. "You didn't ask how I hurt my wrist," Cora said as they left the county road and headed up into the mountains.

He glanced over at her. His first thought was that she'd been spying on someone. Everyone in the county knew that she kept binoculars handy and had even bought herself some night-vision ones. If the grapevine could be believed, she loved learning people's secrets and then cashing in on them. That highly illegal quirk had almost gotten her killed last year, but Davy doubted it had stopped her.

"Gardening?" he asked, clearly joking.

She cackled. "Yep, winter gardening." She was still chuckling when she said, "The road is going to get a lot worse, I'll warn you right now. Best hang on. The cabin's all hell and gone back in here. Place has been empty for years. I figure she'll go there like an animal returns to its den."

Even though she'd been right about Jesse working as Debra Watney at the hospital, he still wasn't sure that she wasn't leading him on a fool's errand back up here in the mountains. He could feel time slipping away.

"It's not far now," Cora said, sitting up to strain to see into the glow of the headlights.

At first he didn't even see the road. But then he saw the fresh tire tracks in the snow. Only one set. Pine trees stood like towering snow-covered walls on each side as the road narrowed to a Jeep trail.

"I'm trying to decide if we should walk the last part or

drive right up to the cabin," Cora said as she shifted into four-wheel drive. "Not sure it makes a difference, since if I know Jesse, she'll be expecting us."

He shot her a look. "What are you saying?"

"If she wants your girlfriend dead…" Again he thought about correcting her. They weren't boyfriend and girlfriend. He wasn't sure what they were. "Then she would have killed her at your house. Why bring her up here unless she was waiting for someone?"

"Jud isn't going to show up, but she might not know that," Davy said. He could feel Cora's gaze swing to him.

"Probably won't make a difference to Jesse which man shows up. I suspect she was planning to kill that boyfriend of hers anyway. He was the kind she would eventually squish beneath her boot. She'd much rather you see her kill Carla."

Davy felt his stomach roil. He was beginning to wonder about Cora and if she even knew what she was talking about, when a cabin came into view in the headlights.

Chapter Twenty-Five

Carla realized that Jesse had heard something. She had her head cocked, listening, and didn't seem surprised when headlights cut through the grime-coated glass of the front window. "Stay here!" she ordered and moved to the door.

Carla knew she didn't have long. She slid across the mattress, then reached over to grab the branding iron from the edge of the fireplace. She had just enough time to hide the iron next to her before Jesse turned.

The blonde's face hardened to stone. "You moved."

"I'm freezing. I moved closer to the fire."

Jesse studied her for a moment before glancing at the fire.

Carla held her breath, afraid she would see that the branding iron was no longer leaning against the soot-coated rocks.

At the sound of boots on the porch, both of their gazes were drawn toward the front door. Jesse quickly came back over to her to point the gun at Carla's head.

"I figured someone would come looking for you," Jesse said. "Hope it's your cowboy. If his PI brothers are worth their salt, then they know about me by now—and that I had family up here in the mountains. Thing is," she said, frowning, "the place isn't that easy to find."

CORA PARKED AND turned off the engine. There was no sneaking up on the cabin. Anyone inside would know that they had company. The headlights went off, pitching them into darkness.

The only light that flickered inside the structure was from a fire. Davy couldn't see anyone through the grime-covered window, but he felt as if they were being watched. No one, however, had come to the door.

He wondered if Carla was here with the woman Cora called Jesse. If so, who was Jesse expecting to come driving up? Jud? "You should stay in the truck," he said to Cora.

The elderly woman harrumphed and was out the pickup door before he could stop her, taking her shotgun with her. He hurried after her. As they reached the porch, he stopped to listen, afraid he'd hear a gunshot.

Cora scaled the rickety porch steps and was almost to the door when Davy heard a female voice call, "Come in!"

Davy recognized it as that of the blonde aide from the hospital, the same one Cora swore was actually Jesse Watney—an alleged killer, and the woman who he knew in his gut had Carla. He reached past Cora, grabbed the door handle, turned it and pushed. The old door groaned and creaked as it swung slowly open.

The fire in the room illuminated the scene before him. Carla sat on an old mattress a few feet from the fireplace, and the blonde stood over her with a gun pointed at Carla's head.

He met Carla's gaze and saw strength and determination in those blue eyes. He hadn't expected anything less. He gave her a small nod—not sure how to get her out of this unharmed, but willing to risk his own life to make it happen.

Cora set her shotgun aside and pushed past him and into the room. Davy could feel his gun where he'd tucked it into the back waistband of his jeans as he was getting out of the pickup. Cora was a loose cannon, but if not for her, he wouldn't have known where to find this place. He just worried about what she would do next and knew he had to be ready.

"Hope you aren't planning to go back to your job at the hospital," Cora was saying, taking obvious delight in the news she was about to impart. "They know you lied about who you are. I would imagine they have already called the sheriff."

"What did you bring this old bat for?" Jesse demanded, seemingly unfazed by the news. "I wasn't going back to that job anyway." Her gaze moved to Davy. "Where's Jud?"

"He had an accident."

"Dead?" she asked. He nodded and she smiled. "One thing less to take care of before I leave town."

"You actually think you're going to get away this time?" Cora demanded, hands on her skinny hips. "The feds are involved. This time you're going down for your crimes. Finally, Debra is going to get what she deserves. Payback for what you did to her."

Jesse frowned, tilting her head as she stared at the older woman. "Why do you care so much?"

"I knew your grandfather and I remember your sister as a child. She was good to her soul," Cora said, her voice breaking. "She deserved better than she got, especially from her twin sister."

Jesse's eyes blazed for a moment and Davy feared she might start shooting—starting with Carla. He swore under his breath, wishing he had insisted on Cora staying in the pickup. He knew he would have had to hog-tie her though.

To his relief, Jesse seemed to tamp down her anger. She shook her head, dismissing Cora as she shifted her gaze to him. "Let's get this over with. I know you have a weapon on you. Toss it over by the fire."

"You need to let Carla go, and we'll all walk out of here," he said. "Carla has nothing to do with this."

Jesse laughed. "She has *everything* to do with this. If it wasn't for her…" She shook her head. "She should have kept her mouth shut about what she saw during the robbery. I warned her. She didn't listen. Her mistake. Now yours for coming up here to try to save her—and worse for bringing this old hag with you."

Cora moved with surprising quickness for her age. She charged like a small tank going into battle. Davy had only an instant to react. He half expected Jesse to pull the trigger and kill Carla before turning the gun on Cora. He drew his weapon, knowing he would probably have only one chance for a clear shot.

For years, he and his brothers had competed against each other firing at tin cans. Davy had always been the better shot. He prayed he still was.

As he raised his gun to aim and fire, he saw Carla reach beside her. As Cora charged Jesse, Carla lifted what looked like an old branding iron. In one fluid movement, she swung it high across her body, striking Jesse's arm with the gun.

The sound of the gunshot was deafening in the small room. Davy had thought the blow with the branding iron would dislodge the gun from Jesse's hand, but he was wrong. He heard her cry of pain, then one like a war cry as she swung the gun at Cora, who was inches away from tackling her. The blow to the side of Cora's head sent her headlong into the floor next to Jesse.

Davy saw it all happen in what felt like an instant before he was looking down the barrel of Jesse's gun, the black hole taking aim at his heart. He fired first. But she still got off a shot before his bullet hit her in the throat. He felt the bullet whiz past his head to lodge in the door behind him.

Blood was spurting from Jesse's throat, but she was still standing, the gun still in her hand. Worse, she was starting to turn, to swing the barrel toward Carla, who'd gotten to her knees on the mattress. As he started to fire again, he saw Carla swing the branding iron in both hands like a batter going for a home run.

The makeshift weapon caught Jesse in the knees. She opened her mouth as if to scream, but only emitted a gurgling sound as she crumpled to the floor next to Cora.

Davy lowered his gun as Carla pried the gun from Jesse's grip and tossed it aside. Davy rushed to her and dropped down next to her to take her in his arms. He'd never been more relieved in his life. This could have gone so much worse. Carla clung to him so tightly that he hoped she'd never let him go.

"Cora?" she asked after a few moments.

"I'm too mean to die" came the answer from the floor as the older woman pushed herself up into a sitting position and flinched as she touched the knot on the side of her head. "Is she dead?" Cora asked of Jesse, before prodding her with a boot toe.

The worn wooden floor was bright red with blood. He could see Jesse's eyes, wide open, lifeless. "She's gone."

"Thank goodness," Cora said and sighed.

"I can't believe you found me," Carla said against his chest.

"It was all Cora's doing. If I hadn't run into her at the hospital…" Davy pulled back a little to look at Carla. Her gaze went to his shoulder and his blood-soaked coat sleeve.

"You're shot," she cried.

"That was from Jud back at the house. That's what I was doing at the hospital—getting it bandaged up."

"He'll live," Cora said. "I just texted the cops. Told them to send a wagon for the body and an ambulance for one of the Colt boys who's been winged."

"Davy," he said. "I'm Davy Colt."

The elderly woman shrugged as if it was all the same to her. "I'm just glad you're a decent shot. I used to listen to the lot of you shooting tin cans by the hour." She shook her head. "All you Colt boys, you're all the same to me. Wild and incorrigible." But there was a twinkle in her eye.

Chapter Twenty-Six

Carla's emotions veered off in every direction. She was so thankful to be alive. So thankful that Davy was alive. She would be forever grateful to Cora for helping them. The bank's money had been recovered—at least most of it—from the cabin where Jesse had taken her. Both Jud and Jesse were dead. She didn't know how to feel about that—guilty for being relieved that they were gone, angry that they'd done what they had, guilty for not being sorry that two people were dead and that she might have played a part in it.

She'd met with Agents Grover and Deeds one final time. Grover didn't quite apologize, but at least he'd told her that she was no longer a suspect. A former employee at the bank had finally confessed that she'd given Jesse information while she'd been in labor at the hospital. She said that the woman she knew as Debra Watney had asked a lot of questions after learning that she had worked there. The woman said she had thought the aide was just trying to keep her mind off the labor. She had had no idea she was giving away information that would be used in the robbery—and key the agents to an inside job.

While Carla felt for the woman, she was grateful that she herself was no longer a suspect. Her boss had called to say that her job was waiting for her whenever she felt up to coming back.

For days all she'd wanted was for her life, and Davy's, to return to normal. Normal meant she would go back to the bank, back to her house alone each night, back to spending her days crossing items off her to-do lists.

For Davy it would mean catching up on the rodeo circuit. The holiday was winding down. It was time. Yet neither of them mentioned it. Since coming out of the mountains, they'd spent every minute of the past few days together at her house. One of Davy's brothers fixed the back door with a better lock and dead bolt and cleaned up the place.

If they ignored the bullet holes in the kitchen wall and refrigerator, they could almost pretend that none of it had happened.

But Carla couldn't pretend that things were going to change. Doc Hull had put her in a walking cast and given her a scooter that she could use at work. She was able to get around by herself with little trouble, and it wouldn't be all that long before even the walking cast would come off.

They'd fallen into a pattern over the days. Lying in bed in the morning until they felt like getting up. Having a breakfast one or both of them prepared. Making love. Cooking and going back to bed to make love again. She loved lying with Davy in her double bed together, her head on his shoulder, her cheek pressed against his skin.

"I love you, Carla. I've always loved you." It was the day before he was to leave. He turned to kiss her deeply. "I was so afraid that I'd lost you. I never want to let you go again." His blue gaze met hers and she felt that fire ignite at her center again.

"I love you, Davy. Always you."

"Come with me," he said, his expression brightening as if the idea had just come to him. He leaned on one elbow so he could look at her face. "We're both still young. We have plenty of time to settle down. We can spend the next few years traveling around the country."

She stared at him, unable to believe what he was suggesting—again. He'd suggested this ten years ago. Didn't he remember how that had ended? "Davy, I have a job. A house. A—" She'd almost said *life*. "A…house that's paid for." These days living in this house, the two of them acting like a real married couple, had she let herself dream that he might see the life they could have here? That he might want it?

But from the look on his face, it was the last thing he wanted. He rose from the bed, his face suddenly stiff, his expression cold. "You thought that I would quit the rodeo." He shook his head, the look ripping apart her heart. "I told you. I'm not ready to quit. I thought…"

"I thought since you were talking about only a couple more years…"

"That I would change my mind."

There was no reason to lie. He knew from her disappointed expression that she'd hoped he would change his mind. She should have known better. One last night after making love ten years ago, they'd lain in bed talking. He'd romanticized about the two of them on the rodeo circuit going places she'd never been, seeing country she might never see again, eating food that she would never have in Lonesome, meeting people, being together.

At the time, she'd been tempted to chuck her life here and hit the road with him. But she wasn't that girl from ten years ago and she certainly wasn't going to chuck it all now, she told herself.

"You never considered coming with me, did you?"

She met his gaze and felt her heart shatter. When she spoke, her voice broke with emotion. "My job, my house…

I can't just pick up and leave like you can. I have *responsibilities*." She rose from the bed to go to him, snatching up her shirt and pulling it on as she did. "Please." How could he not see how much this was killing her? How could he walk away from her now? She tried to cup his cheek, but he took a step back. "Davy, I love you."

"You love me?" he asked as he grabbed up his jeans and pulled them on. "How is that possible, since you want me to be someone I'm not? Or do you love the idea of me? Rodeo cowboy Davy Colt. Because if you loved me, you'd love all of me, whether you agreed with it or not. Hasn't it always been about you trying to change me, so I fit into this perfect picture you have of marriage and our lives together?"

"I could say the same about you," she said, drawing back from him. "You want me to give up everything for you. What's the difference?"

"You're not your job, Carla. Or are you going to tell me that your dream is to work as an executive loan officer in a bank in Lonesome, Montana?"

She took a step back as if he'd slapped her. "You know how I ended up in Lonesome working at the bank. I had to change my plans because it was the right thing to do."

He nodded and took a step toward her, taking her shoulders in his hands. "You had to change your plans. How about changing them for us?"

She'd never wanted to say yes more than she did at that moment. "I'm not like you, footloose and fancy-free to go and do whatever you please."

He shook his head and let go of her to pull on his boots. "You can't blame your mother, Carla. She's been gone now for over five years. But you're still here. Why?"

He made it sound as if she'd chosen the path of least resistance. As if she lacked courage. "I'm not like you."

"You're right about that," he said. "I've spent my life

taking chances, drawing rank bucking horses that will either put me in the money or the dirt or the hospital. Betting on myself, fighting the odds, testing myself over and over again against eighteen-hundred-pound animals. In all that time, you've never taken a chance. Not one. Not on me," he said. "Not even on yourself."

She watched him snatch up his Stetson. Their gazes met and held for a moment. She could see him waiting for her to say something. To ask him to stay. But she couldn't do that any more than she could ten years ago, she told herself.

"I swore I wouldn't let you break my heart again," he said, his voice cracking. "This time, it is all on me. Goodbye, Carla."

She stood there, shaken to her core. Only minutes ago they'd been locked in each other's arms, promising to love each other forever. What had happened? She heard him drive away in his new pickup, furious with him and what he'd said, furious with herself and how much of what he said might be true. Either way, her heart was breaking all over again.

It wasn't until the sound of his pickup engine died off in the distance that she let herself break down and cry.

DAVY WENT DOWN to the office the next morning. He'd smelled coffee and knew he'd find someone there working.

James was behind their father's large old desk. He looked up, not seeming surprised. "Packing up to go?" he asked.

Davy helped himself to a cup of coffee from the pot that was usually going—except when something happened that called for them to dip into their father's blackberry brandy. "You were right."

James put aside his work to give Davy his full attention. "I'm always right, but you'll have to enlighten me why this time." Then he seemed to see his brother's face. "You and Carla. She didn't take it well, you returning to the circuit?"

He shook his head. "I actually thought I could talk her into going with me. Just for even a year, and if she hated it, I would have quit and come back here."

"Did you tell her that?"

"What would be the point? She's settled. My life isn't for her even if I quit the rodeo. There was nothing I could say."

"I'm sorry," James said. "I know how you feel about her."

All Davy could do was nod, his chest aching from the heartbreak when he thought about how much he loved her. "These days together… So tell me about Dad's case," he said, wanting to change the subject. "Willie thought he could get a copy of the file—or at least get a look at it."

James shook his head. "It's missing."

"You know it's those Osterman brothers' doing. Both Osterman sheriffs were crooked as a dog's hind leg. So there's nothing we can do?"

"There's a good chance there wouldn't have been anything helpful in the file anyway," James said.

"Or there could be something someone wanted to stay hidden," Davy argued. "Why get rid of it otherwise?"

Before James could respond, Willie came in the door, followed quickly by their brother Tommy. One look at Davy and Willie said, "Sorry, bro. I get it, I do. But if after all this you still can't find a way to be together—"

"You've never been in love," Davy said to Willie as his brothers came in the door on a gust of winter-cold air and snow.

Willie looked as if he wanted to argue, but conceded the point since they all knew it was true. Their older brother guarded his heart closely when it came to women. "If it hurts as bad as you look, then I never want to fall in love."

"How's this sheriff's deputy gig going?" Davy asked him, again anxious to change the subject.

"Good," Willie said, sounding almost surprised himself. "I like it. I have a lot to learn and I'm definitely a rookie at this point, but…" He smiled. "I'm a fast learner."

"We were just talking about Dad's case," James told them.

"I guess James told you that the file on the accident is missing," Willie said. "But I did find out something interesting. I think Dad's pickup might still be in Evidence. I just need to find out where if that's the case."

"I'm not sure I want to see his pickup if you find it," Tommy said with a shudder. "I don't even want to think about the kind of damage the train did. Anyway, what could you hope to find in it after all this time?"

Willie shook his head. "I don't know, but if I can find the pickup, I'm definitely going to. So, you're leaving," he said to Davy, clasping his brother's shoulder. "Hope they give you some decent broncs. Do you know who's supplying the stock for your first ride?"

Davy was grateful that the conversation didn't return to Carla and his broken heart. Not that he could stop thinking about her. He could still smell her on his skin and ached at the thought that he might never hold her again.

Chapter Twenty-Seven

A few days after Davy walked out of her life, Carla got up,
showered, dressed and headed for the bank. She'd cried
until there were no more tears. She'd also had a lot of time
to think about the robbery and the times she'd escaped
death. Mostly she thought about Davy and what he'd said
to her before he'd left her house.

Before driving to the bank, she'd looked around her
house. She loved what she'd done with the place since she'd
moved in. But having Davy live with her there made it feel
too empty now. A friend had suggested she get a cat. Carla
had laughed, even though she loved cats.

"Life is about choices and consequences," her mother
used to say. Carla couldn't agree more as she walked into
the bank and went straight toward her office. But she didn't
enter it at first. Instead, she stopped in the doorway, taking
in the space as if seeing it for the first time.

She'd been proud of this accomplishment because it was
a symbol of her hard work and what she'd given up to get
here. Back then her office had been a place of comfort
and safety. She knew her job and did it efficiently. She'd
always thought that one day she might move up and be a
branch manager. Maybe it wasn't what she'd set out to do,
but she'd accepted it.

Just as she'd accepted that she and Davy Colt would never be together.

Shoving away the thought, she stepped in to walk behind her desk, but she didn't sit down. Instead, she stared at the open doorway, remembering Judson Bruckner standing there the first time he'd come to the bank for money. He'd looked so nervous, so unsure of himself, so scared.

And then him later in the Santa costume.

Her boss suddenly filled the doorway, startling her for a moment.

Appearing uncomfortable, he stepped in and closed the door behind him. "I know I've already tried to talk you out of this, but I have to try one last time," he said. "We have trauma experts you can talk to about your fears."

Carla chuckled. "I'm not afraid of working in the bank or of another robbery." She shook her head. "It's personal, like I told you. All the robbery did was make me realize what I really want out of life."

"If you're sure I can't talk you out of this," he said.

"No, I've made up my mind. It's definitely out of my comfort zone and it will be the first time that I don't have a plan or know what the future holds. But I'm not scared anymore and that's a really good feeling." She smiled. "I've never felt so free."

"Well, if you change your mind or need a job in the future…" He turned to walk toward the door.

"Thank you. I appreciate that." But she didn't see herself coming back here. She'd put away money for years. With the sale of her house, she would have plenty to live on for a long while, since she'd never lived extravagantly and she didn't really see that changing.

As her boss opened the door to leave, she dragged her gaze to the box she'd brought to clean out her desk. Before Christmas, she couldn't wait to get back here to this job, to the routine, to the comfortable life she'd managed to make for herself here in Lonesome. A safe, secure life. She realized the past few days that keeping Davy in her heart had also been part of her protection from moving on with her life. He'd been safe there, just under the branding iron tattoo. And she'd been happy enough with that.

Then Judson Bruckner had walked into the bank, and everything had changed. He brought Davy—the real live cowboy—back into her life. How had she thought that after everything she could just walk back into her old life that easily? She'd almost been killed—not once, but numerous times—since she'd left this office. But oddly, that wasn't what had jolted her into making a decision about that life.

She'd lived in fear, she'd realized, long before the bank robbery. She'd feared disappointing her mother, feared becoming like her, feared veering off the path she'd set for herself. She'd feared what it would mean loving the rodeo cowboy part of Davy, who would always get on the back of a rank horse and try to ride it.

Her biggest fear had been taking a risk and following her heart.

Carla opened a drawer and began to take out her personal items and put them into the box.

"I'll leave you to it then," her boss said, having stopped in the open doorway. "I wish you all the luck in the world."

Luck? She smiled and thanked him. She was lucky to be alive, but it would take more than luck to get what she wanted. It would take true love, the kind that compromised, that changed dreams, that didn't always give you what you thought you wanted. But gave a woman what she needed soul deep. While that scared her, nothing could hold her back. Not anymore.

DAVY COULDN'T COUNT how many times he'd almost turned around and gone back to Lonesome. He hated the way he'd left. He regretted the things he'd said to Carla. He felt as if he'd burned their last bridge. There was no going back because they'd reached an impasse—*just like ten years ago*, he told himself as he drove toward Arlington, Texas.

So he'd kept going, even though his heart wasn't in it— even when he'd drawn a horse he'd been wanting to ride for a long time. He told himself that Carla loved the idea of him—but not the man he was. She needed a man who wore a suit to work, who got off every night at five and mowed the lawn on the weekends.

But even as he thought it, his heart broke even worse to think of her with another man. He asked himself if this really had anything to do with the rodeo. Was he being unreasonable? What was another two years on the circuit? What if he didn't want to quit even after that?

He stopped in Cheyenne, Wyoming, for gas. The sun was starting to set. He found himself looking back up the highway toward Montana. Regret seemed to weigh him down even more. He was weary from the miles pulling his horse trailer across the country. Why had he fought so hard to do this? He'd always planned that one day he'd quit rodeo and raise rough stock. He had the land and had saved enough money to make it happen.

But it had always been down the road. He'd wanted a few more years riding bucking horses that were determined to toss him into the dirt more often than not. Man against beast. It was something that, whether Carla liked it or not, was in his genes, he told himself.

So why wasn't he excited like he usually was when he hit the road? He needed these Texas-sanctioned rodeos. He had to earn enough wins to count toward circuit standings. He had wanted desperately to draw a horse named

Pearl that weighed close to fifteen hundred pounds and was said to send cowboys to the Pearly Gates. Pearl had never been successfully ridden. He'd told himself he had to try to change that if he got the chance.

Gas tank full, he climbed behind the wheel, determined to make it to Dodge City, Kansas, before he pulled over and climbed into his horse-trailer camper to sleep.

CARLA WAS PACKING her car for the trip to Arlington, Texas, before the next snowstorm hit. A light dusting of flakes drifted down. She planned to be there when Davy rode and was hurrying to finish when she heard a vehicle pull into her drive. Turning, she blinked.

Through the falling snow, she couldn't see the driver behind the wheel. She didn't have to. She knew this shiny new truck intimately. Carla felt goose bumps race over her. Davy? Her mind whirled. What was he doing back here? Had something happened?

The pickup door swung open, and he stepped out. He adjusted his Stetson and seemed to hesitate, but only for a moment as he started toward her.

Carla realized that she hadn't moved, that she'd barely taken a breath.

"Going somewhere?" he asked. Snow was beginning to collect on his Stetson.

She glanced back at her SUV, now loaded with only what she'd thought she'd need on the road. When she turned back, he was almost to her.

"Thought I'd see what life was like on the open road," she said, surprised that her voice sounded almost normal around the lump in her throat. What was he doing here? "I was going to start in Arlington. Don't you have a ride there?"

He took a step closer. The love she saw in his blue eyes

was her undoing. She felt tears rush to her eyes even as snowflakes caught on her lashes. All she got out was his name before she was in his arms. He kissed her like there was no tomorrow.

When he finally drew back, he asked, "You really quit your job?"

"It was just a job." He grinned at that. "Davy—"

He touched a finger to her lips. "There's something I need to say to you first. I got down the road. Almost made it to Dodge City when I realized my heart was no longer in rodeo. I'd left it in Montana with you. Carla, I love you, have for years, always thinking that one day I'd come back and we'd be together."

"But I was coming to you."

He laughed. "I see that." His smile broadened even as he shook his head. "Coming so close to almost losing you made me realize what I really want. What I've always wanted. I said you were afraid to live life? Well, I was the one who was hanging on to what had become familiar as well. So I turned around and I came home. I want a life with you."

"But you can have that and rodeo too," she said, motioning toward her packed car as snow began to fall harder. "I've already talked to a Realtor about selling the house—"

Davy shook his head. "You can't sell it. We're going to need somewhere to live until our house is built on the ranch. I'm not going back, Carla. This is where I belong. It's what I've always wanted." His gaze met hers. "You. This isn't how probably either of us pictured this…" He dropped down into the snow on one knee. "Will you marry me?"

"Davy." She was laughing as she dropped down next to him. "Are you sure?"

"I've never been more sure of anything in my life," he

said and kissed her. As far as winter kisses went, this was the best one yet.

"Was that a yes?" Davy asked, pulling back from the kiss.

"No, this is a yes," she said, and cupping his handsome face, she drew him to her for another kiss.

That's where his brothers found the two of them after James got a call from someone who'd just seen Davy drive past pulling his horse trailer. It didn't take them long to figure out where Davy was headed—if true.

"What are you two kids doing?" James demanded as he and his brothers climbed out of their rig and walked toward where the two were kneeling in the snow. Snowflakes whirled around them all as Davy and Carla got to their feet, laughing.

"We're getting married," Davy announced and put a protective arm around her. "Anyone have a problem with that?"

"About damned time," James said. The Colt brothers all laughed.

"No problem at all," Willie said.

"I think this calls for blackberry brandy down at Dad's office," Tommy said. It had become a celebration ritual, and now Carla was part of it—and part of this big, rowdy family. She couldn't believe this was happening, especially since she'd always planned her life down to the minute.

She looked over at Davy. For so long she'd pictured their perfect life together. She laughed now, realizing she had no idea what was ahead for the two of them. More surprising, she'd never felt more free or more excited. All she knew was that with Davy—and this family of his—it would be a wild ride.

* * * * *

CANYON
KIDNAPPING

CINDI MYERS

Chapter One

Climbing walls of rock or ice was all about conquering
obstacles, Sheri Stevens thought as she watched competitors in the Eagle Mountain Ice Festival tackle the
challenging routes up the walls of Caspar Canyon. The
realization that she could face tough things that frightened her and emerge victorious had drawn her to the
sport four years ago, and in that time she had grown
stronger and more confident than she had ever imagined would be possible. She had learned how to carry
the pain of the past without letting it defeat her.

She didn't say these things to the people who stopped
by the Picksie Chix booth at the ice festival. They would
discover that aspect of the sport soon enough—or not.
"Climbing is terrific exercise and a lot of fun," she
told the two teenage girls who approached the booth.
They wore matching fake-fur-trimmed parkas and Ugg
boots against the February chill. "Once you've finished
a challenging climb, you'll know you can conquer anything."

"We saw you up there earlier," the taller of the two
girls, a high school junior named Monica, said.

"You were amazing," her friend, Lexie, said. "Didn't
you win a medal or something?"

"I'm in the running for a medal in the time trials," Sheri said. She had won her class in the annual ice climbing competition last year and hoped to repeat her victory this year. "There is another competitive climb tomorrow and exhibition climbs on Sunday."

"Good luck." Monica picked up one of the Picksie Chix brochures.

"I'm teaching a free women's climbing clinic Sunday at one," Sheri said. "You should both come."

"Maybe we will," Lexie said. "Though I don't know if my mom could handle it. She won't even come watch the other climbers, it freaks her out so much."

"Invite your mom to come with you to my clinic," Sheri said. "She can see all the safety precautions we take, and she can even try climbing herself."

Lexie wrinkled her nose. "Isn't she a little old to take up a sport like climbing?"

"I was thirty before I ever tried it," Sheri said. "And there are people in their sixties and seventies who are still climbing."

The girls looked as if they didn't believe her, but were polite enough not to say so. "Maybe we'll see you tomorrow," Monica said, and the two wandered off.

Kim Lazaro arrived to take over manning the booth. "I saw your climb earlier," she said. "You looked great up there."

"Thanks," Sheri said. "I haven't had as much time to practice as I'd like, but I was pleased with how things went this morning."

"All that climbing you do for Search and Rescue has to help," Kim said. "From what I read in the paper, you folks have been busy this winter."

"It hasn't slowed down all year," Sheri said.

"Honestly, woman, I couldn't keep up with your schedule," Kim said. "When do you sleep?"

Sheri laughed. "I guess I'm just someone who likes to keep busy." She checked her watch. "And in a few minutes I'm due over at the Search and Rescue booth." In addition to answering questions about search and rescue, the booth volunteers handed out applications to potential volunteers and sold T-shirts to raise money for the group, which always operated on a shoestring.

She said goodbye to Kim and headed across the open area at the entrance to the canyon, where various local organizations and businesses had set up booths. She passed the booth for the local barbecue place, a big iron smoker on a trailer filling the canyon with the scent of cooking ribs and brisket. Hundreds of people filled the area, mingling among the booths or gathering closer to the base of the cliffs to watch the climbers make their way up and down the canyon walls, over flows of ice tinted pink and green and blue and orange by minerals in the water.

Sheri paused as a familiar figure—fellow SAR volunteer Eldon Ramsey—started up a route dubbed Free Style. Though relatively new to the sport, he was a good climber, and making a terrific start.

"Mommy!"

The child's shout stopped Sheri's breath and she looked around, heart pounding. A little girl raced toward her, dark hair flying out behind her. *It isn't Claire*, Sheri reminded herself, and tried to bring her breathing back under control. But this little girl was about the age Claire would be now, and seeing her sent a sharp ache through Sheri.

The little girl stopped short just a few feet from Sheri

and looked up at her in obvious confusion. "I was looking for my mom," she said. She was about eight years
old, with straight dark hair that hung past her shoulders,
and big brown eyes fringed with black lashes.

"What's your mom's name?" Sheri asked. She looked
around, hoping to spot a woman who was obviously
searching for a lost child. "I'll help you find her."

"It's okay." A man hurried up and took the little girl's
hand. He was about forty, with thinning brown hair and
a narrow face. He wore dark aviator glasses and a blue
windbreaker over tan chinos and scuffed hiking boots.

"I want my mom!" the little girl insisted, and tried
to pull out of the man's grasp.

"Dawn, you need to calm down," the man said. "I
told you I'd take you to your mother, but you have to be-
have." He glanced up at Sheri. "Sorry about that." Then
he scooped the child into his arms and walked away.

The little girl watched Sheri over the man's shoulders, her eyes brimming with tears. Sheri's own eyes
burned, but she blinked rapidly to clear them. This kind
of thing had happened before, but it always shook her.
When she was fifty, she would probably still be seeing young women and automatically calculating if they
were the same age her daughter, Claire, would have
been if she had lived. She would never stop wondering
what Claire would have been like at eight or eighteen
or twenty-eight or forty-eight. There would come a day
when no one else on earth would remember her daughter, but Sheri would never forget.

She watched the man and the girl until they disappeared in the crowd, then gathered herself and continued toward the Eagle Mountain Search and Rescue
booth. She was waylaid twice, once by a fellow teacher

at Eagle Mountain High School, and once by two of her students, who wanted to talk about her climb this morning. By the time she broke free she was already late for her shift at the booth, but consoled herself that the volunteer schedules were staggered, so even if the person ahead of her on the roster had to leave, someone would be there.

"I'm sorry I'm late," she said, as soon as she approached the booth, which was manned by SAR Lieutenant Carrie Andrews and trainee Austen Morrissey. "I kept getting stopped by people who wanted to talk."

"No problem," Carrie said. "We've sold six T-shirts this morning."

"It's going to take a lot more to pay for the new vehicle the captain wants," Austen said.

"It all adds up. Plus, every one we sell is one less I have to pack up and take back to headquarters when the festival is over." Carrie looked past Sheri and smiled. "Good morning, Sheriff," she said. "Sergeant Walker."

Sheri turned to see Sheriff Travis Walker and his brother, Gage, closing in on the booth. Both men were in uniform, apparently patrolling the festival. But neither returned Carrie's smile. "How many volunteers do you have here today?" Travis asked.

Carrie looked around. "There's me and Sheri and Austen. Eldon is climbing right now and Tony is spotting for him. I think I saw Danny and Ted around somewhere. Why?"

"We've had a report of a missing little girl," Travis said. "I left the parents with Deputy Douglas and thought we could organize a search."

"Of course," Carrie said. "We can shut the booth

down and I can radio whoever is here." She picked up a radio from the corner of the booth.

"Tell them the little girl is eight years old, fifty-five pounds, about fifty inches tall, with long brown hair and brown eyes," the sheriff said. "Her name is Dawn Sheffield."

The name jolted Sheri. "I think I just saw her," she said.

"Where?" Gage asked. "When?"

Sheri checked her watch. "About half an hour ago. Halfway between this booth and the one for Picksie Chix. I stopped to watch Eldon begin his climb and this little girl came running up to me. She thought I was her mom, but realized her mistake as she got closer. A man came up and promised to take her to her mother. He called her Dawn." Her stomach twisted. "I thought he was her father. He certainly acted as if he knew her, and she didn't seem afraid of him." Not afraid, just unhappy. Sheri had thought she was a typical tired kid, having a bit of a temper tantrum. Why hadn't she seen there was more to the girl's mood than that?

"What did this man look like?" Travis asked.

Sheri considered, wanting to give a clear, accurate description. "He was about forty, maybe five-ten or five-eleven, medium build, thinning brown hair. He was wearing dark glasses—aviator style—a blue windbreaker, tan chinos and hiking boots."

"Dawn's father is blond, and six-three," Gage said.

"I've already sent deputies to man the festival entrance and exits," Travis said. "But if you saw him half an hour ago, there's a good chance he's already left. In the meantime, get some of your people circulating among the crowds, looking for Dawn or the man she was with." He looked at Sheri. "I'd like you to come with me and talk to the parents. I want to find out if they know anyone who fits the description of the man you saw. Particularly anyone who might want to harm their daughter."

Sheri nodded, her mouth dry. She didn't want anything to happen to that little girl.

She especially didn't want to be the person who could have saved her, and didn't.

DETECTIVE ERIK LESTER, Colorado Bureau of Investigation, had lost all patience with Carl Westover. He had dealt with tougher crooks than Westover. He had apprehended men who were smarter than Carl, and those who were more devious. Carl wasn't tough or smart or devious—he was just annoying. He was the type of person who thought he deserved a lot more than he had ever earned. Carl thought life wasn't fair and wasted most of his time trying to shift the odds in his favor. He did this by manipulating and taking advantage of other people. He had embezzled several hundred thousand dollars from the corporation he worked for, blown the money on fancy cars and vacations, then whined to anyone who would listen about how unfairly he had been treated when he was arrested for his crimes.

Now Carl had skipped town instead of showing up for his court date and Erik had to go after him. As far as Erik was concerned, Carl was wasting his time. The man hadn't even made his pursuit very challenging. He used his credit card to purchase gas and had made a beeline for the one place he was probably sure he would find refuge—his sister's second home in Eagle Mountain, Colorado. Erik fully expected to find Carl taking it easy on his sister's sofa.

Erik didn't want to be in Eagle Mountain dealing with Carl's whiny self. But he had a job to do and he was determined to do it well. So he had made the drive from Denver over several snowy mountain passes. He would have enjoyed the winter scenery if he had been headed out on vacation, but right now the trip was one more thing to add to the list of the ways Carl had annoyed him. Midmorning on a Friday in late February found him ringing the doorbell at Melissa and Brandon Sheffield's mountain getaway, a six-thousand-square-foot chalet with breathtaking views.

No one answered the bell, so Erik knocked. Then he knocked harder. No sound of movement within the house. He moved over to a large picture window and peered inside. The massive great room appeared to be empty. A child's doll lay on the leather sofa, next to a blanket, and a coffee mug sat on the top of the wooden trunk in front of the sofa, but no fire burned in the fireplace and everything gave the appearance of being unoccupied.

Frowning, Erik turned away from the door and headed back to his car. He'd look up the number for the Sheffields and give them a call. "Are you looking for Mel and Brand?" A slim woman dressed in leggings and a puffy jacket, a yoga mat tucked under one arm, paused next to the SUV in her driveway next door. "I think they went to the ice festival. I saw them leave a little while ago."

"Do you know if Melissa's brother is visiting?" Erik asked. "I was hoping to talk to him."

The woman shook her head, blond ponytail swaying.

"I don't think so. It was just the two of them and their little girl when they left this morning."

"Thanks." Erik got into his car and pulled away before the woman could ask who he was and what he wanted with Melissa's brother. Not that he couldn't lie with the best of them but it was easier to avoid awkward questions in the first place.

He was wondering how he'd find out where the ice festival was when he spotted a large banner hanging over the street as he entered Eagle Mountain. "Welcome to the thirtieth annual Ice Festival," it proclaimed. "Caspar Canyon, February 25–27." His Toyota's GPS obligingly provided directions to Caspar Canyon.

He saw the crowd for the festival long before he saw the canyon itself. The road was lined with cars, and adjacent fields had been turned into parking lots. The turnoff to the canyon was closed, and a uniformed officer directed him to turn around and park in a lot. Erik thought of flashing his badge and announcing that he was looking for a fugitive, but that was a good way to panic people needlessly. The last thing he wanted was for Carl to have any warning that Erik was here. With luck, the two of them would have a quiet conversation and Erik would lead Carl back to his vehicle and they'd be on their way. He had handcuffs if he needed to use them, but it would be easier on everyone if he didn't have to. Carl had no history of violence. He was a dishonest man, but he had never physically hurt anyone, so Erik didn't expect trouble.

Metal gates blocked off the entrance to the canyon and people were lined up waiting to enter. Beyond the entrance, he could see vendors' booths and a glimpse of high rock walls coated in ice, ropes dangling from

the ice, and people dangling from the ropes. He estimated the crowd in his view at a couple of hundred
people, with more farther into the canyon. He hoped
he wouldn't have too much trouble tracking down the
Sheffields, and after that, locating Carl.

The line he was in wasn't moving. "What's going
on?" a man behind him asked.

"They're not letting people in," a woman beside him
answered. "The cops have closed it down."

Erik made his way to the front of the line, ignoring
disgruntled remarks from a few people he passed. He
approached a man in a sheriff's department uniform
and held up his badge. "What's going on, Deputy?"
he asked.

"A little girl has gone missing," the man, whose name
badge identified him as Deputy Doyle, said. "We're not
letting anyone in or out while we search for her and the
man who may have taken her."

"How old a child?" Erik asked. "What does she look
like?"

"She's eight. Long dark hair and brown eyes. Her
name is Dawn Sheffield."

Erik felt cold all over. He didn't believe it was a coincidence that the Sheffields' daughter had gone missing at the same time Melissa Sheffield's brother was
fleeing criminal charges and known to be headed this
way. In his experience, crimes like this were always
connected. "I might have information that could help,"
Erik said. "Could someone take me to the Sheffields?"

He had thought Carl was too dumb to be a real danger to anyone, but maybe Erik was the one who wasn't
so smart. He, of all people, ought to know that danger

could lurk in the most unexpected places, and not realizing that could lead to the worst of all consequences.

SHERIFF WALKER AND Gage escorted Sheri to the first aid tent, where a couple sat with Deputy Jamie Douglas. The woman, her dark hair cut in an asymmetrical style that set off her elfin features, stood when they entered the tent. "Have you found her?" she asked.

Travis shook his head. "This is Sheri Stevens," he said. "She saw a girl we think may be Dawn. Sheri, this is Brandon and Melissa Sheffield."

"Where was this?" Brandon Sheffield, a tall, broad-shouldered blond who looked as if he'd be more at home in a logging camp than a boardroom, turned eagerly to Sheri. "Was she all right? Was she afraid?"

"The child I saw was asking for her mother, but otherwise she seemed fine." Sheri chose her words carefully. She wanted to tell the truth, but she didn't want to upset this mother and father any more than she could help. "She was a very pretty little girl, with long dark hair, parted in the middle, and big brown eyes. She was with a man with thinning brown hair. He called her Dawn and she seemed to know him, though I never heard her address him by name."

"That sounds like Dawn," Brandon said. "And Carl." He turned to his wife. "Don't you think that sounds like Carl?"

"Who is Carl?" Gage asked.

"My wife's brother," Brandon said. "Dawn wouldn't be afraid of him. To her, he's just her uncle."

"Why would your brother take Dawn without your knowing about it?" Travis asked Melissa.

"He wouldn't." She looked up at her husband.

"Brand, I'm sure you're wrong. Carl wouldn't do something like that."

Brandon ignored her protest and turned to the officers. "Carl is in trouble for embezzling money from his former employer," he said. "He asked me for one hundred thousand dollars to pay his legal fees and when I refused, he got angry. Maybe he took Dawn to get back at me."

"No. My brother wouldn't do something like that," Melissa said. "And the whole business with the money— it was just a misunderstanding. I don't know why you wouldn't give him the money he needed. He would have paid me back."

"Right. Like he paid back the money I lent him to buy his last house, or the loan you gave him before we were married."

Watching these two argue made Sheri's stomach hurt. They were both afraid and hurting, but instead of coming together to present a united front, they were already pulling away. She wanted to tell them to stop it—they didn't realize the damage they were doing. She knew too well how easy it was to blame the person you were closest to for all the pain you were feeling—and how the damage hurtful words inflicted could never be undone.

But she was a stranger to these people. The last thing they wanted was advice from her, especially when the counsel came in the form of "don't make the same mistake I did."

"Do you have a picture of your brother?" Travis asked.

"Not with me," Melissa said.

"I think I do." Brandon took out his phone. "I took

a lot of pictures when we were all together at Melissa's parents' place last Christmas." He swiped through several photos, then angled the phone toward them. "Carl is the one in the middle, next to Melissa."

Sheri stared at the man in the photo. He was smiling, and looked a little younger, but it was the same man. "That's the man I saw with the little girl," she said.

Brandon turned the phone toward himself and scrolled once more. "Is this the little girl you saw?" he asked, and showed her a photograph of a smiling child, her long dark hair whipped by a breeze, dressed in shorts and a T-shirt, on the deck of a boat.

Sheri nodded. "Yes, that's her."

Melissa Sheffield began to cry, and sank into a chair. Brandon hesitated, then put his arm around his wife. "It's going to be okay," he said. "Now that we know who has Melissa, we can find him. He can't have gone far in such a short time."

"I'm sure Carl would never hurt Dawn," Melissa said. "He loves her."

"I don't think Carl is violent," Brandon said. "He's greedy and manipulative, but he's not violent. And he does love Dawn."

Melissa pulled away from her husband. "Carl is not greedy and manipulative," she said. "He hasn't had the same advantages you've had and people always underestimate him."

"Do you have any idea where your brother might have taken Dawn?" Travis asked. "A friend's house? Someplace else he's frequented?"

"We're the only people he knows here," Melissa said.

The sheriff turned to Sheri. "What, exactly, did he say when you saw him?" he asked.

She relayed as much as she could remember of the brief exchange. "He told the little girl he was going to take her to her mother. But he didn't say where or when."

"What kind of vehicle does your brother drive?" Gage asked.

"The last time I saw him, he had a Lexus, I think?" Melissa looked to her husband for confirmation.

"He drives a Lexus LS. Black," Brandon said. "Or he did last month. He leases vehicles and switches them out pretty often."

"When was the last time you spoke to your brother, Mrs. Sheffield?" Travis asked.

"A few days ago. We talk and text regularly. He was getting ready for his trial and he seemed in good spirits."

"He was out on bail and was upset I wouldn't give him the money he wanted," Brandon said. "Apparently, he'd already blown the money he stole on fancy vacations and new suits and no telling what else."

"He didn't steal any money!" Melissa protested.

"Did he make any threats to you or your wife, when you refused to give him the money?" Travis asked.

"No!" Melissa jumped up again. "You're making him sound like some hardened criminal and he isn't. If Dawn is with Carl, I'm sure he'll bring her back to us soon."

"He whined about me not having any faith in him, but he didn't make threats," Brandon said. He looked at his wife. "I hope you're right. All I want is for Dawn to be safe."

"I don't believe he did this," Melissa said. She turned to Sheri. "You may have seen Dawn with Carl, but that doesn't mean Carl took her anywhere. Maybe he really was taking her to me, but before he could find me, someone else intercepted them. Or maybe Dawn ran away, Carl lost track of her in the crowd and someone else took her."

"Then why didn't he come to us and tell us what happened?" Brandon asked.

"Because he knew you'd accuse him of doing something awful. You've never liked him and he knows it."

"Did your brother mention he was coming to see you?" Gage asked.

Melissa shook her head, and hugged her arms over her chest. "Carl is family. He doesn't have to wait for an invitation to come see me. He's always welcome. He probably wanted to surprise me."

"Have you tried calling him?" Travis asked.

Brandon took out his phone again. "There's no signal down here in this canyon."

"When you get to someplace with a signal, I want you to call him," Travis said. "If you reach him, please ask him to stop by the sheriff's department and give a statement."

"Of course," Melissa said. "I'm sure he'll want to do everything he can to help." She shook her head. "But I can't believe the man you saw really was Carl. Lots of men have brown hair."

"Carl Westover is here, all right."

They all turned to look at the man who spoke—a tall, dark-haired man with olive skin and a strong jaw. Sheri stared at him, dizzy and disoriented.

He stared back, eyes burning into hers. "Sheri!" He didn't try to hide his shock at seeing her. "What are you doing here?"

"I live here." The words came out with more force than she intended. She worked to rein in her agitation. "What are you doing here, Erik?"

Erik looked at the others, and fixed on the sheriff. He held out his hand. "Detective Erik Lester, Colorado Bureau of Investigation," he introduced himself.

"Sheriff Travis Walker." The sheriff shook Erik's hand, then examined the credentials he offered.

"I'm here because I've been tracking Carl Westover ever since he jumped bail and failed to appear for his trial yesterday," Erik said. "His credit card receipts showed he was headed to Eagle Mountain, I presumed to visit his sister." He looked to Melissa. "Carl didn't tell you he was coming?"

"No. I already told these people that."

"I stopped by the Sheffields' house before I came here," Erik said. "I didn't see any sign of Carl and the neighbor I talked to hadn't seen him."

"He was seen approximately forty-five minutes ago with his niece," Travis said.

"Who saw him?" Erik said. "I'd like to talk to them."

"I saw him," Sheri said. She really couldn't believe this was happening. Erik was the last person she wanted to talk to.

"Do you two know each other?" Gage asked.

Sheri stood up straighter, her eyes fixed on Erik. "You could say that," she said. "Erik is my ex-husband."

Chapter Two

Seeing Sheri again had shaken Erik more than he wanted to admit. Of all the people he would have gone out of his way to avoid running into, her name was at the top of the list. Not because he didn't want to face her—he wouldn't have minded keeping in touch after their divorce, but she had insisted on a clean break. Just another way she had rejected him.

He pulled back from the silent criticism. He had done his share of ugly things in the last couple of years of their marriage. There was plenty of blame to go around on all sides. At the time she had made her statement about wanting a clean break, he had put it down to her attempt to cope with Claire's death by making a fresh start. He had even agreed that might be a good idea.

Seeing her now, he was struck by how much she looked the same—and how different she was. She was thinner, but not skinny. There was a lot of muscle definition in the arms showing in her tight Lycra shirt and the thighs beneath purple athletic leggings. She looked fit and healthy. She had cut her hair short, and though he had always loved her long blond hair, the new style suited her. He could still read the pain in her eyes when she met his gaze, but maybe that was only because he knew her so well. Or at least he had, once upon a time.

"What did Carl look like when you saw him?" he asked. Keeping their focus on the business at hand was the best way to get through the awkwardness, he thought. "What was he wearing?"

Nothing stood out about the outfit she described. "You're wasting your time looking for Carl." Melissa Sheffield stood. "He wouldn't hurt Dawn—I know he wouldn't. Meanwhile, whoever did take her is getting farther and farther away."

"Do you know of anyone else who might take your daughter?" Travis asked. "Someone with a grudge against you? A business rival? A disgruntled employee? Has anyone made threats against you?"

"No." Brandon Sheffield shook his head. Erik had met him only once before, but Sheffield had struck him as smart—and someone who saw his brother-in-law for the con man he was, despite his wife's rosy view of her younger brother. "No one has made threats—not against me, or my daughter."

"We have dozens of people from the sheriff's department and with the local search and rescue organization looking for your daughter," Travis said. "We've issued an Amber Alert for a missing child, which goes out to other law enforcement agencies and transportation companies. Now that we have a good description of Dawn and of your brother we'll share that information as well. There's a good chance someone will see them."

Erik was sure Melissa was going to protest again that her brother hadn't taken Dawn, but at a look from her husband she merely pressed her lips together and nodded.

A big blond sheriff's deputy joined them. "We've

searched the entire canyon and no one reports seeing the little girl—either by herself or with someone else," he said. "No one has entered or left since we shut down the entrance, but people are starting to complain."

Travis nodded. "Open things back up, but keep a couple of deputies on the entrance, just in case whoever has the girl managed to evade the searchers and tries to slip out."

"There's a photographer from the paper here and he's agreed to share all the crowd photos he took, and there's a guy here with a drone who's been filming a competition," the deputy said. "He's agreed to turn over copies of all his footage. Oh, and Tony Meisner, the SAR captain, wants to talk to you. He thinks he saw the girl over by the restroom, a little before she was reported missing."

"Where is Tony now?" Gage asked.

"He's at the SAR tent." The deputy pointed in the direction of the exhibitors. "He said he would wait for you there."

Travis nodded. "Good thinking on the photos and video," he said. He turned to Sheri. "We'll need you to come by the station and give us a formal statement."

"Of course," she said. "Anything I can do to help."

"Mr. and Mrs. Sheffield, you can return to your home," Travis said to the couple. "We'll let you know if we hear anything about your daughter. We'll send a deputy with you, to check for any sign of your brother."

Again, Erik thought Melissa would object, but her husband cut her off. "Of course. Whatever you need to do."

"Someone at the station will take your statement when you're ready," Gage told Sheri. He looked at Erik.

"It would be helpful if you'd share what you know about Carl Westover."

"Of course."

The officers and the Sheffields left. Sheri turned away also, but Erik followed. "Which way did Carl and the girl head when they left you?" he asked.

"I don't know," she said. "I wasn't paying attention."

"I don't believe that. You always pay attention. Especially when a child is involved."

Because the one time she hadn't, a tragedy had happened. Sheri had never been able to forgive herself for that brief lapse, no matter how many times Erik and others told her Claire's death wasn't her fault. Accidents happened all the time, for no reason.

The glare she directed at him definitely wasn't friendly or forgiving. Fine. She hated his guts. He still had a job to do. "Which direction?" he prodded.

She halted and closed her eyes. "They headed toward the entrance," she said. "He was carrying the little girl—Dawn. She wasn't fighting him, but she didn't look happy. I thought she was just a tired child having a little tantrum. I thought he was taking her to her mother."

She was blaming herself for something she had no control over, the same way she had done after Claire's death. She probably wouldn't listen to him now, any more than she had then, but he had to try to steer her thoughts in another direction. "Anyone would have thought that," Erik said. "If I didn't know Carl, I would have thought that."

"What kind of man is he?" she asked. "Would he hurt her? Her mother says not, but maybe that's just because she can't bear to think the worst of her brother."

"He's never been violent before," Erik said. "He was accused of embezzling a lot of money. It's not a victimless crime, but it is nonviolent. There's nothing in his past that would indicate to me he would hurt a child, especially a family member. From what you described, Dawn wasn't afraid of him."

"She wasn't," Sheri said. She put her fist to her mouth and shook her head. "But what if we're wrong?" Tears gleamed in her eyes. Erik fought the urge to put his arm around her and pull her close. He had a feeling she wouldn't welcome the gesture.

"Don't focus on the worst possible outcome," he said. "Carl is a self-centered jerk, but so far all he's done is spirit his niece away from her parents. He could be waiting back at the house for them right now."

She nodded and took a deep breath. "This is just hard for me. Dawn is the same age Claire would be now."

"I realize that," he said. "Did you think I didn't?"

"I don't know what you think or feel," she said. "You never would tell me."

Just like that, they'd gone back in time four years, sniping at each other in a game of "he said, she said" no one could ever win. "Where are you going now?" he asked.

"To the sheriff's department, to give my statement. Not that it's any concern of yours."

"Of course not." Except that he was concerned. A piece of paper said they were no longer married, and they hadn't set eyes on each other in two years, but part of him still thought of her as his wife. He would never admit it to anyone, and he knew they'd never get back together. But even though he didn't like to talk about his feelings, he could acknowledge he had them. And right now, standing close enough to her to touch, in-haling the soft scent of her and feeling her pain like fingernails tearing at his insides, he knew that divorce hadn't excised that part of his heart. "Go on, then," he said. "But I'll need to talk to you later."

She waved her hand in a gesture that could have meant "fine" or "goodbye" or "good riddance" as she moved away from him. *It was good to see you*, he wanted to say, though he doubted she would agree.

AFTER ERIK LEFT SHERI, he went in search of the Search and Rescue booth. He found Sheriff Walker and his ser-geant there with a tall, thin man with streaks of silver in his thick, dark hair. They looked up at his approach. "This is Detective Lester, with the Colorado Bureau of Investigation," Walker said by way of introduction. "And this is Tony Meisner, captain of Eagle Mountain Search and Rescue. He saw Dawn Sheffield with a man shortly before Sheri ran into them."

"Do you mind repeating what you told the sheriff?" Erik asked.

"There's not a lot to tell," Meisner said. "I was on my way to the men's room when I saw a little girl play-ing on the picnic tables right next to the portable toi-lets. She was climbing up and down the tables, the way kids do. I only noticed her because my nephew broke his arm doing just that. I looked around for a parent and spotted a man watching her. I was about to go up to him and suggest what she was doing was dangerous when he called to her. The little girl looked up, smiled at him and ran to him and put her arms around him. She certainly wasn't upset or afraid. I figured he was her dad." He looked to the deputies. "She definitely knew who this guy was."

"What did the man look like?" Erik asked.

Meisner described Carl Westover to a T, including the Western Casing logo on the left side of the windbreaker he wore—a detail Sheri had missed. "Western Casing was the company Carl Westover worked for," Erik said.

"I know I would have recognized the man and the girl if I had seen them again when we searched the canyon," Tony said. "They must have already left by the time the alarm was raised."

"I'm sure once Carl had the girl, he got out of here as soon as possible," Erik said.

"I can't believe the only two people who remember seeing them are with Search and Rescue," Tony said. "Maybe it's just that we're trained to assess situations."

"Sheri is with Search and Rescue?" Erik asked.

"She's our training officer this year," Tony said. "A terrific volunteer. One of our best climbers."

Erik tried to connect this picture with the woman he had known. Sheri had always been fit, but never what he would call athletic. "You mean rock climbing?" he asked.

"Rocks, ice—she's really good," Tony said. "She's competing this weekend and will probably take a medal. Every volunteer trains for climbing work—it's pretty much required, working in these mountains or canyons—but if I need someone who's fearless and technically very proficient, Sheri is my go-to. And she's a great training officer. Very patient and encouraging."

Fearless. Patient. Encouraging. Not the first words Erik thought of when it came to Sheri. But he supposed four years could change a person. A few seconds could change a person, if those seconds resulted in tragedy.

The sheriff told Meisner he could go, then motioned for Erik to follow him away from the booth. "If you've been following Westover, you know him better than we do," Travis said. "What do you think he's up to?"

"His sister said he asked her husband for money," Erik said. "Brandon Sheffield owns a computer software company that's worth millions. Carl is one of these people who think the world owes him. He did a lousy job of covering his tracks when he embezzled from Western Casing, but he's continued to deny stealing the money, while at the same time whining about how he wasn't paid what he was worth and was owed bonuses he never received, etc., etc. He might have taken the girl intending to force the Sheffields to pay his legal fees."

"Why does he need money for his legal fees if he stole a bunch from his employer?" Sergeant Walker—who must be the sheriff's brother, they looked enough alike—asked.

"He blew all the money he stole on vacations, wine, dinner out—who knows," Erik said. "But he doesn't have anything left."

"So we wait for some kind of ransom note," Gage said.

"We don't wait," Travis said. "We keep looking. But I won't be surprised if the Sheffields hear from him very soon. He may try to make it look like someone else took the girl, but the more I hear, the more I think it's him."

"I think so, too," Erik said.

"When were you and Sheri married?" Gage asked.

His marriage wasn't something Erik ever talked about, but after Sheri's dramatic announcement, the questions were bound to come. "We split a couple of years ago."

"About the time she moved to Eagle Mountain," Gage said. "I went out with her a couple of times before I got married and she never mentioned an ex. Then again, we didn't date that long."

"Is she dating anyone now?" Erik regretted the question as soon as he asked it. Sheri's personal life was none of his business.

"Not that I know of," Gage said. "And it's hard to keep a secret like that around here. I know a couple of guys who were interested, but she turned a cold shoulder. Then again, she's pretty involved in Search and Rescue and she teaches high school. That probably doesn't leave much time for a social life."

Erik didn't like the way something inside him relaxed when he learned Sheri was unattached. He had never been the possessive type and he had zero claim on Sheri now. He ought to be wishing she had found someone and was happy.

"I'd appreciate it if you'd share your file on Westover," Travis said. "Do you plan on sticking around for a while?"

"I'm here until Westover is arrested," Erik said. "Even if he didn't kidnap his niece, he's a fugitive and my job is to haul him back to Denver for his trial." He pulled out his wallet, removed a business card and passed it to the sheriff. "There's my contact information. Call me anytime. And let me know if there's anything I can do to help."

"Where are you staying?" Travis asked.

"I don't know. I just got to town. I was hoping to pick

up Westover at his sister's house and head straight back to Denver, but no such luck."

"The Ranch Motel on the highway is clean," Travis said. "If you wanted something fancier, there are a few bed-and-breakfasts in town. The Alpiner is good, though with the ice festival, they're probably booked up. The local real estate office keeps a list of private vacation rentals, too."

"I'll try the real estate office. I prefer something private." And he had no idea how long he would be in town.

He said goodbye to the officers and made his way through the crowd toward the mouth of the canyon. He stopped to watch a woman climbing up what looked to him to be a sheet of ice. Sheri did that—and was good at it? How had he been married to her for six years and never known that side of her?

He was going to be in Eagle Mountain a little while longer. Maybe he should take the opportunity to get to know his ex-wife better. Not with a view of getting back together—they were long past that point. But they had spent six years together, and they had shared a child, and they would always share the grief over that child's death. When they parted ways again, it was nice to think they could do so on better terms.

SHERI'S CLIMB ON the second day of competition was up a route called Snakebite, a long, steep climb navigating a tricky column of ice. After yesterday's climb she was second in the standings and had a good chance to take the lead—if she didn't let her unexpected reunion with Erik mess with her head.

She had spent more than an hour at the sheriff's

department late yesterday, going over everything she could remember about those few moments with Dawn and her uncle. Erik hadn't been there, but she kept replaying the shock of seeing him again. He had looked good—even more handsome than she remembered him, lean and edgy. She had been attracted to him from the moment they met, in a gym near the school where she had been doing her student teaching in a suburb of Denver. She had fallen for him so hard—and the falling-out had been just as hard. Having him step back into her life after all this time was such a shock. She hadn't slept well, her mind racing with thoughts of Erik, and Claire, and a life that seemed so distant now.

But strong coffee and a long hot shower had put those memories back into the box where they belonged. Today she was going to put her ex-husband out of her mind and focus on the ice. She double-checked all of her equipment and mentally ran through the climb, picturing herself making each move, each placement of her hands and feet, all the way up the ice.

"Good luck!" Her fellow Picksie Chix member Susie Fellini rushed up to hug her. "You're going to do great!" Susie said.

Then it was time. Sheri started up, all her focus on the ice and the movements she had made so many times they were instinctual—place her foot here, reach her hand up there, clip into a piton, shift her weight, lean and stretch. Sink one ax in, then the next. The cold seeped into her, but the exertion of the climb warmed her. The noise of the crowd below receded as she climbed higher and calm flooded her. This was what climbing gave her, this sense of peace and control.

Then she was at the top, the announcer giving her

time as 13.260. Triumph surged through her and she thrust her arms into the air. For now, at least, she led the standings for women.

Friends and spectators she didn't know gathered to offer their congratulations. "I'm impressed." The deep, resonant voice brought her up short and she turned to find Erik standing just behind her. Had he really come to see her climb? The thought sent an unwelcome flutter through her.

"I only caught part of it, but you looked like you knew what you were doing," he said.

As compliments went, it wasn't up there with "you were amazing" but Erik had never been overly effusive. "I'm happy with the climb," she said. "If you'd like to see more, I'm doing an exhibition climb tomorrow, the last day of the festival. You should come."

"I'd like that," he said. "What time are you climbing?"

"One o'clock." Prime time, when all the various winners would be on display, as it were, for the crowds who gathered within the canyon and along the rim.

"I'll be there," he said.

"Good." Suddenly, she really wanted him to see her—to see what she was capable of. When they had last been together, she had been so broken. She wanted him to know she was past that. She would never fully heal—how could you heal from the loss of a child?—but she was alive, and doing well. No one gave medals for that kind of victory, but having Erik see all she had accomplished would be its own reward.

"I stopped by because you need to come to the sheriff's department and look at some photographs," he said.

So much for thinking his presence here was about

anything but work. "I'm a little busy right now," she said, and began gathering up her gear.

"When you're done, then."

"Why didn't they ask me to do this yesterday when I was giving my statement?" she asked.

"It just came up."

"Why are you telling me this, instead of a deputy?"

"They've asked me to help with the investigation."

She said nothing, but squatted to unbuckle her crampons.

"I hear you're on the Search and Rescue squad," Erik said.

She glared at him. She did not want to make conversation with him. "Does that have anything to do with your case?" she asked.

His expression was unreadable. And to think that once upon a time she had believed she knew him so well. "I'll see you at the sheriff's department later," he said, then turned and left.

"Who was that man you were talking to after your climb?" Susie intercepted Sheri as she trudged toward the parking lot, laden with gear.

"Just somebody I used to know," Sheri said.

"A really good-looking somebody. Is he a climber?"

"No." Erik ran and lifted weights, but those were things he did to keep in shape for his job, not because he enjoyed them the way she enjoyed climbing.

"Too bad."

"What do you mean?"

"Oh, you know—if you try to have a relationship with a nonclimber, they end up complaining about all the time you spend climbing," Susie said. "They just don't get it. You've been there, right?"

"Yeah, that is a problem," Sheri said. Actually, she hadn't dated anyone seriously since she had started climbing, so she had no idea if what Susie said was true or not. She had tried to meet new men, and had even gone on a few outings to dinner or the movies, but nothing had clicked, and at last she had given up trying. She wasn't comfortable letting anyone get that close.

They reached her car and Susie helped Sheri load her gear. "Are you coming to the party tonight?" Susie asked. Saturday night of the festival always featured a big bash at the Elks Lodge.

"I don't know," Sheri said. "I have other stuff I need to do first."

"I sort of agreed to meet this Swedish climber and his friends," Susie said. "They're really cute. I could introduce you."

Sheri forced a smile. "Maybe." She wasn't in a partying mood, but she didn't want to waste time debating with Susie, who would try to change her mind.

"I promise if you show up it will be worth it," Susie said. "These guys are hot—and smart. One of them is a physicist."

Sheri waved goodbye and pulled out of the lot. She wanted to go home, take a long hot shower, then climb into bed and surrender to the dark mood that had haunted her since little Dawn Sheffield had disappeared. Which was the exact last thing she should allow herself to do. Instead, she turned her car toward the sheriff's department. She might as well get her next encounter with Erik over with.

She relaxed a little when Deputy Jamie Douglas came out to greet her in the lobby of the sheriff's department. But her hope that she'd been saved from talking to Erik was dashed when Jamie escorted her to a room where Sheriff Travis Walker and Erik waited.

Both men stood as she entered the room. "Thank you for stopping by," Travis said. "This won't take long."

The three of them sat at a plain metal table in a gray-walled room that was the very definition of drab. Erik sat across from her, a manila folder in front of him. "I'm going to lay out six photographs," he said. "I want to know if any of them is the man you saw with the little girl yesterday."

"I already identified Carl from the photo Mr. Sheffield showed me yesterday," Sheri said.

"We want to be certain of the identification," Travis said. "If you don't see the man who was with Dawn in the photo array, we want to know that, too."

She waited while he laid out the photos in a line in front of her, like a dealer in a casino. She took her time studying the images. All the men were similar, middle-aged with thinning brown hair. When she came to the fourth photograph, she felt a jolt of recognition. This image was different from the photograph Brandon Sheffield had showed her on his phone—the man in this picture was scowling, less well-dressed, but she was sure he was the same man she had seen with the little girl yesterday. Still, she made herself consider the other two images as well.

Then she sat back and pointed to the fourth photo. "That one," she said. "That's the man I saw."

"Are you sure?" Erik asked.

"Yes, I'm sure."

Erik gathered up the photos. "Thank you."

"Is that the uncle?" she asked. "The man they think took Dawn?"

"I'm not at liberty—" began Erik.

"Yes," said Travis. At least he wasn't going to shut her out. Then again, Erik had had plenty of practice excluding her from what he knew or felt.

Jamie reappeared in the doorway. "Mr. and Mrs. Sheffield are here and asking to see you, Sheriff," she said.

Travis started to stand, but Melissa Sheffield pushed past Jamie into the room, followed by her husband. "Carl texted fifteen minutes ago," she said. "He has Dawn. I can't believe he has Dawn."

Chapter Three

Melissa Sheffield's anguish filled the small room, its sharpness a physical sensation to Sheri. Memory of that feeling flooded her. She wanted to look away from such suffering, but could not.

"What did your brother say, exactly?" Erik's voice, firm yet calm, cut through the hysteria that seemed to Sheri to shimmer around Melissa.

Melissa bit her lip, then thrust the phone at him. He took it, glanced at the screen, then read out loud: "'I have Dawn. She's fine, but if you want her to stay that way, transfer one million dollars to this account now. CH86000000111.'" Erik looked up. "That sounds like a Swiss bank account. Does your brother have a Swiss account?"

"I don't know anything about that," she said.

"Are you sure Carl sent that text?" Travis asked.

"It's from his number," Melissa said.

Erik scrolled down the phone screen. "You didn't answer him?"

"No. Brand thought we should come here first." She turned to her husband. "But we have to send him the money."

"That's ridiculous." Brandon frowned at Erik and

Travis. "You can use this text to find him, can't you?" he asked.

"If you had paid him the money he asked for before, this wouldn't have happened," Melissa said.

Brandon winced. "Melissa…" he began.

She turned away. "Carl must be desperate to do this," she said. "I know he wouldn't hurt Dawn, but what if the stress has made him snap? What if he isn't in his right mind? You have to do something."

"Have you had any other communication from Carl?" Erik asked.

"No," she said.

"No," Brandon echoed.

"It's only been twenty-six hours since he was seen at the ice park," Erik said. "No one has reported seeing him and the Amber Alert has been widely distributed. I think that's an indication that he went to ground very quickly. Is there any place near here where he might hide—a vacation home or a friend's place?"

"I can't think of any place," Melissa said.

"Our house is the only place he's ever stayed in the area," Brandon said. He sent a worried look to his wife. "What if we pretend we want to pay the money, but we insist on paying in cash? We could arrange a meeting."

"Yes!" Melissa clutched his arm. "We could insist he bring Dawn and exchange her for the money."

"We could try," Erik said. "Do you think he would fall for it?"

"He wants the money," she said. "He doesn't really want Dawn."

"He might suspect a trap," Travis said.

"At least some of the money should be real," Melissa said. "If he sees that he'll be more likely to cooperate."

"He doesn't deserve a dime," Brandon said.

"We're talking about our daughter!"

"Are you saying I don't care about Dawn?"

"Stop!" Sheri hadn't meant to vent her frustration out loud, but seeing these two tear at each other when so much was at stake was too much to bear. Aware that everyone was staring at her now, she pushed on. "Your daughter needs both of you," she said. "The two of you will be stronger together than you could ever be apart."

Melissa stared, and Sheri was sure she was going to tell her to mind her own business. Sheri wouldn't blame her if she did. Instead, after a moment Melissa turned to her husband. "I'm sorry," she said. "I'm just so upset."

Brandon caressed his wife's shoulders. "I know."

Erik returned the phone to Melissa. "Send a reply," he said. "Tell him you'll give him the money. Tell him… Tell him your husband doesn't want to give it to him, but you'll liquidate some assets and bring him the cash without Brandon knowing about it. That can be your excuse for not wiring the money to a bank. Do you think he'll believe that?"

"Yes. He'll know Brandon won't want to pay him. And Carl knows I have some stocks in my name. Not a million dollars, but he doesn't know that."

"Good," Erik said. "Send him the text."

They fell silent, the tap of her nails on the screen of the phone the only sound. She hit Send and looked up. "What do we do now?" she asked.

"Now, we wait," Erik said.

As PHYSICALLY TOUGH as she might be now, Sheri was still as emotionally transparent as ever, Erik thought as he watched her observe the Sheffields snipe at each other. He knew as well as he had known anything that Sheri was reliving all the arguments the two of them had had in the months and years following Claire's death. They'd been like two warring planets sharing an orbit, unable to keep from colliding over and over. They should have been united by their shared pain, but their methods of coping with that pain had caused them to clash. He had known as well as she had that it was wrong, but neither of them could stop themselves.

When she had called on the Sheffields to come together for the sake of their daughter, Erik wondered if she wished someone had said the same thing to the two of them. Would it have made any difference? Or did how a couple reacted to stress show the true nature of their relationship? He and Sheri had started off great together, but maybe they were never really all that compatible in the first place. When faced with a real trial, their marriage had crumbled. Maybe losing Claire had only hastened the inevitable.

"I'd better go." Sheri pushed back from the table and stood.

"We'll be in touch if we have more questions," Erik said.

She nodded, not looking at him, and hurried from the room.

Melissa Sheffield sat in the chair Sheri had vacated. She held her phone, staring at the screen as if willing it to display a new message. "How are we going to fake a million dollars in cash?" Brandon Sheffield asked.

"We'll figure that out once we arrange the meeting," the sheriff said. "Tell him you'll need time to gather up the cash."

The phone in Melissa's hand buzzed and she almost

dropped it. "It's Carl!" she yelped, and fumbled to un-
lock the screen. She stared at the message in silence,
then tossed the phone on the table. "He says no." She
swiveled to face her husband, who stood, back against
the wall. "He says it has to be a transfer to that bank
account and it has to come from you. You have to pay
him. It's the only way to get Dawn back."

"And what happens after I pay him?" Brandon
straightened. "How do we even know he'll give Dawn
back to us, unharmed?"

"Carl would never hurt Dawn," Melissa said.

"Then why did he kidnap her? Why is he threatening her?"

"Because he's desperate and you gave him no
choice!" She started crying, hiccupping, ugly sobs that
made Erik look away.

Brandon had looked away from his wife, too. He
caught Erik's eye. "I want my daughter back safe," he
said. "And I'd do anything to save her. But Carl has been
leeching off me ever since Melissa and I got married.
No matter what I give him, it's never enough. If I give
him a million today, what's to keep him for asking for
two million next time?"

"I agree you shouldn't pay the ransom," Erik said.
"Especially not without a guarantee that Dawn will be
returned to you unharmed."

Another loud sob broke from Melissa. Brandon
moved closer. "Is there any way to trace his location
from those texts?" he asked the sheriff.

"We'll ask his service provider to try," Travis said.
"But that can be tough to do even in cities with lots
of towers. The rugged terrain around here presents
more challenges."

Melissa wiped at her eyes and picked up her phone again. "What should I tell Carl?" she asked.

"Tell him to call you," Erik said. "Tell him you can't send the money until you're sure that Dawn is all right. Tell him you want to talk to your daughter."

"Yes!" She began typing. "I do want to talk to Dawn. Poor baby. She must be terrified."

"Tell him if he hurts one hair on my little girl's head I will personally rip him apart with my bare hands," Brandon said.

"I will tell him so such thing." She finished typing and hit Send.

"We're contacting every hotel, motel, campground and other lodging within a two-hundred-mile radius," Travis said.

"I checked with my office," Erik said. "He hasn't used his credit cards. Do you know if he had any cash with him?"

Melissa shook her head. "I hadn't talked to him since last week, when he called to ask for money to pay his legal bills."

"If he only wanted a hundred thousand then, why is he asking for a million dollars now?" Erik asked.

"Because Carl never has enough," Brandon said. "And he's angry that I refused to give him the hundred thousand, so he's getting back at me by asking for even more." He stared at Melissa, who sat hunched over her phone, her back to him. "He won't get away with this. Kidnapping is a felony. He'll go to prison for a long time."

Melissa only hunched her shoulders more. Erik didn't bother pointing out that the embezzlement Carl Westover was already accused of was also a felony, but the penalty for kidnapping and extortion would add considerably to his sentence. From what Erik knew of Carl, he had a sharp mind. He would know what he was risking by taking Dawn. Which meant Melissa was right—Carl was desperate. Whether he was desperate enough to hurt a niece he supposedly loved remained to be seen.

Someone knocked on the door and Travis opened it to Deputy Jamie Douglas. She glanced at the Sheffields, then asked to speak to the sheriff alone. Travis stepped out and closed the door.

Brandon sat at the opposite end of the table and buried his head in his hands. He looked totally drained, his skin pasty and sagging, eyes hollowed. Melissa, mascara smeared and lipstick faded, continued to stare at her phone. Erik wondered if she was even aware of anyone else in the room.

The door opened and the sheriff returned. Erik and Brandon looked up. "Someone has reported a car off the highway up on Dixon Pass," he said. "It matches the description of Carl Westover's current lease vehicle, the Lexus LS."

"What do you mean, off the highway?" Brandon asked. "Is it parked? Is anyone in it?"

Travis glanced at Erik, then away. "The car is in the canyon below the roadway. Search and Rescue are on their way now."

SHERI HAD BEEN thinking of drawing a hot bath and pouring a large glass of wine when the call came for volunteers to respond to a report of a vehicle off the side of Dixon Pass. She could have opted out, using the excuse that she was too tired from competing in the ice festival earlier that day, but a car in the canyon meant rescuers would have to climb down to reach any survivors, sometimes a long way, and sometimes in very rugged terrain. Everyone on Search and Rescue trained for the work, but only a handful of members, including Sheri, could handle the difficult stuff easily. And how many of that group would already be celebrating at the after-party for the festival, their blood alcohol high enough that they would have to excuse themselves from this call?

She changed into insulated winter gear, donned her bright blue Search and Rescue parka and texted Tony that she was on her way.

She spotted the flashing lights of emergency vehicles as she crested the top of the pass, red and blue strobes lighting up the snowbanks of the left side of the road in the growing darkness. She parked at the end of a row of cars on the right shoulder and climbed out, the cold that had descended with nightfall hitting her like a slap and making her draw her parka more tightly around her.

She walked up the road to where Tony and Lieutenant Carrie Andrews conferred. Several other volunteers—Danny Irwin, Eldon Ramsey, Ted Carruthers, and Austen Morrissey—stood nearby. Tony looked up at Sheri's approach and motioned for the others to join them. "A passing motorist noticed the tracks over the edge about half an hour ago," Tony said. "He stopped to take a look and saw the top of the car in the creek at the bottom of the canyon. He had to drive to the top of the pass to get a signal and call for help."

"It's in the creek?" Ted made a face. The water would be ice cold this time of year. Anyone landing in

it, whether someone thrown from the vehicle or a res-
cuer who had to wade through the water to get to anyone in the car, would be risking hypothermia.

"I took a look and the vehicle is lying on its side in
the water," Tony said. "From what I remember, the creek
at that point is less than a foot deep. There's a crust of
ice the vehicle broke through, but the water is running
fast enough in that narrow section that the creek hasn't
frozen solid."

"It's a fairly gentle slope down into the canyon,"
Carrie said. "Lots of loose rock, so running some ropes
down will make climbing up and down a lot easier. The
trickiest part will be getting a litter up."

"Do we know who's in the car?" Danny asked. "How
many? What ages?"

Tony shook his head. "I didn't see anyone moving
around when I looked," he said.

Not something they wanted to hear—no one calling
for help or trying to get out of the car could mean the
driver and any passengers were either dead, or so seriously injured that they were unconscious.

"Sheri, you and Danny go down first," Tony said.
"Assess the situation and let us know what you need."

"Ted and I will handle the ropes up top," Carrie said.

As they gathered the gear they would need to descend, a new set of flashing lights moved toward them
on the highway. A black-and-white Rayford County
Sheriff's Department SUV pulled in alongside them
and Sheriff Walker leaned out the driver's side window.
"What have you got?"

"A vehicle in the creek down there." Tony nodded
toward the canyon. "We don't know anything else."

"Someone called in the license plate and it matches a vehicle we're looking for," Travis said.

"Oh?" Tony asked. "Who's that? Should we be worried?"

"You should be careful," Travis said. "If the plate number is right, it could belong to a kidnapper."

"Carl Westover?" Sheri had been listening to the conversation. Now she turned and faced the others. "That's his car down there?"

"We think so." The answer came not from the sheriff but from Erik, who had stepped out of the sheriff's SUV on the passenger side. "He may have Dawn Sheffield with him."

"We'll know more in a few minutes," Tony said. He turned back to help Austen with the ropes.

Five minutes later, they had everything set up for the descent into the canyon. "Are you ready?" Carrie asked, looking at Danny and Sheri.

"Ready." She checked her safety lines, clipped in and started her descent. As Carrie had said, this wasn't a particularly challenging or frightening climb, though the loose rock did make some spots tricky.

Ten minutes later, she was standing in the ice on the bank of the creek, studying the wrecked vehicle in front of her. The stillness and silence of the area struck her—not a good sign. She scanned the area around the wreckage, but saw no sign that anyone had been thrown from the vehicle as it tumbled from the roadway above.

"A Lexus." Danny came up beside her and gave a low whistle. "Sweet ride."

"Let's hope the fancy ride came with fancy safety features," Sheri said. She braced herself, then waded into the water.

Her boots kept her dry for the first few steps, then icy fingers of water seeped in, down her ankles, and wrapped around her toes. The water was so cold it hurt, and she gritted her teeth against the pain. Only a few more minutes. All she had to do was reach up and open the passenger door.

Danny followed and hoisted himself up onto the vehicle. Working together, the two of them succeeded in wrenching open the door, which had been badly dented on the trip down into the canyon. Danny leaned in, legs dangling, and emerged soon after. "There's nobody in there," he said.

"They must have been thrown." Sheri jogged to the bank and hauled herself out again, then jogged down the bank, scanning the area. "Carl!" she shouted. "Dawn!"

Danny caught up with her, a hand on her shoulder. "There's nobody here," he said.

"How do you know?"

"The seat belts are all unfastened. The windshield and side windows are cracked and crazed, but none of them are busted out."

"Did they manage to get out on their own?" She looked around. "Where did they go?"

"The only footprints I saw were our own." He shook his head. "I don't think anyone was in that car when it went over."

"What have you found?"

They both turned to see Erik striding toward him. "What are you doing down here?" she asked. He was wearing a helmet and climbing harness, which looked out of place with his street clothes, though at least he was wearing good boots.

"I'm investigating a possible crime scene and hoping

to apprehend a criminal suspect." He looked around. "Are Carl and Dawn in there?"

"No one's in there," Danny said. "I don't think they were—at least not when the car went over."

"We have to look," Sheri said. "We have to make sure." She cupped her hands to her mouth and shouted, "Dawn! Dawn Sheffield!"

She walked away from the others, and took out a flashlight, widened its beam and played it over the ground on both sides of the creek. No footprints but hers and Danny's. Nothing that would have been made by a little girl.

While she searched, Erik and Danny returned to the vehicle. Erik climbed up as Danny had done, and looked inside. By the time he and Danny returned to the bank, Sheri had rejoined them. "The keys are in the ignition," Erik said. "I don't see any luggage or clothing or other personal items. The glove box is empty."

"He took everything out before he sent the vehicle over the edge," Danny said.

"Why are you so sure of that?" Erik asked.

Danny looked back up the slope. "It's an odd place to go off the road. The highway is wider here than a lot of other places, there's no sharp curve, no blind spot, no steep grade and no shadowed area that would collect ice. No avalanche chute."

"I don't remember a vehicle going off at this spot before," Sheri said.

"The shoulder is just wide enough here to safely exit the vehicle without being in traffic," Danny said. "The slope down to the creek starts out gradual, then gets steeper. Get the car started rolling toward the edge and gravity would do the rest."

"Why do something like that?" Sheri asked.

"The Amber Alert includes a description of Carl's car," Erik said. "He would want to get rid of it as soon as possible. It's only bad luck someone spotted the tracks on the side of the road and got curious. Otherwise, it could have been months before the car was found."

"So he ditched his car," Sheri said. "Then what? He's got a little girl and maybe some luggage. We're eight miles from town."

"Someone might have picked them up," Danny said. "Someone who hasn't seen the news and doesn't get alerts on their phone. A man and his little girl look harmless enough."

"We'll put out a bulletin," Erik said. He looked back at the vehicle. "And we'll arrange for a wrecker to haul the vehicle out of the creek."

"We'd better head up top and get into dry shoes," Danny said. "Sheri, you go first. Erik can follow and I'll be cleanup man."

They made the trek up top. Carrie met Sheri at the end of the rope. "There's no one there," Sheri said. "We think the car was dumped and the driver and passenger hitched a ride from a passing motorist."

"The plate number and description match the car leased to Carl Westover," Erik said when he emerged at road level a few moments later. He removed the helmet and stripped off the harness and handed them to Austen. "He knew every law enforcement agency in the state was looking for him and his car, so he got rid of it."

"You won't be needing us anymore," Tony said.

Sheri started to follow Danny toward their cars, but Erik touched her elbow. "Hang on a sec," he said.

She sent him a questioning look, but said nothing, waiting.

"Do you mind if I stop by later?" he asked. "Just to get your feedback on all this." He gestured to take in the scene.

She wanted to tell him no, but she was curious to know what he found. She was invested in Dawn Sheffield's safety now, even if getting involved wasn't such a good idea. "All right. I'm in the Spruce Condos on the east side of town. 4A."

"Thanks. I won't be too late."

She probably wouldn't have time for that bath, but she might open the wine, she thought as she hiked back to her car. A little liquid courage might be just the thing for her first time alone with her ex in two years.

Chapter Four

Sheri had finished one glass of wine and was contemplating a second when Erik knocked on her door. "Come on in," she said, and led the way into the living room of her condo. "You can hang your coat in the closet there." She indicated a closet that held everything from skis to some of her climbing gear, plus winter coats.

He removed his jacket to reveal a denim-blue sweater. She recognized that sweater. She had given it to him for Christmas five years ago. A lifetime ago.

"Can I get you something?" she asked. "I'm having wine."

"That would be good. Thanks." He sank onto the sofa and rubbed one hand across his face.

"Is everything okay?" she asked as she filled two wineglasses. "You look exhausted."

"More frustrated. I'm pretty sure Carl Westover hasn't gone too far, but we haven't turned up a single sighting of him or Dawn."

"My heart goes out to her parents." Sheri handed him one of the glasses, then settled on the opposite end of the sofa.

"I wish I had as much faith as the mother that her

brother won't hurt her little girl." He sipped from his glass and nodded. "This is good wine."

"You don't really think Carl would hurt his niece, do you? When I saw them, she didn't seem afraid of him at all."

"Unfortunately, my line of work gives you a jaundiced view of people in general. And anyone who would take a child away from loving parents for the purposes of extorting money has already crossed a big moral barrier."

"What are you doing back in investigations?" she asked. "When did you leave teaching?" Erik had starting teaching at the state's law enforcement academy the year before their divorce was final. He had said the opportunity was too good to pass up.

He set the wineglass on the table beside him and angled toward her. "I thought teaching would get me away from the emotional side of law enforcement. After Claire died, I had a harder time than I expected dealing with the criminals I investigated. The last case I worked was a pedophile ring. They were making and selling videos of kids." He shook his head. "It almost broke me. I couldn't deal."

She stared at him, feeling sick. "You never told me." She leaned toward him. "We were still married then. Why didn't you tell me?"

"You were struggling so much—I couldn't add to that. I thought I could handle it on my own." He picked up the wineglass and took a long drink. "I went to counseling for a while. It helped."

"Was this while we were still married, too?"

"After. I'd been teaching a little while then, but I was still having a hard time emotionally. Leaving fieldwork helped, but there were still days where just getting out of bed was such a struggle."

She nodded. She knew all about those days. After Claire died she had spent so many months wondering why she had to keep living when her daughter was gone.

"You say the counseling helped?" She never would have expected Erik to seek professional counseling. He was always the tough guy, able to handle whatever came along.

"It did," he said. "I've kept it up, though I don't see my therapist as often. She's the one who encouraged me to return to investigation. Carl Westover was my first assignment. Dealing with an embezzler seemed like a good way to ease back in. And then he had to kidnap a kid." He drained the rest of the wine and set the glass aside. "What about you?" he asked. "Did you try counseling?"

She shook her head. "I took up climbing."

He nodded. "Pushing yourself physically can help focus your mind. I spent a lot of time at the gym that first year after Claire died."

She hadn't known that, either. Those months she had lived at the bottom of a well of grief, unable to see anything around her. "When I'm tackling a tough climb, I can't think about anything else but my next move, and the move after that," she said. "It's like a meditation, emptying my mind of everything else."

"Everyone says you're very good," he said.

Did that mean he had been asking about her? "I discovered I have a talent, plus I've worked very hard to get better."

"And the search and rescue work? How did you get into that?"

"When I took the teaching job here two years ago Tony, the captain, saw me when I was climbing one day and asked if I'd be interested. He said they were always looking for climbers to add to the team. It sounded intriguing, so I attended a training session and I was hooked."

"What do you like about it?" he asked.

"It's physically and emotionally demanding. Intense. But you're working as a team and everyone is focused on the same goal. And you save lives. When a rescue is successful, it's such a tremendous feeling of victory."

"And the unsuccessful rescues?"

"They're hard. But again, you're not dealing with the hard stuff alone. Everyone on the team is watching out for each other."

"We should have done that after Claire died," he said. "Watched out for each other. I don't know why we didn't. Why we couldn't."

His words caught her off guard. This was a side of Erik she had never seen—one willing to talk about the hard emotions, almost as if he had been wanting to discuss this with her. She had grown so used to the hard, closed-off man he had become at the end of their marriage that she wasn't sure how to react. "We were both hurting so badly, I guess," she said. Now she was the one who struggled for words. She had wanted him to be there for her so badly in those days after the accident—but how selfish was that, when she hadn't given him any support in his own grief?

"I know you felt guilty about what happened," he said. "You shouldn't be. That's one thing therapy drilled in to me. The feeling is natural, but it's a lie."

"I was her mother. I was supposed to look out for her. And I was right there."

"She was an active, curious four-year-old. You turned your back for half a second and she ran into the street and was struck by that car. She had never done anything like that before, so how could you have predicted it."

She nodded, her throat too constricted to speak. Everything he said was true. She had said it herself over and over. But she couldn't shake the feeling that she should have known. Claire was only four. And Sheri was her mother. A mother should know better.

He moved over and put his arm around her. She rested her head on his shoulder, surprised to feel her cheeks were wet. "Sometimes I dream about that day," she said. "But in my dreams I yank her back. The car goes by and Claire is still there, in my arms."

She pressed her face into the sweater and breathed in the familiar scent of him—salt and spice and clean skin. She had heard that the sense of smell remained when all others deserted you. When she was very old, she was sure she would still recognize Erik by the scent of him.

He held her tighter, his arms around her so reassuring. She thought he might have kissed the top of her head, but maybe she only imagined that. It was something he used to do.

"I'm sorry," he said after a moment. "I'm sorry I wasn't a better husband."

"I'm sorry I wasn't a better wife." The words were muffled, so she raised her head and wiped at her eyes with one hand. "We were both pretty awful to each other at the end."

"We'd been through something awful. Something no parents should ever have to face."

"I think about that woman sometimes. Margaret Freeble." The driver whose car had struck Claire when the little girl darted out from between two parked cars.

"What about her?"

"It must be so awful for her. I was so angry and I said some terrible things to her. But I know now the accident wasn't her fault. It was just…an accident."

"Maybe you should write to her and tell her that."

The thought had never occurred to her. She stared at him. "Seriously? I don't even know her address."

"I could probably find it out. It might make her feel better. And it might help you, too."

"Now you sound like a therapist."

"Maybe I've learned a few things."

His arm was still around her, and she was suddenly conscious of how close they were, his body warm against hers. An unsettling longing to be closer swept through her. Though they had been divorced for two years, and their relationship had been in trouble for two years before that, her body still remembered what is was like to be loved by this man.

She sat up straighter and pressed against the arm of the sofa, putting as much distance between them as possible. "What did you come here to talk to me about?" she asked.

Some dark emotion passed across his face—hurt? anger?—but he looked away, and moved over a few inches on the sofa. "I wanted to know what you saw when you first came upon Carl's car in that gulch," he said.

She frowned. "It was just a car, lying on its side. Pretty dented up. The windows were cracked but not blown out. There were no personal belongings scattered about, which should have been my first clue that no one was in the vehicle when it went down there. Usually there is stuff scattered around—papers, clothing, food wrappers—whatever is in the car gets shaken out on the way down or when any survivors get out. Danny said he looked in the glove box and it was empty too."

"Carl probably thought that would slow us down on identifying him as the driver, though he left the license tags in place. Maybe he just took everything out as a matter of course. He'd wiped the interior clean, too. We didn't find a single clear fingerprint."

"Why would he go to all that trouble?" she asked. "He must know he would be identified—by his sister, if by no one else."

"I've been studying Carl for three months now," Erik said. "He has an outsized opinion of himself. He was sure he could get away with stealing large amounts of money from his employer. When he was arrested he seemed more upset that the people he worked with had suspected him all along than that we were charging him with a crime. Even after his arrest, he was sure the charges would be dropped, or that the judge and jury would believe his story and not the evidence. Maybe that ego is operating here. He sees himself as a dangerous fugitive, on the run from the law."

"He's playing a character in a movie," she said. "He crashes his car and wipes it clean to slow down his pursuers."

"But he doesn't remove the license plates." Erik nodded. "That's the kind of overlooked detail that has tripped him up all along. He stole a lot of money from his employer, but instead of tucking it away and carrying on as usual, he immediately began spending it lavishly. Naturally, everyone wondered where he had gotten the funds for a new car, new suits and a fancy vacation. It might have taken us a little longer to pin the crime on him if he had been more careful."

"What's going to happen now that he's contacted his sister?" she asked.

"Maybe we can persuade him to come out of hiding for the money. Greed has driven him all along. Or maybe someone will spot him and Dawn and report them to law enforcement. We'll keep looking and sooner or later he'll make a mistake."

She nodded. Erik had always been dogged in pursuit of any criminal he was after. His devotion to duty had annoyed her sometimes, because it meant she didn't come first in every aspect of his life. Now that she was working search and rescue, she understood that better. When people's lives were at stake, your personal concerns had to be set aside for a while. That kind of compartmentalization enabled you to do the job. If a person thought only about her children or spouse, she would never descend into canyons or climb perilous mountains to rescue a stranger, knowing it meant risking depriving her loved ones of a partner or parent.

He stood. "Thanks for the wine. And the talk. Hashing all this out with someone else helps, I think."

She stood also, and walked him to the door. "Good luck," she said. She wanted to say more—that it was good to see him again, and that she was glad they were on better terms now. But the words stuck in her throat. Because she was afraid of saying the wrong thing? Afraid he might misinterpret her words? Both?

"Good night," he said, and then he was gone, the door closing softly behind him.

She leaned against the door and closed her eyes. Erik had been so kind and understanding tonight, so smart and perceptive—the man she had first fallen in love with.

Was she so pathetic, so starved for attention that the smallest kindness from a man had her wanting him to take her to bed?

Or was what she was feeling more nostalgia for what had been, for a life before grief and anger had stolen the part of her away that could forget herself in lovemaking? How wonderful to be that woman again, if only for a few hours.

But she wasn't that woman, and Erik wasn't that man. As much as she knew how well he could love her, she also knew how deeply they could hurt each other. Ignoring that seemed a recipe for disaster. She had a lot of training in saving other people from their mistakes, but she had a feeling rescuing herself could be much harder.

THE RENTAL ERIK HAD ended up in had two things in its favor—the price was cheap, since the owners were in the middle of remodeling, with construction confined mostly to the exterior—and the bedroom was dark and quiet, at the back of the house, which boded well for sleeping in on mornings after a late night. His job came with a lot of late nights, so he valued anything that could help him be less sleep-deprived. He was sound asleep ten o'clock Sunday morning when the blare of his phone startled him awake. He groped on the nightstand and answered, "Hello?"

"Erik, this is Gage." The sergeant's easygoing voice sounded wide awake. "We got a call someone spotted

Carl and Dawn at a motel in Junction. By the time the local cops got there, they had cleared out, but I thought you might want to go with me to talk to the woman who called it in, and anyone at the motel who might have seen them."

"Yes. Great." Erik sat up on the side of the bed and scrubbed at his face.

"I'll be by in a few minutes to pick you up," Gage said.

"Give me more than a few minutes. Twenty." He needed a shower and a shave and a large cup of strong coffee.

"See you in twenty."

Gage was waiting at the curb when Erik emerged from the house twenty minutes later, coffee mug in hand, sunglasses hiding his bloodshot eyes. Gage looked amused as Erik slid into the passenger seat of the SUV. "Late night?"

"I didn't sleep well." He had lain awake far too many hours, wondering if he should have stayed with Sheri. He didn't think he had imagined the old heat between them, and he had wanted her badly. But he hadn't wanted to screw up this new closeness by asking for too much too soon, so he had made himself leave. Then he had replayed the whole evening over and over in his head, and imagined what might have happened if he had stayed. He could have woken up beside her this morning, instead of in a cold, impersonal rental.

"The woman who called in the sighting lives behind the States Inn," Gage said. "She said she saw a man and a girl that fit the description from the Amber Alert outside one of the rooms this morning. The motel owner says the man registered as Mark Freeman and told her he and his daughter were on their way to visit his mother in Albuquerque. They checked out about nine o'clock."

"Did the clerk at the motel agree that they fit the description from the Amber Alert?" Erik asked.

"She said she didn't see the girl, but the man was about forty and had brown hair, so maybe. At least if this checks out we know he's on the move. That gives us something to go on."

Erik nodded. Sometimes you got lucky. Other times, you spent a lot of effort chasing leads that went nowhere.

Fayette Roubideaux was a full-figured peroxide blonde who managed a local discount store and grew vegetables in her backyard. "I was watering the tomatoes when I saw the man and the girl," she told Erik and Gage, after she had checked their ID and escorted them into said yard. She gestured to where a row of motel rooms were visible across a ditch, on the other side of a chain-link fence. "I noticed because the girl was crying. She wanted to go swimming and the man kept telling her the pool was closed. Which it is, because you know, it's February." She shrugged. "Kids."

"Describe them for me," Erik said.

"Well, the man was a pretty average white guy—middle-aged, kind of shaggy brown hair. He had on khaki pants and a kind of dark jacket. The little girl had long hair, about the same color of brown."

"Dark brown or light brown?" Erik asked.

"Light. Almost dishwater blond. She was wearing a pink snowsuit."

Erik showed her a picture of Dawn. "Was this the girl you saw?" he asked.

The woman frowned at the photograph. "Maybe?

Only her hair was a lot lighter, and she looked younger to me. I mean, they were way over on the other side of the fence."

A picture of Carl produced even less certainty. "I didn't really pay much attention to him," she said. "He was just, you know, ordinary."

"Thank you, Ms. Roubideaux," Erik said. "We appreciate you calling this in."

"Do you think it's the people you're looking for?" she asked.

"We'll definitely follow up on it," Erik said.

They returned to Gage's SUV and drove to the motel. "I'm not convinced it's them," Gage said.

"Let's see what the motel clerk says."

The motel clerk, Darius Haskins, shook his head when shown a photo of Carl Westover. "Freeman had less of a chin and more of a nose than this guy," he said.

"What kind of car was he driving?" Gage asked.

"A Toyota Sienna. I remember because my sister just got one."

He provided Freeman's driver's license, plate number and credit card information and Erik called it in when they were back at Gage's SUV. "It checks out," Erik said after a few minutes. "The vehicle is registered to Mark Freeman of Tecumseh, Nebraska. No wants or warrants. Forty years old, five-ten, two hundred pounds. Divorced. Parents Susan and Martin Freeman of Albuquerque."

Gage put the SUV in gear. "We had to check it out."

"We did." A great deal of investigations involved legwork like this that led nowhere, but ruling out possibilities was important, too.

"Are you hungry?" Gage asked. "I know a place that has really good Mexican food."

Erik's stomach growled. Dinner had been a very long time ago. "That sounds great." They might as well get some good out of this road trip.

SHERI SEARCHED THE crowd around the base of the canyon walls for Erik. It was almost one o'clock and she hadn't spotted him yet. She should have told him to come down here, where she would start the climb. Was he in the spectator area up top?

"Oh, don't you look adorable?" Susie jogged up, grinning. "The wings are an especially nice touch."

Sheri brushed self-consciously at the fairy wings that fluttered at her back. Many of the competition winners donned costumes for the exhibition climbs and this was hers, along with a bright pink skin suit and a short tulle tutu. She had spotted several superheroes, a skeleton and what might have been an eagle among her fellow climbers. "Thanks. Um, you remember that guy you saw me talking to yesterday? The one you asked about? Have you seen him around today?"

"Sorry, no. And he's the type of man a woman notices, right? Why? Is he supposed to be here?"

"He said he would come to watch me climb today."

"Then he'd better hurry. You're almost up."

Sure enough, the announcer called her name. Cheers and clanging cowbells greeted the announcement, and she moved to her starting point and clipped in.

She was taking a route known as Ice Dancer. It wasn't the most difficult route, but it was one of the most beautiful, with mineral deposits creating a rainbow effect in the ice. The melodic strains of Florence and the Machine filled the canyon as she ascended through panels of pink, orange and green-tinged ice. The effect to the spectators should be like a real-life fairy floating up a frozen waterfall.

Near the top the ice jutted out in an overhang that could be tricky. It was something she had climbed a dozen times, but it was still exciting enough to make the crowd ooh and aah as she worked her way over it. And then she was at the top, just as the music ended. Cheers echoed through the canyon and Sheri executed a deep curtsy that set her wings to fluttering.

And still no Erik. She shook hands and accepted hugs from friends, fans and well-wishers, all the while searching for him among the many smiling faces.

"Your guy was a no-show, huh?" Susie made a sad face. "I told you—if they're not climbers, they just don't get it. You should have come to the party and let me introduce you to those Swedish guys. They were super nice." She sighed. "Too bad Sweden is so far away."

Sheri shrugged. "No big deal. Hey, I have to go run my clinic now." The free climbing clinics were designed to introduce novices to the sport of ice climbing. They were staged in the beginner area at the other end of the canyon and were always very popular, even more so when organizers could boast an instructor who had won at this year's festival.

Sheri lugged her gear to the beginner area, stopping repeatedly to accept congratulations. As she moved, her disappointment morphed to anger. So much for thinking Erik had changed. This was just like him, to fail to show today. Sure, it was just a climbing exhibition. But it was a big deal to her. It would have meant so much to have him here.

Maybe something had come up with work. She would understand that. But if that was the case, why hadn't he texted or called? The signal in the canyon itself was pretty much nonexistent, but up top it was great. She had checked and he hadn't tried to contact her.

Lexie and Monica were waiting for her at the beginner wall, along with a petite, curly haired older version of Lexie. "Ms. Stevens, this is my mom," Lexie said. "She decided she wants to try climbing after all."

"I'm Alice," Lexie's mom introduced herself. "I wanted to show these girls that you're never too old to try new things."

"With that attitude, you can't lose," Sheri said. She turned to greet the other nine women and girls who had signed up for the clinic. "We're going to have a great time this afternoon," she told them. "And you're going to find out you're all capable of a lot more than you ever believed possible."

As always, climbing worked its magic, the hurt and anger over Erik's failure to show pushed aside as she demonstrated equipment and technique, then helped each participant make her first climb. The joy on the women's faces as they conquered fear and uncertainty and reached the top of the beginner wall filled Sheri with pride. Everyone left with a packet of information about the climbing area, equipment providers and Picksie Chix to help them continue to pursue the sport.

All in all, Sheri decided as she lugged her gear toward the parking lot, it had been a good day. Erik was one man, and she knew better than to think she could lean on him. Better to take pride in standing on her own.

GAGE SLOWED THE SUV, then stopped to allow a line of traffic to pass as he waited to make the turn onto Eagle Mountain's main street. "Is there always this much traffic on a Sunday afternoon?" Erik asked.

Gage glanced at the dashboard clock. "The climbing festival just let out," he said. "It will clear out in a few minutes."

Dread washed over Erik in a sick wave. He swore.

"It's just a few minutes," Gage said. "What are you in such a hurry to do?"

"The climbing festival. I told Sheri I'd be there today to watch her climb."

"She'll understand about work, won't she?"

Erik shook his head and pulled out his phone.

"Right. I forgot she's your ex-wife, not your wife," Gage said. "Less likely to be forgiving. Or so I've heard."

Erik tried to think of a text that sounded apologetic enough, then shook his head and stuffed the phone back into his pocket. This would require groveling in person. "I can't believe I forgot," he said.

"Is that where you were last night?" Gage asked. "With Sheri? Not that it's any of my business."

"You're right. It's none of your business." But there was no heat behind the words.

"Tell her I dragged you out of town before you had a chance to get in touch with her," Gage said. "She knows me—she'll believe you."

Erik shook his head. "I have a history of this kind of thing." Letting her down. Not that he did so on purpose, but for so many years he hadn't been very good at reading what was really important to Sheri—and she hadn't helped him out by telling him. They were married, so he was supposed to know. Except he hadn't.

But climbing was important to her. She'd been clear about that. And he had genuinely wanted to see her doing more of something she so clearly loved. He had just…forgotten. Blame lack of sleep or a focus on the job or the fact that he was out of the habit of pleasing anyone but himself. It didn't matter. She would be upset and he would have to apologize.

Gage dropped him at his Jeep and wished him good luck, then Erik drove the few blocks to Sheri's apartment. Her car was in the lot in front of her building. With a heavy heart, he climbed the steps to her front door and rang the bell.

Sheri opened the door. Her face was flushed, her hair was tousled, and she was wearing a form-fitting pink leotard that made him forget himself for a moment. He studied the way the garment clung to her curves, then focused on her shoulders. "Are those wings?" he asked.

"It's my costume for the exhibition climb," she said. "You'd know that if you'd been there."

"Look, I'm sorry," he said. "I'm so wound up in this case, I spaced it. I—"

He didn't get any further. Sheri slammed the door in his face, and he heard the solid *Thunk!* of a dead bolt being shot home. He sighed. It was the reaction he had been expecting, but he had held out hope that this time things would be different. The two of them didn't have to keep repeating the same old patterns. Except it seemed they did.

He turned and trudged back to his car. He and Sheri had lost more than their daughter the day of Claire's accident. They could never get their child back, but he

had hoped they could recover some of their old feelings for each other.

It seemed he was wrong about that, too.

Chapter Five

The sheriff formally introduced Erik to his department at Monday morning's staff meeting. Every available deputy had gathered with Erik and the sheriff at a conference room table scattered with coffee mugs and to-go cups. A whiteboard at the front of the room listed the information they had about the kidnapping case so far.

"I've requested assistance from the Colorado Bureau of Investigation on this kidnapping case and they've agreed to post Detective Lester with us for the time being," Travis said. "He's been investigating the embezzlement case against the suspected kidnapper, Carl Westover, and is familiar with him. Erik, why don't you bring us up to date on what we're dealing with."

Erik thanked the sheriff and presented a summary of the events so far, from the embezzlement charges against Carl to his fleeing town, with Erik in pursuit, to the kidnapping of his niece and the demand for a million dollars, along with him dumping his car in the canyon and his refusal to accept the ransom in cash or in person. "Carl Westover is of above-average intelligence, but he's also overconfident and sloppy," Erik said. "He's impulsive, vain, greedy and immature. My feeling is he came to Eagle Mountain to plead for more money from his sister, but before he could do that, he spotted his niece wandering away from her parents and hit upon what he no doubt thought of as a brilliant plan to get even more money, and maybe a little revenge on the brother-in-law, who was thwarting him. He didn't think it through."

"The numbered account had to be arranged well ahead of time," Deputy Ronin Doyle pointed out.

"He may have already had that to stash away some of the money he embezzled from his former employer," Erik said. "Though I'll admit, that message to his sister was the first I had heard of such an account."

"What is Carl into that he needs so much money?" Gage asked.

"He's got tens of thousands of dollars in legal bills," Deputy Dwight Prentice said. "That might panic anyone."

"That might panic an ordinary person with a well-functioning conscience," Erik said. "That isn't Carl."

"Why did he steal the money from his employer in the first place?" Deputy Jamie Douglas asked. "Does he have a drug habit? A gambling problem?"

"We haven't uncovered any evidence of anything like that," Erik said. "I think he figured out how lax the accounting safeguards were at Western Casing. He saw the opportunity to help himself to some extra cash and took it. If he had stuck to small amounts here and there, he might have gotten away with it for years. But he got greedy."

"So is greed the reason he's asking a million dollars for his niece?" Deputy Shane Ellis asked.

"I think so," Erik said. "Carl has a very grandiose

view of himself. He believes he deserves to be a millionaire, so why not make it so?"

"His sister thinks he wants to stick it to her husband," Travis said.

Erik nodded. "That's probably part of it. There's no love lost between those two."

"But kidnapping his niece hurts his sister, too," Jamie said. "And they're supposed to be close."

"She seems to care a great deal about him, but I don't know if he feels as close to her," Erik said. "I don't know if he's capable of that kind of attachment."

"As far as we know, he hasn't answered his sister's text, asking to talk to him," Travis said.

"There's nothing to keep the two of them from talking when we're not around," Dwight said.

"She came to us right away with the first text," Erik said. "I think she wants our help getting her daughter back."

"What about her contention that her brother would never harm his niece?" Travis asked. "If he doesn't get the money he wants, would he hurt her, out of frustration or spite?"

"I don't know," Erik admitted. "People are unpredictable, and people in desperate situations are even more volatile. All I can say is that Carl hasn't shown any tendency to violence in the past. I'd even say he's a rather passive person. That's another reason I think this kidnapping was on impulse. He saw what he thought would be an easy opportunity and took it. He probably expected his brother-in-law to cave right away and he had planned to send Dawn back to her parents in a couple of days and be on his way."

"When was the last time you spoke to Mrs. Sheffield?" Gage asked.

"About fifteen minutes before this meeting started," Erik said. "She said she hasn't received a reply to her text. She was very upset." The memory of Melissa's distress was a heavy weight in his stomach.

"Carl's car didn't turn up anything significant," Travis said. "Some long dark hair in the back seat that might have come from Dawn, but he had wiped the whole thing pretty clean."

"We've gotten calls from people who think they've seen Carl or Dawn, or both of them," Gage said. "But none of them have panned out, including the one Erik and I checked out in Junction yesterday."

"I'm still following up on a few more of those sightings," Jamie said. "There are a lot of dark-haired little girls around, and Carl's a very ordinary-looking man."

"Our best bet is going to be finding whoever picked them up after Carl sent his car into the canyon," Travis said. "A man and a child thumbing a ride in winter on that stretch of highway is going to stand out. I want to know what story he gave the driver, and where that person dropped them off."

"What if he didn't catch a ride?" Erik asked. "Is there anywhere he could have walked to from there?"

"Not for ten miles," Gage said. "That's all public land on both sides of the highway—all cliffs and gorges. Some mine ruins in the high country, but no roads, and any trails to them are under twelve feet of snow. The only way Carl and Dawn got out of there was if someone gave them a ride."

"Maybe he has an accomplice," Shane said.

"Maybe." Travis looked to Erik. "Has Carl worked with anyone before?"

"No. We weren't able to find any close friends and while he can be personable, he's not charismatic enough to have followers. One of the reasons he got caught embezzling the money he took is because most of his coworkers didn't like him. They were only too happy to provide evidence against him."

"Any other family?" Gage asked. "An ex-wife? Other siblings?"

"None," Erik said. "Just him and Melissa."

"Find out where she was yesterday before she came here," Travis said. "Just to cover all our bases."

"I'll find out," Erik said. "I was planning on talking to her again today anyway."

Someone knocked on the conference room door, then the office manager, Adelaide Kinkaid, peered around the door. Midsixties, with short white hair, bifocals with red plastic rims and dangling earrings shaped like strawberries, Adelaide seemed out of place in the formality of a sheriff's department—but apparently only to Erik, as everyone else accepted her as a vital part of the team. "Angie Searle is on the phone," Adelaide said now. "She has what sounds like legitimate information about Carl Westover and Dawn Sheffield."

The sheriff and Erik both stood. "Who is Angie Searle?" Erik asked.

"She owns some cabins up by Reflection Lake," Adelaide said. "They're mostly used by fishermen."

"I thought she was closed this time of year," Travis said. He moved into the hallway, Erik close behind.

"She opens up after Christmas for ice fishermen and cross-country skiers," Adelaide said, leading the way down the hall. "When this guy and his daughter rented one of the cabins it struck her as odd. Then she saw the news this morning and thought she'd better call."

Travis turned off into his office and moved behind his desk. Erik stood in the doorway, Adelaide beside him.

Travis picked up his phone. "Hello. This is Sheriff Walker."

He listened to the person on the other end of the line for several minutes, his face betraying nothing. Finally he said, "Thank you for contacting us. We'll be out there right away."

He replaced the receiver and looked to Erik. "About nine o'clock last night she rented a cabin to a man who introduced himself as Adam Smith, and his daughter, Dee. He paid cash for one night. She didn't think anything of it until she noticed this morning that he didn't have a car. Then she heard a news report and decided to contact us." He took his jacket from a hook by the door. "Gage can ride with me," he said. "You're welcome to follow."

Erik stayed close to the sheriff's SUV on the drive into the mountains, determined not to get lost on the winding back roads. The weather was cold but clear, and the roads were freshly plowed, but still it took thirty minutes to reach Lakeside Cabins—a sextet of small, green-painted log cabins arranged in a semicircle across the highway from an iced-in lake. Several fishermen stood or sat on the ice, fishing.

Angie Searle was a short, round woman with the bright red hair of a twenty-year-old and the wrinkled complexion of a seventy-year-old. She met them at the door to the cabin that was marked Office, a half-smoked cigarette clenched between her bright red lips.

"Cabin Four," she said by way of greeting. "I've been watching it ever since I called and no one has made a peep. My guess is they're sleeping in. The little girl, especially, looked worn out when they checked in."

"Thanks," Travis said. "Do you have a key we could use?"

She dug in the pocket of her hoodie and pulled out an old-fashioned brass key attached to a six-inch circle of green plastic. "All the rooms have security chains, too," she said. "But nothing special. Don't do any more damage than you have to."

"Go back inside and stay there, please," Travis said, in a voice that brooked no argument.

"Anything for you, sugar," Angie said. She flicked cigarette ash on the snow beside the steps, then went back inside.

Gage snickered. "I may have to start calling you Sheriff Sugar."

"Try it and I'll rip those sergeant stripes off your uniform myself," Travis said.

Gage smirked at Erik, but kept quiet. Travis started toward the cabin. "Gage, check the back," he said. "Erik, back me up."

Erik drew his pistol from the shoulder holster beneath his jacket. "Yes, sir."

Travis knocked on the door of Cabin Four. No answer. "Mr. Smith?" he called. "Dawn?"

Still no answer. Travis inserted the key in the lock and shoved. The door opened easily, onto an empty room.

Travis moved into the cabin, Erik behind him. Both

beds were unmade, and towels littered the floor of the adjacent bathroom. Travis holstered his gun and Erik did likewise. Gage joined them.

"They've been gone a while," Erik said. The room was cold—the heating had been off for several hours, he estimated.

"They probably left before Angie opened up this morning," Travis said. He pulled back the covers on the nearest bed. Gage moved over to check the dresser drawers.

They found nothing—not so much as a fast-food wrapper. "Let's check outside," Travis said.

They examined the snow around the cabin, then trailed to the road, where Erik spotted a set of child-sized footprints on the shoulder. Just two prints there in the snow. "These could belong to Dawn," he said. "They look right for an eight-year-old girl."

Gage photographed the impressions, but they found nothing else. "Did they set out on foot, or did their ride from the night before return and pick them up?" Gage asked.

"My guess is the latter." Erik stared down the highway, which was empty of traffic. "Carl isn't the rugged outdoors type."

"Fishermen get up early," Gage said. "Maybe one of them saw something."

They crossed the road, then ventured onto the ice to interview the three people fishing there. One of them, Steve Gadwell, said he was staying in Cabin Six, but had not heard or seen anyone else in any of the other cabins. The other two men had driven up earlier that morning, but didn't remember any other cars pulling into the cabins.

"Let's talk to Angie," Travis said, and led the way back to the office.

When the sheriff told Angie the occupants of Cabin Four had left, she said a string of very bad words, then lit a cigarette and settled back in her desk chair. "I guess you want me to tell you everything that happened."

Travis settled into the chair on the other side of the desk. Gage stood in the doorway and Erik leaned against a credenza a few feet from Gage. The room was small, stuffed with furniture, stacks of paper, a box of yellowing brochures, a folding cot and a small wire cage. Angie saw him eyeing the cage. "We had a skunk under Cabin Six last fall. I borrowed that cage and baited it with cat food to catch the critter before he caused too much trouble." She took a long drag on the cigarette and returned her attention to Travis.

"I was back there, watching TV, about nine last night." She pointed to a door behind her. "I've got an apartment back there. There's a bell across the driveway that goes off when anyone drives in. I've only got one cabin rented right now, to Mr. Gadwell. He's a regular, from Denver. Fishes all day and goes to bed early. I heard the driveway bell about nine, so I got up and came out here to see what was what. A man was ringing the bell by then. I yelled at him to hold his horses, and went to answer it."

"What did he look like?" Travis asked.

"Middle-aged, a little pudgy, not too tall." She shrugged. "Brown hair. Brown eyes. Ordinary. He asked if I would rent him a cabin and I said yes and told him the price. He took out a wad of cash and peeled off four twenties. I took a good look at them, but they seemed real. He signed his name as Adam Smith."

"What about the girl?" Erik asked.

"I didn't see her at first. He'd finished filling out the registration card when the door opened and the kid came in. He whipped around and said 'I told you to wait outside.' And she said something about being cold. Then he looked at me and said. 'My daughter, Dee.' I said, 'Hello, Dee,' but she didn't answer, just kind of glared." She shrugged. "I figured she was grumpy about being dragged out here in the middle of the night. Well, not the middle of the night, but nine o'clock is kind of late for a kid that age."

"Mr. Smith only paid for one night?" Travis asked.

"Yes. I asked him if he was here to fish and he said no, he was just passing through. Which was odd in itself, since this place isn't on the way to anywhere, but I figured it was just his way of telling me to mind my own business."

"Did they have luggage with them?" Travis asked.

"No, but I figured it was in their vehicle. I didn't actually see a car or truck, but how else would they get up here? This isn't a place you can easily walk to. And he didn't have a backpack or anything."

"You say you heard a bell when he arrived?" Travis asked. "The kind where it rings if a car drives over it?"

"That's right. I definitely heard the bell."

"Did you hear it again after Mr. Smith came into the office?" Travis asked.

She frowned. "I don't think so. But we were talking, and it rings loudest back in my apartment, so I know to come out here when someone arrives."

"What about this morning?" Travis asked. "Did you hear anyone this morning?"

"No. And I've been by myself all morning, so I'm sure I would have heard it."

"Can you give us a description of what they were wearing?" Travis asked.

The description matched the one Sheri had given of the man and girl she had encountered at the ice festival, which matched the description Melissa Sheffield had given of her daughter's clothing.

"Do you remember anything else about Mr. Smith or the little girl?" Erik asked.

"No. But when I heard that report on the radio I realized it could be them." She looked fierce. "Don't tell me he did anything awful to that girl in that cabin."

"We don't have any reason to believe he's harmed her," Travis said.

Erik knew that the most innocent-seeming relationships could turn out to be twisted, but nothing in Carl's history pointed to any sexual interest in children.

"That's good to know," Angie said.

"We'll want you to look at a photo lineup later," Travis said. "When can you come in to the sheriff's department?"

"My help comes in at one," she said. "I can drive down then."

"We would appreciate it," Travis said. "And we'll need to look over the cabin for evidence. Don't go inside or let anyone else in until I get some officers up here to investigate."

"Got it." She stubbed out her cigarette. "Anything else?"

Travis handed her his card. "Let us know if you think of anything else. And if you happen to see the man or the girl again, call us right away, but don't engage with them."

"Right." She stood and followed them to the door. "The radio said he kidnapped that girl. Is that right?"

"We think so, yes."

"Poor thing. Wish I had known. But I try not to pay more attention to the news than I have to."

They said goodbye and returned to their vehicles. "I'll bet she didn't hear a bell this morning because Carl's ride picked them up at the road," Gage said.

"And took him where?" Erik gazed across at the icy lake, and the snowy spires rising around it. Carl Westover had lived in cities all his life. Erik hadn't even come across any indication that he had so much as attended scout camp as a kid. Erik would have expected him to immediately run to the nearest town of any size, not here where there was nothing and no one.

But there was someone helping him. If they found that person, maybe they would find Carl.

SHERI WOKE LATE Monday morning, fuzzy headed from not enough sleep, still angry at Erik, and angrier with herself for caring so much. She had hardly ever thought about him in the last year or so, so why should anything he said or did matter so much to her now? She made a cup of strong coffee and scrambled some eggs, then headed to school, sure that lesson plans and her students' own dramas would demand all her focus.

By the time the first lunch bell rang at eleven thirty, she was feeling much better. The last student had filed from her classroom and she was gathering her belongings to take her off period when Erik appeared in the doorway. He was dressed in what she thought of as his detective clothes—a dark suit, crisp white shirt and tie. The rather severe look suited him, emphasizing his elegant features. "Hello," he said. "I wondered if you'd have lunch with me."

"No thank you." She grabbed a tote bag and began stuffing random books into it, not because she needed any of them, but so that he would see that she was too busy to talk to him.

He moved into the room, and she caught the scent of his aftershave as he approached. Something expensive and French she had given to him for Christmas a few months before they divorced. Why would he be wearing that scent now? He stopped beside her and leaned over the desk, one hand planted firmly on the book she had been reaching for. "I don't want any animosity between us," he said. "I made a mistake yesterday. I admit it. Gage called with a lead on Carl Westover—a lead that turned out to be a dead end, but we still had to go to Junction to check it out. I should have called you and told you but I didn't."

"You forgot all about me." She winced at how petulant that sounded.

"All right. I forgot." He leaned closer, the sleeve of his jacket brushing her bare arm. "You haven't been a part of my life for two years. I have regrets about that, I truly do. But is it so hard to believe I would forget about an event we mentioned in passing?"

"No, but…"

"But what?"

She almost didn't say but then thought he was being honest with her, so she should be honest with him. "Climbing is important to me. I wanted you to be there."

"I hope I'll have the opportunity to see you climb again. Now, will you have lunch with me?"

"Yes." She set the tote bag of books aside and picked up her purse. "The students are allowed to leave campus for lunch, so they'll be at every restaurant within walking distance."

"There's a barbecue place just as you come into town. Is it any good?"

"Very."

"Then we'll go there."

He drove to the barbecue restaurant and they ordered sliced beef sandwiches and potato chips, then ate sitting in the front seat of his car, the engine running to keep the heat going. The windows fogged and the space felt closed in and intimate. "I remember when we used to do this all the time when you first started teaching," he said.

She smiled, remembering as well. He would surprise her at least once a week by showing up to take her to lunch. They couldn't afford anything fancy, so often they ate sandwiches he had made, and sat in the front seat of his car and talked. And sometimes made out. Once he had persuaded her to have sex in the car, the possibility of getting caught adding to the thrill of the encounter.

"Do you like teaching here?" he asked, pulling her mind back to the present, away from such dangerous memories.

"Yes. I was a little worried about moving to a smaller school district, but it's been great." She crunched a potato chip, salt making her mouth water. "It's easier to get to know my students and the rest of the faculty, and the administration encourages us to be creative with our lesson plans. If I want to teach outside one day, I can, or if I want to take them somewhere local on a field trip, or do a special project, I have the principal's support. The students are great, too. You still get troubled children, but they don't get lost in the crowd, and it's easier to reach them. There are fewer temptations for them, also."

He arranged dill pickle slices atop his sandwich. "I always thought students were lucky to have a teacher like you. Maybe I would have done better in school if I had thought anyone there cared about how I was doing."

"They probably did care, but teenagers can't always see that."

"I can't blame all my problems in school on the teachers." He wiped his hands on a napkin and scrunched it into a ball. "I wasted a lot of my time not studying, and looking for ways to get into trouble. It's a wonder I didn't end up in jail." She had heard the stories before, but liked hearing them again, fascinated by the transformation from potential juvenile delinquent to cop. In college, he had discovered an interest in true crime, which led to studying criminal justice and forensics, where he had learned there were many more jobs for law enforcement officers than for forensic scientists.

"This place isn't what I was expecting," he said. "Eagle Mountain, I mean."

"It's a small town, but it isn't backward or unsophisticated," she said. "The average person here has more years of education, a higher income, volunteers more hours and contributes more to charity. And if you're interested in any kind of recreation—skiing, climbing, running, biking, rafting, hunting and fishing, hiking, photography—this is the place to be. If you're bored here, you have no one to blame but yourself."

"So I'm coming to understand. It's been a pleasant surprise."

They ate in silence for a while. When they were almost done, she asked the question that had been at the back of her mind almost since that first day. "How long are you going to be in town?"

"I don't know. Until we find Dawn and Carl, or until their trail goes cold."

The idea that Dawn might never be found sent a chill through her. "You won't just give up looking for a child," she said, daring him to contradict her.

"Of course not."

Of course he wouldn't. But she had needed to hear him say it. She checked her watch. "I should be getting back."

"Yeah. Me, too." He started the engine and drove back to the school. Students walked across the parking lot in noisy, laughing groups.

Erik parked, got out and walked to the building with her. "I can only imagine what Melissa is going through," she said. "To have your child just disappear, and then to know someone you trusted took her and wants to trade her for money. She must be half out of her mind with worry."

"And Brandon," he said. "When I saw him, he looked really rough. I'm going to their house this afternoon to interview them."

"Of course he's worried." But a father's worry wasn't the same as a mother's worry. She had seen that with Erik. She had grieved for Claire as she might grieve for an essential part of herself, which is what her daughter had been.

They reached the door of her classroom and stopped. "It's good to see you again," he said. "To see you looking so strong."

Strong. Not *beautiful* or *healthy* or *good.* She liked the word. It spoke of overcoming weakness or a debilitating condition—exactly what she felt she had done. "Thank you."

A bell rang. "My lunch break is almost over," she said.

"I have to go, too." He touched her arm. "Are we good now? Can we be friends?"

She hesitated. She had loved Erik more than she had loved anyone except their daughter. And she had hated him with the same depth and ferocity. Could she find a balance between the two? "I'll try," she said.

"I've never known you to give less than your full effort," he said. He kissed her cheek—a move that would surely have half the students and most of the administration who heard of it talking. But the kiss felt good. Warm and familiar and a little thrilling. The start of something, though she didn't want to think further than that.

Chapter Six

A large black SUV, registered to Brandon Sheffield, sat in the driveway of the Sheffield home when Erik arrived after his lunch with Sheri. He walked past the vehicle on his way to the front door and put his hand on the hood—it was cold, so the SUV had been sitting here a little while. Though the driveway had been plowed, the walk was unshoveled, and there were no shoe prints on its surface. Erik picked his way through the packed snow and rang the bell beside the door. A computer-printed sign held in place by a thumbtack read Please Respect Our Privacy. No Media.

Erik pressed the bell a second time, the deep, sonorous gong sounding through the house. Footsteps shuffled toward the door, followed by the sound of locks turning. Brandon Sheffield, in rumpled khakis and a faded maroon sweatshirt, his hair disheveled and several days' growth of beard softening his jaw, stared out. "Have you heard something?" he asked, the words weighted with both hope and dread.

"I'm sorry, no," Erik said. "I had a few more questions for you and your wife."

"Come in." Brandon held the door open wider. "Melissa isn't here. A neighbor invited her to Junction for lunch and a movie. I told her to go, to try to take her mind off everything. We've both been a mess."

Erik followed him into the great room, which looked much the same as when he had last seen it, though someone had set the child's doll up on the mantel, and two bed pillows and a blanket were spread on the sofa. Brandon sat on the blanket and leaned forward, elbows on knees, head in his hands. "We haven't heard anything else out of Carl," he said. "And then the whole business with the car being dumped—do you think someone else is behind this and they're just using Carl as a front?"

"Why do you think that?" Erik asked.

"It just seems like Carl would need help to pull this off," Brandon said. "If he dumped the car, how is he getting around? And if he wants the money, why stop communicating with us?"

"Where were you and your wife between three and seven p.m. Saturday?" Erik asked.

Brandon raised his head to stare at Erik. "We were here."

"You're sure about that."

"Of course I'm sure. What is this about?"

"You and your wife were both here, together, the entire time Saturday afternoon and evening?" Erik asked.

"I was in my office, trying to get some work done, though I've been too distracted to accomplish much. Melissa was here, then she stuck her head in the office to let me know she was going for a walk, then planned to take a shower and try to get some sleep."

"She didn't go anywhere in the car?" Erik asked. "Maybe she changed her mind and went for a drive instead of a walk."

"My office is located at the front of the house and

my desk faces the front window," he said. "I can see the driveway from there and the car never moved."

"Would you show me?"

"Why? What is this about?"

"We agree with you that Carl needed someone to drive him from the location where he ditched the car to a fishing camp in the mountains where we have established that he and Dawn spent Saturday night," Erik said.

"Melissa didn't drive him. She wouldn't. The man kidnapped our daughter!" His voice rose and he raked a hand through his hair.

"I'm ruling out as many people as I can in order to focus on the most likely accomplices," Erik said. "Let's take a look at your office."

Brandon led the way to a sparsely furnished front room, the only furniture a desk and chair, boxes lining the walls on two sides. He pointed out the front window. "See? No one could move the car without me knowing about it."

The window looked onto the front yard, the SUV in the driveway clearly visible on the right side. "Thank you," Erik said, and walked back to the great room.

Brandon sank onto the sofa again. "Does Carl have a friend who would help him?" Erik said. "Not necessarily someone who knew about the kidnapping. Maybe he called a friend—a girlfriend, maybe—and said he was stranded after an accident and needed a ride."

"He isn't dating anyone that I know about, and I've never heard him mention a friend," Brandon said. "But it's not like I know him that well. I don't like the man. I only tolerated him for Melissa's sake."

"Would Melissa know about his friends?"

"Probably. The two of them are pretty close. I don't know why. They're nothing alike. He's greedy and manipulative—she isn't like that."

"Tell me about the time he asked for money from you, before all this."

"It was about a month ago." Brandon leaned back against the cushions and sighed. "He didn't even have the guts to ask me to my face—he got Melissa to do the begging for him, which is typical. I came home from a short business trip to Vegas and she was waiting with a good bottle of wine and a steak dinner. I should have known then something was up, but I thought she had just missed me. She waited until I was in a good mood, then started in by saying she had spoken to Carl that day and she was so worried about him. His legal bills were so much higher than he had expected. She said she thought we should help him out by advancing him some money to pay for his defense."

"What did you say?" Erik asked.

"I said no. And I tried to change the subject, but Melissa wasn't having it. She said Carl was sure he would prove he was innocent of the charges and he would pay us back. I reminded her he had never paid us back the other two times I had loaned him money—once to get out from under a loan he had taken out for a bad real estate investment, and another time to pay off a car Melissa said was going to be repossessed. I had a bad feeling about that last one—I'm pretty sure that car was a lease, too. Carl let it go back and spent the money on a vacation to Aruba or something. I told Melissa then I would never give another dime to her brother, but he must have pressured her pretty hard."

"How did she react when you refused this new loan?" Erik asked.

"She cried. Then she got angry and didn't speak to me for about three days. But I meant what I said—he doesn't get another dime from me."

"Do you agree with Melissa, that Carl is innocent?"

Brandon snorted. "No, I don't. But I'll never persuade her of that. She has a real blind spot when it comes to her brother. She believes all the lies he's told her. And she's not the only one. He can be very charming when he wants to be. But I've always seen through that charm."

"What does she say about him taking Dawn?" Erik wanted to get Brandon's perspective on his wife's attitude.

"She's horrified, of course. Confused. I am, too. I have zero respect for Carl and wouldn't trust him to water my plants while I was on vacation, but I would never in a million years think he would hurt Dawn. I still don't believe he would hurt her. That's the only thing that's keeping me sane. And I know Dawn loves her uncle, so I'm praying that is keeping her from being too afraid."

"Is Carl friends with anyone here locally?" Erik asked.

"Not that I know of. I really don't think he's spent much time here at all—just a couple of short visits when we were here. But again, I'm not close to him. He doesn't confide in me and I don't keep tabs on him. I wish I did."

Erik rose. "Thank you for your time," he said. "Let your wife know I'd like to speak to her also. Maybe she knows someone her brother is close to."

"I'll have her contact you as soon as she gets home. We both want to do whatever it takes to keep Dawn safe and get her back with us, where she belongs. If I thought giving Carl money would do it, I wouldn't hesitate to shell out a million dollars or more. Melissa thinks that would solve everything, but I don't agree."

"It can be hard when a couple aren't on the same page with these decisions," Erik said. "But my experience has been that paying off an extortionist only encourages him to try for a bigger payout the next time."

"Maybe you could mention that to Melissa when you talk to her." Brandon walked with him to the front door. "I know this kind of thing can tear couples apart and I'm determined not to let that happen."

Erik got in the car and drove to the end of the cul-de-sac, where he sat and made notes on his interview with Brandon, and admired the view of snow-covered mountains. Maybe Melissa Sheffield would have a name for him—a girlfriend or a former coworker or someone Carl might have called to help him. Someone who could give them a clue about Carl's intentions or where he might be headed next.

He reviewed his notes on the case, looking for anything he had overlooked. He had missed this aspect of law enforcement work—sifting through clues and putting the pieces of a case together to form a correct picture of the crime. Whether it was tracking down a guilty party or working to build a case against the person that would lead to a just conviction, he thrived on investigative work. While teaching had its rewards, it had felt good to dig back into real police work. After almost four years away, he had felt emotionally strong enough to handle investigations again and so far that was proving true. Some cases, especially those involving children, would always be tough, but now he was even more inspired to find justice for those young victims.

He pondered Brandon's last words to him, about intending to keep his marriage together. If he could have seen what was coming, in those early days after Claire's death, would he have worked harder to save his marriage? Would his efforts have made any difference? If they had stayed together, maybe had another child, would that have helped them to heal faster?

Or had they had to go through all the pain and misery to get to the healing they needed? Teaching had taught him lessons he wouldn't have learned any other way, and Sheri had discovered a talent for climbing and a calling to volunteer in search and rescue. He didn't know if they were better people for all they had gone through, but they were different people. They didn't hate each other anymore, which was a gift in itself, considering how bad things had been between them in the end.

It was good to have Sheri back in his life. In some ways, she knew him better than anyone. She had been his closest friend and probably still was. If nothing else came from this painful kidnapping, he would always be grateful for that.

"Ms. Stevens!" A trio of Sheri's students hailed her as she headed toward her car after school let out on Tuesday. She waited while they caught up with her. "Congratulations on winning the ice climbing competition last weekend," a tall brunette, Ella, said.

"We heard your name on the radio," Maxine, forward on the varsity basketball team, said.

"Thank you," Sheri said. "I won in my category, not the overall competition,"

"Still, it's a big deal," the third girl, an outgoing blonde named Tressa, said. "Especially since you were competing with a lot of younger women."

Sheri suppressed a laugh. She supposed to these girls her thirty-two years must seem ancient. "I think of it as having had time to gain more experience than some of my competitors," she said. It was a diplomatic answer, though not very true, since most people who climbed competitively started the sport at a much younger age than she had.

"We just wanted to say how cool we think it is," Ella said.

The three girls hurried away and Sheri continued toward her car. She slowed as she neared the dusty blue Jeep, startled to see a woman in a long black down coat standing beside the vehicle.

The woman turned to face her, then pushed back the hood. Sheri relaxed a little and hurried forward.

"I'm sorry to bother you," Melissa Sheffield said. "Someone told me this was your car and I hoped if I waited here I could catch you."

"Of course." Despite her stylish coat and expensive haircut, Melissa looked beaten down, her eye makeup smudged, her nail polish chipped. "What did you want to see me about?"

"I wanted to talk to you about Dawn. Can we go somewhere for coffee?"

"Sure. Do you know the Bean and Bakery, on Main?"

Melissa nodded. "I think so. I can follow you there."

Sheri drove to the coffee shop and parked across the street. By the time she walked to the front door, Melissa was waiting. They ordered drinks, then found a table near the back. "I know you've been over all this before, but would you mind telling me about what you saw at the ice park on Friday?" Melissa asked when they were settled with their drinks. "I think it would help me to know how Dawn looked and acted. And how Carl looked and acted. It's so unlike him to do something like this that I'm having a hard time accepting it."

"Of course." Sheri sipped her coffee, gathering her thoughts. "I noticed Dawn first. She's such a pretty child." She didn't add that she was always drawn to girls who were the same age Claire would have been. "She actually ran into me—I think she just saw a woman's legs and mistook me for you. Of course she realized her mistake right away. She said she was looking for her mom. Then Carl came up and said he would take her to her mother if she calmed down. He picked her up and carried her off. She didn't resist."

"Did she seem afraid?" Melissa asked. "Or unhappy?"

"She was crying, but I took it as more frustration than fear or sadness. She was impatient with the man. She wanted her mother, but she wasn't afraid."

"Did he seem angry? Or threatening in any way?"

"No. I thought he was a typical parent, trying to get a child to do something she didn't really want to do. Frustrated, maybe a little impatient himself. But not angry. And when the girl went with him, she seemed to me to go willingly. She wasn't fighting him."

Melissa wrapped both hands around her coffee cup, but didn't drink. "Carl adores Dawn. He doesn't have children of his own and she's his only niece, so he spoils her terribly. And she's wild about him. I can't believe he set out to deliberately do this."

Sheri refrained from pointing out that she couldn't see how anyone could accidentally kidnap a child. And that message demanding a million dollars in ransom had certainly been no accident.

"Do you have any brothers or sisters?" Melissa asked.

"I have a brother," Sheri said.

"Then you know. Carl is only two years younger than me and we've always been close."

Sheri didn't know—she rarely spoke to her own brother, not out of any animosity, but they lived very different lives a thousand miles apart. She loved him, but she couldn't say she really knew him.

"When I heard they had found Carl's car, I was terrified," Melissa said. "I was sure there had been a horrible accident. You were there, weren't you? With Search and Rescue?"

"Yes," Sheri said.

"The sheriff's department said Carl deliberately pushed the car into that canyon, but how could that be? He must have lost control and managed to get Dawn and himself out before the car went over the edge."

"There was nothing in the car," Sheri said. "Not even paperwork in the glove box. I imagine Carl thought the car was too noticeable. The description of it was on all the bulletins the sheriff's department distributed."

"Carl loved that car," Melissa said. "He drove over to our house to show it off the day he leased it. He was so proud. Of course, Brandon made Carl feel bad, because he couldn't stop himself from telling Carl what a mistake it is to lease instead of buy. We argued about it afterward. Would it have killed my husband to allow Carl his moment in the sun?"

Sheri didn't have an answer for that. She didn't think Melissa even expected one. The woman had probably sought Sheri out as an alternative to waiting by the phone for word of her daughter. Sheri couldn't blame her for that.

"I think all the stress of being investigated for something that wasn't his fault made Carl snap and do all these things he would never ordinarily do," Melissa said. "I blame that Detective Lester. That man has been harassing Carl mercilessly for months now. I couldn't believe it when he showed up here in Eagle Mountain. The last thing we need is him here. He's just going to make things worse."

"My understanding is that Detective Lester is working with the local sheriff's department to find your daughter and return her safely to you."

"If everyone would just leave Carl alone, he would return Dawn on his own," Melissa said. "If Brandon would give him the money he asked for, Carl would have no reason to keep her."

Sheri stared. "If my brother kidnapped my daughter, I wouldn't be so forgiving," she said. "I would want law enforcement to do everything in their power to find her—and to punish the person who took her."

"Of course I want Dawn back," Melissa said. "But I'm sure Carl will take good care of her. She's probably having fun getting to spend time with her favorite uncle."

Sheri couldn't think how to respond to this, but she didn't have to. Melissa looked over Sheri's shoulder, then stood and gathered her coat and purse. "I have to go," she said. "Thank you for talking to me."

She hurried away. Sheri turned in time to see her slip past Erik, who hurried after her, but returned moments later, looking frustrated.

"I wanted to talk to her, but she brushed me off and drove away before I could stop her," he said as he slid into the chair Melissa had vacated. "What was she doing here with you?"

"I don't understand her," Sheri said. "She asked me to have coffee and said she wanted to talk about Dawn, but she spent most of the time defending her brother."

"Do you have time to talk about it?" he asked.

"Sure. I still have most of my coffee to finish."

"Let me get a drink and you can tell me all about your visit with Melissa."

A few minutes later he returned with a large cup and saucer and sat opposite her. "Melissa told her husband she was going to a movie and lunch with a friend," he said.

"Maybe she did," Sheri said. "She was waiting for me when school let out."

"What did she say?" he asked.

"She wanted to hear about my encounter with Carl and Dawn at the ice park on Friday," Sheri said. "And she asked about Carl's car in the canyon off Dixon Pass. She knew I was with Search and Rescue at the scene." She frowned. "Come to think of it, I wonder who told her that."

"Maybe she talked to another volunteer who mentioned you were there?" Erik shrugged.

"Maybe. She had plenty to say about you, too."

"Oh?" He lifted one eyebrow in question.

"She thinks your harassment—her word—of her brother has driven him over the edge. That and her husband's refusal to give Carl more money have led to him doing uncharacteristic things like kidnapping his niece and wrecking a car she says he loved."

"So her daughter and a car are in the same category?" Erik asked.

"I don't think she meant that, but she isn't as angry with her brother as I would be in her shoes. She says he was accused in Denver of something that wasn't his fault and she seems to think if her husband would just hand over the ransom money Carl has asked for, Carl would return Dawn and everything would be fine. She even said Dawn is probably having fun with her favorite uncle."

"Do you think Melissa could be helping her brother to extort money from Brandon?" Erik asked.

"No!" Sheri shook her head. "Granted, she has a skewed view of her brother's role in this, but she seemed genuinely worried about her daughter and wants her safely returned. Even that remark about Dawn having fun with her uncle sounded more to me like someone trying to reassure herself. And when I saw Dawn, she was begging to go back to her mother. She wants to be with her. From the first, their relationship struck me as close. I can't believe any mother would do something like that."

"You're probably right." He took a long drink of coffee. "I only asked because it looks as if someone is helping Carl. Someone gave him a ride after he pushed his car off the road—someone who isn't talking. And that same person, probably, took him to a group of fishing cabins in the mountains, where he and Dawn spent the night. They left the next morning and all indications are that someone gave them a ride then, too."

"So they're still nearby." Sheri leaned across the table toward him. "How is Dawn? Is she okay?"

"The woman who owns the cabins says she looked fine. She only saw her briefly, but nothing about the interaction between the man, who called himself Adam Smith, and the little girl, whom he called Dee, struck her as odd. I think Melissa is right when she says the two of them get along and Dawn trusts him."

"What about her theory that the stress of his predicament drove Carl to act out of character?" Sheri asked. "Does that kind of thing really happen?"

"I don't know if I agree that it's out of character. Carl has always come across to me as spoiled, vain and selfish. Also manipulative. I think he's the type who would justify almost any behavior to get what he thinks he deserves. That might include 'borrowing' his niece to use as leverage to get her rich dad to pay up. He's used to Melissa doing whatever he wants and I think it's making him angry that she can't persuade Brandon to go along with his requests."

"As much as Melissa loves her brother, I can't believe she'd be any part of this," Sheri said. "I think if Melissa could get her daughter back right now, she'd jump at the chance. What mother wouldn't?"

"You think every mother is good because you were so good." Erik's voice was quiet, but his words hit her with force. "I'm sorry I never told you that before," he added.

She looked away. She hadn't been good enough to save Claire from running into traffic. She hadn't watched her closely enough, or kept hold of her hand, or impressed on her how important it was to watch for cars.

No. She pushed the thoughts away. She wasn't going to think about those things and risk breaking down, the way she had Saturday night. She shoved back her chair. "I'd better go," she said. "I have a Search and Rescue meeting tonight."

"Thanks for telling me about Melissa. She may not like having me around, but I'm going to keep looking for Dawn, and for Carl."

"She doesn't know how lucky she is to have you on her side." She left, before she said too much. For so many years, thinking about Erik had been too painful. He had not been there for her when she needed him most. Now she saw him in a new light, more like the man she had been so attracted to from their very first meeting over a decade ago.

Maybe her problem was she didn't know how to love any other man. And falling for Erik a second time was out of the question. They had proved how unsuited they were for each other deep down. And relationships weren't like tricky climbing routes. You couldn't keep trying the same route over and over and expect to get better results.

Love was more like a dangerous rescue. You got one chance to do things right. If you failed, all you could do was mourn and try to clean up the mess.

Chapter Seven

Sheri was staring down at a stack of essays she needed to grade on Wednesday evening when she received a text from emergency dispatch that a family was missing in the mountains. The lethargy she had been fighting since late afternoon vanished in the familiar adrenaline rush of being needed for a rescue. She changed into outdoor gear, stuffed food and water into her pack and headed for Search and Rescue headquarters, where a dozen other volunteers milled about. Tony whistled to quiet the chatter and filled them in on the details.

"We've got a local couple, Chet and Sarah Cargill, thirty-eight and thirty-four, and their three children—Carter, ten, Simon, eight, and Opal, four. They headed out about ten this morning to snowshoe in the Alexander Basin area. There are some heavily used trails in that area and their car is reportedly still parked at the trailhead. They were supposed to meet up with their best friends and neighbors at six this evening for dinner, but they didn't show. They're not answering their phones and they aren't at home. The neighbors drove up to the trailhead, saw the car, looked around a little, but it was already getting dark and starting to snow harder, so they called for help."

"Do we know which trail they intended to hike?" Ted asked.

"No. Though the neighbors didn't think they'd try anything too difficult with three children."

"It's been snowing all afternoon," Austen said. "There won't be any tracks to follow."

"It could have filled in the trails," someone else said. "Maybe they got lost."

"There are three trails from that trailhead," Carrie said. "We'll caravan up to the trailhead, then set out in groups of three—one for each trail, plus a group on standby at the trailhead to coordinate and provide more assistance when the family is located."

"Why do we have to caravan?" Austen asked. "Why don't we take the Beast?"

The Beast was their nickname for the modified Jeep they used as a Search and Rescue vehicle. Though ten years old and much-battered, it was better equipped than any personal vehicle for navigating rough terrain and holding all their gear.

"The Beast is out of commission," Carrie said. "I got in to warm it up when I first got here tonight and it won't start."

"Maybe the battery's dead," someone said.

"Did you check the terminals?" someone else asked.

"We don't have time for that," Carrie said. "We need to get going. Make sure you all have all the gear you'll need." She ran through the list of supplies they should all have in their packs, then assigned volunteers to each group.

Sheri was paired with Ted and Austen, a trainee who had only recently joined Search and Rescue. "I'll drive," Sheri volunteered, and the three headed for her Jeep.

They stowed gear in the back and Ted slid into the passenger seat and Austen folded his tall frame into the back seat.

"Who takes kids that young out in this weather?" Austen asked as Sheri pulled onto the highway behind Danny Irwin's truck. "And why weren't they in school?"

"Lots of kids around here are used to being outdoors doing stuff in all kinds of weather," Ted said. "And I think the Cargills homeschool. It sounds like they let their friends know where they were going, which was the first smart step."

"Do you know the family?" Sheri asked.

"I've just seen them around, the way you do people in a small town."

Sheri nodded. Though she had only lived in Eagle Mountain two years, she knew a surprising number of people, from teaching, from her rescue work, and simply because she ran into the same faces over and over again, and eventually learned names and little things about all the people around her.

"Let's hope this group doesn't end up like that lost skier we searched for a couple weeks ago," Austen said.

Sheri shuddered. A cross-country skier had been murdered near one of the ski huts. "That murderer has been caught," she said. "I imagine these people got lost when the heavy snow obscured the trail. Hopefully, they're staying put and waiting for help."

"Almost nobody does that," Ted said. "People are always convinced it will be quicker to walk out on their own, even if they aren't sure of the way. They think if they keep walking, eventually they'll see something familiar and everything will be okay."

"It would be hard to sit and wait, not knowing if help was on its way or not," Sheri said.

"I hope for all our sakes we find them soon," Ted said. "Kids shouldn't have to be out on a night like this."

Sheri glanced at the temperature readout on her dash—sixteen degrees Fahrenheit. Even inside the car with the heater running she felt chilled. She didn't want to think what it must be like stuck outside with no shelter.

She followed the line of cars out a county road to the ski trails, about five miles from town. A brown-and-white forest service sign noted these were the Alexander Basin trails. They were popular with hikers in the summer, but saw almost as much use from skiers and snowshoers in the winter.

"Ted, take your group down Goshawk," Tony said, indicating a trail that branched off to the left. "Carrie's group will head down Sharp Shin and Danny's group will take Red-tail Trail. Keep an eye out for any place someone might have wandered off the trail—a downed tree that caused them to divert, a missing marker on a tree, anything like that—and make note to check it out if we don't find them near the main trails."

They set out, walking several lengths apart. Sheri widened the beam of her headlamp and focused on the side of the trail, searching for broken limbs, cloth caught on a branch, a disturbance in the snow or any other sign that someone might have ventured off trail. From time to time she checked for the silver diamond-shaped markers tacked to the trees that denoted the trail. The Cargills should have been able to follow those markers even if snow had obscured the trail.

"Chet! Sarah! Carter!" Ted cupped his hands to his

mouth and shouted the names of the three oldest members of the missing party, and they all strained their ears, listening for a reply. Then they moved on, stopping to call and listen every couple of hundred yards. They moved at a steady pace, but slow enough to carefully examine their surroundings. The most likely reason the Cargills hadn't returned to their car was that they were lost. At some point, they had wandered off the trail, lost sight of those silver diamonds and been unable to find their way back. Figuring out where they had left the trail was the surest way of finding them safe. Traveling with three children would have slowed them down, making them less likely to have wandered very many miles from the trailhead.

"Chet! Sarah! Carter!" Ted's voice was raspy now.

"Let Austen take over calling," Sheri said. She could do it, but men's deeper voices tended to carry further.

"I'm fine," Ted said, and trudged forward once more. Sheri frowned at his back. At sixty, Ted was the oldest active volunteer, and sensitive to anything he took as criticism of his abilities. He was in great shape for his age, but a sixty-year-old was never going to be as physically strong as a thirty-year-old with the same conditioning. That didn't mean he wasn't an asset to the group—his experience alone, with over thirty years in search and rescue, was invaluable. If only he wouldn't be so stubborn about yielding to others who were a little better equipped for certain activities.

The snow had stopped, but wind had picked up, sending the tops of spruce and fir overhead swaying and hitting them with icy force in any clearing. Austen swore and buried his chin farther into his neck gaiter. "We're all going to get frostbite," he complained.

Sheri ignored him. She was cold, too, of course. But if you were going to do this kind of work, you had to accept that you were going to spend much of the time in the cold, the dark, the wind or the wet. Your muscles were going to protest from overuse, you were going to stay up twenty-four hours straight sometimes and after a bad rescue you might not sleep well for months, or might require professional help to deal with some of the things you had seen. For the people who stuck with it, the benefits of rescue work outweighed the negatives. She didn't think that made people like her better than others, only different, and uniquely equipped for this necessary job.

Ted came to a halt and she and Austen stopped behind him. He aimed his light at the side of the trail and pointed. At first, Sheri didn't see anything. Then she recognized a splash of dull blue in the shadows. Ted bent and retrieved what turned out to be a child's mitten. A very small child. Claire had had a pair like that the winter before she died.

"That's not good," Sheri said, thinking of the four-year-old girl who might be risking frostbite. She hoped Mom had brought extra mittens or socks or anything to protect those tiny fingers.

"What were those parents thinking?" Austen asked.

She thought she had grown used to Austen's judgmental nature by now, but this question hit her wrong. "They were thinking they would enjoy a fun family outing in the healthy outdoors," she said. "They're probably more terrified now than the children."

Ted stuffed the mitten in the pocket of his parka. "Let's go," he said. "At least now we know we're headed in the right direction."

When they weren't discussing the search or calling for the Cargills, the silence of the mountains closed around them. Even their steps were muffled by the soft snow. Two saw-whet owls, with calls more like a crying child than a whining saw, sent a chill up Sheri's spine as the birds carried on a late-night conversation.

The radio crackled with messages from the other searchers—no one had found anything so far. Ted reported on the finding of the mitten and Tony ordered the others to move toward the Goshawk Trail, fanning out to take in the territory in between, where the Cargills might have wandered.

"Let's stop and get some water and something to eat," Ted said. He slipped off his pack and dug out a water bottle. "Five minutes."

Sheri drained half of one bottle, then tore the wrapper from a protein bar. The bar was almost frozen and hard to chew, but she needed the fuel after an hour of trudging mostly uphill through the snow. She leaned against a tree trunk and closed her eyes, and focused on her breath. A local woman had given a search and rescue training workshop on using meditation to stay calm and focused in a crisis and Sheri tried to use the techniques when she remembered. Deep breath in…hold for the count of eight. Exhale to the count of eight…

She opened her eyes. "I smell smoke," she said.

Austen and Ted looked at her. Austen pointed his nose up and sniffed, like a beagle trying to catch a scent on a breeze. "I don't smell anything," he said.

"Me, neither," Ted said. "Which direction is it coming from?"

She inhaled again, but the scent was gone. "The wind's changed directions," she said. "I don't smell it anymore." She stuffed the protein bar wrapper back into her pack, then cupped her hands to her mouth. "Chet! Sarah! Carter!"

A faint call made the hair at the back of her neck stand on end. "Chet! Sarah! Carter!" she shouted, trying to make her voice even louder. Then she held her breath. The faint cry came again. "Do you hear that?" she asked.

Austen frowned. "I think it's just another saw-whet."

The cry came again. To Sheri it sounded like *Help!* "That's not an owl," she said.

"No, it isn't." Ted slid back into his pack. "Chet! Sarah! Carter!" he shouted, his voice booming.

"Help!"

"This way!" Sheri said, and started moving to the right. The others fell in behind her, Ted periodically shouting. The answer sounded louder. A woman's voice, or maybe a child's. High-pitched and full of fear and hope.

Sheri almost collided with the boy when he came barreling toward them. He had big dark eyes in a pale face, and wore a red parka and black ski suit. "Have you come to help us?" he asked, staring up at them.

"Yes, we have," Sheri said. "We're with Eagle Mountain Search and Rescue."

"Do you have a doctor with you?" he asked.

"Are you Carter?" Ted asked. "We have people who can help. Where is the rest of your family?"

"This way!" He didn't wait for a response, but turned and took off running. They stumbled after him, racing to keep up.

Sheri smelled smoke again, then spotted the fire— a small blaze almost obscured by a circle of stacked rocks. A woman, wrapped in a foil blanket, sat in front of the fire. Her husband lay sprawled beside her, covered with a second blanket. At first, Sheri didn't see the other two children, then they stuck their heads out from beneath their mother's blanket, like chicks peeking from beneath a hen. "Mom, I found help!" Carter shouted as he jogged up to the fire.

The woman looked past him to the three rescuers, their bright jackets identifying them as SAR. "Thank God!" she said, then burst into tears.

Sheri knelt beside her while Ted went to see to the man. "You're Sarah, right?" Sheri said. She slipped off her pack and dug into the bottom for more protein bars. Chocolate. "You all must be hungry," she said, and handed the bars out to Sarah and all three children, who immediately ripped into them. But Sarah merely held hers. She sniffed and managed a wobbly smile. "I've been terrified," she whispered.

"I know," Sheri said.

"Not for myself," Sarah continued. "But for Chet and the children."

"I know." Sheri looked across the fire to the man on the ground. "What happened?"

"Dad fell and broke his leg," Carter moved in to sit beside his mother. She put her arm around him.

"It's a closed fracture," Ted said. "Probably of the tibia."

"Hurts like the devil," Chet Cargill said.

"We're going to have a paramedic here soon to give you something for the pain and get you stabilized, then we'll get you all out of here," Ted said.

"What happened?" Austen asked as he dug in his

pack and began removing chemical heat packs and more food and water.

"It was snowing hard and we got off the trail somehow," Sarah said. "We were trying to find our way back when Chet just went down and screamed."

"I think he stepped in a hole or something," Carter said. "I heard a snap and thought it was his snowshoe. The snowshoe was wedged under this fallen tree and Dad was just lying there, all white and moaning."

"I didn't know what to do," Sarah said. "I tried to help him, but I was only hurting him worse. But I couldn't just leave him lying there."

"It looks to me like you did an excellent job," Sheri said. "You found a sheltered place to wait, you made camp and you had emergency supplies with you."

Sarah nodded. "We had fire starters and these emergency blankets and a little food and water. The children helped me drag Chet to this flat ground. I know we hurt him, and I think he may have passed out after a while."

"I built the fire," Carter said. "My dad taught me how. You have to dig a pit in the snow and line it with rocks to keep the wind from blowing it out. Plus, the rocks get warm and give off heat."

"You did a great job," Sheri said.

"How did you ever find us?" Sarah asked.

"I smelled the smoke from your fire," Sheri said. "Then we heard you answering our calls."

"How long have you been waiting?" Austen asked as he wrapped another blanket around Carter.

"Chet fell about one o'clock," Sarah said. "We had finished lunch and were heading back, except we were lost."

It was after ten now. The poor woman had been sitting here for nine hours. "We saw what looked like chimney smoke up on that ridge," she said. "I thought about trying to get to it, to ask whoever was there to help, but I couldn't figure out how to get there, and I couldn't leave Chet."

"You did the right thing, staying put," Ted said.

"Which direction was the smoke?" Sheri asked.

"Straight out that way." Sarah pointed to the south. "Higher in elevation than this. It stopped snowing for a while and I could see the smoke rising above the trees."

"Ted, do you know of any cabins up there?" Sheri asked. He had lived in the area most of his life.

"No homes," Ted says. "There's a summer camp. Some church group. But it's shut tight this time of year, only open in the summer."

Sheri stared to the south, but it was much too dark to see anything now.

"Ted! Sheri! Austen!" came a shout in the distance.

"Over here!" Ted stood and began signaling with his light. A few moments later six people marched into the clearing.

Simon, who had crawled from beneath the blanket to stand beside Carter, stared, wide-eyed. "It's like the army!" he said.

Things happened quickly then. Danny, a paramedic, assessed Chet and administered pain medication, then fit his leg in an inflatable splint. They transferred him to a litter. "We'll carry you to the trail, then tow you along, like a sled," Danny explained to an already-groggy Chet. "The trail's pretty smooth, so it should be an easier ride for you."

A volunteer put out the fire while others assisted Sarah and the children. Sarah was exhausted, so one volunteer walked with her, another boosted Simon onto his back, and Sheri carried the four-year-old, Opal. Carter insisted on walking by himself, marching along behind the litter like a little soldier.

Sheri fixed a sling for Opal to ride in, facing Sheri's body. "Put your arms around my neck and your head on my shoulder," she encouraged. "I'm going to zip you up in my parka and we'll both be warm and cozy." It was a tight fit, but she managed, and by the time they reached the trail, the little girl was asleep, her breathing deep and even.

The weight of this child in her arms was such a familiar, visceral sensation Sheri felt detached from herself, floating along the trail in a warm cloud of pheromones. She had had similar feelings in the early months after Claire's birth, during early morning feedings when she would sit in a darkened room and rock her nursing baby, both of them half-asleep and swamped with love.

They moved swiftly once they hit the trail, everyone wanting to reach warmth and safety, and medical care for the family, as soon as possible. A golden glow ahead alerted them they were near the parking area. They emerged into the flood of portable spotlights, a waiting ambulance and several sheriff's department cars.

Sheri relinquished a sleeping Opal back to her mother and others swooped in to tend to the family. Paramedics examined Sarah and her children and announced they had weathered their ordeal well, and prepared Chet for transport. Deputy Jamie Douglas offered to drive the family to the hospital and they set out in the Cargills' van. After a short meeting with Tony, the others agreed to meet up the next day at SAR headquarters and dispersed to make their way home.

"Sheri, wait up!"

She had just pulled out the keys to her Jeep when Erik jogged toward her. Her heart beat faster at the sight of him, dressed in jeans and parka, hair mussed by the wind. How many times after a long call had she wished someone was waiting for her—and here he was. "I was at the sheriff's department, working, when the call came in," he said. "I had a hunch you'd be here."

"I can't believe you came all the way up here," she said. "Especially on a night like this."

"I wanted to make sure you were okay." He searched her face. "You must be exhausted."

"I should be, but I'm too wired to settle down. It's such a rush when things turn out well."

"Do you want to come to my place and talk about it?"

"Yes." She answered without thinking, but didn't wish the word back. Sitting with him somewhere warm, talking to him—that was exactly what she wanted.

Chapter Eight

Erik drove ahead of Sheri to the Airbnb he was renting on a street of older homes three blocks from the sheriff's department. He had been half-afraid she would object to him showing up at the scene of the rescue, or that she would tell him the last thing she wanted to do tonight was spend more time with him. He no longer felt the animosity that had colored every interaction in the last months before their divorce, but he hadn't been as sure about her.

Tonight, however, she had looked at him with a softness in her expression that he hadn't seen since before Claire's death. That look had made him want things he probably shouldn't want, but he wasn't going to pass up the chance to see where this new détente between them led.

He parked in the driveway of the Victorian cottage and waited by the front steps for her to pull in behind him. "This is cute," she said, admiring what was visible of the house in the porch light.

"The owners are in the process of renovating it, so they gave me a good deal on the rental, as long as I need it," he said. "Fortunately, all the construction at this point is outside." He led the way inside, flicking on lights as he went. The furniture was simple and classic, which suited him. "Would you like some wine?" he asked. "Or tea?"

"Tea would be great," she said. She walked around the room, studying the pictures on the wall and the books in the bookcase—none of which belonged to him.

He let her wander and went into the kitchen and put on water for tea. After a moment, she followed him into the room. "That family tonight was so amazing," she said. "You never know how these kinds of calls are going to turn out—too often it's not good. But the Cargills did everything right. They let someone know where they were going to be and when they should be back. They carried emergency supplies with them. They built a fire and stayed put, waiting for help. And those children! So calm and smart. The oldest boy told me how he built the fire. And that little girl was so precious."

He heard the nervous energy behind her words. She had always been like this when she was excited or agitated—unable to sit down and talking a mile a minute. "Are you hungry?" he asked. "I don't have much but I could make a sandwich. Or toast?"

"Do you have jam? Toast with butter and jam sounds so…comforting."

He took the bread from the cabinet. "The butter and jam are in the refrigerator."

She opened the refrigerator and located the butter and a jar of strawberry jam. "Oh my gosh!" she exclaimed, then laughed and pulled out an open box of Twinkies. "I can't believe you still eat these."

He flushed. When they were newlyweds, she had teased him about his affection for what was, to her, a snack food for children and teenagers. He took the box from her and shoved it back into the refrigerator. "Yeah, well, everyone has their guilty pleasures."

"You know you don't have to refrigerate them," she said. "They never go stale."

"I like them cold. They taste better that way."

"I'll take your word for it."

While he prepared the tea, she made toast. It was nice, working side by side like this. The way they had in the early days. How much of this closeness he felt to her right now was nostalgia and how much was attraction to the woman she had become since they'd been apart?

"Let's eat in the living room," he said when the tea was poured. "I'll light the gas fireplace."

They settled next to each other on the sofa, a tray with the tea and toast on the coffee table between them. "I never did hear exactly what happened to the family you were looking for," he said. "Were they lost?"

She nodded. "They got off the trail in the heavy snow and then the dad broke his leg, so they were stuck."

"How did he break his leg?"

"It was a freak accident. His snowshoe caught on something, he fell over sideways and it must have twisted or something. Anyway, it broke. He must have been miserable, but his wife and kids did the best they could to make him comfortable. Fortunately, he should be fine."

"That's good. So many things can go wrong in a situation like that."

She sipped her tea and her face took on a dreamy look. "I carried the little girl, Opal, all the way back. She snuggled right against me and went to sleep. Holding her felt so familiar—almost like holding Claire again." She blinked rapidly and looked away. "I guess that's silly."

"It's not silly. I'm even a little envious."

Her eyes met his. "Do you think about her?" she asked.

"All the time. Every time I see a man with a child that age. Every time I'm driving near a school or where children are playing. I grip the steering wheel, white-knuckled, and slow down to the point I've had other drivers honk their horns and curse me out."

"I could never tell what you were feeling back then. I couldn't keep my emotions in check but you were so...shut down."

"People cope in different ways," he said. Her torrent of emotions had frightened him at times. And they had angered him, as if she was saying she was the only one their daughter's death had hurt—the only one who experienced true grief. "For me, I think I hurt so badly I was afraid to let the grief out—afraid it would destroy me."

She placed her hand over his. "I'm sorry I didn't see that," she said. "I should have."

"It was a hard time for both of us," he said. "We both made mistakes."

She laced her fingers with his, her touch both familiar and new. She had calluses she hadn't had before, and the nails she had once kept painted were short and bare. He raised her hand closer to study it. "Your hands are different," he said. "Stronger."

"I'm stronger now," she said. "Physically, and I think emotionally too." She shifted, bringing them closer together. "You're different, too," she said. "More approachable."

"I thought you were going to say *vulnerable*."

"Would you think that was an insult?"

"Not now. But there was a time I would have."

"Did therapy change that?" she asked.

"Therapy. Maturity." He raised her hand to his lips and kissed her knuckles, not thinking about the gesture, just wanting the taste of her, the heat of her against his lips. "I lost everything that mattered to me—not just Claire, but you, too. That made me see how foolish pride and my desire to be one of those stiff-upper-lip guys who were never affected by anything had been."

"Yes," she said. "I know what you mean. When I had to start over with nothing, I realized how little was really worth holding on to. Not things or reputation or caring what other people thought of me. I had to think hard about what I really wanted."

"Tell me what you want," he said.

She turned to him. "Right now, I want you," she said, her voice low and husky.

"I never stopped wanting you," he said, and kissed her.

THAT KISS WAS like an undertow, pulling her off her feet and sweeping her away. Erik reached to drag her closer as she slid toward him, their bodies pressed together, their mouths communicating without words, the messages both familiar and brand-new. She climbed into his lap, needing to be closer still. His hands caressed her, kindling the excitement of long abstinence.

She slid her hands beneath his sweater, thrilling at the feel of his still-hard abdomen. She shoved the fabric up farther and kissed her way across his chest. He shifted beneath her, the hard ridge of his erection pressed against her crotch. In answer, she reached between them and lowered his zipper.

His hand around her wrist stilled her. "Why don't we go into the bedroom?" he asked.

She was going to protest they could stay here on the sofa—why waste time? But as she shifted position her foot hit the coffee table, almost upending her tea mug. "That's a good idea," she said.

She slid off him and he stood, then hauled her to her feet alongside him. Instead of leading her to the bedroom, he pulled her close once more, and pressed his mouth to hers in a lingering kiss. For the second time that evening, she felt lifted out of her body, floating on a surge of warm emotion and a memory of past happiness.

But this time that was accompanied by an eagerness for the future. She and Erik had both confessed they weren't the same people they had been three years ago, when they had last made love. How would that change their approach to sex? How wonderful that they had a chance to find out.

At last he raised his head, looking as dazed as she felt. He didn't say anything, merely took her hand and tugged her out of the room.

His bedroom was dark and a little chilly. He moved around the bed, switching on lamps, then turned back the covers. "Is it too cold in here?" he asked.

"I think we'll find a way to warm up," she said, then pulled her fleece top over her head.

He quickly moved in to help her with the remaining layers—silk long underwear, fitted tank, panties and socks. When she was naked and shivering, she slid under the covers and sat, hugging her knees to her chest, to watch him undress.

He was a gorgeous man. All lean muscle and grace. She found herself searching his body for all the things she remembered—the small scar on his abdomen from surgery to remove his appendix when he was seventeen. The mole on the left side of his upper back.

Then her eyes locked to something new—a small tattoo of a butterfly above his left hip bone. She stared. The symbol seemed so out of place. Had some girl-friend persuaded him to get it? Someone he had loved after her?

He noticed her staring, and looked down at the butterfly. "It's in memory of Claire," he said. "I had it done a few months after we split up. She was so beautiful, and with us for such a short time."

Something inside her broke at that, and the emotion that followed wasn't grief, but love. She held up her arms, and he came to her. For a long moment, they held each other, together in grief in a way they had never been in the early days after Claire's passing.

Then he began to kiss her again, sexy, coaxing ca-resses, his lips against her temple, her throat, the curve of her breast. Desire, more potent than ever, surged back, and she arched against him, wanting him so badly.

He lay down and pulled her down with him. She closed her eyes, ready to lose herself in him, but a nag-ging thought made her look at him again. "Wait," she said. "What about protection?" Her face heated, and her embarrassment embarrassed her. Maybe it was the awkwardness of having this discussion with *him*. "Do you have anything?"

"Just a minute."

He got up and went into the bathroom, and came back a few moments later with a condom in a foil packet.

"When the owners of this place said it came fully furnished, they weren't kidding," he said. "I laughed when I first saw the box in the medicine cabinet, but now I'm very grateful."

He unwrapped the condom and slid it on, then she pulled him to her—on top of her. She wrapped her legs around his hips and welcomed him into her, stretched and filled and complete in a way she hadn't been for too long.

They quickly found a rhythm that, while familiar, felt new. They had to discover each other again. Their bodies had changed, and they had changed—but the delight they took in each other hadn't changed. "You are so gorgeous," he said as he stroked the side of her breast, then flicked his thumb across her erect nipple. "So perfect."

Not perfect, but right now she felt perfect for him. She cupped his buttocks and urged him deeper, appreciating the dazed joy on his face, until she fell into a trance of her own, all her focus on the tension building within her, the way his hands and mouth moving over her and his erection moving in her made her feel.

Her climax shattered her, light and heat shuddering through her, so overwhelming that when at last she came back to herself, her face was wet with tears. Then he cried out with his own release and she held him as he tensed, then relaxed. He opened his eyes and smiled down on her, then leaned down to kiss her, blotting the tears with his lips, and saying nothing, because what words could ever say what they felt?

After a while he withdrew, removed the condom and disposed of it, then lay beside her once more and pulled her close. She curled into him, her head resting in the hollow of his shoulder, breathing in the scent of him, utterly relaxed and happier than she could remember being.

She thought he had fallen asleep, then he said, "I might owe Carl Westover a debt of thanks when this is over. Though I'll never let him know."

"Does he know you're investigating him?" she asked.

"He knows. I questioned him several times when he was in custody. I have no idea if he knows I'm involved in this case, though."

She rose up on one elbow and looked at him. "Can I see your tattoo again?"

In answer, he pulled back the covers and she slid down for a closer look at the butterfly above his hip bone. Inked in purple, blue and black, it was about two inches across, with the name "Claire" worked in script along one wing. "I imagine that draws some questions from women," she said.

"I wouldn't know. You're the first woman to see it."

He must have read the question in her eyes, even if she couldn't say it. "There hasn't been anyone since you," he said. "I messed things up so badly with you, I wasn't ready to risk that again."

She lay down again, holding him tightly. She didn't want to let go of this moment, didn't want to let go of him, even while a voice in the back of her mind whispered that she would surely have to.

ERIK WOKE AT six the next morning to the unfamiliar, but not unwelcome, sensation of a woman in bed beside him. He carefully rolled over, not wanting to disturb Sheri, and watched her sleep, an eager voyeur wanting to memorize everything about her, from the way a lock of hair curled around her ear to the frown line etched between her eyes even in sleep. That line hadn't been there before and he wished he had the ability to take it away.

She opened her eyes and looked up at him. "Good morning," she said.

"Good morning." He kissed the tip of her nose and she laughed and batted him away. "I haven't even brushed my teeth." He had known she would say that. It was what she always said. The thought sent a thrill of satisfaction through him.

"What time is it?" she asked, and rolled over to look at the bedside clock.

"What time do you have to be at the school?" he asked.

"Eight. I'll need to go home and change clothes."

"We have a little time." He slid down and began kissing his way along her shoulder.

She pushed him away. "I'll be right back."

"There's an extra toothbrush in the medicine cabinet," he called after her.

She returned a few moments later, breath minty fresh, and it was his turn to freshen up before he once more slid under the sheets. He would have liked to take his time, reacquainting himself with every inch of her body, but they were both on a schedule this morning, since he had a meeting at the sheriff's department at eight thirty.

She had her own ideas about how things should progress, and soon had him on his back, helpless as she kissed her way down his body, her mouth quickly bringing him to the brink, trembling with need. He clutched her shoulder in a warning that things were progressing beyond his control and she smiled up at him, then plucked the condom he'd retrieved from the bathroom from his hand, opened the package and rolled it on with an agonizing slowness that had him clenching his muscles, holding back.

Then she slid up and impaled herself on him, stealing his breath and his ability to think as she rode him. She grasped his hand and brought it down to her center. He was a man who could take a hint, and soon had her panting with need as well. They didn't waste time after that, driving toward their climaxes that, while not simultaneous, were definitely mutually satisfying.

"Awake now?" he asked, knowing he probably sounded a little smug.

"Not for long, if we keep lying here like this."

"Just a little longer." He tightened his arm around her shoulder. He wanted to savor the feel of her, naked and warm, against him.

She fell silent, the kind of silence that had weight to it. She was thinking, and not necessarily of good things. "What is it?" he asked, dreading the answer, but still wanting to know what was going on in her head. Not asking that question enough had been one of the things that had led to them growing apart before.

"Last night, you didn't ask if I've had lovers since we divorced," she said.

"It's none of my business." It didn't matter to him. He had never seen the value in worrying about the past.

"Well, I haven't." She traced circular patterns across his chest with the tip of one finger. "I guess, like you, I wasn't ready to risk it."

This from a woman who routinely risked her life to climb cliffs or ice, or to rescue strangers. But he knew what she meant—emotional jeopardy felt far more dangerous. Broken bones could heal; a broken spirit didn't always recover.

He kissed her forehead and glanced at the clock. Almost seven already. "I'll make coffee," he said. "Then you'd better go."

He was dressed and pouring the coffee when she joined him in the kitchen, all traces of last night's makeup removed, most of the wrinkles smoothed from last night's clothes. She had taken a quick shower, the ends of her hair wet and her skin smelling of his bath gel. He handed her a mug—cream and sugar, the way she had always taken it before. She sipped and smiled, but made no comment about his memory.

"Will you have dinner with me tonight?" he asked. "A real dinner, not just toast and tea."

"As long as I don't get a rescue call, yes. I'd like that."

"Same here. As long as Carl doesn't decide to make a move and we have to go after him."

She frowned. Thinking again. "What is it?" he asked.

She shook her head. "It's probably nothing, but last night, when we found the Cargills, Sarah said something that was a little odd."

"Oh?" he prompted.

"She said while they were waiting for someone to find them, they spotted smoke up on the ridge above them—like smoke from a chimney. She thought about trying to get up there, but she couldn't see how to do it, and she didn't want to leave her husband. Ted, one of the other volunteers, who's lived in the area for decades, said no one lives up there. There's just a summer camp, and it's closed this time of year."

"It's not that far from the fishing camp where Carl

and Dawn stayed two nights ago," he said. "It might be worth checking out."

She set aside her coffee mug. "I want to come with you."

"You have to teach."

"I can call in a sub. I do that sometimes, after a rescue like last night. The school understands."

"I'll need to talk to the sheriff. This is his jurisdiction. I'm here as an adviser."

She pressed her lips together, but didn't argue. "I'll let you know," he said. "Can I call you at school?"

"Text me," she said. "I'll answer on my break." She put a hand on his arm. "I'm not just being nosy. I really want to help Dawn."

"I know." Having her with him might be good, especially if Dawn was there. Children often responded better to women, and Sheri had always been especially good with children.

They kissed goodbye and he got ready for the day. He was tired, but more relaxed than he had been in recent memory. Good sex would do that. So would settling unfinished business, which was what last night and this morning had felt like, as if he had been waiting all this time for the next chapter in his story with Sheri. He had no idea how things would turn out. He didn't dare think that far ahead. But they were moving forward again, and that was a gift he had never expected to receive.

The sheriff's department was already abuzz with activity when he arrived. "The meeting you're here for has been canceled, Detective Lester," Adelaide informed him as he passed her desk.

"What's going on?" Erik asked. Two deputies rushed past him and out the door.

"Two women robbed a bank in Junction and are headed this way," Adelaide said. "Junction police are in pursuit and have asked for our assistance. We're setting up roadblocks on all the routes into town."

Erik continued down the hall to the sheriff's office. Travis was shrugging into his jacket when Erik stopped in the doorway. "Did Adelaide tell you what's going on?" Travis asked.

"Yes. I just need to run one thing by you before you leave."

"Walk and talk," Travis said, and led the way out of the office.

Erik walked with him toward the back lot, where Travis's SUV was parked, and relayed Sheri's story about the possible smoke from the closed summer camp. "It's probably nothing, but I'd like to check it out," he concluded.

"I don't have a problem with that, as long as you don't approach anyone who's up there. Carl knows you, so even a glimpse of you might set him off, or cause him to flee."

"I won't approach," Erik promised. "I'll let you know if it's worth sending a team up there for a closer look. And I'm thinking about taking Sheri with me. If we do find the little girl, she would be good to have along."

The sheriff considered this a moment, then nodded. "All right."

He left and Erik returned to his Jeep to text Sheri. We're on. When are you free?

By the time he was back at his rental, he had her

answer. My substitute comes in at noon. I can meet
you then.

My place, as soon after noon as you can be there.

He hit Send and leaned back against the counter. He
didn't know if anything would come of this trip into
the mountains, but it felt good to be taking some kind
of action. It felt even better to be doing it with Sheri
by his side.

Chapter Nine

As Erik steered his Jeep up the winding mountain road, Sheri had a flashback to another trip they had made together. A year into their marriage, they had spent a weekend away at a cabin outside Estes Park. They had been like two kids running away from home, giddy with the chance to escape the pressures of jobs and every-day responsibilities. They had spent three days eating decadent meals, hiking new trails, soaking in the hot tub and making love.

Claire had been conceived on that trip, which only added to Sheri's fond memories of that place. Looking back, she could hardly believe she had ever been such a carefree, joyful person, blissfully unaware of the pain the future would bring.

"Do you remember that trip we took to that cabin outside of Estes Park?" Erik asked.

The question didn't even surprise her—for so many years he had done this, mentioning something that had popped into her head. "I was just thinking about that," she said.

"We should have done that more," he said. "Taken time off to get away."

"Would it have made a difference?"

"I don't know. Maybe."

They fell silent again, probably both thinking of all the mistakes they had made that could never be undone. Sheri didn't feel guilty, merely sad that things hadn't worked out differently.

"How far to the turnoff?" Erik interrupted her thoughts.

She checked the directions from Ted that she had written down. "You'll turn left on Forest Service Road 261A, twelve miles after your turn onto County Road 302."

He glanced at the odometer. "Another couple of miles, then."

She had called Ted this morning to get the directions, saying only that she and Erik wanted to take a drive up there. "Are you and that cop an item?" he'd asked.

"An item?" The old-fashioned term made her grimace. It made her think of gossip, or a notice in the paper.

"I saw the two of you last night," Ted said. "I thought there might be something between you."

There was a lot between her and Erik, but she couldn't begin to define what, exactly. "A lady never kisses and tells," she said.

Ted laughed. "Be careful up there," he said. "The road in probably isn't plowed."

Erik slowed for the turn onto the forest road. The narrow track had been plowed at some point, though not recently, and he shifted into four-wheel drive and steered carefully in the tracks made by other travelers. "It looks like this road gets a fair amount of traffic," he said.

"Ted told me people come up here to ski or run snowmobiles," she said. "The camp is five miles in. There's a sign for King's Kids."

Moments later, a rustic wooden sign jutting from a snowbank announced "King's Kids Youth Camp, next left."

Erik turned at the next left and came to a stop in front of a six-foot wall of snow. "I guess Ted was right when he said the road in wasn't plowed," she said.

He shut off the engine and unfastened his seat belt. "You wait here and I'll walk up and check things out."

"Oh, I'm going with you." She unclipped her own belt and pushed open her door. "The first rule of wilderness survival is 'don't separate.'"

"Sitting in a warm car is not exactly wilderness survival," he said. "I'll even leave you the keys."

"I'm coming with you." She pulled her pack from the back seat and shrugged into it.

He shook his head, but didn't argue, merely looked around, then led the way to a slight break in the snow, past where the plow had shoved most of the buildup from the road. He scrambled over a low wall of frozen slush and turned to give her a hand, but she was already over. Together they made their way through the trees, staying parallel to the main drive into the camp, which was covered in two feet of unpacked snow. Even in the trees, where the snow was less deep, walking was a slog, continually breaking through the icy crust and sinking knee-deep in drifts. "One thing for sure," she said. "If anyone else came this way, we'd be able to see it."

"Depends on when they were here," he said. "That snow yesterday laid down a good five or six inches."

"It annoys me that you are right so much of the time," she said.

"I've made my share of mistakes." The look he sent her made her shiver—but not in a bad way.

The drive made a sweeping left turn and the first building appeared—a large structure of logs painted the muted green she associated with the forest service and summer camps everywhere. She stopped and sniffed the air. "I don't smell any smoke."

"I don't see any signs of movement, or any footprints in the snow. Let's keep to the cover of the trees and get closer."

Carefully, they picked their way past what she assumed was the lodge or office, toward a cluster of smaller cabins. Still no smoke and no footprints. Erik stopped and pulled the hood of his parka over his head, and a neck gaiter over his mouth. With his sunglasses, this all but obscured his face. "Just in case Carl is here, I don't want him to get a good look at me," he said. "If he says anything, we're two hikers out exploring."

She followed his example and pulled up her hood and gaiter as well. He set out across the clearing and she followed, heart pounding. There probably wasn't anyone here to see them, but she couldn't shake the idea that a kidnapper might be watching them, not pleased to see them.

They approached the first cabin, a structure about ten feet square, the windows covered with padlocked wooden shutters, another padlock on the front door. Snow was piled to the top of the porch railings and obscured the steps. They circled the cabin, but all looked undisturbed.

There were ten cabins in total, identical right down to the snow piled on the front porches. "Sarah Cargill must have been mistaken about the smoke," Sheri said as they headed around the side of the last cabin. "I'm sorry I dragged you out here for nothing."

Erik stopped so abruptly she collided with him. "Someone has been here," he said, his voice low. He reached into his parka and drew out a pistol.

She stared at the weapon, then wrenched her gaze to the cabin. It looked like all the others. "What are you seeing that I don't?" she asked.

"Look at the snow beneath that back window," he said. "Someone has tried to make it look like the rest of the area, but it's too neat and even, and there are marks, like from a pine bough. And the lock is cut. Whoever did it fit the pieces back together, but they don't quite meet."

He was right. The padlock on the shutters hung crooked, the hasp in two pieces.

Erik made a wide berth around the window, pausing halfway to fish something out of the snow. He held up a pair of bolt cutters. "I'm betting these came from somewhere on the property," he said. "A toolshed or something." He set the cutters to one side, then came to stand under the window, very close to the cabin. He stared up at the lock, then reached up with gloved hands and carefully unhooked it. "I'm going to look inside," he said.

He pocketed the lock, then folded back the shutters. The window sash rose easily, and within seconds he had heaved himself over the sill.

Sheri didn't wait, but followed him. He scowled, but only said, "Don't touch anything."

Whoever had been here hadn't tried to hide their presence. Dirty dishes were piled on the table and a trash can in the corner overflowed with wrappers. Downstairs one of two double beds was unmade, sheets trailing to the floor. Ashes filled the fireplace. Erik leaned down and held his hand over the hearth. "Cold," he said.

"The room is cold, too," she said. "I think whoever was here has been gone a while."

"I'm going to look upstairs." He motioned toward a ladder that led to a loft. She waited until he was up there before she followed. She emerged onto a wooden platform furnished with a row of twin beds. The end bed showed signs of having been slept in, the indentation of a small body on the pillow and mattress.

Sheri stared at that child-sized imprint. "They were here," she said. "Carl slept downstairs, and Dawn slept up here."

"We don't know it was them," he said. "Wasn't there some serial murderer hiding out in this area a couple of weeks ago?"

"He was traveling alone, and he was captured more than two weeks ago," she said. "This looks more recent." She bent and laid a hand on the bed.

"Please don't touch anything," Erik said.

She pulled back her hand and straightened, then a scrap of blue paper caught her eye, wedged between two logs, just to the left of the headboard. "Erik, look at this."

He joined her, then reached out and plucked the paper from where it was wedged. Still wearing gloves, he opened it and laid it on the blanket. They bent, heads together, and read the neatly printed note: *To whoever finds this. My uncle says we are going to Mexico. I don't want to go and...* The note ended abruptly, as if whoever had been writing it had been interrupted.

Sheri was still staring at the note when she felt Erik's

gaze on her. She turned her head and their eyes met. "I'm sure Dawn wrote this," she said.

"What makes you so sure?"

"It mentions her uncle. That has to be Carl."

He took a clear envelope from the pocket of his parka, unfolded it and held it open. "Slide it in here," he said. "But carefully. Handle it by the edges."

She did as he asked and he labeled the envelope with the date, time and location, then had her sign her name. Then he slipped the envelope into his inside coat pocket. "What made you look there?" he asked.

"Do you remember how Claire used to hide things around her room?"

"Like a squirrel." He swallowed, the play of strong emotion so clear on his face. She took his hand and squeezed it, then turned away.

"We should tell someone," she said. "Maybe they can be tracked."

They exited the cabin the way they had come in. Erik closed the shutters over the window and rehung the padlock. Then they retraced their steps back to the road leading into the camp.

"They must have left yesterday," Erik said as they trudged along. "After Mrs. Cargill saw the smoke, but before the snow stopped."

"I don't think the snow stopped until early this morning," Sheri said.

"That gives them a lot of hours. And they didn't walk out of here. Well, they may have walked out of the camp, but someone must have picked them up on the road."

"The same person who gave them a ride before?" she asked.

"Either that, or Carl has a whole network of friends we don't know about."

They reached the wall of snow that blocked the drive and made their way around it. They were almost to the car once more when Erik stopped again and swore. Sheri followed his gaze and her heart sank. "The tires!" All four tires on the Jeep were flat, the rims sinking into the snow. She looked around them, but saw no one.

"Who did this?" she asked.

"It could be Carl," Erik said. He moved closer to the Jeep and stared down at clear footprints in the snow. "He knows me. If he spotted me before I put my jacket hood up, he probably recognized me."

"But we thought he was long gone." Her stomach lurched at the thought of a criminal deliberately stranding them.

"I think he's probably gone now." Erik moved to study a fresh set of tire tracks that had pulled over just behind his Jeep. "Studded snow tires," he said. "They could have swung in here to pick up Carl and Dawn." He pointed to two sets of footprints—one large and one small. "They were probably waiting somewhere close when we showed up. Carl punctured my tires to make sure I couldn't follow too close." He pulled out his cell phone. "No signal. No surprise there. Carl probably knew that, too."

"What are we going to do?" Sheri hugged her arms around her middle. Already, she felt colder. She had been looking forward to returning to the warm car.

"The sheriff knows where I was headed," he said. "And you told your friend Ted. When we don't show up in a few hours, someone will raise the alarm and come looking for us."

A few hours was a long time to wait in the cold, even in the Jeep with the heater running. She groaned.

Erik took out a small notebook. "I'll leave a note on the Jeep and we'll go back to the camp," he said. "We'll try to break into one of the other cabins. I'd just as soon not disturb the cabin Carl was in."

"I guess if you're a cop, it's okay," she said.

"My being a cop doesn't make it okay," he said. "But this being an emergency does. I'll pay for a new lock and we'll clean up after ourselves." He finished writing his note and left it under the windshield wiper, then turned to her. "Let's go. We might as well try to make ourselves comfortable."

ERIK CHOSE THE cabin closest to the main lodge for their refuge. "It will be easier for the sheriff's deputies to find us here," he explained.

"But how are we going to get in?" Sheri eyed the padlock on the door.

"The same way whoever broke into the other cabin got in. With those bolt cutters."

"I'm coming with you to get them," Sheri said.

"I won't argue with that," Erik said. "I don't intend to let you out of my sight as long as there's a chance Carl—or whoever ruined my tires—is still around."

She paled. "You don't think he's still here, do you?"

"I don't think so, but we won't take any chances." He gave her a brief hug, then they set out for the other cabin. He retrieved the bolt cutters, keeping his gloves on and grasping them high on the handles, well above where someone would usually hold them. Back at the cabin he severed the lock and pushed open the door.

"This doesn't look too bad," Sheri said. She stood in

the middle of the room and turned a slow circle. Unlike the cabin the intruder had stayed in, this one was furnished with four sets of bunk beds, arranged on three walls, with a dusty iron woodstove on the fourth wall, and a large wooden table and chairs in the center of the room. "Spartan, but in good shape."

"I saw a bunch of firewood by the lodge," he said. "Let's get some."

Together, they carried armloads of wood and dumped them in the wood box by the stove, then removed their gloves, hats and parkas. He started a fire while she searched the single closet in one corner of the room. This yielded a pile of blankets, a Scrabble game, a teakettle, a stack of plastic cups and a half-empty jar of instant coffee. She filled the kettle from a water bottle in her pack and set it on top of the stove, then laid out beef jerky, two candy bars and two packets of hot cocoa mix. "You can have coffee, hot chocolate or mix them for mocha," she said.

"A hot drink sounds good," he said. "Though it may be a while before this fire is hot enough to boil water." He rose from in front of the stove and joined her at the table. "So much for our dinner date."

"I'll take a rain check," she said. She surveyed the items on the table in front of them. "I suppose we could play Scrabble while we wait."

"I have a better idea." He pulled her close and kissed her. She relaxed against him, and wrapped her arms around his neck.

"I like the way you think," she said, smiling up at him.

He kissed her again, then looked around for someplace more comfortable. They could spread the blankets on one of the bunks, though it wasn't the most romantic setup. "This isn't exactly like the cabin in Estes Park," he said.

"No, this is like the place we stayed on that lake in Idaho," she said. "The one where we had booked this deluxe cabin and ended up in an old toolshed or something."

He laughed. "Oh, I remember. What was their story—that the cabin we were supposed to have had burned down the week before and they were booked up?"

She nodded. "Something like that. Then they put us in that building they were using to store old furniture."

"Everything was mismatched and had all the romance of, well, a toolshed."

"We probably should have complained, but we were so glad just to be somewhere together that we didn't." She slid her hands beneath his sweater, her fingers warm against his skin. "We had a great time just being together."

"We did." He cradled the back of her head. "How did we lose that?"

"You know how," she said. "After we lost Claire, we could never be that innocent and carefree again."

"I think one of the worst things about those first months after she died was that I hurt so much myself— but I also hurt for you. I knew you were suffering and there was nothing I could do to fix it. I felt so empty and useless."

"You should have told me," she said.

"I didn't have the words."

She pulled his head down to hers, their foreheads touching, a moment of such tenderness he felt a tightness in the back of his throat, grief for all the time they had wasted, and gratitude that at least they had this moment.

He didn't know how long they stood like that, the fire crackling in the stove, warmth gradually filling the cabin, a deeper heat spreading through him. She reached down and lowered his zipper, and began kissing the side of his neck, stoking the fire within.

Then a pounding on the door made her yelp and jump away. He had the presence of mind to zip his pants as Gage Walker shouted, "Erik, is that you in there?"

Chapter Ten

When Erik hadn't checked in with Travis after a couple
of hours, the sheriff had been concerned enough to send
Gage to look for him. Gage had spotted Erik's Jeep, and
smoke from the wood stove had led him to the cabin
where he and Sheri were sheltering.

A sweep of King's Kids camp turned up nothing that
would prove Carl and Dawn had been there. Deputies
collected some fibers and hairs and carefully preserved
them, but at this point the sheriff felt they couldn't justify the expense of DNA testing, and Erik's bosses with
the state agreed.

The next morning, Erik decided to question the Sheffields again, but rather than talk to them in their home,
he asked them to come to the sheriff's department. "If
they're hiding something, I want to make them a little
uneasy," he explained to the sheriff.

"What do you think they're hiding?" Travis asked.

"I don't know," he admitted. "Maybe they've had
some communication from Carl that they haven't shared
with us. Maybe before he took Dawn he made a threat
or said something that hinted he might do something
like this and they don't want to admit they didn't take
him seriously. Or maybe they have an idea who might

be helping him and are protecting that person for some reason. I'd like a uniformed deputy to be in the room when I question them, as another way to impress upon them that this is a serious part of the investigation."

"Deputy Douglas," Travis said. "She looks sympathetic, but she won't stand for anything out of line."

Melissa Sheffield answered Erik's call to the couple's landline. "Do you have any news?" she asked.

"We've had one small development," Erik said. "I'd like to talk to you and your husband about it. Can you be at the sheriff's department at ten thirty?"

"Why do we have to come there?" she asked. "Why can't you come here?"

"I need you and your husband to be here. I can send a deputy to pick you up if you like."

"Absolutely not. I really don't see why we have to talk to you at all. Our daughter is missing and instead of spending your time out looking for her, you're wasting time interrogating us as if we were somehow involved. It's disgraceful."

Her voice caught and he pictured her working up to full-blown sobbing. He couldn't decide if this was real distress or an act to make him back off. It didn't matter. He wasn't going to give ground. "We are working very hard to see that Dawn is safely returned to you," he said. "You are the one person who knows more about her kidnapper than anyone. Without even realizing it, you may have the key that will help us find him and Dawn. It's very important that you help us—that you help Dawn—by coming to the sheriff's department and talking to us."

"I've told you everything I know. Answering more

questions isn't going to help. You're just harassing us, the way you did my brother."

"Detective?" Brandon Sheffield's voice broke in. "What time do you need to see us?"

"Ten thirty. At the sheriff's department in Eagle Mountain."

"We'll be there," Brandon said.

"Thank you."

Brandon hung up and Erik opened his notebook to prepare for the interview. He didn't envy Sheffield the argument he would probably have with his wife. Erik didn't know what kind of person she was under normal circumstances, but stress didn't bring out the best in anyone.

At ten thirty-five Adelaide announced that the Sheffields had arrived, and Erik sent Jamie to escort them from the lobby to the interview room. He wondered if the five-minute delay in their arrival had been deliberate. Given the absence of traffic on most local roads, coupled with Melissa's objection to having to come here to speak with him, he decided it probably was.

The door to the interview room opened and Melissa swept in, head high, like a model striding down the catwalk. She wore fitted leather trousers, a leather jacket, black leather boots and a black turtleneck sweater. She looked like a glamorous cat burglar. Brandon followed, shoulders hunched, deep shadows beneath his eyes. Unlike his wife, he hadn't dressed to impress. He wore the same wrinkled khakis and flannel shirt he'd had on when Erik had visited his house on Monday.

Deputy Douglas closed the door behind her as she entered and remained standing as the Sheffields advanced toward Erik, who stood behind the gray steel table in the center of the room. "Please, have a seat," he said, indicating the two chairs across from him.

"I told Brandon we should have our lawyer with us," Melissa said.

"You may certainly do that," Erik said. "How soon can your attorney be here?"

"He's in Denver," she said. "I'm sure he would have to clear his schedule and travel here."

"Time is very important in a case like this," Erik said. "The sooner you can provide the information I need, the better our chances of finding Carl right away."

Brandon put a hand on his wife's shoulder. "Let's see what the detective needs to know," he said. He pulled out a chair and she sat in it, then he took his place beside her.

Erik consulted his notes, a touch of drama he really didn't need. "Yesterday, we received information that someone was occupying a cabin at a closed summer camp a few miles from the fishing cabins where Carl and Dawn were last seen," he said. "By the time we got to the camp, whoever had been there was gone, but we found this note." He slid the small piece of paper in its clear evidence envelope toward them. "Do you recognize this handwriting?" he asked.

Brandon leaned forward and read the note out loud. "My uncle is taking me to Mexico and I don't want to go." He looked up, eyes wide. "Do you think Dawn wrote this?"

"Do you recognize the handwriting?" Erik asked again.

Brandon looked down at the note once more. "I don't know. I think it could be Dawn's handwriting. Mel, what do you think?"

"I think it's ridiculous to think an eight-year-old has any kind of definable handwriting," Melissa said. "Anyone could have written that note. Maybe one of the campers who stay there in the summer."

Erik took the note and tucked it back into his folder. Brandon watched him, looking sadder than ever. "Has Carl ever been to Mexico?" he asked.

Brandon looked at his wife. "Mel?"

"I have no idea if Carl has been to Mexico."

"I understood the two of you are close," Erik said. "Has he ever mentioned traveling to Mexico, either for work or for a vacation?"

"I don't believe so. No."

"Maybe Dawn misunderstood," Brandon said. "Maybe he meant New Mexico."

"Why New Mexico?" Erik asked.

"Really, Brand, that's stretching things," Melissa said. "Dawn is smart enough not to confuse a state with a country."

Brandon ignored her. "Carl dated a woman from Santa Fe for a while," he said.

"When was this?" Erik asked. "What was her name?"

"Last year sometime. He brought her to a barbecue at our house in Denver." He looked to his wife once more. "Don't you remember, Mel? A very pretty woman. What was her name? Margery or Maude. Something with an *M*."

"I don't remember," Melissa said.

Erik hadn't uncovered anyone like that in his recent investigations of Carl's activities. "Are they still seeing each other?" he asked.

"I don't think so," Brandon said. "I haven't heard him talk about her in months."

"When was the last time Carl was in New Mexico?" Erik asked. "Do you know?"

"I don't," Brandon said. "Mel, has he mentioned New Mexico to you?"

"No." She folded her arms over her chest. "You're wasting your time," she said. "Why aren't you out looking for Dawn?"

"Every law enforcement officer in this state and the surrounding states are on the lookout for a man and a girl meeting Carl's and Dawn's descriptions," Erik said. "It would be much more helpful if we were able to pinpoint the most likely locations Carl would run to. Did he have a favorite vacation spot? A best friend or other relative he would turn to for help? Has he mentioned anyplace lately? Maybe he said something like 'when my trial is over, I'm going to...'"

Brandon shook his head. "If he did, I don't remember," he said.

"He didn't." Melissa turned on her husband. "Instead of trying to guess where Carl might be hiding, we should text him and tell him we have the money he wants. We can wire it to his account and I'm sure he'll return Dawn to us."

"Mel, a million dollars isn't a sum I can pull together in a matter of hours, even if I did think it would help," Brandon said. "And what's to stop Carl from taking the money and keeping Dawn? He might think he can keep squeezing us by threatening her."

"Carl wouldn't do that. Why do you have such a horrible opinion of my brother?"

"How can you not have a horrible opinion of him?" Brandon's voice rose and he stood, his chair scraping the floor as he shoved it back. "He kidnapped our daughter. Any ounce of sympathy I might have ever had for him vanished when he did that."

"Mrs. Sheffield, do you have any idea who might be helping your brother evade authorities?" Erik asked. "Someone picked him up when he dumped his car in the canyon, and that same person may have provided transportation from the fishing cabins to the summer camp and away from there, too."

"I don't know. And I'm done here." She stood also and stalked to the door, but Jamie stepped in front of it.

"Are you holding us prisoner now?" Melissa asked. "What are you charging us with?"

"Mel, calm down," Brandon said. "You're not making this any easier."

"Why should I make 'this' easy on anyone?" she asked. "Our little girl in missing. There's nothing easy about that."

"You're free to go," Erik said. "If you think of anything that might help, no matter how small, contact me at any time,"

"We will," Brandon said, and led his wife from the room.

Erik sat at the table once more. Finding a woman in Santa Fe whose first name began with *M* was going to be impossible without more information.

Jamie returned to the room. "Do you think the Sheffields were telling the truth?" he asked.

"He is. And she probably is, too," Jamie said. "But then, some people are very good liars."

"She's angry with me, and with her husband," Erik

said. "She's furious with everyone but her brother, the man who kidnapped her daughter."

"Maybe admitting he's guilty is too hard for her," Jamie said. "She has this image of him built up in her mind and even though he's not living up to that image, she's not ready to let it go."

"She wants her daughter safe, but she doesn't want her brother punished."

"Something like that," Jamie said. "Family relationships can be pretty complicated."

"I love my brother, but if he stole my kid I'd punish him myself," Erik said. "I wouldn't be defending him to law enforcement officers who were trying to help me."

"But you're a cop. Not everyone sees us the same way."

True enough. He gathered his papers and stood. "Thanks for your help. And for sharing your impressions."

"What are you going to do now?"

"I'm going to go over everything we know again and hope something comes to light that I missed before. We may have no choice but to wait for Carl to make the next move."

WHEN ERIK TEXTED Sheri Thursday afternoon and suggested they have their delayed dinner that night, she fought an internal battle for five minutes. Yes, she had already agreed to have dinner with him, and part of her ached to see him again. Yet what she thought of as the more rational part of herself was alarmed by the easy way he had slipped back into her life. Could good sex (okay, great sex) now make up for the pain he had caused her in the past? He said he had changed, that therapy had helped him to see how he had failed her, but was that really true, or something he said because he wanted her back in his bed?

I'm exhausted and need to take a break tonight, she texted back.

OK.

She stared at the two-letter reply and tried to figure out what it meant. Was he really okay with not seeing her? Was that a good thing or a bad thing? He hadn't even tried to change her mind. Was he respecting her choices or did he not care as deeply as she thought?

"Arrgh!" She was as bad as one of her students, over-thinking everything, analyzing every word and gesture for some clue as to where this relationship was going. Sometimes OK just meant OK. She tossed the phone to one side and turned back to the laptop, open to the student essays she really should be grading. Three. She would do three of them, then call it a night. She opened the first file. She had assigned her class to write about someone in their life whom they admired. The first girl wrote about her grandfather and, except for an unfortunate overuse of the word *great*, it was well done. The next student, a boy, wrote about his mom, who was raising him and his sister by herself since their father had died. It was touching and well-written, and earned him an A.

The last of the three was authored by another girl, who had chosen to write about her younger brother, who had battled a brain tumor, multiple surgeries and che-motherapy since the age of seven. "He has overcome so much and remained positive and strong the whole time," she wrote. "I would do anything for him, and I know he would do the same for me."

Sheri wondered what it would be like to have that kind of bond with another person. She loved her brother and enjoyed being with him, but they could go years without seeing each other. They had grown up together, but each in their own sphere of different interests and different friends. When she had married Erik, she believed she had found the one person who would always be there for her, but it hadn't worked out that way. What if the person you felt that way about wasn't a romantic partner, but a sibling?

She shut down the laptop and was contemplating which frozen meal to reheat for dinner when a text from Search and Rescue came in: South Falls slide caught two vehicles. One a school van.

South Falls was a notorious avalanche chute on Dixon Pass. The highway department regularly launched explosives to clear the chute in order to prevent exactly this kind of accident, but nature didn't always operate on a schedule. Quickly, she changed clothes and gathered her gear, her mind racing. A school van meant students were involved, probably returning from a sports activity. Had the van been swept off the road altogether, or was it trapped in snow packed like concrete around the vehicle? Was anyone injured? She prayed no one was dead.

Focus, she reminded herself. She couldn't prevent what had already happened. Her job was to show up and help in any way she could.

Chapter Eleven

The fifteen-passenger van lay on its side thirty yards below the road, wedged against a large boulder and almost completely buried in snow and debris. The second vehicle, a black Ford Expedition with a single occupant, was still on the roadway, also buried in snow. By the time Search and Rescue arrived, in the once-more-operational Beast, sheriff's deputies had closed the road and sent for equipment to clear the blockage. Sheri searched for Erik, but didn't see him in the glow of red and blue oscillating lights.

"Let's get some lines run down to the van," Carrie directed. Tony was out of town so as lieutenant, Carrie was in charge. "I want two people down there to assess the situation. Sheri, you and Hannah go."

Hannah Richards, a paramedic, shouldered a pack full of medical gear and helped Sheri stock her own pack with things they might need—cervical collars, splints and various other braces and bandages. They would assess who needed to be transported on a litter and who could walk out on their own. And if necessary, who would be brought up later, in a body bag.

While Hannah and Sheri packed, Ted and Eldon Ramsey inspected the South Falls chute. If they determined it held enough snow to run again, the rescuers would have to wait for the highway department to come out and clear it before they could do much more. The last thing anyone wanted was for accident victims to be pulled from the vehicles only to be swept away by a second slide.

"We don't think it's going to run again," Ted reported when he and Eldon returned to the group at the edge of the road. By this time one of the sheriff's deputies had shoveled enough snow away from the SUV for the driver to roll down the window and speak to them.

The woman's voice carried well in the clear night air and Sheri was startled to hear Melissa Sheffield say, "I'm all right. I'm just a little shaken. I was driving along and suddenly I couldn't see anything but white, and the car wasn't moving. It was the strangest sensation."

Sheri hurried to the SUV. "Ms. Sheffield, what are you doing out here alone?" she asked.

Melissa stared at her a long moment, then apparently recognized her. "I couldn't sit still," she said. "So I went for a drive."

"This really isn't the place to go for a casual drive at night," Ted said.

"Were you looking for Dawn?" Sheri asked. It was the kind of thing she would have done.

Some of the tension left Melissa's expression. "Yes. I thought I could find that summer camp the detective told us about—the one where he thought Dawn and Carl were staying. But everything is so confusing in the dark. I got lost and had to turn around and head home."

Sheri reached in and patted the other woman's shoulder. She thought sometimes she had been drawn to rescue work as a way to combat the feeling of helplessness Melissa was experiencing now.

Austen and Ryan emerged from the canyon, where they had been running rope lines, and Sheri rejoined them and the others. "It's a nice, easy slope," Ryan said. "The snow's packed enough you can walk right down."

"Did you hear anything from the van?" Carrie asked.

Ryan grimaced. "I heard kids crying. Don't know if they're hurt or just scared."

"We're going to get some shovels and picks and follow you back down," Austen said.

Hannah and Sheri started down. Ryan was right. They were able to walk down, like walking down a ramp, holding on to the rope for balance. Only the roof of the white van was visible, buried in the snow, the top of the boulder it rested against barely poking above the sea of white. Past the boulder the drop-off was dizzying, hundreds of yards of emptiness to jagged rocks below. Sheri fought a wave of nausea and forced her gaze back to the van. Austen and Ryan followed and began attacking the wall of snow around the vehicle with picks and shovels.

"Hello!" Sheri shouted. "Hang on tight and we're coming to get you!"

A clamor rose from the van, a sound like a beehive suddenly disturbed. The words were mostly unintelligible, though Sheri thought she heard "Help!" and "Thank God!"

The men carved a path to the rear of the van. Faces appeared at the fogged window. "Do you see a red handle?" Hannah called. "Press down on that and see if you can open the window."

Moments later, the window popped open, then fell

away, and two girls immediately climbed out into the snow. "Whoa! Whoa!" Sheri moved to block any more exits. "Wait a minute and let's do this safely." She switched on her headlamp, leaned her head and shoulders into the emergency exit and surveyed the scene. Half a dozen pairs of eyes stared back at her, some frightened, a few more curious. "Who are the adults here?" she asked.

"I'm Coach Dellafield." A woman with curly sandy hair and freckles moved down the aisle, holding on to the seat backs to pull herself along the angled floor. "The driver, Mr. Fox, has a bad bump on his head and he's trapped by the seat belt," she said. "One of the girls may have broken her arm. I think everyone else is okay."

Relief surged through Sheri. That was great news. "Give us a few minutes and we'll have you out of here," she said, and withdrew.

"I heard," Hannah, who had been standing right behind her, said. "Let's get everyone mobile out and I'll go in and see to the driver."

"How stable is this van?" Sheri asked Ryan.

"It's wedged solid against that boulder and the snow is like a mold, holding it in," Ryan said. "For the time being, you're as good as it gets."

She looked past him, to where the two girls who had climbed out stood. They wore light jackets and track pants and hopped up and down in an attempt to keep warm. "We're going to have some people lead you up to the road," she said. "You do exactly what they tell you to do."

"Yes, ma'am," they said, meek now that they were out in the open, perhaps struck by how lucky they had been to avoid a much more serious accident.

Five more girls climbed out of the van and joined the procession to the top, walking up like climbing stairs. Then Hannah and Sheri entered the van and approached Ms. Dellafield, who sat in the aisle near the front of the van with an ashen-faced girl with black braids who cradled her arm. "I need to take a look at that arm," Hannah said gently. "I know it probably hurts to move it, but if I put it in a splint, you'll soon feel much better."

Eyes brimming with tears, the girl allowed Hannah to examine her arm while Sheri moved past them to the driver. Blood stained his Eagle Mountain Eagles sweatshirt and matted his graying hair, but he was conscious. Sheri introduced herself and took his pulse. A little fast, but steady. "What's your name?" she asked.

"Hank Fox."

"What happened, Mr. Fox?"

"We were on our way home from a basketball tournament in Durango. We had just come over the summit and I saw a few chunks of ice hit the road in front of me. I braked—but gently. I know better than to slam on the brakes up here. I mainly tapped the brakes to warn the driver I knew was behind me. The next thing I know we're swamped in this cloud of white. I didn't even have time to steer before we were carried over the edge. The van tilted and I was thrown sideways and bashed my head. I must have blacked out for a few seconds. The next thing I knew, everything went still. I couldn't see anything but white. Someone yelled that we were buried alive and I tell you, that set everyone off. I realized about that time that I had blood all over me and I panicked and started yelling." He made a face. "I'm sure that didn't help calm things down." He tried to look around, but the seat belt held him tight against the seat. "How are the girls?"

"Everyone is fine. One girl with a possible broken arm, but looks like you're the most seriously injured."

"It's just a bump on the head," he said. "I'll be fine."

Hannah moved up to join them. "I put a splint on Schuyler's arm and Mrs. Delafield and Austen are going to help her walk up to the top," she said. "They're sending down a litter for Mr. Fox."

Sheri moved aside to allow Hannah to examine the van driver, then exited the van altogether when Ted and Eldon arrived with the litter and tools to cut away the safety belt and free Mr. Fox from the vehicle. She returned up top in time to see several of the girls reunited with frantic parents who had learned of the accident from friends or neighbors and driven up to learn the fate of their daughters. This time, the news was all good.

Sheri sat on the back bumper of the Beast and watched as dads and daughters hugged and moms and daughters wept. These parents had feared the very worst—their children being taken from them—and now knew the joy of having their children returned, safe. Even Schuyler, cradling her injured arm, was smiling now, surrounded by family and friends, a momentary celebrity who would emerge from this with a story she would tell for the rest of her life.

Carrie sat on the bumper next to Sheri. "I meant to ask," Sheri said. "Did they figure out why the Beast wasn't running the other night?"

Carrie shook her head. "Just temperamental, I guess. The poor thing only has almost three hundred thousand miles on it. It's long overdue to be replaced, but that will take a major fundraising drive. Probably sooner rather than later, so get ready."

Sheri nodded. Fundraising wasn't her favorite part of search and rescue work, but it was necessary.

Carrie watched as a mom and dad loaded one of the basketball players into their car. "I dread calls like this," she said. "Anything with children ties me in knots. I can't help but think of my own kids." Carrie had a son and daughter, both in elementary school. Sheri had forgotten that. Carrie glanced at her. "They say being a mom makes you tough, but you don't hear very often about how vulnerable it makes you, also."

Sheri nodded. She thought about telling Carrie that she had had a daughter, too. She knew all about that vulnerability. But she didn't say anything. That was a part of herself she didn't talk about.

"Every time we get a call with children involved, I tell myself I'm going to have to give this up," Carrie continued. "I almost quit last spring, after that ATV rollover on Spark Mountain Road."

That accident had involved an ATV with a mom and dad and their two children that had taken a curve too fast and rolled down the mountain. The parents had survived the accident but both children had been killed. Sheri had been in Denver visiting family when it happened and had been relieved not to be involved. "That must have been traumatic for everyone involved," she said.

Carrie nodded. "I saw a counselor for a couple of months afterward. I thought about quitting but the next time a call went out—no kids that time—I had to go, you know? It's like, I'm addicted to rescue work."

Sheri knew. The adrenaline rush, the high when

a rescue went well and some innate need to well, *be needed*, all combined to keep a certain kind of person coming back time after time to endure all the hardships and sometimes disappointments of search and rescue work. They had all attended a lecture once by a psychologist who had studied search and rescue volunteers. He told them that success in the field required a positive mental attitude in the face of danger and extreme difficulty. It was the same trait that allowed some people to survive grave injuries or terrible ordeals when all the odds said they wouldn't make it. Sheri would have never said she possessed that kind of attitude, but she supposed when it came down to it, she did.

"Tonight was good," Sheri said. "Everyone is going to be all right." She squeezed Carrie's arm. "Us, too."

Carrie nodded, and stood. "Come on. We'd better load up and get home."

They helped the others gather their equipment and stow it in the Beast. The road crew had freed Melissa Sheffield's vehicle and she had driven away, and the plows cleared the rest of the snow. The road reopened and the law enforcement vehicles left. The SAR crew returned to headquarters, then dispersed to their own homes. Sheri drove to her place, wondering if a glass of wine and a movie would be enough to help her settle down and sleep.

A familiar Jeep was parked in her driveway. As she emerged from her vehicle, the driver's door opened and Erik got out and moved toward her. "I heard about the accident up on the pass," he said. "I heard it was kids." He searched her face, and worry etched the lines around his eyes and mouth deeper.

"It was kids," she said. "But everyone is okay."

"Thank God." He held out his arms and she went to him. She didn't want to want him this way, but she was so glad he was here. She didn't have to tell him what she felt or why. She didn't have to keep quiet about Claire or pretend there wasn't a hole in her heart where her daughter had been. Erik knew her in a way no one else did, and for now that was enough.

SHERI WAS CLEANING her bathroom Saturday morning when the doorbell sounded over Adele blaring from a smart speaker in the adjacent bedroom. It took a few more seconds for the sounds to register and by this time whoever was out there was pounding on the door. She stripped off her rubber gloves, silenced the music and hurried to check the door. She was startled to see Melissa Sheffield looking back at her, the other woman's expression hidden by a pair of oversize sunglasses.

Sheri unlocked and opened the door. "Mrs. Sheffield?"

"May I come in?"

"Of course." Sheri stepped back and Melissa, dressed in high-heeled black boots, a slim black maxi skirt and a long black puffer coat, moved past her into the living room. "Can I get you something?" Sheri asked. "Tea, or I could make coffee."

Melissa took off her gloves, tugging carefully at each finger. When she turned to Sheri, her eyes were bloodshot, devoid of makeup. "I've done something very bad," she said. "I did it for the right reasons, but still." She made a helpless gesture with her hands.

"What do you want me to do?" Sheri asked. "I mean, shouldn't you go to the sheriff's office and tell them? Or, I don't know, a priest or something?"

"I came to you because you seem sympathetic, and because, well, I need rescuing. That's what you do, isn't it? Search and rescue?"

The dazed expression Melissa wore worried Sheri. "Why don't you take off your coat and have a seat," she said.

Melissa hesitated, then moved to the sofa. She sat on the edge of the cushions, knees together, hands folded primly in her lap. Sheri sat beside her, the space of one cushion between them. "My brother needs help," Melissa said. "I've always been the one to help him. That's all I was trying to do this time. I need you to make the law enforcement officers believe that."

"What did you do?" Sheri asked, a knot forming in her stomach.

"Dawn was never in any danger," Mel continued. "It's been very upsetting for people to ever believe that she was. Carl is not a violent person. He simply isn't. And he loves Dawn. And she's a very…resilient child. She'll take all of this in stride…eventually."

The bad feeling in Sheri's stomach and chest was growing. "What will Dawn understand?" she asked. "What exactly have you done?"

"Carl needed money for his legal expenses," she continued. "Because of these horrible accusations against him, he'd lost his job. He had to be able to defend himself, so he asked Brand and I for the money. It wasn't an unreasonable request. We're his family and families support one another." She pressed her lips together, the lines around her mouth deepening, making her look older and more severe. "Brand refused. I couldn't believe it. It's not as if I'm an extravagant person who goes around wasting his money on silly impulses. I was asking for the money for my brother. For family. But he refused to give Carl one dime."

"What did you do?" Sheri asked again, trying to remain calm. She thought she knew what was coming, but she needed to hear it from Melissa's own lips.

"Brand loves Dawn. I do, too, but sometimes I think she's the only person he truly does love. He's certainly not close to his siblings the way I am to Carl. Carl and I realized that if Dawn was kidnapped, Brand would pay anything to get her back." She glanced at Sheri, clearly annoyed. "No one was supposed to know Carl was the kidnapper, but you ruined that when you spotted him with Dawn at the ice festival. I really think that if it had been anyone but Carl, Brand would have paid the money with no fuss." She sighed. "I don't know why he has to be so difficult. This could have all been over with so much sooner."

Sheri stared at Melissa, questions tumbling over themselves in her head like clothes in a dryer: What kind of mother thought setting her daughter up to be kidnapped—even a pretend kidnapping—was a good idea? Why ask for a million dollars? If Carl was so great, why had he ever agreed to such an outrageous plan? And are you out of your mind?

The question she asked was: "So you weren't worried about your daughter?" Had all that motherly concern and tears been fake?

"Dawn is fine. She's crazy about Carl, and I know he wouldn't let anything happen to her."

Sheri remembered the little girl who had grabbed onto her at the ice festival, and the way she had said, "I want my mom." And the note she had found in the cabin at the closed summer camp. *My uncle is taking me to Mexico and I don't want to go.* "Were you the one who picked up Carl and Dawn when he sent his car into the canyon?" Sheri asked.

"Yes. He wasn't very happy with me that day. Carl really loved that car. But I pointed out with a million dollars, he could buy all the cars he wanted. I had checked out the fishing cabins ahead of time—I knew he and Dawn would be safe there. But he called me that night and told me the woman who ran the place had seen Dawn—which wasn't supposed to happen— and I decided to move them to the summer camp. Not as comfortable, but it would do for a few nights while I worked on Brand."

"Did you puncture Detective Lester's tires?"

Melissa looked her in the eye, completely calm. "I have no idea what you're talking about."

Sheri was sure she was lying, but that didn't really matter, because she believed Melissa was telling the truth about everything else. "Where did you take them after the summer camp?" she asked.

"That's what I need to tell the sheriff," Melissa said. "This has gone on too long. Dawn is very unhappy with me and I need to make it up to her. I'll find a way to make it up to Carl, too. But it's time for this to stop."

Sheri walked to the door and made sure the lock was turned. She didn't want Melissa leaving. She took out her phone. "I'll call Erik," she said.

"I don't want to talk to him," Melissa said. "I want to talk to the sheriff."

"Fine, then I'll call the sheriff." She would text Erik. She wasn't about to leave him out of all of this.

Chapter Twelve

When Sheri told Erik that the person trapped in the second vehicle on Dixon Pass was Melissa Sheffield, he wanted to bring Dawn's mother in for questioning again. But he decided to wait. He would have more leverage to pressure her if he could find someone else connected to Carl who could speak to his intentions. Maybe Carl had mentioned his plan to get money from his brother-in-law to a former coworker or a woman he had dated. And there was the bank account to investigate, too. Erik had put in a request to the FBI for help tracking down the bank associated with the account and needed to follow up on that. Melissa could wait a little while longer.

He devoted himself to contacting Carl Westover's former coworkers, neighbors and known associates and questioning them about a former girlfriend whose name began with *M*, and any trips to Mexico or New Mexico. He asked about foreign bank accounts, and if Carl had ever mentioned wanting to get back at his brother-in-law for refusing to help him.

"Carl was the kind of person who talked big but didn't ever do anything," a former coworker told Erik. "He was mad at his brother-in-law, but the threats, if you could call them that, were more along the lines of 'he'll be sorry he ever treated me this way.'"

"What did he say, exactly?" Erik asked.

"Oh, he said a lot of things, but he was just blowing hot air."

"Can you remember anything specific?"

The man thought for a moment. "Well, okay. One time—last time I saw him, in fact — he said he was going to show Brandon. When Carl ended up more famous and richer than Brandon ever thought about, he'd come crawling to Carl to help him, and Carl would throw him out. See what I mean—a lot of hot air."

"Did he ever talk about his niece, Dawn?" Erik asked.

"Not that I remember. The only family I ever heard him mention was his sister."

"What did he say about her?"

"Oh, just that she had promised to help him fight the charges against him and prove he was innocent. I know they talked a lot on the phone and seemed close."

"Unnaturally close?" Erik asked.

"No. Nothing like that. I think he looked up to her."

Erik thanked the man and hung up the phone. To some people, *famous* and *notorious* were synonymous. Kidnapping was one way to get your name in the news, but it seemed a stretch to cite Carl's conversation with his old coworker as evidence that he had been planning to abduct his niece for some time.

He checked the clock. It was getting late, and so far he had accomplished nothing today. Time to contact Melissa and find out what she had to say about her activities yesterday. He tried her cell phone number, but got no answer, so he called the phone at their home. Brandon answered.

"I don't know where Melissa is," Brandon said after Erik asked for Melissa. "Her car is gone."

"How long has she been gone?" Erik asked.

"I woke up this morning and she wasn't here. I didn't worry at first. She left a note saying she couldn't sleep and she was going out driving. She does that sometimes. She says it helps her think. But that was hours and hours ago and I haven't heard anything." His voice broke and it was a long moment before he continued. "Do you think Carl took her, too?"

"Has Carl threatened to kidnap your wife, also?" Erik asked.

"No, but what else could have happened to her? She's never stayed away all day like this—not without telling me where she was going ahead of time."

"Have you tried calling her?"

"Several times. All my calls go straight to voice mail."

"Was your wife at home last night?" Erik asked.

"Yes. We went to bed together at eleven."

"Did the two of you argue? Maybe she left this morning because she was angry, and that's why she's not answering your calls."

The man on the other end of the line didn't speak for several seconds. "Mr. Sheffield? Are you still there?"

"I'm here. Melissa and I argue all the time lately. She's angry that I won't hand over money to Carl every time he holds out his hand and she isn't one to hide her feelings. But we didn't talk about that last night. When we said good-night she gave no indication that she was any more upset with me than she has been."

Erik remembered those days—terrible arguments interspersed with attempts to pretend everything was normal. But those efforts always felt perfunctory, even desperate, with no real warmth behind them. He and Sheri hadn't been able to find their way back to the closeness that had once characterized their marriage. "Did Melissa go out yesterday afternoon or evening?" he asked.

Another pause, then, "Yes. She went out for a few hours."

"What time?"

"She left about five o'clock."

"And how long was she gone?"

"Three hours. When she got home she said she had to wait while the highway crew cleared an avalanche up on Dixon Pass."

"Did she say where she had been, that she was on the other side of Dixon Pass?"

"She said she was trying to find Dawn." His voice broke. "Detective, are we ever going to see our little girl again? I dreamed last night we were attending her funeral. You don't think that was a premonition, do you?"

"I don't believe in premonitions," Erik said. He had lived the hell of attending his child's funeral and no dream could have prepared him for that moment. Neither he nor Sheri had had any warning that Claire would be taken from them. "And we haven't seen anything to indicate that Carl has done anything to harm your daughter," he added.

"You're right. I can't give up hope. Do you want me to come to the station and file some kind of missing persons report on Melissa?"

"I think it's too soon for that. Keep trying her phone, and let us know as soon as she gets home."

"All right."

Erik ended the call and looked up to find the sheriff standing in the doorway. "I heard part of that," Travis said. "And I saw the report about Melissa Sheffield being caught in the avalanche last night. What is she playing at?"

"I don't know," Erik said. "I've been suspicious of Melissa for a while now. I wonder if she's in this with her brother—the two of them teaming up to extort money from her husband. It would explain who has been helping him move around."

"She has alibis for at least some of the times when Carl was being driven from place to place," Travis said.

"You and I both know alibis can be faked." Find the right person to lie for you, or rearrange the facts just slightly to be in your favor. "From my time spent investigating Carl, I know he's a skilled manipulator. I suspect his sister shares his talent."

"It's getting late," Travis said. "Go home and sleep on it. See if any new ideas come to you."

What he wanted was to see Sheri. She was home to him—she always had been. Finding her again had made him realize how true that was. He had believed all the emptiness inside him was because they had lost Claire. He would always mourn his daughter, but the space he had been trying to fill was the one where Sheri belonged. He only hoped he could make her see that, too.

Erik had just pulled into the driveway of his rental when his phone pinged. He smiled when he saw the message was from Sheri, then the smile changed to anger as he read the text: Melissa Sheffield is at my house now. She says she helped her brother and knows where he is now. She wants to talk to the sheriff. I think you should come, too.

His phone rang with a call from the sheriff as Erik was composing his reply. "I just heard from Sheri Stevens," Travis said. "Melissa Sheffield showed up at her house a few minutes ago to confess that she and her brother have been working together."

"Sheri texted me the same." Erik stood. "I want to be there when you question Melissa."

"Meet me there. I'll have a couple of deputies wait outside the house, in case we decide to take her into custody."

Erik backed his Jeep out of the driveway, mind racing. So he had been right to suspect Melissa had helped her brother, but he still couldn't understand why she would do such a thing. Why arrange for your own daughter to be kidnapped. Money? Revenge? He shook his head to clear it. None of that really mattered right now. The question they needed Melissa to answer was where Carl and Dawn were now. They needed to bring the girl home, or to some place she would be safe.

MELISSA REFUSED SHERI'S offers of tea and wine, preferring to pace, still wearing her puffy coat, though the house wasn't cold. She examined the books on Sheri's shelves and the decorative items on her tables with the air of a woman who was shopping at a store she didn't like. Sheri tried asking her more questions—about Carl, about Dawn, about what she thought would happen next, but was greeted with only silence or "I don't want to talk about that."

When lights swept across the front windows as a car

pulled into the driveway, relief surged through Sheri and she hurried to look out. Sheriff Travis Walker moved into the glow from the front porch, bareheaded and wearing a leather jacket with a shearling collar. Behind him was Erik in his black parka.

She unfastened the locks and pulled open the door, wanting to throw her arms around both of them, but settling for "Thank you for coming."

Melissa had finally shed the coat and sat on the edge of the sofa, posed like an elegant statue, knees together, hands folded, head up. She wore a maroon cowl-necked sweater that looked expensive, the deeply rolled collar accentuating the fine bones of her face. She looked beautiful and vulnerable, not the sort of woman who would use her own daughter as a pawn in a sick game to get money for her brother.

Erik and Travis sat on chairs across from her, while Sheri took another chair, out of the circle they made. "I understand you have some things you want to tell us," he said.

"Yes," Melissa answered.

Travis removed a small recorder from his jacket pocket and set it on the table between them. Then he recited the Miranda warning Sheri had heard on countless television episodes and told Melissa he was recording everything. Melissa eyed the recorder like a mouse might view a trap, but indicated she understood her rights. She smoothed her hands, carefully manicured with pearl pink polish, down her thighs and began to talk.

She told them everything she had told Sheri, filling in details as Travis asked for them.

"Why a million dollars?" Travis asked. "When Carl had requested only a hundred thousand before?"

"I know that sounds like an outrageous sum to a lot of people," Melissa said. "But a million dollars hardly makes a dent in Brand's fortune. In addition to the money he's made from his software company, he inherited quite a lot from his grandparents, and will get even more when his parents die. Carl and I come from a much more modest background. In addition to his legal fees, Carl will need money to start over once his name is cleared. He would like to start his own business. Instead of asking Brand for more money then, why not get it all up front? And as I was telling Sheri earlier, this was supposed to be an anonymous crime. Brand wasn't supposed to know who had Dawn. A million sounded like a sum an experienced kidnapper would ask for, don't you think?" She tilted her head to one side, a coquettish gesture that sent a shiver up Sheri's spine.

Erik shifted in his chair, but remained silent, his eyes fixed on Melissa, revealing nothing of his thoughts. Sheri had resented his ability to hide his feelings so well when they were married, but she saw its usefulness now. "Your husband told us your car never left the driveway the day your brother dumped his car," Travis said. "Was he lying?"

"Brand is a terrible liar—he was telling the truth. I told him I was going for a walk, then borrowed a neighbor's car. I told her the battery in mine had died and we were waiting for the road service to deliver a new one, but that in the meantime I needed to get something from the store. She didn't question me, just handed over the keys. People here are very trusting and helpful."

She managed to make something good sound like

a fault. "How did your daughter react when she saw you?" Erik spoke for the first time, asking a question Sheri had wondered about also.

"Dawn was happy to see me. I told her she was going to stay with Uncle Carl a little while longer but they would have a good time together and we would be back together soon."

"And she accepted that?" Erik asked.

"She whined that she wasn't having a good time, but children are like that. Easily bored. I reassured her. After all, I'm her mother."

You don't deserve her, Sheri thought, but said nothing.

"Where did you take your brother and your daughter after they left the summer camp?" Travis asked.

"There's a group of summer cabins in the national forest up there somewhere," Melissa said. "I found it when I was driving around. I told Carl he would be safe in that spot and that I would bring him some more food and supplies today, but when I went up there this afternoon, he was gone. That's when I decided I had to come clean. If he's not going to cooperate with me, I wasn't going to help him anymore."

"So you didn't pick up Carl and Dawn and take them to another location?" Travis asked.

"No. When I got to the cabin, they were gone. I can show you where it is if you like." She leaned forward. "I'm really worried about them. Carl is a very capable man, very smart, but he's not an outdoorsman. He's the type who'll get lost in the woods. He doesn't like hiking, or being cold, or doing any of the things he must have had to do after he left that hiding place."

"Do you have any idea where he might have gone?" Travis asked.

"None. I'm completely in the dark."

Travis stood. "We need you to come to the station now."

Melissa stared up at them, wide-eyed, somehow looking younger than her years. "Am I under arrest?"

"Not at this time, but we want to talk to you more about your brother's motive and possible next move."

"I'm always happy to help the police," she said. "Though I'll want to contact my lawyer."

"You can call your attorney from the sheriff's department."

"You can contact your husband, too," Erik said. "He's been very worried about you."

"I don't want to talk to Brand right now," Melissa said. "He's already so upset about Dawn. He wouldn't understand that what happened was just a…a prank that got out of hand."

Sheri had trouble not gaping at the woman. Kidnapping a child and trying to extort a million dollars was not a "prank."

"When we do find Carl, we may need you to persuade him to give himself up and release your daughter unharmed," Travis said. "We hope you can help us with that. Will you talk to him?"

"Of course." She stood, her smile still in place, though Sheri thought it looked a little harder. "Carl will listen to me. He always has."

MELISSA BALKED AT riding with Travis in his SUV, but he ignored her protests. "I'll have a deputy pick up your car later," he said.

"Will he be coming along, too?" Melissa asked, indicating Erik.

"Detective Lester will follow in his own vehicle."

Melissa folded her arms over her chest. "I'm not going to get into any car with a man who is a stranger to me," she said. "I've heard too many stories about what can happen to a woman who does something like that."

Travis's jaw tightened. Erik half expected him to tell Melissa that in that case, she was under arrest, but Sheri spoke up. "I'll come with you," she said. She moved closer to Melissa. "I'm sure Mrs. Sheffield would feel more comfortable with another woman along. Someone who understands what she's going through."

"Yes." Melissa looked grateful and took Sheri's hand. "That would make me feel better."

Erik caught Sheri's eye and read the revulsion behind her feigned sympathy. Like him, Melissa Sheffield's actions disgusted her. But also like him, Sheri would do anything to help Melissa's daughter.

"I need to search you and make sure you aren't carrying a weapon," Travis said.

"That's outrageous," she protested.

"Standard procedure," Travis said.

"I'll do it," Erik said. She already loathed him, and he didn't care what she thought. Melissa could play the distraught mother card all she wanted, but considering the crimes she had already confessed to, he wouldn't put it past her to be armed. "Arms up, legs apart," he ordered. "This will only take a moment."

She was ready to make a fuss, but Sheri put a hand on her arm. "Remember, this is for Dawn," she said.

Melissa clenched her jaw, but nodded, and allowed

him to pat her down. "No weapon," he said when he was done.

She glared at him as Sheri walked with her to Travis's SUV. The two women climbed in the back seat and when he was sure they were settled, Erik headed for his Jeep. He would have preferred to have Sheri ride with him, but he appreciated how she was helping them manage Melissa. He and Travis were on the same page when it came to treating Dawn's mother with kid gloves, for the time being. If they could keep her in a cooperative mood, they had a better chance of learning everything she knew about Carl's whereabouts and plans. Justice would come for her soon enough, but right now saving a child took priority.

No one spoke on the short ride to the sheriff's department. Sheri watched Melissa out of the corner of her eye, trying to read her mood, and failing. Before tonight, she had projected her own feelings onto the other woman. She had believed that Melissa must be as distressed over her daughter's abduction as Sheri would have been. Part of her shock now came from realizing she had been so wrong.

At the sheriff's department, Travis and a deputy escorted Melissa to a small gray room furnished only with a table and two chairs. Melissa glanced around the space, lip curled as if she had tasted sour milk. "I'd prefer to wait in the lobby," she said.

"Here will be fine," Travis said. "I'll have someone bring you a phone. Ms. Stevens, come with me."

They left Melissa with the deputy. Erik met them in the hall. "While Mrs. Sheffield talks to her lawyer, you and I can interview Ms. Stevens," Travis said. "Take her into Interview B and I'll meet you in five."

Erik led the way to a room identical to the one in which they had left Melissa. Sheri told herself she had nothing to be nervous about, but the stark room and Travis's characterization of this as a formal interview had her on edge. Erik said nothing until the door closed behind them, then he turned to her. "Are you okay?"

"Yes." She hugged her arms to her chest. "I'm having a hard time wrapping my head around a mother doing that to her child."

He slipped his arm around her and pulled her close. "You've been a big help with her so far."

The door opened and Erik moved away again as Travis entered the room. "I have two deputies with Mrs. Sheffield," he said. "I'm sure she's already telling her attorney how poorly she's being treated." He gestured to the table. "Let's sit and you can tell us what she told you."

Erik sat next to Sheri, facing Travis across the table. His presence steadied her as she related everything Melissa had told her. "So her story is that she drove to the summer cabins where Carl and Dawn were supposedly staying, and they weren't there?" Travis asked. "He had just walked away?"

"That's what she said." Sheri twisted her hands together. "She said he wasn't an outdoorsman. She was afraid he would get lost and that's what prompted her to confess to me."

"Why you?" Travis asked.

"I don't know, really. I suppose it's because I'm another woman and until now, I've been sympathetic to her?"

"Or because she thought she could manipulate you into sympathizing with her actions," Erik said.

"Where are these summer cabins?" Travis asked.

"She didn't say."

"There are several groups of cabins like that in the county," Travis said. "We'll have to look at a map and pinpoint those closest to the camp where they last stayed, then send deputies to check for any signs Carl and Dawn were there."

"They may have been there, but if they left, I doubt it was because Carl decided to strike out on his own," Erik said. "He's had big sister chauffeuring him all over the county for the last few days. Why set out on foot now, especially since she indicated he was expecting her to pick him up?"

"Maybe something spooked him," Travis said.

"Or Melissa is lying." Erik angled toward Sheri. "Did she say anything to indicate she knows where Carl is now?"

"No. She says she doesn't know."

"What's her motive for lying?" Travis asked.

"She realizes we're closing in and wants to distance herself from her brother," Erik said.

"So she's helped him all this time and now she's cutting him loose?" Travis asked. "And then she readily admits her part in the crime. It feels like something is missing from this story."

"I think Melissa knows where Carl is, but she thinks if she keeps stonewalling we'll find him on our own," Erik said. "Then she can plead that he manipulated her into helping him and that, ultimately, he's mostly responsible for everything that happened."

"Huh." Travis turned his attention to Sheri. "Did Melissa say anything else you haven't told us yet?"

"No. Except..." She bit her lower lip, hesitating.

"What is it?" Erik asked.

"It wasn't anything she said, it's just... If I thought I knew where my daughter was and suddenly I didn't—if it was possible she was lost in the woods—I'd be frantic. Melissa is a little nervous. She's impatient and irritated. But she isn't scared. And she's scarcely mentioned Dawn. That feels off to me."

"Some people are more reserved than others," Travis said. "But I see your point." He stood. "I'm going to have Gage search for cabins where Carl and Dawn might have been, then I'll meet you in Interview B. Let's see if Melissa has anything more to say. Ms. Stevens, I can have someone take you home."

"Would it be all right if I stayed here for a while?" Sheri asked. "Maybe I could be useful, since Melissa seems comfortable with me."

Travis nodded. "Suit yourself. But you could be here a while."

He left the room and Sheri turned to Erik. "It's not as if I would get any sleep at home," she said. "What is going to happen to Melissa?"

"She'll be charged, eventually," Erik said. "Right now we want her to tell us as much as she can, and help us find Dawn. If she believes we're sympathetic, and willing to go easy on her, the chances are greater that she'll cooperate."

"Do you think this is all a game to her?" Sheri asked. "When she was telling me everything that had happened, before you and Travis arrived, I got the sense that she was almost proud that she had orchestrated everything so well. She didn't have any qualms about trying to trick her husband into handing over a million dollars to her brother. What kind of marriage is that?"

"Not the kind I want." His eyes met hers. She saw his fatigue there, and sadness. "Not the kind we ever had, even at our worst." He stood. "Come on. You can wait in the space I'm using as an office. I'll get you some coffee and you can make yourself at home. I think the sheriff was right—it's going to be a long night."

Chapter Thirteen

Melissa sat at the conference room table, legs and arms crossed, one foot moving in time to some rhythm only she could hear. When Travis and Erik entered, she jumped up. "My attorney has advised me not to talk to you until he arrives," she said.

"When will that be?" Travis asked.

"Not before tomorrow, I imagine. He has to drive over from Denver." She smiled. "Why don't we all go home and we can meet to discuss this tomorrow."

"What about Dawn?" Erik asked.

The smile vanished. "What about her?"

"Aren't you concerned about where she might be?" Erik moved to stand in front of her. "You said you thought Carl had left the cabin with her and could be lost."

"I'm assuming you're going to be looking for them," she said.

"Where is this cabin where you say you left them last?" Travis asked.

"I don't think it has an address," she said. "But I'm sure you'll be able to find it. It's not far from the King's Kids camp—in that same general area, off one of those forest service side roads."

"Could you take us there?" he asked.

"I'm sure I could, though I can't promise I could find it in the dark."

"Is there really a cabin?" Erik asked. "Or did you make up that story so we would intensify our search for your brother in that area?"

"You keep reassuring me you're doing everything you can to find my little girl. Are you saying that's not the case? Why should I resort to made-up stories to get you to do your job?" She turned to the sheriff. "Do you have people looking for Carl and Dawn, or not?"

"I have people looking for them." He pulled out one of the chairs. "Have a seat."

"No. I want to go home."

"You need to wait here for a bit," he said.

"Wait for what? I've had enough of this. I want to go home." She started for the door. Erik knew there were two deputies stationed outside who would stop her if she tried to leave, but before she could try that, the door opened and Brandon Sheffield burst in. "Mel, are you all right?" He gripped her shoulders. "I came as soon as the sheriff called to tell me you were being questioned."

"I'm fine." Melissa shrugged out of his grasp. "You're just in time to take me home. I'm exhausted."

"Your wife has admitted to helping her brother to abduct your daughter in order to extort money from you," Travis said.

Brandon gaped at him.

"*Abduct* is a very inflammatory word," Melissa said. "As is *extort*."

Brandon stared at her. "What is he talking about?" he asked.

"Carl needed that money and you were wrong to refuse to help him," she said. "He came up with a very simple plan to get the money and I agreed to help. If you had paid up, Dawn wouldn't have been away for more than one night at most, and you know how much she enjoys spending time with Carl, so you see how that really isn't an abduction, don't you?" She turned to Travis. "And the whole thing was really Carl's idea. I only agreed to go along to protect Dawn."

"You have a funny way of protecting your daughter," Erik said. So much for keeping her cooperative. He'd had more than enough of her pretending she was innocent.

"You *helped* Carl?" Brandon asked. "To kidnap our daughter and hold her for ransom?"

"I'm not going to say another word until my lawyer gets here," she said. "Except that you can't believe everything they tell you." She nodded to the sheriff. "He's trying to paint me as some monster and I'm not. And Dawn is fine and has been this whole time."

Brandon took a step toward her. "You took our daughter away from her home and kept her away in order to what—teach me a lesson? Extract revenge? You thought your brother's greed was more important than our child's well-being?"

She backed away. "I told you not to listen to them," she said. "And if you had given Carl the money he asked for to begin with, this never would have happened, so you're every bit as much to blame as I am."

Brandon lunged toward her. Travis and a deputy pulled him off. "I'm sorry," he said. "I'll control myself." He sent his wife a look of loathing. "Where is Dawn now?" he asked. "Do you know?"

She said nothing, merely shook her head. Brandon

turned to Travis. "We're searching for your daughter now," the sheriff said. "We're hoping Mrs. Sheffield will tell us if she knows where they are. She's indicated she believes your daughter and her brother may be lost in the woods somewhere."

"It's twenty degrees out there!" he said, his voice rising. "There's two feet of snow on the ground. Melissa! If you know where they are, tell us!"

A knock on the door interrupted. The deputy opened the door and Gage leaned in. "There's been a development." He glanced toward Melissa and Brandon.

Travis left the room, Erik behind him. "We got a call about some vandalism up on Marietta Peak," Gage said. "There's a satellite tower up there and the provider has had problems with people stealing the solar batteries that run the transmission equipment. So they installed an alarm and cameras. The alarm went off about ninety minutes ago. They downloaded footage from the camera and sent it right over to us. I think you ought to see it."

"Why? What's on it?" Travis asked.

"I want you to take a look and draw your own conclusions," Gage said.

They followed Gage to his desk, and leaned over to watch the grainy black-and-white video that played on Gage's laptop screen. "This was taken at night, so the resolution is lousy," Gage said.

Two figures emerged from the shadows and approached the door of a small building—one figure tall and bulky, one very short. The larger figure fumbled at the door, then stepped back and pulled something from his pocket. There was no sound, but Erik recognized the bright flash of gunfire. The second figure, behind the first, raised its hands, as if to cover its ears. Then the first figure shoved against the door. It opened, and the two figures went inside. The clip ended.

Gage straightened. "What do you think?"

"Where is this, exactly?" Erik asked.

"About six miles from the summer camp," Gage said. "There's a good dirt road up there."

"You think it's Carl and Dawn," Erik said.

"Don't you? The sizes are right. Who else is going to be up there with a kid? And stay there? The satellite company is monitoring the camera feed and they say the two of them haven't left."

"Why did they wait ninety minutes to notify us?" Travis asked.

"They had to get a supervisor to look at the footage or something," Gage said. "Then they probably had a meeting to decide whether to handle it themselves or call us in."

Travis shook his head. "What's the building they broke into?" he asked.

"It houses the transmitter, maybe some other things. It's heated and air-conditioned so the equipment doesn't malfunction. There's probably enough room in there to camp out for a night or two. Out of the weather."

"And it's not an obvious hideout," Travis said. He stepped back from the computer. "We need to get up there with a team. A hostage negotiator, for sure."

Gage frowned. "Carl is armed. We don't want to go in with the cavalry and spook him into hurting the kid."

"What are the chances of getting to the tower without him noticing?"

"Close to zero. Nothing is up there but the satellite tower and that building. There's no other reason for anyone to come to that spot and he would hear any vehicle long before it got there. The company that owns the equipment wanted to send some workers to it and I had to impress upon them the stupidity of going anywhere near an armed man who might possibly be holding a hostage."

"We could hike up," Erik said.

"We could." Gage paused. "We've already sent a couple of deputies on foot to watch the place. They're instructed not to confront Carl, but to keep track of him if he and the girl leave."

"What if we get Melissa to talk to Carl?" Travis said. "He and his sister are close. Maybe she can persuade him to give himself up, or at least send the girl out."

"I don't trust Melissa to stick to any script we give her," Erik said. "And Carl may not feel so charitable toward her if he thinks she's betrayed him to us."

"We'll get a professional negotiator up there, too," Travis said. "But I think Melissa has the best chance of getting through to him."

Erik didn't like it, but he also didn't see an alternative. "All right," he said. "I'll do whatever I can to help."

"Contact CBI about a hostage negotiator," Travis said. "Gage, get two more deputies up there to keep eyes on that building, but tell them not to let Carl see them. I'll talk to SWAT." He checked his watch. "Be ready to go in thirty minutes."

SHERI WAS CONTEMPLATING stretching out on the floor or Erik's office space and trying to take a nap when he stuck his head in the door. "Come with me a minute," he said.

"Where are we going?" she asked as she followed him down the hallway.

"We think we've found Carl and Dawn. We're going to talk to Melissa and I think it would be a good idea if you were there." He glanced at her. "You're the sympathetic ear that will pressure her to do the right thing."

"And what is the right thing?"

"Help us by talking to her brother." He pushed open the door to the room where Melissa waited. Brandon stood against the wall on the opposite side of the room, arms crossed, frowning at his wife, who managed to look serene in spite of the tension that filled the air like fog. The sheriff loomed over her, while a pair of deputies waited on either side of the door.

"Are you familiar with Marietta Peak?" Travis asked Melissa.

She looked up at him. "No. Where is that?"

"Not far from the summer camp where we know Carl and Dawn last stayed," Travis said. "There's some satellite equipment up there, and a building housing equipment. A little less than two hours ago, two people broke into the building. We have the surveillance tapes and we believe the intruders were Carl and Dawn."

"Well, thank God you've found them," Melissa said.

Brandon straightened. "Is it really them? Is Dawn all right?"

"The video is poor quality, but we believe it could be them," Travis said. "Dawn appears to be okay, but again, the quality of the images is poor and we only glimpsed her. We got a better look at the man." He turned back to Melissa. "Did you know Carl and Dawn were there?"

"Of course not," she said. "I already told you, the last time I saw them was when I dropped them off at that group of summer cabins. Why don't you people believe me?"

Because you've proven you can lie so well, Erik thought.

"What are you going to do?" Brandon asked. "How are you going to rescue my little girl?"

"We want you to come with us to Marietta Peak," Travis said to Melissa. "Tell your brother all of this is over. He needs to release Dawn and turn himself in."

She stood. "Of course. That's what I've wanted ever since I went to Sheri's house. I just want this to be over."

"I'm coming, too," Brandon said.

Travis studied him. "You have to stay back a safe distance and not interfere."

Brandon nodded. "All I want is to take Dawn home once she's safe."

"I want to come, too." Sheri's face heated as everyone turned to look at her, but she forged on. "I'm not a paramedic, but I do have first aid training. I can check Dawn and make sure she's really okay."

"Of course she's okay," Melissa said. "Carl would never hurt her."

"Of course not," Sheri agreed. "But you know how children are—they're always coming down with sore throats or colds. If something like that has happened, I know you'd want Dawn treated right away."

Melissa seemed to consider this, then nodded. "She's right. I want Sheri to come. In the car with me." She gave the sheriff a long look that clearly said she didn't trust him.

"Same instructions for you," Travis told Sheri. "Stay back and don't interfere."

She nodded. "Yes, sir."

A caravan of vehicles left the sheriff's department, the sheriff in the lead with Erik, Melissa and Sheri with him. Two patrol cars with deputies followed, with Brandon Sheffield's SUV behind. As Travis fastened his seat belt, Erik got a call that a hostage negotiator was on the way from Junction.

"Let's let Melissa talk to her brother first," Travis said. "We may not need the negotiator, but keep her on standby."

They drove in silence into the mountains outside town. Whenever Sheri glanced over at Melissa, the other woman was staring out the window at the darkness, her expression unreadable.

Halfway up Marietta Peak, they gathered at a staging area. Half a dozen law enforcement vehicles were parked in the trees, their open doors casting yellow light onto the snow. Men and women in uniform or black SWAT gear milled about in the cold, their breath forming clouds, like speech bubbles with no words. "Are you sure this is out of sight of the building up there?" Erik asked as Travis shut off the engine.

"The tower is on the other side of the peak," Travis said. "And the trees provide cover." He and Erik both got out of the car.

"What about us?" Melissa asked.

"You can wait here," Travis said.

She opened her mouth to argue, but Sheri said, "We can use the time to run through what you're going to say to your brother."

Melissa glared at her. "I don't need to *rehearse*. I'm just going to tell him to give up this silly game. It's time for Dawn to come home."

"You obviously know your brother better than anyone," Sheri said. "How do you think he's going to respond?"

"He'll whine. He'll talk about how none of this is his fault. But he'll know I'm right and in the end he'll do what I tell him. He doesn't like getting on my bad side."

So much for Melissa's contention that Carl had come up with this plan and she had just gone along to protect her daughter. Clearly Melissa was the dominant personality in this relationship. "Does he respond to flattery?" Sheri asked. "Maybe you should start with that—talk about how much he loves Dawn and how you know he only wants what's best for her."

"I think I know how to talk to my own brother. I don't need your help." She looked around. "Where did the sheriff go?"

"I think he's over there with those other officers." Sheri indicated the group of uniformed men and women at the edge of the spotlight.

"I want to hear what they're talking about." Melissa groped at the door. "How do we get out of here?"

"I don't think we do," Sheri said. "That's the thing about cop cars—you don't get out of the back seat until they let you." She didn't like the idea of being stuck in this vehicle with a woman she was beginning to believe was unbalanced. But she was in this too deep to back out now. This was a second chance for her to save a little girl in danger. Maybe doing so would help assuage some of the guilt she still suffered over Claire's accident.

Whatever happened, none of them were going to come out of this predicament untouched. She only hoped a little girl didn't suffer because of the folly of the adults involved.

Erik and Travis met Gage on the edge of the crowd. "Dwight and Shane report no sign of Carl or Dawn," Gage said. "I think they're tucked in for the night. There are no windows in that building. We could probably surround the place without him knowing about it, especially with the darkness for cover."

"Do it," Travis said. "But stay as far back as you can and still have the building well in sight. I'm going to take Melissa closer and get her to talk to Carl."

Erik and Travis returned to the car. Erik opened the back passenger door and Melissa hurried out, pulling her coat tightly around her. "What do you mean, walking off and leaving us trapped back there?" she demanded.

Sheri and Travis came around the car and joined them. "What's going on?" Melissa demanded. "What are we waiting for?"

"Carl and Dawn are in a small building at the top of the peak," Travis said. "We know Carl has a pistol. He used it to shoot the lock off the building. What kind of gun is it?"

Erik expected her to say she didn't know, but Melissa surprised him. "It's a Taurus 9mm," she said. "I didn't like the idea of him having it, but he insisted I buy it for him. But don't worry—he won't use it on you. He's not that kind of man at all."

"We need to get going," Travis said. "It's another mile up to the tower." He glanced at Melissa's high-heeled boots. "Can you make the hike?"

"That won't be necessary." She took out a cell phone. "I can call Carl."

Chapter Fourteen

Erik stared at the phone in Melissa's hand. "That's not the cell phone you were using the other day," he said.

"I bought this so that Carl and I could communicate without anyone knowing," she said. "It should come in handy now."

As soon as she had made her call, Erik planned to seize that phone. No telling what kind of incriminating evidence her phone records would provide.

She punched in a number and waited. When he answered, Carl's agitation was evident, his voice clear despite Melissa's effort to press the phone more tightly to her cheek. "Mel? Mel, where are you? You were supposed to be here hours ago."

So much for her story about having arranged to meet Carl at a summer cabin and his leaving on his own, and her claim that she hadn't known where he was. Carl had clearly expected to rendezvous with her here. "Carl, I'm here on Marietta Peak," she said. "With a lot of sheriff's deputies. You need to give yourself up."

"What are you talking about?" He sounded frantic. "You want me to just turn myself in? What are you doing to me?"

"It's for the best," she said. "How is Dawn?"

"Dawn isn't good. She's sick. I think she's running a fever. All this running around in the cold isn't good for her. I told you—"

"Don't lie, Carl," she chided. "You're terrible at it. I'm sure Dawn will be fine. Send her out of the building and tell her to walk down the road toward the lights."

"I'm not going to send a sick child out into the dark and cold on top of a mountain." Erik was relieved to hear that at least one of this pair had a little sense where the child was concerned.

Melissa sighed. "Fine. Then I'll come and get her." She ended the call. "I guess we're going to have to walk up there after all."

She and Travis started toward the road leading up to the summit. Sheri took a few steps after them, but Erik grabbed her arm to stop her. "You can't go up there," he said.

She pulled her arm away. "You heard him. That little girl is sick. I'm not a paramedic, but I do have basic first aid training. The least I can do is assess her."

He was prepared to tell her all the reasons she had no business getting anywhere near an armed kidnapper when Melissa called back to them. "I want Sheri to come with us," she said. "At least then I'll have someone up there who is on my side."

Sheri's expression softened. "Don't worry," she said softly, close enough that maybe Erik was the only one who heard. Then she strode past him to join the sheriff and Melissa. He fell into step behind them, prepared to do whatever it took to protect Sheri. She might be used to risking her safety for others, but he didn't know if he could ever grow accustomed to standing by and watching while she put her life on the line.

SHERI FELT ERIK'S gaze burning into her as she hiked up the mountain just behind the sheriff and Melissa. The road was snow-packed and rutted, and the sheriff had warned they would be making the climb in the dark. "We don't want to be a target," he had said. Melissa had looked alarmed, but Sheri had merely nodded.

She had made this kind of climb before, up rougher trails, in worse weather. Lives had been on the line in those situations, too, but this time everything felt more urgent. If any of them said or did the wrong thing, Carl might snap and Dawn could be hurt. Sheri wanted Dawn safe, but how safe would she be with a mother like Melissa?

Sheri saw the faint outline of the tower against the moonlit sky first, then the red light blinking steadily on the top. A concrete cube of a building squatted at the base of the tower, sides glowing the color of butter in the moonlight. The sheriff halted them two hundred feet from the tower. Sheri hoped this was out of the range of a pistol shot.

"What should I do now?" Melissa asked.

"Call Carl again," Travis said.

Melissa slipped the phone from her pocket and hit a button. Carl's voice broke the silence. "What is going on out there, Mel? What are you doing?"

"I'm here with the sheriff," Melissa said. "Right outside that little building you're in. Send Dawn out to me."

"And then what?" he asked. "The cops come in and shoot me?"

"They're not going to shoot you," she said. "Once Dawn is safe with me, you'll surrender and we'll get this all sorted out down at the sheriff's department."

"The cops hate me," he said. "They think I'm someone who would harm a child. Why did I let you talk me into this?"

"Don't be ridiculous. This was your idea originally. I just agreed to help."

"That's what you told them, isn't it? Well, you can forget about me sending Dawn back out to you!"

Afraid he was going to hang up, Sheri grabbed the phone from Melissa. "Mr. Westover!" she said. "Please don't hang up. My name is Sheri Stevens. I'm with Eagle Mountain Search and Rescue. I'm not a law enforcement officer. I'm not armed. I don't mean you any harm. But I'm trained to give medical care in the field. Can I come in and check on Dawn, just to reassure you that she's all right? I can tell you're very concerned about her. It's obvious you care about her."

"Is this some kind of trick?" he asked.

"No. I promise it isn't. I'll come by myself. Just me and my medical kit, to take care of Dawn."

He hesitated and she bit her lip, praying he would let her in. She stared at the little building, wishing she could see what was going on in there.

"All right," he said. "But just you. No one else. I have a gun. I don't want to use it, but I will if I have to, to protect myself."

"Understood."

He ended the call. Sheri returned the phone to Melissa. "That's a wonderful idea," Melissa said.

"It's a terrible idea." Erik pulled her around to face him. "You can't do this," he said.

"I have to," she said.

"No you don't. I've been in enough situations like this to know what will happen. I'm beginning to believe that Carl doesn't want to hurt his niece, but you're a stranger to him. You'll make the perfect hostage. He'll try to use you to get what he wants."

"I know." That knowledge ought to frighten her, but it didn't. All she could think of was Dawn. "I have to help that little girl," she said.

"We're all here to help her," Erik said.

"But right now, I'm the only one who can do anything," she said. She leaned closer to him, her voice low, the words urgent. "Please. I couldn't save Claire, but now I have a chance to save Dawn. It's a chance I have to take."

"I agree with Erik," the sheriff said. "Getting involved in this is a bad idea."

"No, this is our best chance," Sheri said. She didn't wait for him to say more, but turned and ran toward the building. By the time the others recovered from their shock and sprinted after her, she was already pounding on the door. "Mr. Westover! Carl! It's Sheri Stevens. Please let me in."

"No!" Erik shouted as the door to the building opened and Sheri was pulled inside. The door slammed and he stared at it, anger and terror warring in his chest.

"All we can do now is wait," Travis said. "I'm going to talk to the SWAT commander about strategy." He pulled out his radio and turned away, but before he could make a connection, Brandon Sheffield and two deputies arrived. Brandon ignored the rest of them and headed for his wife. "Melissa, what is going on?" he asked.

"Now is not the time to discuss this," she said. She tried to turn away, but he grabbed her arm and pulled her back.

One of the deputies started to step in, but Travis motioned him back. "Let's see what they have to say."

Erik understood. In the heat of the moment, one or both of them might say something revealing. Something incriminating.

"You could have prevented all of this, if you hadn't been so miserly," Melissa said.

"All of what?" Brandon asked. "Are you trying to justify what Carl did by shifting blame? Because that is going too far."

"You're the one who's gone too far!" she retorted. "Turning down a perfectly reasonable request—"

Travis's phone rang and he answered, then caught Erik's eye. *It's Carl*, he mouthed.

Erik moved closer to listen in. "I'm sending Dawn out," Carl said. "I wanted you to know so you don't do anything stupid like shoot her, thinking it's me."

"No one is shooting anyone," Travis said. "What about Ms. Stevens?"

"She's staying with me. She's my ticket out of here."

"IF YOU WANT DAWN, you're going to have to do things my way." Carl clutched the phone with white-knuckled fingers, and paced back and forth in the small shed. The square building had unfinished sheetrock walls and concrete floors that were crowded with an array of gray metal boxes that hummed and clicked in harmony with the heating unit mounted high on one wall. The constant drone was giving Sheri a headache.

"What's going on?" Beside her, Dawn wiggled closer and whispered in Sheri's ear. Her skin was hot to the touch and her eyes were bright with fever. The thermometer Sheri had pulled from her backpack registered a temperature of 102 degrees. The number had alarmed Carl enough that he had pulled out his phone and called the sheriff and made his offer to release the child, in exchange for Sheri. "Am I going to get to go home?" Dawn asked.

"I hope so." Sheri smoothed the girl's hair, soft as only a child's hair can be. The idea of being stuck in this small space with Carl didn't appeal to her, but she told herself it would be worth it to save this little girl. Carl was still talking to the sheriff, though he had moved farther away from them and another machine had kicked on, its louder whine drowning out his words.

Carl pocketed the phone and came to stand in front of them. "How are you doing, kiddo?" he asked Dawn.

"I don't feel good." She buried her head against Sheri's shoulder. "I want to go home."

"Then that's just where you're going." Carl knelt in front of them. Traces of the confident man Sheri had encountered at the ice festival remained, but the past few days as a fugitive had taken their toll. His eyes were red-rimmed, and a shadow of beard darkened his jaw. He smelled of stale sweat and his skin was pasty. "Give me a hug and then we'll go over to the door. I'll open it and you walk out to the people waiting out there." He touched her shoulder. "I'm sorry you're not feeling well. I was hoping we'd have a better time than this. You know I love you, don't you?"

Dawn nodded, her head rubbing against Sheri's jacket. "I love you, too, but I want my mom."

"Your mom is right outside," Carl said. "So are a lot of other people, but don't let them scare you. Now give me a hug."

She moved away from Sheri and wrapped her uncle

in a hug. Carl lingered a moment, his arms around her, then released her and stood, and offered his hand. She took it and he led her to the door. He waited a moment, then slowly pulled it open, staying out of sight behind the door. "Go on, honey," he said to Dawn.

The little girl didn't look back, but took a few steps into the darkness, then began to run.

Carl closed the door and sagged against it, eyes closed. Sheri watched him, wondering what was going through his head right now. People who knew him kept saying he wasn't the violent type, but she could clearly see the bulge of the pistol in a holster at his hip. Was he desperate enough to use it?

He opened his eyes and met her gaze. "You're the woman I met at the ice festival, aren't you?" he asked. "The one who identified me to the cops."

She shifted, uncomfortable sitting on the hard floor, but also uneasy about what those words implied. Was he angry with her for spoiling his plan to remain anonymous? "What happens now?" she asked.

"The sheriff said they're bringing in a negotiator for me to talk to." He slid down the door until he was sitting on the floor with his back to it, knees up. "I'm sure he or she will try to talk me into turning myself in, but it's too late for that."

"Why do you say that?" Sheri folded her legs under her, trying to get more comfortable. Though the air in the room was warm, cold seeped up through the concrete floor.

"When I was just facing embezzlement charges, it wasn't so bad," he said. "I could have beat those, or made some kind of plea. But kidnapping a kid?" He shook his head. "They'll send me to prison for the rest of my life for that."

"Why did you do it?" she asked.

He blew out a breath. "First of all, I didn't kidnap my niece. Not really. I mean, it's not kidnapping if the parents—well, at least her mom—knew where she was the whole time. That's what Mel told me, anyway. This was all her idea. The plan was that I'd take Dawn with me for a few hours, maybe overnight, and pretend to be a kidnapper. I'd send a text demanding money. Mel would freak out and plead with Brandon to pay the money. He might balk at first, but he would eventually cave. Mel was sure of that. Once the money was safely socked away in the account Mel helped me set up, I'd show up with Dawn and say I found her and everybody would be happy."

"Weren't you worried Dawn would tell police what really happened?"

"Mel promised that wouldn't happen. She said she would explain to Dawn that this was a big secret. She said if Dawn did say anything, Mel would tell them she was just confused. No one would believe a little kid over the word of her own mother."

Sheri wasn't so sure of that, but didn't see the point of mentioning it. "What about the gun?" she asked. "If this was so innocent, why do you have that?"

The lines on either side of his mouth deepened. "Mel bought that gun and insisted I take it. I didn't want to, but she said I might need it to protect myself while Dawn and I were waiting for Brandon to transfer the money. She insisted on it."

Sheri wondered if Mel had done this to make her brother look guiltier. "Melissa told the sheriff everything was your idea," she said. "She insisted you persuaded her to go along."

He slumped farther, wrists resting loosely on his knees. "I guess I ought to be surprised by that, but I'm not. Melissa has always been very good at looking out for number one, for all she's been a big help to me over the years."

"Do you really think the cops will let you walk out of here?" she asked.

"They'll have to. They won't want to risk you getting hurt. I really don't want to hurt you, but as long as I can make them believe I will, I have the upper hand. At least now I know Dawn is safe. I never would have harmed her."

"You should give yourself up," she said. "Tell the police what you told me. Don't let your sister let you take all the blame."

"Yeah, I tried surrendering once before and that didn't work out so well for me."

"When did you try to surrender?" she asked, confused.

"When they charged me with stealing that money from Western Casing."

"You didn't steal it?"

He grimaced. "I borrowed it. I was going to pay it back."

"How?"

"I'd have found a way. There was no reason to treat me like a criminal. That Detective Lester wouldn't leave me alone. He was constantly questioning me, talking to my neighbors and friends, women I used to date. I thought that kind of harassment was illegal. He just wouldn't let it go."

Erik had always been dogged in his pursuit of justice. It had made him great at his job, though more than once his devotion to his work had made Sheri feel left out. After Claire had died, he had worked endless hours of overtime. She had convinced herself it was because he didn't want to be with her. With time, she had come to see it was his way of trying to outrun grief.

"He's not going to quit pursuing you if you manage to get away," she said.

"He won't know where to find me," Carl said.

"If you leave the country, you'll be an international fugitive," she said. "Do you really think that will be any better?"

He glared at her. "Shut up. I'm done talking to you." He turned away, a gesture that struck her as childish.

She took the opportunity to study the room more closely. There were no windows, no openings of any kind, other than the door he was sitting in front of. She mentally reviewed the equipment in her backpack that might be used as a weapon. She had a pair of angled bandage scissors, but they wouldn't be much defense against a real weapon, like a knife or gun.

Maybe the hostage negotiator really would talk him into surrendering, or at least letting her go. For all his bravado, Carl struck her as a weak man. Weak enough to allow his sister to talk him into what seemed to her a very flawed plan. Had Melissa really believed it would work? Or did she have some other motive for putting her brother—and her daughter—in such danger?

BRANDON SHEFFIELD HELD his daughter on his lap in the back seat of a sheriff's department SUV, one arm around her, relief in every line of his face. Melissa sat by his side, smiling at the girl. "We need to ask Dawn a few questions," Travis said as he and Erik approached the open door of the vehicle.

"We need to get her to a doctor," Brandon said. "She's burning up with fever."

"This will only take a few minutes," Travis said. "And she's the only one who can give us the information we need."

"Just a few questions," Brandon said. "You can save the rest for when she's better."

Travis squatted beside the open door. "Hello, Dawn," he said. "I'm Sheriff Walker. Did your uncle Carl say where he planned to go next?"

Dawn leaned in closer to her father. "He said he wanted to go to Mexico, because it's warm there."

"Did he mention anything else? Did he say why he came here?"

"He said Mama told us to wait here for her."

"Obviously, she's confused," Melissa said. "The poor child is burning up. No one could think clearly in that condition."

Brandon frowned at his wife. "Did Uncle Carl talk to your mother on the phone?" he asked.

"Lots of times," Dawn said. "And Mom came to see us and drove us places." She turned to look at Melissa. "Mama, why did you keep going away? Why didn't you let me come home with you?"

Melissa managed a weak smile. "You're confused, sweetie," she said. "Of course Mama didn't leave you."

Dawn squirmed. "I have to go to the bathroom," she said.

"I'll take you," Melissa opened her car door. "We'll

have to go in the woods, but you know how to do that. Then we can leave here and go home."

"Deputy Douglas will go with you," Travis said. He looked around for Jamie, spotted her and waved her over.

But Melissa hadn't waited. She had hold of Dawn's hand and the two were hurrying toward the trees at the edge of the clearing. "Go after them, Jamie," Travis said to the deputy. "Make sure Melissa doesn't try anything."

"Are you going to arrest my wife?" Brandon asked.

"She's admitted she helped her brother carry out this plan to extort money from you," Travis said. "We'll need to take her into custody."

"I can't believe she'd do something like that," Brandon said, his face slack. He didn't sound angry. Erik thought that would come later. For now he was in shock, his world turned upside down.

"You should consult an attorney," Erik said.

Brandon nodded. "I'll find a good criminal defense lawyer to represent Melissa."

"You should find an attorney to represent yourself and your daughter," Erik said.

Brandon's eyes met his, clarity flashing beneath the shock. He nodded. "You're right. I will."

Jamie jogged toward them, Dawn in her arms. She stopped before them, out of breath. "Dawn came out of the woods," Jamie said. "But Mrs. Sheffield didn't."

Chapter Fifteen

"Why hasn't that hostage negotiator called?" Carl stared at his phone. "Don't they realize they have to deal with me?"

"Maybe you could call them," Sheri said. "Or call your sister. Ask her what's going on."

He nodded and punched in a number. Sheri could hear the ringing, then a man's voice answered. "Hello, Carl."

"Who is this? What are you doing with Mel's phone?"

"Mel isn't here." Sheri recognized Erik's voice and felt a surge of, if not relief, a lessening of her anxiety. Erik was very good at his job. He was going to do everything in his power to keep her safe. To keep everyone safe. "She took Dawn into the woods to use the bathroom and apparently decided to run away," Erik said. "She left you to deal with this on your own, Carl."

"No! She wouldn't do that. You're lying to try to get me to cooperate."

"I'm not lying," Erik said. "Melissa is gone. She told us that this was all your fault. You were the one who came up with the idea of kidnapping your niece and asking Brandon to pay a big ransom, and Melissa only helped because you threatened her."

"That's not true!" Carl moaned and hugged his arm across his stomach, nearly bent double. "This was Melissa's idea. She told me it would be easy. Brandon would never know it was me. No one would suspect me. She said she could convince Dawn not to say anything. She set up the offshore account for the ransom and everything. She said it would only take a few hours."

"It's been a lot more than a few hours," Erik said.

"Mel told me she would take care of it!" Carl's voice rose. "I wanted to stop after that first night, but she told me she would fix everything if I was patient."

"Why did you decide to hide up here in that equipment shed?" Erik asked.

"I didn't decide. Mel told me I had to wait here. She dropped us off this morning and said she would be back in a few hours."

"That's not the story she's telling, Carl," Erik said. "If you want to clear this up, you need to release Sheri and come out and talk to us."

"Then you'll arrest me."

"We'll take you to the sheriff's department and you can contact a lawyer to help you."

"Trying to pay for a lawyer is what got me into this mess in the first place!"

"All right. Calm down. It's going to be okay. Let me talk to Sheri."

"No."

"I want to make sure she's all right."

"I'm fine," Sheri called, hoping Erik would hear her.

"Shut up," Carl said. He punched the button to end the call and threw the phone across the room. It hit the wall hard, the screen shattering.

Sheri stared at the damaged phone. "What are you going to do if they want to talk to you again?" she asked.

"I'm done talking." He sank to the floor and buried his face in his hands. "I'm a dead man," he said. "They'll send me to jail for the rest of my life for this. I can't survive in prison. There are murderers and rapists and really dangerous people in there. They'll eat me alive."

Sheri scooted closer. "If you don't get out there and tell your story, they'll only have Melissa's side of things to go on," she said. "Melissa is putting all the blame on you. That's not right."

He raised his head, tears streaming down his face. "They won't believe me," he said. "They'll believe Melissa. She's beautiful and smart and rich. She gets away with things. She always has." He reached to his side and pulled out the gun.

Sheri drew back. "What are you doing with that?"

He looked at the weapon in his hand. "I didn't want to do this, but I'm already in so deep I don't think it matters." He pointed the pistol at her. "If I hold this to your head and stand in the door of this building, do you think they'll let me go free?"

She stared in horror—at the gun, and then at the hand that held it, a hand that shook, ever so slightly. "That isn't a good idea, Carl," she said.

His free hand lashed out and took hold of her. "It's the only idea I've got."

ERIK HIT THE redial button on Melissa's phone, but no one answered. He looked around, hoping to spot the hostage negotiator his bosses had promised to send, but so far she hadn't shown. The whole side of the mountain was lit up with portable lights, teams of law enforcement officers swarming the area, searching for Melissa Sheffield or waiting for orders on how to deal with Carl Westover.

Brandon and Dawn, escorted by a victim's advocate from the county, had left, on their way to the emergency room to have Dawn examined. Erik had been on his way to the sheriff's SUV to place Melissa's phone in an evidence bag when Carl had called. He had tried to keep the kidnapper talking as long as possible, hoping that word of his sister's betrayal would spur him to want to come out and present his own version of events. But it had only ended up making him angry.

He spotted Travis, phone to his ear, several hundred yards away. Gage was with him, both standing with their backs to the equipment shed. Erik moved out of the reach of the lights, to the back side of the building where Carl was holed up with Sheri. Crusted snow crunched under his feet, but he was confident the constant hum of machinery in the building would prevent anyone inside from hearing his approach. Constructed of cinder blocks painted dark brown, the flat-roofed shed had no windows or back door. The only opening was a louvered vent that was too small for an adult to squeeze through.

He crept up to the back wall and put his ear to the vent, but all he heard was the hum of machinery. He straightened, and pulled his coat more tightly around him. It was even colder here in the darkness, morning still several hours away. Was Melissa regretting her choice of footwear about now? Her high-heeled boots weren't made for fleeing through snowy woods, and how did she expect to reach safety with so many law enforcement personnel searching for her?

People did all kinds of desperate things when they were cornered, he knew. He had known criminals who ate evidence, one who jumped into an ice-cold lake and attempted to swim away, and one who insisted he suffered a split personality and didn't have any idea why all these officers were pointing their guns at him. Sometimes the desperate moves even paid off—the lake swimmer had made it all away across the lake and into a nearby town before he was caught shoplifting from a store. The local cops who arrested him had no idea they were dealing with a dangerous felon until Erik and a fellow agent showed up.

He stepped back from the building and studied it again. They were never going to get in there using force. They would have to find a way to persuade Carl to come out. He returned to the front of the building and found Travis. "Any sign of that negotiator?" the sheriff asked.

"Let me check." Erik pulled out his phone and saw that he had a text. He read it and swore. "The negotiator made it to Eagle Mountain, but then she got lost on some back road and ran out of gas. She's waiting for a deputy to pick her up—as soon as he figures out where she is, since she doesn't know." He stuffed the phone back into his pocket. "Looks like we're on our own. And Carl isn't answering his phone." He related his brief conversation with the kidnapper. "We're going to have to find a way to force him out," Erik concluded.

"I'll get in touch with the satellite company and see about shutting down their equipment," Travis said. "Once it starts to get cold in there, Carl might feel differently about moving to a nice warm cell."

"Right." Of course, anything they did to Carl, Sheri would suffer as well. But Erik knew she was tough. She wouldn't complain about a little cold or hunger if it resulted in her freedom. Though he was definitely going to have a few things to say about her putting herself in danger the way she had—right after he kissed her breathless.

Travis left to find a quieter place to make his call. Gage joined Erik. "We've got a sniper focused on the door," he said. "If Carl comes out with Sheri, the sniper will try to get a clear shot at just Carl."

Erik's stomach flipped at the idea of a bullet anywhere near Sheri. He forced the thought away. "Let's hope it doesn't come to that."

Travis returned. "The satellite company has agreed to cooperate, but it will take a bit to get everything ready to shut down," he said. "In the meantime, I'm going to try talking to Carl. Do you have his number?"

Erik consulted Melissa's phone and read off the number. Travis punched it in and they waited, the buzzing ring loud in the sudden stillness. Travis hung up on the twelfth ring. "I didn't hear any ringing in there," Gage said, and nodded toward the building.

"Those cinder block walls are pretty thick," Erik said. "And with the machinery running, I don't think you could hear anything."

"The machinery should be shutting down any minute now," Travis said. He and Gage discussed the positioning of various deputies while Erik stared at the door of the building. What was going on in there? What if Carl wasn't as nonviolent and passive as everyone believed? What if he tried to hurt Sheri, just when the two of them had found each other again?

Silence descended like a hammer as the machinery in the building abruptly shut off. Travis raised a hand to his mouth. "Carl! This is Sheriff Travis Walker. You are surrounded. Open the door and throw out your weapon!"

Erik held his breath, ears straining. No answer came. No sign of movement. Were Carl and Sheri still in there? Still alive?

Pop! Pop! The shots sounded small and almost innocent, like a cap pistol or a firecracker, but Erik almost doubled over from the pain in his chest as he recognized the gunfire for what it was. "Sheri!" The shout tore from his throat and he staggered toward the building.

Gage wrapped him up in a bear hug and dragged him back, even as the door to the building swung open. Everyone froze.

"It's okay!" Sheri called. "I'm okay. But Carl…" Her voice broke. "Carl isn't okay."

Erik broke free of Gage's grip and ran to her, arriving in time to catch her as she sagged. They clung together, her face buried against his shoulder. "I thought he was going to shoot me," she whispered. "Instead, he shot himself."

He looked past her, to where Carl lay crumpled on the concrete floor, then a tide of law enforcement personnel swept past them. He moved out of the way, taking Sheri with him.

"What happened?" Travis asked the question, standing at Erik's shoulder.

Sheri straightened, and swiped at her tear-stained cheeks. "He was very upset when he learned his sister had deserted him. He said the situation was hopeless. When he took out the gun, I thought he intended to kill me, but then he… He shot himself." Fresh tears welled. Erik gripped her hand.

"We'll need a statement," Travis said. "While it's still fresh in your mind."

"Of course." She sniffed, then took the handkerchief Erik handed her. "How is Dawn?"

"She's fine. She's with her father, who was taking her to be checked out by a doctor."

"That's good." She dabbed at her eyes. "Did Melissa really run away?"

"She did," Travis said. "But we'll find her." He looked at Erik. "Take her to the station. Someone there can take her statement. Then take her home."

"I need a vehicle," Erik said.

Travis dug out his keys and tossed them to Erik. "I'll get a ride back with Gage."

Erik led Sheri to the SUV and helped her into the front seat. But instead of moving to the driver's seat, he leaned over her. "Don't you ever do anything like that again," he said, his voice rough. "When I heard those shots, I thought I was going to die."

She pressed her palm to his cheek. "You would have done the same thing—to save that little girl. I know you would have."

"I'm a cop," he said. "That's part of the job."

"And I was a mother. That's part of my job, too. It doesn't matter that Dawn wasn't my child. I had to protect her."

They leaned in, foreheads pressed together. "I love you," he said. "Even at the worst times, before the divorce, I still loved you. I just couldn't figure out how to live with you and my grief, too."

"I know." She pressed her lips to his, a brief, soft kiss. "I love you, too."

"I want to try again," he said. "I think we belong together."

"Yes." Another kiss. "We're stronger now. I think we can do this."

He wrapped his arms around her and dragged her to him, and kissed her with a fierceness born of fear of losing her and joy at having her restored to him. It was a very long time before they pulled apart, and longer still before he moved out of her arms and around to the driver's seat, to finish out the rest of what had to be done on this long night.

Epilogue

A week after the showdown on Marietta Peak, the sheriff contacted Erik and asked him to stop by the office. "I thought you would want an update on the case and I prefer to do it in person," Travis said.

When Erik showed up with Sheri in tow, the sheriff fixed his gaze on the diamond ring on the third finger of Sheri's left hand and said, "I take it the rumors are true that you're going to be staying in town?"

"I'm being transferred to the Junction office, effective immediately," Erik said.

"Erik and I are getting married," Sheri said, somewhat unnecessarily, Erik thought, since everyone in town seemed to be aware of the news, judging by the chorus of congratulations the two of them received wherever they went.

Travis nodded. "Congratulations."

"Is that what you wanted to see me about?" Erik asked.

"No. I wanted to let you know Colorado State Patrol picked up Melissa Sheffield this morning."

Sheri gasped. "Where?" She flushed. "That is, if you're allowed to tell me."

"She was buying gas at a store in Trinidad, near the

New Mexico state line," Travis said. "A clerk recognized her picture from the news stories. She's being held there and will be transported to Junction tomorrow."

"That's a relief," Sheri said. "I didn't like the idea of her running free."

"We're still pulling together the case against her, but I doubt she'll be free again for a very long time," Travis said.

"Here's one more thing you can add to your files." Erik handed over a thin folder. "I just received this this morning as well. It's a report from the FBI on the numbered account Brandon was instructed to wire the ransom money to. Melissa set it up in Carl's name, but what Carl probably didn't know was that she had also set up a second account in her own name. Anything deposited in the first account would be automatically transferred to the second."

"She was picked up with a forged passport and an airline ticket to Buenos Aires," Travis said.

"I think she planned this all along," Erik said. "If Brandon had paid out the cash, Melissa would have found a way to have Carl identified as the kidnapper. She would have unspooled her story about being forced to help him and he would have been arrested and sent to prison. After a suitable amount of time, she would have disappeared to Buenos Aires or some point beyond, with a new identity and a million dollars to smooth the way."

"I almost feel sorry for Carl," Sheri said.

"Don't," Erik said. "He knew what his sister was like, but he let greed get the better of his judgment."

"Sheriff, there's someone here to see you," Adelaide

interrupted them. "All of you." She turned and motioned to someone down the hall.

A moment later, Dawn Sheffield appeared in the doorway, her father close behind. "Hello!" Sheri smiled and leaned toward the little girl. "It's good to see you again."

Dawn looked like a different child now, pink-cheeked and smiling, her long brown hair pulled back from her face. She wore jeans and a pink sweater and a pink parka and white snow boots. "I made you this," she said, and thrust an envelope at Sheri.

"We were going to stop by the school after this," Brandon said. "We didn't expect to find you here."

"I made this, too," Dawn said, and handed Travis another envelope.

Sheri opened her envelope and took out a card with a drawing of colorful cliffs in blue and white and green, a tiny figure perched near the top of one cliff. "That's you, climbing the ice," Dawn said. "I watched you before...well, before everything happened."

"It's perfect." Sheri's eyes shone. She reached out and pulled Dawn to her. "Thank you so much. I'll treasure this."

"Thank you," Dawn said. She took a deep breath. "I know Uncle Carl let me go because you offered to take my place."

"Your uncle loved you," Sheri said. "He never would have hurt you."

Dawn nodded, and turned to the sheriff. "Thank you to you and all your officers, too," she said.

"You're very welcome." Travis stood his card, which showed a mountain with a tower at the top and several men and women with big stars on their chests.

"How are you doing?" Erik asked Brandon.

"Okay." Brandon nodded. "It's been tough, but Dawn and I are seeing a family therapist and I've consulted attorneys." He glanced at Travis. "The sheriff shared that Carl's accomplice was apprehended earlier today. I have a lot of mixed feelings about all of this, but we'll get through it." He patted his daughter's shoulder. "Dawn and I are headed back to Denver today. We just wanted to stop by and say thank you again for everything."

"We'll keep you posted," Travis said. "Stop by anytime you're in town."

"I've already listed the house," Brandon said. "Too many bad memories there for both of us. I think we'll get a new place. Someplace the two of us can make a fresh start."

They left and Erik and Sheri followed them out. In the car, Sheri admired the card once more. "I hope she'll be all right," she said. "That's a lot to go through at such a young age. At any age, really."

"Her father will help her," Erik said. "They'll help each other." He took her hand and squeezed it. "I like what he said, about fresh starts."

"Yes." She turned her palm up and laced her fingers with his. "Are we really going to do this and not screw up?"

"We're going to be a family again." He glanced at her. "I always wanted more children, didn't you?"

Her smile pierced him, full of joy and pain and hope. "Yes. I'd like that. The idea terrifies me, but I still want to try."

"So much of life is terrifying like that," he said. "But you know how to be brave. You've done it for years." He kissed her knuckles. "We'll be brave together this time." The wedding vows would mean even more when he said them this time. Now he knew the cost of all he had given away before. Now that they were together again, they were never going to let each other go.

* * * * *

COMING SOON!

We really hope you enjoyed reading this book.
If you're looking for more romance, be sure to
head to the shops when new books are
available on

Thursday 8th
December

To see which titles are coming soon, please visit
millsandboon.co.uk/nextmonth

LET'S TALK

Romance

For exclusive extracts, competitions
and special offers, find us online:

- f facebook.com/millsandboon
- 🐦 @MillsandBoon
- 📷 @MillsandBoonUK

Get in touch on 01413 063232

For all the latest titles coming soon, visit

millsandboon.co.uk/nextmonth

JOIN US ON SOCIAL MEDIA!

Stay up to date with our latest releases, author news and gossip, special offers and discounts, and all the behind-the-scenes action from Mills & Boon...

 @millsandboon

 @millsandboonuk

 facebook.com/millsandboon

 @millsandboonuk

It might just be true love...

GET YOUR ROMANCE FIX!

Get the latest romance news, exclusive author interviews, story extracts and much more!

MILLS & BOON

Desire

Indulge in secrets and scandal, intense drama and plenty of sizzling hot action with powerful and passionate heroes who have it all: wealth, status, good looks…everything but the right woman.

MILLS & BOON

MODERN

Power and Passion

Prepare to be swept off your feet by sophisticated, sexy and seductive heroes, in some of the world's most glamourous and romantic locations, where power and passion collide.

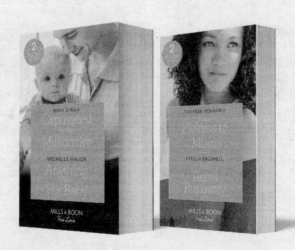